STRANGE FIRE

ALSO BY TOMMY WALLACH

We All Looked Up
Thanks for the Trouble

TOMMY WALLACH
STRANGE FIRE

The Anchor & Sophia: Book One

SIMON & SCHUSTER BFYR

New York   London   Toronto   Sydney   New Delhi

An imprint of Simon & Schuster Children's Publishing Division
1230 Avenue of the Americas, New York, New York 10020

This book is a work of fiction. Any references to historical events,
real people, or real places are used fictitiously. Other names, characters, places,
and events are products of the author's imagination, and any resemblance
to actual events or places or persons, living or dead, is entirely coincidental.
Text copyright © 2017 by Tommy Wallach
Jacket photography copyright © 2017 by Thinkstock.com
Jacket photo retouching by We Monsters
All rights reserved, including the right of reproduction in whole or in part in any form.
SIMON & SCHUSTER BFYR is a trademark of Simon & Schuster, Inc.

For information about special discounts for bulk purchases, please contact
Simon & Schuster Special Sales at 1-866-506-1949 or business@simonandschuster.com.
The Simon & Schuster Speakers Bureau can bring authors to your live event.
For more information or to book an event, contact the Simon & Schuster
Speakers Bureau at 1-866-248-3049 or visit our website at www.simonspeakers.com.
Book design by Lucy Ruth Cummins
Map art by Ryan Thompson
The text for this book was set in Adobe Jenson Pro.
Manufactured in the United States of America
First Edition
2 4 6 8 10 9 7 5 3 1
Library of Congress Cataloging-in-Publication Data
Names: Wallach, Tommy, author.
Title: Strange fire / Tommy Wallach.
Description: First edition. | New York : Simon & Schuster Books for Young Readers, [2017]. |
Series: The Anchor and Sophia ; 1 | Summary: Clive and Clover Hamill, sons of a well-respected
Descendant minister, discover a community intent on rediscovering the blasphemous technologies of
the past, setting into motion a holy war that will endanger their relationship and humanity itself.
Identifiers: LCCN 2017002649| ISBN 9781481468381 (hardback) |
ISBN 9781481468404 (eBook)
Subjects: | CYAC: Clergy—Fiction. | Brothers—Fiction. |
Technology—Fiction. | Science fiction.
Classification: LCC PZ7.W158855 Str 2017 | DDC [Fic]—dc23
LC record available at https://lccn.loc.gov/2017002649

For the doubtful

ACKNOWLEDGMENTS

Thank you to Krista Vitola and Christian Trimmer, editors in arms. Thank you to Lucy Ruth Cummins, Ryan Thompson, Jenica Nasworthy, Alison Velea, Valerie Shea, and the whole design and production team at Simon & Schuster. Thank you to my sensitivity reader. Thanks to the MacDowell Colony, where this book was started almost three years ago. And finally, thanks to Mom and Ellen, for everything else.

Let us rather choose
Arm'd with Hell flames and fury all at once
O're Heav'ns high Towrs to force resistless way,
Turning our Tortures into horrid Arms
Against the Torturer; when to meet the noise
Of his Almighty Engin he shall hear
Infernal Thunder, and for Lightning see
Black fire and horror shot with equal rage
Among his Angels; and his Throne it self
Mixt with Tartarean Sulphur, and strange fire,
His own invented Torments.

—Milton, *Paradise Lost*, Book 2

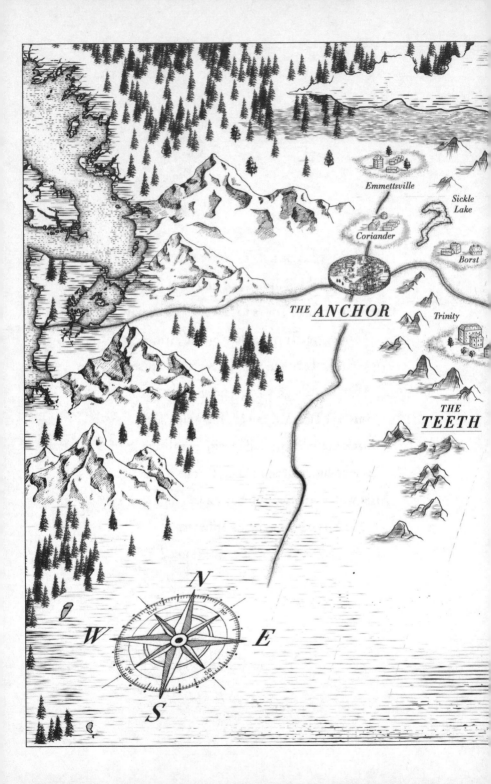

STRANGE FIRE

Prologue

FLORIAN PARKS WAS SITTING IN THE GANTRY watchtower, whittling a wooden doll for his little sister, when he first spotted the travelers over the pointed tips of the palisade. He was so surprised that he cut the figurine's nose clean off. An hour later they appeared again, marching along the river. They were close enough to make out individually this time: about twenty people altogether, men and women both, each one bedraggled and gaunt as a beggar. They had no pack animals or wagons, just a single handcart they kept near the center of their procession. It was clear they'd been traveling for a long time.

They crossed the bridge and stopped a dozen feet from the town gate. One of them stepped forward. He had lank silver hair and a thick beard, and he walked with a pronounced limp.

"Hail and good evening," he said. His voice was surprisingly powerful, reeking of a practiced, if rusty, authority.

"Same to you," Florian responded.

"We are a band of travelers in search of a place to lay our heads for the night. We were hoping to find such a thing behind your walls."

Florian hesitated. His sense of charity warred against that pessimism born of having known a few too many bad men. "There sure are an awful lot of you."

"We have shekels, if that's your concern," said another of the strangers.

Florian frowned; the word was distantly familiar. "Shekels?"

"Currency," the man explained. "Bronze and silver."

Florian spat a gob of chew into the corner of the tower, which was long since stained rust red with the stuff. He doubted the strangers actually had anything of value on them, but he also didn't see how they could be much of a threat. Utter exhaustion was written all over their faces, and they didn't have a single sword or bow between them.

"Gimme a tick," he said, and quickly clambered down from the watchtower. The gate was braced on the Gantry side with a large iron rod. Florian lifted it off the brackets and set it to lean against the palisade.

"Just give it a push," he shouted, and stood back as the gate swung open.

"Welcome to Gantry," he said. "I'm Florian Parks."

They each gave their names as they passed, but Florian managed to remember only that of their leader, Seftika Onoma. When they'd all passed through the gate, a couple of them helped him to replace the buttress rod.

"Mr. Onoma," Florian said, "I should bring you straight to the mayor. The rest of you can sit a spell at the Hare. Grant—that is, the proprietor—won't have space for all of you to sleep, but you can at least get warm by the fire until we sort things out."

After introducing the strangers at the Hare (and confirming that they did indeed have a fair bit of silver on them), Florian went up the hill with Seftika. They moved slowly, on account of the old man's limp.

TOMMY WALLACH

"Your town is rather well situated, isn't it?" Seftika said.

"You've got a good eye. That's why the Wesah don't bother us. Water all the way around, and cliffs, too. That bridge is pretty much the only way in. Here we are."

The mayor's house was twice the size of any other in town, built of red brick and mortar instead of the usual wood. Florian could tell that Seftika was impressed by it.

"Constantine built that thing with his own two hands. He's got all kinds of workshops in the back, too. Says he likes to tinker."

Florian knocked. After a moment, the door was answered by the mayor's daughter, Denise. She was a pretty thing, hair always braided elaborately, neck smooth as planed rosewood. He always got a little tongue-tied around her.

"Evening, Denise. We've got a guest here. That is, we have a whole lot of guests. About twenty, all told. This here is their leader, Seftika Onoma, of . . ." Florian realized he'd yet to ask where the strangers had come from.

"The Anchor," Seftika said.

"The Anchor?" Denise said. "What's that?"

"It's a city."

"Huh. Never heard of it. But I imagine there's plenty of things out there I never heard of, eh? Just let me tell Papa you're here."

She returned a moment later and ushered them into the house, down a hallway, and out onto the back patio. Constantine was sitting in a rocking chair, smoking a pipe.

"Evening, Florian," he said. "And a pleasure to meet you, Mr. Onoma."

"Thank you, sir," Seftika replied.

"So my daughter tells me you're from the Anchor."

"That's right."

"And you've brought a few friends with you."

"Yes."

The mayor took a leisurely suck on his pipe, exhaling the fragrant smoke in a narrow stream. "Interesting. I'm bettin' there's a story there, eh?"

"There is."

"I'll warn you even before you start, I got an ear for liars. Comes from having three daughters. They're always trying to pull something over on me." He winked at Denise, who blushed prettily. Florian couldn't help but wonder exactly what her father might be referring to.

"I have no interest in lying to you, sir," Seftika said.

"Good." The mayor leaned back in his chair and closed his eyes. "Then start talking."

Seftika sat down cross-legged on the deck and took a deep breath. "Duncan Leibowitz, Epistem of the Anchor Library, was terribly ill …"

He tossed and turned. He sweated and swore. He cried out for water, then threw up whatever he drank. He prayed to God and in the same breath cursed a creator who would inflict such suffering on his creations. He was tormented by visions of the Conflagration, of the Daughter turning her face away from him in shame, of demons descending from the skies to torment those he loved. He sensed the dark angel of death perched just at the edge of his vision, patient as a vulture, brutal as a hawk.

And yet, through it all, the scientist in him remained awake and aware.

Decades earlier, just after taking his holy orders as a monk, Leibowitz had been assigned to the Library's chemistry department. He accomplished little of note in that position, choosing to focus his efforts on the sort of politicking that allowed one to rise through the ranks of the institution, rather than on synthesizing a more efficient fertilizer or a less toxic solvent. It took him nearly a quarter of a century to achieve his goal: just shy of his fiftieth year, he was named Epistem, the most senior position in the Library, answerable only to the Archbishop and God. His business now was exclusively bureaucratic in nature: meetings with Church officials and the Anchor city council, delegating his attendants in response to specific calls for consultation, appearing at parties and functions.

He couldn't have said when he began to grow nostalgic for his days as a lowly attendant, toiling alone in a dank chamber over a flask and a crucible, the hours passing by unheeded. It stole over him slowly—this sense that life was passing him by, that he would die having produced nothing of lasting value. Then the plague came, carried up the coast by traders from Sudamir and left at Edgewise docks with the rest of their cargo. And as it began to spread across the Descendancy, as town after town saw its population decimated, the funeral pyres wafting pestilential smoke across the countryside, Leibowitz finally understood what God wanted of him.

Unbeknownst to even his closest associates, he built a small laboratory in his private offices and began poring over every volume in the anathema stacks, page by page, line by line. It took him months to find what he was looking for: a reference to a medicine invented by the first generation of men, a sort of panacea, cultivated from the same mold that grew on bread left out to rot. The procedure for synthesizing this elixir was terribly complex, and more than two years passed before Leibowitz even managed to assemble all the necessary ingredients. Another year later, he finally produced a viable dose.

At that point, Leibowitz faced a critical question: Who would he test his invention on? He had to tread carefully; his experiments had never been formally approved by a writ from the Church, which meant he was already guilty of blasphemy. If his potion wasn't a rousing success, he would almost certainly end up excommunicated.

There was only one plausible solution.

That Sunday, Leibowitz traveled to St. Ivan's Hospital and spent the morning walking among the sick and the dying. He held their cold, clammy hands to his lips. He leaned down to kiss their foreheads.

By the time he went to bed that night, he could already feel the fever taking hold.

He waited as long as he could before taking the medicine; the plague needed time to incubate, to reach its full strength. Only after three days, when he felt any further delay might prove fatal, did he fetch the vial and syringe.

He injected the solution, then lay back on his bed and fell into a dreamless sleep.

When he woke again, it was to a bright, clear morning and a bright, clear head. He felt as if he'd spent the past few days slowly drowning, trapped beneath a thick layer of ice, desperate for air. And at the last possible moment, he'd managed to break back through to the surface. He laughed like a madman. He wept with joy. God had granted him a miracle. Producing the antidote on a large scale would be difficult—perhaps impossible. But so many lives would be saved as a result—they really had no choice but to try.

Those were the exact words he used when he presented his discovery to the Archbishop—*we really have no choice but to try.*

But it turned out the Archbishop saw things rather differently, and the two men spent the entire night arguing. The Epistem asked how the Church could so cavalierly consign thousands of men, women, and children to death. The Archbishop countered that the Lord and his Daughter determined the appropriate time for every mortal being's passing. The Epistem then asked why the Archbishop bothered to eat or drink, if he was unafraid of death. The Archbishop said that eating and drinking were natural acts, while the work Leibowitz had done was not. The Epistem asked what the purpose of the Library was, if not to improve the lives of the people. The Archbishop answered that it was Scripture, not science, that determined the definition of "improvement." Back and forth the debate went, in an ever-widening gyre, until it encompassed the very nature of faith, of knowledge, of divinity, of mercy, of providence, and of the Descendancy itself.

But when all was said and done, the Library was subordinate to the Church. The Archbishop's word was final, and that word was *no.*

Over the next few weeks, Leibowitz found it more and more difficult to sleep. He spurned the company of others, and when forced to socialize, would be either cold and taciturn or needlessly quarrelsome. The despair he'd subjugated to his scientific work reasserted itself. And one night, as he lay awake into the wee hours, he began to compose an essay in his mind. It would come to be known as *A*

Treatise on Knowledge, and within a week, every monk in the Library would've read it. The *Treatise* told the story of the Epistem's past five years—how he'd labored to discover the cure, how he'd made the difficult decision to test it on himself, how he'd brought his triumph to the Archbishop, and how he'd been rebuffed.

He'd hoped to sway opinion within the Library against the Archbishop. He didn't realize that his letter amounted to a declaration of war.

The Archbishop quickly called together the Gloria—his council of bishops—and they agreed to formally name the Epistem a heretic. Within a few days, Leibowitz had been taken from the Library in chains, and a new Epistem had been installed in his place. The official word given to the people was that he'd succumbed to the plague.

Leibowitz's story would've ended there, if not for the fact that a few dozen attendants had read the *Treatise* and been moved by it. Before the former Epistem's execution could be carried out, these intrepid few staged a daring escape, successfully spiriting him out of the city.

They were alive, but they no longer had a home. Not only because the Archbishop would be looking for them, but because they'd lost their faith. They decided to travel east until they reached territory where they were no longer criminals on the run, where they were no longer anyone at all. And in that place, they would find a way to start again.

The silence stretched out for a long time after that. Constantine's eyes were closed, and if not for the smoke periodically leaking out from around his pipe, Florian would've thought he was asleep.

TOMMY WALLACH

"I've put most of it together," he eventually said, "but I do have one last question."

"Please," said Seftika.

"Can you teach us some of the things you know?"

Florian didn't have the slightest idea what the mayor was talking about, but the stranger seemed to understand.

"Give us fifty years, maybe a hundred, and we will improve your lives in ways you can't begin to imagine. We will flood your streets with light even in the dead of night. We will show you how to soar above the clouds. We will make your farms more productive, your sicknesses less deadly, your horses stronger."

"What about our booze?"

Seftika smiled. "We can make a shine so strong it'll melt a snail down to slime."

"You willing to shake on that?"

"Indeed I am."

The two men stood up and shook hands. And Florian realized that Seftika wasn't nearly as decrepit as he'd at first appeared. In fact, it almost seemed as if his shabbiness were a sort of disguise, one he could slough away like a snakeskin. With a good wash and a fresh set of clothes, a trimmed beard and a haircut, he would look completely different—formidable, commanding even.

Florian chuckled. He'd never been the fastest calf to the teat, but he always got there eventually. "Seftika Onoma?" he said. "Where'd you come up with that one?"

"It means 'false name' in an ancient tongue," the stranger replied, looking almost sheepish. "But now that we're to be neighbors, I hope you'll call me Duncan."

Part I
BROTHERS

What hath God wrought?
—*Samuel Morse, 1844*
(the first official message sent over the Washington-Baltimore telegraph line,
quoting from the Book of Numbers)

1. Clover

LOVER HAMILL ATTEMPTED TO CALCULATE HIS SHARE of the modest birthday pie his mother had just brought out from the wagon. Three hundred and sixty degrees of pie divided by nine people was forty degrees each, but that would only be if the slices were cut evenly, which they seldom were. Clive, being the man of the hour, would be in charge of dividing the pie up, and that didn't bode well for his younger brother. It wasn't that Clive would apportion himself the largest piece—though no one could have blamed him for doing so on his own birthday—but that he would undoubtedly give outsize pieces to their mother for making the pie in the first place, and to their father and Eddie and Burns because the men needed to keep their strength up, and to Michael because he'd throw a tantrum otherwise, and to Gemma and Flora just because they were girls. Clover figured he would be lucky to end up with a twenty-degree slice. Given that the height of the pie was about four inches and the radius about five, his share would amount to . . . roughly seventeen cubic inches of pie.

Attendant Bernstein could have taken the math even further—reckoning the caloric content of the pie based on its constituent ingredients, for example—but Clover hadn't yet received the education to carry out such a calculation.

His mother put the pie down on the trestle table. A lone beeswax candle was sunk into the middle of the doughy lattice, but the breeze had already put out the flame. Everything would have been so much better back at their house in the Anchor. The pie would have been a cake at least twice the size of this one, and the room would have been pitch dark but for the candle flames spitting shadows over the walls, and everyone would have been warm and comfortable and clean.

But they weren't at home. They were on the road. And on the road, you took what you could get.

Clover realized he'd missed the first couple of lines of the "Birthday Hymn." He joined in just in time to wish his brother long life and happiness—*in the name of the Father and the Daughter and Holy Gravity*. Clive closed his eyes, looking prayerful and solemn even though he was probably only wishing for an extra-special present from Gemma tonight, and then he made a show of trying to blow out the candle. Everybody laughed.

"Eighteen years old." Honor Daniel Hamill gave a little whistle, then clapped a firm hand on Clive's shoulder. "I never thought I'd see the day."

"He doesn't look like a man to me," Burns said, in that way he had of joking and not joking at the same time.

Eddie Poplin squinted into the horizon. "We should get moving," he said. "Only a couple hours of light left."

TOMMY WALLACH

Eddie was Gemma, Flora, and Michael's father, as well as the ministry's official handyman (or, more technically, "factotum"—a word Clover had always liked, but that he liked even more now that he knew enough Latin to translate it: "do everything").

As Clover finished his meager helping of pie (the slice had been closer to fifteen degrees than twenty, and the bottom was burnt from the pot), he watched his brother head off with the other men, toward the clearing where the gathering would be held. Clive gave Gemma a little wave good-bye, and she waved right back, smiling coyly.

Some dark burrowing demon of jealousy quickened in Clover's belly; he felt like taking a swing at someone, or throwing up. Maybe he would've, too, if not for the pair of arms that wrapped around him from behind, still powdered with flour. He made sure Gemma wasn't watching, then allowed himself to relax into his mother's embrace, softening like stale bread brought back to life with a bit of water and a few minutes in the oven.

"You look a hundred feet off the ground, darling. Everything all right?"

"Sure, Ma."

Ellen Hamill followed her son's line of sight, out to where the men had begun laying out the tent poles.

"You know your time's gonna come. Two years is nothing."

"I know."

She turned him around and gripped him by the shoulders. Of the million injustices the Lord had visited on Clover, perhaps the most painful was his height—where Clive seemed destined to take after their father, who towered over almost everyone he met, Clover had gotten the literal short end of the stick. Face-to-face with his mother, his eyes were on the exact same level as hers.

"You believe this or not, but growing up isn't all roses and kittens. Your brother might be a man in the eyes of God now, but being a man means bearing a man's responsibilities."

"I could bear 'em."

"I'm not saying you couldn't. I'm saying you should enjoy the fact that you don't have to. It doesn't last." There was a deep tenderness in his mother's eyes, such that he had to look away. "You know your father and I are awful proud of you, don't you?"

"I know *you* are."

"Daniel is too. He's just not good at showing it."

"He shows it to Clive."

"Clive's chosen a simpler path. Or not simpler, maybe, but one your father understands. You getting noticed by the Library, learning all those things . . . I think you scare him a little."

Clover rolled his eyes at this obvious lie. "What's there to be scared about? I barely learn anything. You wouldn't believe how many rules they've got."

"There's nothing wrong with rules, Clover. What does the Filia tell us about knowledge?"

There were a number of verses his mother could've been referring to, but Clover knew her tastes well enough by now. When it came to the Gospels, she'd take Jiehae and Ivan over Armelle (and she *never* wanted to hear any Nelson). "Learning is a lightening," he quoted.

"That's right." She drew him into a hug. "I just don't want you to float away before you have to."

TOMMY WALLACH

"I won't."

She gave him one last squeeze. "You should get started tuning. The work'll be good for you."

"Yes, Ma."

He wiped his pie-sticky hands on his trousers and headed for the small wagon. Down in the clearing, the men had smoothed out the canvas, which lay on the grass like some sort of huge, flat mushroom. Burns had taken off his shirt, revealing his heavily muscled chest and the quilt of scars that were the origin of his nickname (if you could call it a nickname, given that nobody knew his actual name). Though they'd been on the road together for nearly four months, Clover still didn't trust the man. Burns was a sergeant in the Descendancy Protectorate, tasked with keeping them safe as they preached the word of God along the Tails. But they'd been on plenty of tours before this one, and they'd always gotten by without any protecting. Was the world really getting more dangerous, or was Burns's presence yet another example of the Protectorate's increasing involvement in the doings of the Church?

Clive said he'd heard all sorts of rumors about the sergeant back in the Anchor: that he'd been born outside the Descendancy, that he'd been married to a captured Wesah warrior woman, that he once pulled out a man's eyeball in a bar fight. But so far as Clover could see, all the sergeant ever seemed to do was make off-color jokes and brood. And why didn't he ever bow his head during service, or sing along with the hymns? What was he looking for when he scanned the crowds that gathered beneath the tent to worship, his eyes narrowed like those of some hungry bird of prey?

Eddie and Honor Hamill finished fitting together the pieces

that made up the tent's main post, and then all four men dove under the fabric, little lumps moving like feet beneath a bedsheet. The tent seemed to lift itself up by the center, as if the devil himself had reached down from the sky, pinched the sheet of canvas, and pulled. They emerged through the front flap a minute later, red-faced and sweating. Raising the tent was hard work, and now that Clive was a man, he'd have to do it before every gathering.

It was some slight consolation, anyway.

Inside the small wagon, the soft leather cases in which the instruments were kept were roped tightly to the walls. Clover unpicked the knots and laid them all out in a row, and then he pulled out the tuning fork—a gift from his father on his tenth birthday.

Not a lot of things stay constant in this world, Honor Hamill had said. *But this will.*

And it was true. No matter the time of day or the orientation of the stars or the clemency of the weather, the fork rang out its piercing G like a call to arms against chaos.

Clover tapped the metal against the wooden floor of the wagon. There was something magical about the way the sound just appeared, pulled out of the very air. Not for the first time, he considered the question of just what made one tone different from another. If he'd had to put it into words, he would've said it had something to do with how fast the note shook in your ear—only that wasn't quite right. He'd asked Attendant Bernstein to explain it to him once, but it turned out acoustics was yet another subject he was too young to learn about.

He began with his own instrument, the mandolin, then went on to Gemma's fiddle, his father's bass, and his brother's guitar. It

TOMMY WALLACH

was anxious, delicate work. They only had so many extra strings to last them through the tour, and given the heat of the days and the changes in humidity and elevation as they'd passed over the Teeth—the mountain range to the east of the Anchor—breaks were inevitable. Two tours back, Clive had had to play a five-stringed guitar for a whole month.

Luckily, today was a good day, and all the strings remained intact. Clover put the guitar back in its case and began carrying the instruments one by one to the tent, which was now fully stretched out and staked. Inside, Eddie was hanging the big annulus, while Clive and the two younger Poplin children cleared away any rocks that might trip someone up during the dancing. Just as Clover was making his last trip from the wagon, Gemma came in with a couple mugs of pine tea. She handed one to her father, then offered the other to Clover.

"What about Clive?" he asked.

"I already made him one. It's his birthday, isn't it?"

"Sure is."

But she was always looking out for Clive first. Didn't matter that it was his birthday one bit.

Gemma Poplin was seventeen years old, born right smack-dab between the two brothers. Clover thought about her in ways he knew he wasn't supposed to—not just because lustful thoughts weren't holy, but because she wasn't his to think about. Eddie had been Honor Hamill's best friend since they were boys; it only made sense for their firstborn children to marry. Clive knew this, of course, and as a result, he treated Gemma exactly the same way he did all the girls who fawned over him: not mean or anything, just careless, the way you treated anything that had been handed to you, that you'd never had to fight for.

Of course, even if Gemma *hadn't* been promised to Clive, it wasn't as if she ever would've fallen for Clover. No girl wanted a husband younger than herself, especially one with all the social graces of a wild dog.

So he would always be the little brother in Gemma's eyes, however much he wished it different.

"Something got you blue?" Gemma asked.

Clover hoisted the double bass up onto the platform, then hopped back to the ground. "Everybody keeps asking me that. What would I be blue about?"

"I don't know. Your brother turning eighteen, maybe? I know it's not easy—"

"I'm fine."

"Good. 'Cause I won't be dancing with any moody boys tonight." She leaned over (an inch taller than him, of course) and whispered in his ear. "You'll save one for me, won't you?"

Clover couldn't help but smile. "Slowest song there is."

Gemma put on a bit of an outerlands accent. "Then I'll be waitin' for you in the darkest corner of the room." She gave a little flash of the eyes, then turned on her heel and swept out of the tent.

They talked to each other like that, but it was just playing at words. They wouldn't ever meet in the darkest corner of the room. And if they danced tonight, it would be like a couple of kissing cousins, not sweethearts.

All part of the good Lord's plan, Clover's father would say. But that thought was seldom as comforting as he made it out to be. In fact, a good portion of the time, the good Lord's plan seemed a downright mess.

TOMMY WALLACH

2. Clive

I T WASN'T AS IF CLIVE HAD EXPECTED TO WAKE UP ON HIS eighteenth birthday and find himself transformed, but he'd hoped he would at least *feel* a little different. More mature, maybe. More confident in his convictions. Less anxious about the future.

But no: he woke into the same body and the same mind he'd always had. He said the same morning prayer and sat down to the same breakfast. His pre-gathering duties had shifted, from helping his mother and the other children clean up after dinner to helping the men prepare the tent, but this turned out to be a terrifically unfavorable trade. He didn't have much to add to Eddie and Honor Hamill's conversation about the fraught political situation back in the Anchor, and though he had plenty of questions he wanted to ask Burns, there was something about the sergeant that discouraged idle chatter. Clive missed being up at the big wagon, where Michael and Flora would be running around tickling each other, and Clover would be going on and on about some tree or beetle, and Gemma would be all smiles and sweet looks.

Clive glanced uphill and saw her, long blond hair tinted rose by the last rays of sunset, and felt such a complicated snarl of emotions that he couldn't have separated out the strands if he'd wanted to.

"So how many people we expecting tonight?" Burns asked. Clive was glad to have his train of thought interrupted.

"Should be a good turnout," Eddie said. "Amestown proper's got about four hundred souls, and there's twice that number working the land nearby."

"That's a lot of people to keep track of."

"You expecting trouble?" Clive asked.

"Maybe. Amestown's been part of the Descendancy for five years now, and they still haven't sent a shekel in taxes."

"It's hardscrabble out here," Eddie said, an edge to his voice, as if he were speaking up for one of his own children. "There's nothing extra to go around."

"It's the principle of the thing. We haven't asserted our authority, so they don't respect us."

"We don't have to assert our authority," Honor Hamill said. "That's what God is for."

Burns snorted. "Well, God's got a bad habit of not showing up when you ask him to. So we mortals occasionally have to make our own plans."

Clive covered his mouth so his father wouldn't see him smirking.

"Your plans are your own, Sergeant. We work for the Church, not the Protectorate. And I'll thank you not to fill my son's head with nonsense."

"My apologies, Honor," Burns said, but Clive could tell he wasn't really sorry.

They finished raising the tent just as the shadows of the trees at the edge of the clearing began to stretch out and dissolve into the general darkness. Soon after, Clive spotted the first lantern bouncing up the path from town. Eddie was right that there was likely to be a big crowd at the gathering. Though Amestown had a local novice who ran Sunday services, there hadn't been an official visit from an Honor since the town's incorporation. In these times, and at such a remove from the Anchor, nobody within ten miles was likely to pass up the opportunity for a little bit of preaching and a bigger bit of dancing.

The whole ministry was in the tent now, helping to get all the last details squared away. Clive sat on the edge of the stage, looking over his father's notes for the evening's sermon—Honor Hamill insisted his son provide him with at least three constructive suggestions every week—but he was finding it difficult to concentrate. Gemma's younger brother, Michael, was making a big show of trying to play Honor Hamill's double bass.

"These strings hurt my fingers," he said.

"Because it's too big for you," his twin sister, Flora, chided. "That's why you play mandolin and I play fiddle."

"But I'm bored of the mandolin. Clover won't teach me any new songs."

"I told you," Clover said, "nothing new until you can play 'I Came Me Down to Ground' without making any flubs."

"But it's so haaaard!" Michael turned the last word into a good three-syllable moan. He and Flora were both ten years old, so cute it made you want to kick them in the shins sometimes. They were still new to music, and only allowed to play tambourine and shaker during gatherings.

"You think the mandolin is hard?" Clive asked, putting his father's notes aside.

"It *is* hard!" Michael said.

"How hard?" Clive reached out and caught the boy around the waist, lifting him up off the ground. "As hard as I'd have to throw you to hit the top of this tent?"

"Don't do it!" Michael squealed.

"Do it!" his sister squealed even more loudly.

Clive rolled Michael out onto the grass, tickling him mercilessly. "I would, but your da would give me hell if I broke all your toes."

"You would not!" Michael said through his giggles.

"Try me sometime. You'll see what you get." Finally he allowed the boy to escape his clutches. "Now you and your sister better scoot. Gathering's gonna start soon."

The first few parishioners had already found their spots close to the stage, and more were streaming in all the time. They were dressed in their Sunday best: long muslin dresses dyed yellow and red, white linen shirts, straw hats, even a couple of suits. Though a couple of chairs had been carried up from town to accommodate the oldest members of the congregation, the majority of the crowd sat on wool blankets on the ground. Each family arrived with at least one tallow dip—all of which would be lit and set in brackets pinned to the inside of the tent—and a basket full to the brim with food and liquor; Descendant gatherings were about religion, sure, but there wasn't anything in the Filia about keeping sober.

Clive went out behind the tent, hoping to finish reading over his father's sermon, but his brother followed right on his heels.

"It's not a joke, you know," Clover said. "That boy refuses to practice."

"You mean Michael? He's young. He'll come around to it."

"But he's lazy!"

"He's *ten*! Don't be so hard on him."

Clive turned his attention back to the sermon, but he could sense his brother still had more to say. Something had been weighing on Clover all day; Clive had never seen him look so joyless in the face of a sugar cake. It had to be the fact that Clive had turned eighteen. Here was the one math problem Clover couldn't solve: How was it that no matter how much older he got, his brother managed to remain even older?

"Clover, I'm sorry if today's been tough on you, but you have to underst—"

"Are you gonna marry Gemma when we get home?"

The words had come quickly, tumbling over one another like rocks in a landslide; already, Clover looked as if he wished he could put them all back in his mouth again. Once upon a time, Clive's younger brother had talked about his crush on Gemma openly, as if it were the most unembarrassing thing in the world. But as soon as it became clear that Honor Hamill and Eddie had more or less promised their firstborn children to each other, Clover had gone quiet. For the last two years, in spite of sleeping just a couple of feet away from each other every night, Clive and his brother had managed to avoid the subject of girls entirely—all so they wouldn't have to have this exact conversation.

"I don't think anyone wants us to get married before I get my robes," Clive said, choosing his words carefully.

"But you *do* want to marry her."

A question without a question mark, to which Clive could only provide an answer that wasn't an answer.

"It's what we're meant to do."

His brother took a moment to absorb this, then turned and stepped back through the tent flap without another word. Clive called out after him, but he knew it wouldn't do any good: Clover was nothing if not stubborn.

He gave up on his father's sermon. Too many questions were bouncing around inside his head: Why had he made it sound as if he saw his impending marriage as a burden, rather than a blessing? Why did the thought of being Gemma's husband fill him with such a terrible feeling of disquiet? And if he did marry her—no, *when* he married her—how long would it take his brother to forgive him? Would they ever get back to the easy affinity of childhood, when the only things they argued over were where to build the tree fort, or who would play the hero in their games of bandits and soldiers?

A bell rang from inside the tent, signaling that the gathering was about to begin. There would be time to wrestle with all these questions later—*wounds heal, doubts fester*, as the Filia had it. For now, there was the Lord's work to do.

TOMMY WALLACH

3. Clover

EDDIE OPENED UP THE SERVICE A FEW MINUTES later. Though it had taken him a few years to grow comfortable speaking in front of a crowd, he'd eventually absorbed Honor Hamill's dictum that "every human being has the word of God inside him somewhere." These days, he almost seemed to enjoy it. The congregation recited the Trinity Prayer along with him:

> *Father in the ground*
> *Whose fist is the Daughter*
> *Whose love is Gravity*
> *Thank you for your gift*
> *Release us not into darkness*
> *But hold us to your mantle*
> *As you always have*
> *And always will*
> *Forever and ever*
> *World without end*
> *Amen*

Then Honor Hamill came out from the back of the tent, dressed in his robes the color of flames. He gave the audience a big smile, the kind that made everyone want to smile along with him. Clover's father had been a traveling minister for more than twenty years—making him the most senior Honor currently working the roads. Rumor had it that he would be nominated to the Gloria when they finished this tour of the Tails, and Clover hoped with all his heart that those rumors were true. At sixteen, he'd already been on a dozen tours, and he'd just about had it with life on the road. It also meant he would finally be able to dedicate himself to his studies at the Library full-time.

"Good people of Amestown," Honor Hamill began, "it is such a pleasure to be here with you tonight. The Church sends its apologies that we haven't been able to get an Honor out this way for so long, but I'll do my best to make it worth the wait." The laughter that greeted this statement was polite at best; Clover's father was many things, but hilarious wasn't one of them. "I was pleased to see that the mill our engineers helped you all build is still going strong, and from what I hear, you had a bountiful harvest this past summer. Glory be to God." He applauded for them, which gave them an excuse to applaud for themselves. "I'm going to try to keep things brief tonight, so we can get around to the music and the dancing. But talk is like liquor; if you're gonna go short, you gotta go strong. Ladies and gentlemen, the Book of Nelson will be our moonshine tonight." A low rumble ran through the audience; Nelson wasn't exactly a crowd-pleaser, particularly among those newer to the faith.

Honor Hamill produced his Filia from the shelf under the

TOMMY WALLACH

ambo. It was a work of art—bound in red leather, with a shiny gold-leaf annulus on the cover. "Let me attempt to describe to you the glory of the Daughter," Honor Hamill read, "though no words could ever do justice to the terrible beauty of that creature as she fell from the infernal heavens like some radiant bird of prey. She wore a cloak of crimson fire, but as she approached, all the colors of the rainbow appeared within that crimson. The blue of summer skies. The green of fresh shoots breaking from the loam. Bronzes and silvers and golds more scintillant than any jewels known to man. And when she landed, she gave off a light so bright that it illuminated the farthest reaches of every cavern, every home, and every soul. All the works of man fell away like the veils they were, and humanity stood naked before her. And the Lord said, 'Behold, for I have sent my only daughter to you, to cleanse this world of sin.' But for Noach, who had been warned to build a stronghold deep in the crust of heaven, there to keep his family and two of each animal that walked the Earth, all others burned in the great Conflagration. Even babes and children melted away like wax, their flesh running in rivers through the streets, for they had been tainted by the fruit of those times, as Aleph was said to have been tainted by the nectar of the Great Tree. And the name of that nectar was science, and its sweetness was the sweetness of death."

Clover shivered—he'd always hated that passage.

Honor Hamill gave the dark words time to breathe, to expand in the hearts and minds of the assembly. "There are truths in the Book of Nelson," he said at last. "Truths that must be carried with us every hour of every day." Finally he closed the front cover of his Filia, and it was as if the whole congregation exhaled at once. "My family and I, along with a few other good people I'm lucky to call friends, have been out on the road for almost four months now. Amestown represents the farthest reach of our circuit, the outermost limit of the Lord's Descendancy as it stands today. Tomorrow we begin the long journey back home. But tonight is important for another reason. It is my eldest son's eighteenth birthday. And it is for him that I read from the Book of Nelson. He left the Anchor as a boy, but he will return as a man. And a man doesn't shy away from hard truths."

Clover felt another stab of jealousy as his father beamed down at Clive.

"I fear for him," Honor Hamill went on to say, looking back up at the audience. "As I fear for all of us. Time rushes forward, and it requires all our strength not to be dragged along with it. We must surrender to that divine energy that binds us to the earth, that holds the moon and sun at their safe and proper distance. We must resist the devil who beckons us upward, with promises of so-called progress. In the name of the Father below us . . ."

"In the name of the Father below us . . . ," the congregation repeated.

". . . the Daughter beside us . . ."

". . . the Daughter beside us . . ."

". . . and the Holy Force of Gravity."

". . . and the Holy Force of Gravity."

"Amen."

"Amen."

TOMMY WALLACH

From the back of the stage, Clover watched Clive step forward to take his solo. The gathering was in full swing, everyone dancing and clapping along with the music, their faces orangey-red in the flickering candlelight. In the enclosed space made by the canvas, the stench of moonshine and the reek of sweat battled for supremacy.

Clover's father, his body mostly hidden behind the double bass, gave him a pointed look. Clover had lost track of the progression, chopping the wrong chord on the downbeat for the last few measures. For some reason, the puniness of the mandolin embarrassed him tonight, as if he'd shown up for a sword fight with a butter knife. Clive stepped back and made room for Gemma to take a solo on the fiddle, and as they passed each other, they shared a smile: man to woman, Aleph to Eva, ready to engender nations.

"I'm feeling fit to pass out," Clover said to his father, once the song was finished.

"I think we can manage the last few without you," Honor Hamill said. "Get yourself to bed."

"Thanks, Da."

Clover put his mandolin away and left the tent. Just outside, a handful of people were congregated around the tables where the food and libations had been laid out. Beneath one, a corpulent, thick-bearded man was already asleep and muttering. Nearby, a couple of teenagers were in the process of slipping away into the woods at the edge of the field, advertising their misbehavior with loud giggles. Clover wondered why it always seemed that everybody in the world was having more fun than him. Why did loneliness stick to the spirit like sap, so that even when you were surrounded by hundreds of people, you could end up feeling entirely on your own?

The urge struck him suddenly, and he acted before he could think better of it. Making sure no one was watching, he threw out the dregs of his old mug of pine tea and filled it up to the brim with shine. The alcohol burned like the Daughter going down, but after a few mouthfuls, everything turned warm and numb and sleepy. Within minutes, he could hardly remember what he'd been so sad about. What did it matter if Clive was a man now? What did *anything* matter?

He drifted like a dandelion seed back into the tent. Gemma was singing "What a Weight." Her skin shimmered with sweat, and her voice was a lightning bolt.

I'm gonna tell her I love her tonight, Clover thought. *My brother be damned.*

"That's a fine specimen, ain't it?" said a man standing nearby. His shirt was unbuttoned a few inches too far down his chest, and the red crackle around his pupils advertised his advanced state of inebriation.

"Sure is," Clover said.

"The things I could do to her."

"All of 'em," Clover added, enjoying the novel experience of being taken for a normal teenage boy, rather than the prudish son of an Honor.

"Between you and me"—the man leaned closer, but went on speaking at a normal volume—"I say we've put up with these fanatics long enough. All this mumbo jumbo about God's Daughter and how we should give 'em money for that fancy city of theirs? It's horseshit, plain and simple."

Even through the increasingly dense fog induced by the shine,

TOMMY WALLACH

Clover was shocked. He'd heard the adults talk about how difficult it was for the Descendancy to maintain its authority out at the fringes of its territory, but he'd never actually heard someone speak so disrespectfully about the Church.

"You don't believe in tithing?" he asked.

"Tithe is just another word for tax, which is just another word for thievery."

"But the Anchor built that new mill of yours, and they advise your farmers—"

The man waved this argument away like a bad smell. "We were doing just fine before they came along. Better, even. And now we always got to be worried they're gonna get wind of what's going on out east. I mean, if these folks had shown up just a few days ago, they mighta caught sight of that fire, and then what? They'd bring the hammer down, believe you me."

"The Descendancy doesn't believe in violence."

"They say that, sure, but then what do they have that Protectumate for?"

"Protectorate," Clover corrected. "And what fire are you talking about?"

"You didn't hear? Riley was bringing the you-know-what over from the pumphouse, and he gets it too close to the—"

At that moment, a woman standing nearby suddenly slapped the man in the back of he head. "What kinda crazy are you talking, Dominic? You oughta be ashamed of yourself. And him a member of this fine ministry and all."

"What's that?" Dominic said.

"Didn't you see him up there playing the mandolin?" The

woman leaned down and pinched Clover's cheek. Her breath stank of shine. "And ain't he cute as a button?" She straightened up and took Dominic by the arm. "Come on. We gotta get you home."

Dominic put his weight onto the woman's shoulder and they stumbled off together. Clover closed his eyes, trying to get his swimming head around everything he'd just heard. He needed to lie down.

In his drunken state, it took him nearly half an hour to set up the tent, during which time he tried to put together a mental list of all the questions brought up by his short conversation with Dominic. Who was Riley? What was you-know-what? What was a pumphouse? Why had there been a fire, and what would it matter if someone had seen it?

He lay down inside the tent with every intention of staying awake long enough to consider these questions more deeply. But the moment his head hit the pillow, all of them dissolved, and he was out cold.

4. Clive

MY, BUT THERE WERE A LOT OF PRETTY GIRLS IN THE crowd tonight: small girls and big girls, older girls and younger girls, light-haired girls and dark-haired girls, light-skinned girls and dark-skinned girls. Girls who danced like they had the devil on their minds and girls who danced like they wouldn't give up their first kiss until they were standing beneath the bridal arch. Each one made beautiful by the candle-light and the shine and the music.

But there was one more beautiful than the others, because she was making such an effort to catch Clive's eye. She wore her chestnut hair in a long plait that snaked down her neck and over her chest, limning the décolletage of a white cotton dress so tatty it was almost improper. She fingered the end of the plait coyly as she swayed along with the music, and her smile was like a promise.

After the next song, Gemma started up a reel on the fiddle, to give the rest of the band a break. And could it be a coincidence that the girl chose that precise moment to slip out of the tent?

Outside, a few dozen people were milling around, talking and laughing. Clive spotted the girl sauntering around the edge of the tent, away from the crowd, and began to follow her.

"Someone's got mischief on his mind," Burns said.

The sergeant was leaning up against the tight canvas of the tent, smoking a cigarillo.

"I don't know what you mean."

"I ain't judging, Clivey. Truth be told, I've got some mischief of my own to attend to. Perhaps you'd like to join in on the fun? I could use a second."

"What are you planning?"

"Sorry, but I can't tell you that. I can only show you." He took one last drag on the cigarillo, then flicked the stub away. "I'm not saying it'll be more fun than a grope and a giggle with a willing local, but it'll certainly be more instructive."

The laughter and shouting of the assembly seemed to dim. Gemma's fiddle was a distant birdsong. Clive thought of the thousand things he could say in objection—*My father wouldn't want me to* or *I'm supposed to be playing at the gathering* or *I don't trust you far as I can throw you, and I doubt I could even pick you up.*

But he didn't say any of it. Not only because he'd been dying to pick the sergeant's brain about the soldiering life ever since they'd started traveling together, but also because Burns had already begun walking away, across the long grass, toward the tree line— and whatever it was he meant by mischief.

TOMMY WALLACH

Branches cracked beneath their feet like brittle old bones. The temperature in these parts could drop precipitously after dark, but tonight was on the warm side, and the forest was abuzz with insects. They congregated at the watering holes of perspiration perpetually forming all over Clive's body.

"Why're we walking through the woods when there's a perfectly good trail?" he asked.

"Your brother would've worked that out already," Burns said.

Clive subdued the flash of anger, resisting the urge to retort. The jibe only stung because it was true. And now that he thought about it, the explanation *was* pretty simple: they weren't taking the trail because they were trying to avoid being seen. A few minutes later, Clive caught sight of a vague constellation floating off in the distance. For a moment, he wondered if he was about to be inducted into some supernatural realm—*Fairies really do exist*, Burns would say—then the lights resolved into a handful of candle flames seen through sooty windows.

"Amestown," Clive said. "But isn't everyone at the gathering?"

"Some folks are too old to make the trip. Others don't want to."

"Why not?"

"Whatever your daddy tells you, folks got their own religion in the outerlands, and they ain't near as eager to trade it in as you might expect."

"You mean the totems?"

The totems were little stumps of flaking iron that could be found most everywhere people had built up some kind of township, and even in the woods sometimes. Descendant doctrine had it that they were holy relics, left behind by the children of Noach in memory of their progenitor. But some outlanders believed the totems to be spirits in their own right, leaving burnt offerings and garlands of flowers at their bases—a bunch of silly superstitions, in Clive's opinion.

"Sure. Or else they buy into that whole Jesus story, or they go the Wesah route and decide every squirrel and every other tree is some sort of god."

"If the people don't believe in the teachings of the Church, why did Amestown agree to incorporate?"

"Because we convinced the town council that it was in their best interests to do so—which it was. But most of the folks at that gathering wouldn't mind if the whole Descendancy disappeared tomorrow." Burns stopped and took a folded piece of paper out of his back pocket. "Now where are we going?"

"Is that a map of Amestown? Where'd you get it?"

"One of our engineers made it a couple years back, when he was working on that mill." Burns folded the map up again. "This way."

They turned left, keeping behind the tree line. Clive caught an occasional glimpse of the town through the branches. It was bigger than he'd expected—at least a hundred buildings of one sort or another. The one Burns eventually singled out as their destination was practically a ruin—its porch had rotted through in a dozen places, and where there had once been a small four-paned window, there was now just a frame. Burns approached the door and knocked with his fist rather than his knuckles, so the sound was like a heartbeat.

Nobody answered.

"See anything in that window?" Burns asked.

Clive squinted into the darkness: a half-disintegrated wicker rocking chair, shelves collapsed and moldering, broken pieces of ceramic.

"I don't think anybody's lived here for a long time."

"Shit on a stick." Burns pulled out the map again. "Guess we're going this way, then." He didn't head back toward the woods, but straight down the main road of Amestown.

"I thought you wanted to keep hidden."

"I did. Now I don't. Keep up, Clivey."

Closer to the center of Amestown, the buildings were in much better shape. In fact, some of them were downright impressive. Most towns this far from the capital were pretty backward when it came to construction, but all the homes here had at least one window, and a handful were two stories tall.

Burns stopped in front of a white stucco building with a sign swinging creakily over the entrance: a public house. Light spilled out from the doorway, along with the jangle of an out-of-tune piano.

"After you," Burns said.

"What?" Clive almost laughed. "I'm not going in *there*!"

"Oh no? Why not?"

"Da says places like this are the devil's laboratory."

"Your da's right. But one can't do the Lord's work without spending a little time with the devil."

Clive shook his head. "I'm sorry. I'll just wait for you out here."

Without warning, Burns grabbed hold of Clive's arm just above the elbow, his grip as tight as a manacle. "When you're a high-and-mighty Honor like your daddy, you can be better than places like this. But you came with *me* tonight, and that means you'll damn well do what I tell you to." With that, he pulled Clive forcibly through the swinging doors of the public house.

Inside, a man in a straw hat and no shirt was playing something slow and bawdy on a ramshackle spinet. The instrument was so busted up it looked like the wall behind it was the only thing keeping it upright, but Clive recognized the insignia of Anderson's Music Shop carved into the lid—a gift to Amestown from the Anchor, likely on the occasion of its incorporation. Three or four men sat at the bar, drinking beer and chatting, but it was the woman that caught Clive's attention. He'd never seen so much skin all at once (at least not outside of a bit of spying he'd done back home, around and about the public baths). Seen from the threshold of the tavern, the woman had a kind of rough beauty to her, but as Clive crossed the room, he began to make out the texture of her face, layered like a wedding cake, rouged and mascaraed toward an uncanny approximation of youth. Her dress arced like a child's jumping rope down and across her chest. The plunging crevasse outlined there pulled at his eyes like some demonic misappropriation of Gravity.

He didn't have to be told what she was. Eighteen years of life was plenty of time to learn to recognize sin and money and the places they overlapped. There were women like this back at the Anchor, in spite of the Church's best efforts. They walked the streets of the Third Quarter, pretending to be beggars.

The men at the bar had all gone quiet when they noticed the newcomers, but the pianist was too drunk to notice much of anything, so the cheery off-kilter tonk never stopped.

TOMMY WALLACH

"Can I help you with something?" the bartender asked. He was an older man, silver-haired, with blunt brass rings on most of his fingers.

"A thimble of your strongest," Burns said.

"Sure thing." The bartender unstoppered a bottle and began to pour.

"Say, I just went to visit my old pal Arthur, but his place was all boarded up." Burns's tone was chummy and nonchalant. "I sure hope nothing happened to him. You boys know where he's at?"

The men at the bar shared a series of loaded glances. "You know—" one of them began to say.

"Let me stop you there," Burns interrupted. "See, this ain't my first time around the Tails, if you get my meaning, and one thing I've learned is that whenever someone doesn't answer a question straightaway, he's fixing to lie to you."

The man who'd started to speak stood up, knocking his chair over behind him. "You calling me a liar?"

"Not yet. That's my whole point."

"Well, my whole point is I don't take shit from ugly Anchorite bruisers."

"Diego," the bartender growled, "you shut your mouth and sit your drunk ass back down."

The man called Diego stared hard at Burns for a few seconds more, then grudgingly righted his chair and sat down again. He muttered something in an incomprehensible outerland patois that set the painted woman to cackling.

"You'll have to excuse him," the bartender said. "Diego's protective of Arthur. We all are."

"I understand. I respect blind loyalty." Burns downed the shot on the bar; the bartender immediately refilled it. "Listen, I ain't looking to cause trouble. I just need to visit the old man and make sure he's keeping his promises."

"Art'll have eighty summers behind him come November. Hardly knows where he is half the time."

"Then we won't have a problem. You got my word on that." Burns put out a hand, and after a moment, the bartender shook it.

"He moved a few years ago, to a little shack on a hill about a mile south of town. Keeps a few cows and sheep, makes toys for the kiddies. Widow Moses brings his food out to him once a day, in the mornings. Just follow the main road east until it splits, then head uphill. You'll see it."

"Thank you kindly." Burns reached into his pocket and pulled out a silver shekel. He set it spinning on the bar. "Next round's on me, gentlemen. And make it two for the lady." He tipped his hat to her, and she blushed all the way down to the place Clive was still trying his best not to look.

About half a mile outside of town, they found the spot where the main road sent a narrow envoy up into the hills. Ascending, Clive discerned the golden eyes of an owl glittering between the branches of a tree, just before the creature emitted a loud, eerie hoot and flew off into the night. The trail devolved into a slight browning in the grass underfoot, and before long, the silhouettes of two structures materialized out of the gloom: a small hut that was clearly the old man's home, and a wooden lean-to for the cows a little farther up

TOMMY WALLACH

the hill. A lone heifer was still out grazing. It lowed genially at their approach.

Burns gave a few quick pounds on the door. "Arthur Edwards!"

A clatter from inside. "Who's there?"

"Sergeant Burns of the Descendancy Protectorate. Open up!"

"Unless you wanna see me buck naked, you'll hold your horses." A minute later the door opened, revealing a wizened old man in a white nightshirt and cap. His eyebrows were two wild thatches of silver, and his spine arched like a blade of grass bowing in the breeze.

"Evening, Arthur," Burns said. "Mind if we come inside and take a quick look around?"

"It's the middle of the night. Can't you come back at a reasonable hour?"

"Afraid not. We leave town bright and early tomorrow."

Arthur let out a raspy sigh. "All right. Come on in."

Clive followed Burns into the dingy shack. The only illumination came from the wan moonlight that shone through the cabin's small thick-paned window and the gleam of the moribund embers in the stove.

"I can't see for shit in here," Burns said.

"Patience."

Clive heard the groan of a drawer sliding open, then caught a whiff of bayberry. Arthur opened up the stove and lit the candle off an ember. He set it in a bronze holder nearby, casting the whole of his humble existence in a weak red glow: blankets askew on the narrow bed in the corner, a washbasin and a sliver of soap, half a loaf of bread laid out on a pinewood table next to an empty jar of honey and a sticky carving knife. On the wall opposite the bed, a collection of wicked metal tools hung from hooks above a work surface littered with springs and clasps and wood scraps.

"What are you making here?" Burns said.

"This and that."

"Be specific, Arthur."

"Toys, mostly. Dolls. The occasional flute. Take a look. I've got nothing to hide." He reached up to a shelf and pulled down an unfinished wooden box. There was a crank on the side. "Go ahead." Burns took the box and began turning the crank. A bit of halting music played, tinkling like raindrops on a tin roof, and then a little man leaped out of the top. He wore a golden robe, just like the Archbishop, and his face was screwed up into a ridiculous grimace.

"It's not as good as what I used to make," Arthur said. "The fingers don't listen anymore. I have pains like you wouldn't believe."

Burns put the box down. "And your old pursuits?"

There was a flash of apprehension in the old man's rheumy eyes. "I'm done with all that," he said quietly.

"Glad to hear it." A pregnant pause. "Well, I suppose we'll be going then. Would you mind if I lit my candle off yours, for the journey back?"

"Not at all."

Burns pulled a fresh beeswax candle out of his jacket pocket and lit it. *Strange*, Clive thought. *The sergeant had been happy enough to walk in the dark on the way here.*

Arthur escorted them back outside.

"See you on the next tour," Burns said.

The old man allowed himself a creaky death rattle of a laugh. "Let the Daughter take me before then, eh?"

The door closed behind them, and Burns immediately cut across the pasture toward the cowshed. Clive jogged to catch up. Inside the wooden lean-to, two big cows were lying peacefully on the dirt floor. The air was warm, heavy with the smell of hay and slow-moving animals. One of the cows raised her head, but soon decided the guests were of no consequence and put it right back down again. There was a stall for a horse at the back of the room, empty but for a big mound of hay.

"What are we doing out here?" Clive asked.

The sergeant pointed at the hay. "Move that pile for me," he said.

"Why?"

"You see any horses in here?"

"There's cows."

"And there's a whole field just outside, city boy. Now don't make me ask again."

Clive set to work with a rusty pitchfork he found leaning up against the wall. The cows watched the flying fodder with indifference, but they startled when the pitchfork clanged against metal. Clive knelt down and swept away the last of the hay. A brass ring was set in the middle of a wooden trapdoor.

He looked up at Burns, unable to hide his admiration. "How did you know?"

"Because I'm a misanthrope. Open 'er up."

Clive pulled at the brass ring. Beneath the door, shallow steps descended into a cleanly hewn square of darkness.

"A man his age couldn't dig this," Clive said. "He must've had help."

"A fine observation."

"So what's down there?"

"Only one way to find out." Burns handed the candle to Clive. "I'll be right behind you."

Clive was far from excited at the prospect of plunging blindly into the abyss, but he didn't want to look cowardly in front of Burns. Besides, he couldn't help but be curious about what the old man was hiding.

He counted steps: twelve altogether. At the bottom, he found himself in a room about twice the size of the cowshed up above, and full of strange objects. Some were recognizable from the smithies and woodshops of the Anchor—the clamp, the lathe, the crucible—but Clive had no names for the rest of it. Tiny strips of metal had been melted onto other pieces of metal in mysterious configurations. Copper had been hammered into thread-like strands, which were spooled up or set running from one enigmatic contraption to another. Glass had been blown into strange shapes, and the resulting vessels held various colored liquids.

"What is this place?" he asked.

"Arthur would call it a workshop," Burns said. "Your father would call it a den of sin. They'd both be right." Clive frowned, still uncertain. "It's the anathema, Clivey! In the flesh!"

Of course. The room *literally* reeked of things that should not be known. Burns handed Clive one of the mysterious glass globes. It was affixed to a heavy piece of wood striated with thin bands of metal. One of those copper threads spiraled around within the globe, as if tracing the path of a trapped and frantic firefly. "Hold on to this," he said. "We'll bring it back to the Anchor with us, as evidence."

"What about the rest of it?"

Burns grinned. "Well, that's the fun part." The sergeant got his hands underneath the nearest table, and letting out a sound halfway between and a groan and a roar, he turned the whole thing over. Glass shattered. Metal snapped. There was a hissing sound as one of the infernal liquids was absorbed into the earth, and the sickening smell intensified. The sergeant had an animal joy in his eyes as he reduced the room to fragments and splinters and particles, and Clive had to remind himself that this was a godly, sanctioned destruction. In the space of a minute, Burns had turned the workshop into a ruin.

"That should do it," he said, still panting from the effort. "Let's go."

Clive was all too happy to get back to the surface. He took the steps two at a time. "I can't believe that old man did all of this," he said. "He seemed so frail."

"Plenty of frail men have done plenty worse."

"I know. But that doesn't mean—"

As Clive reached the top step, he felt a sudden shooting pain in his shoulder. He cried out and swatted at his back. His first thought was that he'd been bitten by a spider, only this hurt so much more than a bite should. . . .

Arthur backed away into the corner of the cowshed, his expression an unholy mixture of terror and wrath. He held the carving knife in his palsied right hand, its blade dripping black with blood. And now Clive could feel the warm wetness trickling down his spine and into his pants.

"You monsters," Arthur snarled.

"Oh, it's only you," Burns said. "I was worried those yokels from the inn had followed us." He looked at Clive. "Did the old man poke you with his little pecker? We'll make him pay for that, won't we?"

"Look out!" Clive said. Arthur was on the attack again, heading for Burns this time. But the sergeant saw it coming from a mile away, and delivered a hard fist straight to the old man's nose.

Arthur went down onto his knees, blood pouring from his nostrils. "Oh, you fools," he murmured. "You poor, blind fools."

"We aren't the criminals here, Arthur," Burns said.

"Your leaders are the criminals!" the old man spat back. "Your religion is the criminal! Your dogma and your cant have frozen humanity at a—"

Burns kicked Arthur in the stomach, interrupting the tirade. "If we're so terrible, then why did we show you mercy the *first* time we discovered your little hobby?"

"I spit on your mercy," Arthur said, hawking bloody saliva onto Burns's shoe.

Burns placed that same shoe on the old man's neck. "You gave us your word, Arthur. You lied to your God, and your sovereign protector, and for what? For this?" He grabbed the object Clive had carried up from the workshop. "Do you even know what this is?"

The old man laughed. "Of course I know. I made it with my own hands."

"So what is it?"

"Nothing so extraordinary. Your precious Epistem could make one himself if he wanted to. But I suppose he enjoys keeping you all in the dark."

"You didn't answer my question."

"You wouldn't understand."

TOMMY WALLACH

Burns put more weight on the old man's neck. "Try me."

"Fine! It's a conductive filament of copper built into a glass container to aid in the radiation of light."

"Wrong," Burns said. "It's a weapon."

Clive looked away as soon as he realized what was about to happen. There was a sickening crunch as brittle bone cracked and caved, followed by a vast and terrible silence. Clive felt his eyes drawn back to the old man against his conscious will, as if it were his duty to bear witness to the horror.

A stillness beyond stillness. Eyes open and unblinking. The object was sunk so deeply into the old man's skull, it seemed to have become a part of him.

Clive made the sign of the annulus on his chest, drawing the circle from clavicle to navel and back, as he spoke the Trinity Prayer under his breath.

What had they done?

5. Clover

LOVER WOKE WITH A TERRIBLE POUNDING IN HIS HEAD, and realized it had to be the famous "shinefog" that adults were always going on about. An interesting physiological phenomenon: undoubtedly the headache was related to dehydration, but how could drinking so much fluid make someone dehydrated? His reasoning failed him after that, obliterated by the pain; he felt as if a fissure had opened up in the middle of his brain, and now the two halves were attempting to separate themselves entirely. He sat up with a groan. Clive was still fast asleep on the pallet next to him, which was odd; usually Clover was the later to rise.

He dressed quietly and left the tent. A warm breeze was blowing, hard enough to loose the seeds from nearby dandelions. He caught one in his hands like a firefly, peeking at it through the gap before setting it free again. Though he wouldn't dare tell his father, the little balls of fluff always reminded him of the Filia story about Onan, whom God slew for spilling his seed on the ground. Strange that flowers could get away with things men could not.

The rest of the ministry was already awake, eating breakfast out behind the big wagon. The mornings after gatherings were always a culinary bounty. Parishioners often brought gifts of food to the service, and last night had been no exception: jars of honey and raspberry preserves, plump blueberries and sweet cream, even a small wheel of goat's milk cheese. Clover jammed a bit of everything into his bowl, spooning only a few dollops of thick porridge over the top.

They'd begin the trip back west later today, by way of the Southern Tail this time. There were still months of travel ahead of them, but Clover always enjoyed the feeling of cresting the figurative hill and gazing down on the return journey. Finally you could allow yourself to fantasize about the creature comforts of home without it being a sort of torture. Most of the ministry would be looking forward to warm beds and cozy fireplaces and big dinners, but Clover was most excited about returning to the Library. He'd been rereading the same five books since they left the Anchor, and by now he could recite whole passages from memory—a talent that impressed exactly no one.

"Where's your brother?" Flora asked, just as Clover sat down next to her on the grass. Her pale cheeks were gory with smeared fruit.

"Sleeping."

"After he went to bed all early last night? What a lazybones."

Clover frowned. "He went to bed early?"

"He disappeared just after you did," Honor Hamill said. "We figured he'd earned the break, seeing as it was his birthday and all."

But Clover could remember waking up sometime during the night—probably another side effect of the shine—and noticing that his brother wasn't there. It had been dead silent outside the tent, which meant the gathering had ended. So where had Clive been?

"Now that I think about it," Clover said, "I do remember him coming in, just as I was falling asleep. I must've thought it was a dream."

"Maybe you're still dreaming," Michael said. "Maybe you need me to wake you up." With that, he gave Clover a sharp rap on the forehead.

"Ah!" Clover shouted, raising both hands to his temples; the shinefog had transformed Michael's fist into a sledgehammer.

"What's wrong with you?" his mother said suspiciously.

"Nothing."

She set her bowl aside and came over to where he was sitting. "Stand up."

"What for?"

"I'm not asking."

He rose reluctantly. His mother stared hard into his right eye and then his left, pulling down the skin of his cheeks to get a better look.

"You were *drinking* last night!"

"Ooooooh!" Michael and Flora said at the same time. They loved seeing people get in trouble.

"Just a little," Clover said.

His mother poked him hard in the sternum. "The amount's not the issue!"

"You let Clive drink."

"He's older."

"But you let him do whatever he wants! It's bullshit!"

Clover stalked off, kicking his almost untouched bowl of porridge across the grass as he went, but was drawn up short by his father.

"Clover Hamill, you get back here this instant."

Maybe in a couple of years, he'd have the strength to say no to that voice—but not yet. He turned around, careful not to look at Gemma; the pity in her eyes would only make him feel worse.

"Apologize to your mother," Honor Hamill said.

"Sorry," he said.

"That's right you are. And you'll be cleaning everyone's dishes this morning, just to prove it."

Rage rising like a sun inside him—a bright red disc of fire. He forced it back down, out of sight. The world wasn't just. When would he stop expecting it to be?

"Yes, Da."

After breakfast he carried the bowls in a precarious column to the stream that ran along the western edge of Amestown, a tributary of the great river known as the Ivan. He took off his socks and rolled up the cuffs of his pants, then walked out into the flow. The water was icy cold, clear as glass. Minnows nipped at the particles of food that came off the bowls, clustered around his legs like a living cloud. His feet went numb, and his head finally began to clear of the shinefog.

He didn't go back to the campsite when he'd finished the

washing; it would take at least an hour for the men to fold up the big tent and load the wagons. Instead he walked upstream, his feet sinking deliciously into the soft mud, alert for anything that merited investigation: the jeweled flash of a leaping fish, a puffed-up bullfrog in the rushes, the exposed root structure of an alder. The banks of the stream rose up until they were five or six feet high on either side; in one spot, a small waterfall issued out of an opening in the dirt. Glancing into the hole, Clover saw an incongruous gleam of white. He reached inside and pulled out a fist-size stone of flawless white: quartz crystal, if he wasn't mistaken, polished by the flow of the water over who knew how many decades, just as the Earth itself had been polished into a sphere by the holy force of Gravity. Hypothetically, the stone could be traded with some boy back at the Anchor for candy, or a toy, or maybe even a couple of shekels—but Clover knew he would keep it, adding it to the collection of semiprecious stones and uncut gems he kept beneath his bedroom window.

So caught up was he in admiring his new prize, he didn't hear the footsteps. It was only when a shadow extinguished the sparkle of the crystal that he looked up.

"Hello there."

The man was standing atop the opposite bank of the stream, just a few feet away.

"Hello," Clover said.

"It's good to see you again."

Clover squinted. The man was backlit by the sun, casting his face in shadow. "We've met?"

"We have. I'm Dominic. Remember?"

Finally, the lingering curtain of shinefog parted. This was the man Clover had spoken to last night, about the fire and the pump-house.

"I was about a hundred sheets to the wind last night, wasn't I?" Dominic said.

"I guess."

"And I said some crazy things."

He laughed, so Clover laughed along with him. They went on laughing until the laughter died and then there was only the bur-bling of the creek between them. Dominic sidestepped down the bank and came to stand right at the edge of the water. His eyes were hollow, ringed with sleeplessness, and there was an unhealthy reptilian sheen to his skin. A cricket chirped.

"I'd sure hate to think you took anything I said to heart," he said. "I was just blowing off steam. You didn't repeat any of it to your daddy, did you?"

Clover shook his head.

"And you and me agree it would be best to keep it that way, don't we?"

Clover had never been one for telling lies, but he had a strong feeling what he was supposed to say right now. *You know, I hardly remember a thing you said last night, and even if I did, I wouldn't see any reason to tell anyone else about it. So farewell, stranger, and have a pleasant life.*

But something hijacked the words on their journey from his brain to his mouth. It was the thought of his brother—an adult now, able to drink whatever he wanted, to sneak out in the middle of the night, to marry Gemma if and when it suited him. And here

Clover was, without hardly any rights at all. Lord, but he was sick and tired of being a child. He wanted to be a *man*. And men didn't tell lies out of fear.

"I'm meant to tell my father everything," he said, puffing himself up like a rooster about to crow. "And that's just what I plan on doing."

"I see."

Dominic hesitated, as if teetering on the edge of something momentous. Then he took a step forward, into the stream itself. Clover backed away, but the bank behind him was steep and muddy. He'd never be able to make it to the top before Dominic got hold of him. He looked around for a weapon, but there was nothing close by. All he had was the crystal.

"I'm real sorry about this," Dominic said, as he reached the other side of the creek. One more step and he'd be close enough to strike . . .

"Can I help you, sir?"

Clive stepped out from behind a tree just a dozen yards or so upstream. And for once, Clover was grateful that his brother was tall and strong, intimidating even at eighteen. Dominic took a step backward, out of the flow of the stream, muddying it up as he went.

"I was just saying good morning to your friend here. We met at the gathering last night."

"Well, you've said it, haven't you?"

Dominic put on his smile again, fake as a skull's. "I suppose I have." He turned back to Clover. "Nice to see you again, young man. Glad we could have this talk. I hope you'll remember what I said." With that, he hopped up the bank and disappeared off into the woods. Clover felt a throbbing in his right hand. He looked down and saw that he'd been squeezing the stone so hard it had left a bloodless white patch in the middle of his palm.

"You okay?" Clive asked, extending a hand to pull Clover up out of the streambed.

Clover scrabbled up on his own. "I'm fine." He gave Clive his best accusatory glare. "The real question is how *you* are."

"What do you mean?"

"Where were you last night?"

"Last night? I was, you know, sleeping. Obviously." But Clive had never been a very good liar, and a few seconds later he threw up his hands in surrender. "Fine. You got me. How'd you find out?"

"Doesn't matter. Where were you?"

"Burns said I shouldn't talk about it."

"Burns? What does Burns have to do with anything?"

"He—you have to promise me you won't say anything to Da."

"I promise. Get on with it already."

So Clive told him the story of what had happened in Amestown last night: the broken-down house and the painted lady in the tavern; Arthur Edwards in his nightshirt, with his Archbishop-in-a-box toy; his secret basement, and Burns's wanton destruction; the sharp shock of the old man's knife, and then . . .

If it had come from anyone else, Clover wouldn't have believed it. But Clive would never make up something like that.

"You're saying Burns killed him? Right in front of you?"

"He was just protecting me."

"From an old man?"

"From an old man who'd been doing the devil's work for decades!

I mean, you should've seen the stuff he had down there. I could practically *smell* the sin."

"What kind of stuff was it?"

"Oh no," Clive said. "I've told you more than enough. Now it's your turn."

"My turn?"

Clive gestured off into the woods. "That man I chased off—he was trying to get you to keep your mouth shut about something."

"Last night, at the gathering, he mentioned something about a fire, and someone named Riley. I didn't understand much, to be honest, but I'm sure it'll mean something to Da."

"I'm sure it would," Clive said. "Only you can't tell him."

At first Clover assumed he must have misheard. He and Clive never kept secrets from their parents—not about anything important anyway. "Why not?"

"Because I want to go home," Clive said.

"What does going home have to do with it?"

"He's an Honor, Clover. If you tell him, he'll have to look into it. We'll have to stay out here." There was something ragged and desperate in Clive's voice, and Clover had a flash of insight.

"You're scared!" he said, unable to fully disguise the pleasure he took in that realization.

"Sure, I'm scared! I'm *dead* scared!" Clive grabbed Clover by the shoulders. "What I saw last night—it was awful. And I get the feeling that man you were talking to was thinking about doing something awful too. Everything's all wrong out here, Clover. I can feel it. So let's just forget about it and go home, okay?"

"But Da wouldn't want us to—"

"Promise me! Right now!"

"Fine!" Clover said, wilting in the face of his brother's intensity. He couldn't remember the last time he'd seen Clive so upset. "Fine, I promise."

"Thank the Daughter." Clive clasped one of Clover's hands between his own, squeezing tightly. When he let go, Clover accidentally dropped the crystal. Clive bent down to pick it up. "What's this?"

"I found it in the stream," Clover said.

Clive held the stone up to the sun. "What a beaut. It even lets some light through." Clover hadn't noticed the seams of pink and green veining the crystal. It reminded him of the black opal Bernstein had given him for his thirteenth birthday. *A rainbow in rock,* he'd called it.

"I also found a place where the pike are leaping pretty strong," Clover said.

"Show me."

They spent the next hour exploring the woods and the stream together, talking about a whole lot of nothing. It was almost like old times, back before girls and duties and thoughts of the future had come between them. Back when they were friends first and brothers second.

They were kneeling on the rocks at the edge of the creek, setting leaves with tiny twig passengers to race downstream, when an animal sprinted across the surface of the water, from one bank to the other.

"Did you see that?" Clive said.

"It's a shrew," Clover replied.

"But it walked on water!"

"Actually, they've got these hairs on their feet that trap air bubbles. So it's more like they run on air."

"How do you know that?"

"I read it in this book about rodents they've got in the Library."

Clive shook his head, smiling. "You know just about everything, don't you?"

"Not even close."

"Well it seems that way sometimes. I . . . I'm proud of you, Clover. I'm sorry if I don't say that enough."

Clover felt himself blushing. He hoped his brother wouldn't notice. "It's okay."

"And . . . and I want you to know . . . I'm sorry about Gemma, too."

Suddenly the warm feeling in Clover's chest froze over. He didn't want to talk about Gemma. It had been a mistake to bring her up last night, but he hadn't been able to help himself. Things had just felt so different between her and Clive these past few months. They'd always been flirtatious, of course, but that flirtation had recently taken on a new sort of significance, an intimacy that made Clover feel even more left out than he had before. Now that he knew his brother was definitely going to marry her, he didn't ever want to talk about it again. Talking about it only made it that much more real.

But Clive had clearly struggled to broach the subject, and he planned to see the conversation through to the bitter end. "You

TOMMY WALLACH

know how it is between Da and Eddie," he said. "Everything's been laid out for Gemma and me since . . . since forever, really. I didn't have a say in it."

And here came the rage again, billowing up inside Clover like steam. Did Clive really think that made it better—that he *had* to marry her, that he didn't even *want* her?

"You do have a say, Clive. Of course you do."

"It's not as simple as that. You don't know what it's like."

"*You* don't know!" Clover shouted. "You don't know and you never will!"

He stood up and started walking upstream, back toward camp.

"You don't want to finish the race?" Clive called after him. The hurt was plain in his voice, but Clover didn't care. Everybody hurt. That was just part of life.

"No," he said. "You were gonna win anyway."

6. Clive

CLIVE WAS DOWN IN THE CLEARING, HELPING EDDIE AND Burns load the tent into the big wagon, when he heard Honor Hamill call out in his most thunderous preacher voice.

"Clive Hamill, you get the hell over here."

Eddie gave a little whistle. "Somebody's in hot water."

Clive jogged uphill to the campsite. Behind the small wagon, he found his mother and father speaking in fervent, almost angry tones.

Clive's father noticed him. "Show me your shoulder," he said.

"My shoulder? But . . ." Finally Clive understood. He glared at his brother, who was standing between their parents, looking guilty as all get-out. "You told? But you gave me your word!"

"Leave him out of this," Honor Hamill said. "Let me see your shoulder."

"It's fine."

"Let me see your damn shoulder!"

Grudgingly, Clive took off his shirt. His mother gasped when she saw the wound.

"Clover," Honor Hamill said, "go get the sergeant for me. And keep away afterward."

"Yes, Da."

Clover scurried off, clearly happy to be dismissed.

"It wasn't supposed to—" Clive started to say.

"I don't want to hear a word out of you," his father growled.

"At least Burns did a halfway decent job stitching it up," his mother said, examining the wound more closely. "Did he remember to clean it first?"

"Of course, Ma."

After a couple of minutes of uncomfortable silence, Burns finally appeared. He took one look at Clive's fresh new scar, bared to the world, and let out a long sigh. "I'm about to get a talking to, aren't I?"

"That's all you have to say for yourself?" Honor Hamill strode right up into Burns's face. "You put my son's life at risk and that's all you have to say?"

Burns maintained an impressive serenity in the face of the Honor's rage. "I invited him and he came. He's a man now. It's his decision. No one was supposed to get hurt."

"Talking to Arthur Edwards was *your* job, Burns," Clive's mother said. "Not our boy's."

"Wait," Clive said, "you knew he was going out there last night?"

"Well . . . I only knew . . ." His mother looked to her husband for help. Clearly she'd been caught off guard by the question, and Clive saw an opportunity to take the offensive.

"You knew he was going to kill that old man? Why? What is this all about, anyway?"

Ellen Hamill turned back to Burns, eyes wide. "You *killed* him?"

"He came at us with a knife! I didn't have a choice."

"You did!" Honor Hamill said. "You always have a choice!"

"That's easy for you to say."

"None of this is easy," Clive's mother said.

After that, everybody started talking over everybody else: a cacophony of incrimination and recrimination, rationalization and sanctimony, until finally one voice broke through the rest.

"All of you shut the hell up!"

It was Eddie. He'd come up from the clearing at some point, though Clive hadn't noticed him arrive. Eddie almost never raised his voice, so when he did, you couldn't help but listen.

"Maybe Clive shouldn't have gone, but maybe he should have at that. Maybe, if Burns had been on his own, he'd be dead now." Clive hadn't even thought of that. When he looked over at Burns, the sergeant wouldn't meet his eye. "And, Clive, you have to understand that part of our job as members of the Church is to be on the lookout for misuse of the anathema. That's all Burns was doing last night—his job. Make sense?"

After a moment, Clive nodded.

"Good. Now that we've sorted that out, we have to deal with the much more important question: Just what in God's name are we gonna do next?"

Eddie looked to Honor Hamill, who looked to his wife, who looked to Clive. And Clive, for want of anything better to do,

TOMMY WALLACH

looked to the sky. But there were no answers to be found up there in the blue—only the blank and blameless clouds.

"Should I be worried?" Gemma asked.

"Nah," Clive said, hoping he sounded more certain than he felt.

The two of them were sitting on the lip of the small wagon. Clive could touch the dirt if he stretched out his toes, but Gemma's feet were a good eight inches off the ground.

"Why can't the Protectorate just send soldiers out after we get back?"

"They'd take too long to get here. Things might get covered up."

"If it's so important to Burns, can't he go on his own?"

"Da wouldn't let him. He said it was a responsibility they had to share."

"Of course he did." Gemma kicked the heel of Clive's boot with the toe of her own. "I'm so tired of being on the road."

"We all are. Even Da, I think."

"Momma *always* hated it. Remember that tour we did over to the coast, way back when? Us kids were seeing the ocean for the very first time, jaws down on the sand practically at how beautiful it all was, and then Momma said—"

"'What use could anybody have for so much water?'"

They laughed. It had been doubly funny at the time, because Gemma's mother had been a particularly humorless woman.

"She didn't even realize she'd made a joke," Clive said.

"Oh, I know she wasn't always the most fun, Clive, but I miss her. I miss her all the time."

"I know."

Six years ago Viola Poplin had gone out to harvest summer squash from the family plot outside the Anchor, and nobody ever saw her again. Bandits most likely, who'd killed her for her horse and what few shekels she had on her person. Michael and Flora were only four at the time, young enough to shrug off the hurt, to allow the maternal void to be filled by their older sister and Ellen Hamill. But Gemma had been too old to forget what she'd lost—in a way, it made her the only one of them who was truly motherless.

Something told Clive to take hold of Gemma's hand. It was still a novel sensation; they'd only done it for the first time about a month ago. He'd always thought couples looked silly that way, like overprotective mothers afraid to let their children run free. Now he understood what all the fuss was about. It was more intimate than you'd expect, locking your fingers up in someone else's—a pale but palpable imitation of that greater intimacy that was not to be spoken of, however much it might prey on your mind.

"You know what I've been thinking about?" Gemma asked.

Not what I'm thinking about, Clive thought.

"Tell me," he said.

"I've been wondering what would've happened if our fathers hadn't been friends. Would we have found each other anyway? Walking around the Anchor, just a couple of strangers, you think we would've seen each other and said, 'That one, there, that's the one I'm meant to be with'?"

"I don't know," Clive said. From the slight crumple in Gemma's expression, he recognized his mistake. "I mean, I would've noticed you, of course. I just might not have had the courage to talk to you."

TOMMY WALLACH

"Flatterer." She smiled, giving his hand a little squeeze. "Do you remember the first time you noticed me?"

"I've known you since I was a baby. How could I remember that far back?"

"I'm not talking about the first time you *saw* me. I'm talking about the first time you *noticed* me. You understand the difference?"

"Not really."

Gemma rolled her eyes. "Well, how about I tell you the first time I noticed you?"

"Go on, then."

"It was just after my fourteenth birthday. I was scared to see you, because a couple days before, Da was talking to me about boys, and he said something like, 'How would you feel ending up married to Clive?' And I swear I'd never thought of you like that before. You were like another brother to me, you know? But then I saw you that Sunday at church, all dressed up in that adorable blue suit you used to wear—"

"It's Clover's now."

"—and when you waved to me across the aisle, you gave me this big old grin, and I thought to myself, 'well, Gemma, you could do a whole lot worse.'"

Clive laughed. "That's some faint praise if I ever heard any."

"I didn't mean it that way!"

"I know, I know."

They were quiet for a moment.

"Your turn now. When did you first notice me?"

She was looking up at him, her eyes big and sapphire blue, and because he still didn't have an answer, he leaned over and kissed her. It was their first kiss, and even though Clive had kissed plenty of other girls (seven, to be exact), he was so surprised at the enthusiasm with which he was met that he forgot what to do with his hands or his head or his lips or his tongue, and before he had the chance to remember any of it, Gemma was pulling away.

"All right, lovebirds," Burns said, coming around the side of the wagon, "you finished saying your good-byes?"

"No," Gemma said. "But it'll have to do."

They followed Burns back to the big wagon, which was all packed up and ready for travel. The plan was for the men to ride east in search of this pumphouse, while Clive's mother would take the big wagon and hole up with the children fifteen or twenty miles west along the Southern Tail. The small wagon would have to be left behind, hidden as well as they could manage in the woods outside Amestown, and the men would hitch it up again on their way back.

"You be careful now," Clive's mother said, hugging him so tight he felt his ribs creaking. "I'm not kidding around."

"I will."

Clover was waiting just behind her, still looking guilty as a killer approaching the gallows.

"Here," he said, and offered up the crystal he'd found at the stream.

As angry as Clive still was, he couldn't help but feel touched by the gesture. Ever since he was little, Clover had collected precious stones like this one, hoarding them like a goblin in a fairy tale. He didn't part with them easily.

"Thanks," Clive said, taking the stone.

"Don't lose it, okay? I'll want it back."

"I'll do my best."

After that, Clive was tackled by a dual hug from Michael and Flora, who hadn't yet learned to be ashamed of loving someone unreservedly.

Only one more parting left. He'd only been planning to give Gemma a friendly hug, but she tilted her head at the last moment, catching him with a kiss right there in front of everyone. "When we get home, you can propose to me proper," she whispered in his ear. "Then we can do whatever we want."

She backed away before he could say anything in response, casting her eyes demurely toward the ground. He climbed up onto his horse and urged it into a trot. When he looked back for one last glimpse of her, the sun was so bright in his eyes, she appeared only as a shadow—the faceless outline of a girl, waving good-bye.

7. Clover

CLOVER SAT IN THE BACK OF THE BIG WAGON, TRYING and failing to read a book of poetry, Flora's little head heavy in his lap. Michael was up front in the driver's seat next to Ellen; whenever he was scared, he liked to be close to her. Gemma was passed out on a pile of folded blankets up against the wagon gate. Only a few hours ago, he'd had to watch her kiss Clive good-bye. He could still picture their lips sticking together as they disengaged; just the thought of it made his stomach churn.

Still, however revolting the kiss might've been, it wasn't the source of his current disquiet. He couldn't stop hearing his brother's voice—*You gave me your word.* And while there had been plenty of good reasons to break his promise—because keeping secrets from your parents was a sin, because they had a duty to the Church to investigate any incident involving the anathema, because Clive's odd infatuation with Burns needed to be nipped in the bud—Clover knew his true motivations had been far less noble. Bitterness. Jealousy. A desire to show his parents that Clive was far from the perfect little Honor-in-training he pretended to be.

Now, at Clover's prompting, they'd ridden off into who knew what sort of danger. And what if one of them got hurt, or worse? How would he live with himself knowing that it was all his fault?

"What's wrong?" Flora asked, gazing up from her cozy berth in his lap. Her eyes were a pale, eerie blue—different from those of her siblings. If you stared into them for long enough, you started to get the feeling the girl was a lot older than she looked.

"Nothing. I thought you were sleeping."

"I'm not. And you're a liar."

"Am not."

"You are, though." Flora turned her head to look out the back of the wagon. "Rain'll be here soon."

The sky was gray, aswirl with clouds, promissory.

Suddenly Gemma sat bolt upright, bending into a perfect right angle. Clover's first instinct was to laugh, but then he saw her eyes: pure white, the same color as the crystal he'd given to Clive. She jerked violently and fell onto the wooden floor of the wagon, shaking like a fish freshly pulled out of the water.

Clover crawled to her side, calling out to Flora as he went. "Get up front and tell Ma to stop the wagon. I'll see to your sister."

He'd seen Gemma have plenty of fits over the years, though this was the first time he'd had to take care of her on his own. He rolled her over onto her side, so she didn't end up choking on her own spit, and lifted her head up onto his leg, where it was soft. He didn't know if she could hear him, but he tried talking to her anyway—"Everything's gonna be okay. You're gonna be just fine.

I've got you." It always hurt him to watch her like this; he wished he could take the suffering on himself. She would be so grateful to him that she'd forget all about Clive, and then they'd—

It came without warning: a sharp contraction sent her flexed fist careening into his left eye. His surprise gave way to agony, as Gemma's fingernails tore bright red ribbons of pain down his cheek. He reached for her hand and held it there, trapped against his face, until at last her fingers loosened and her whole body went slack. It was over. She'd wake up in a few minutes with a thumping headache, but it didn't look as if any permanent damage had been done. On impulse, Clover brushed a lock of Gemma's hair back around her ear. So soft . . .

Only then did he notice that the wagon had come to a stop, and that his mother, Michael, and Flora were all watching him from the front seat. Michael's smile grew wider and wider, until it broke into a full-on laugh.

"She punched you! You got beat up by a girl!"

"Michael Poplin, you better hush," Clover's mother said, "or this girl will give *you* a punch in the eye."

A pattering started up on the canvas roof of the wagon: the rain had come. Little droplets darkened the dry red earth they left rutted in their wake. Clover let his head fall back against one of the hickory boughs that arched overhead, and before long, the swaying of the wagon and the thrumming of the rain put him to sleep. His dreams were haunted by a shapeless threat, a red-eyed monster hidden in roiling black fog. When he came to again, the wagon was

TOMMY WALLACH

jostling to a stop at the edge of the road, though the sun wouldn't set for a couple of hours yet.

"This is as far as we go," Ellen said, opening up the gate so they could all get out the back.

"Da said we should spend the night in Laramie," Clover replied.

"I know what he said. But we're safe enough here. Nobody's going to trouble a ministry wagon full of children."

Clover figured he knew the real reason his mother wanted to stop: she didn't like the idea of being any farther away from the men than she had to be.

"That doesn't make any sense, Ma. Five more miles might as well be a hundred, if something goes wrong—"

"Clover!" There was a profound terror in his mother's eyes; for a moment, he wondered if she was going to cry. "Don't you talk about things going wrong," she said, more quietly but with the same intensity. "Don't bring those thoughts into the world. The Daughter will protect them, like she always has." She made the sign of the annulus on her chest.

"Sorry, Ma."

He felt bad about upsetting her, but it wasn't as if talking about something made it any more likely to happen. Besides, the prospect of dying was something they'd all had to come to terms with a long time ago. There'd been so many close calls over the years: the snakebite that kept Clive in a fever-sleep for almost a week, the bandits who stole their gold annulus and a couple of weeks' worth of food at knifepoint, the half-dozen run-ins they'd had with Wesah raiders. Luck had seen them through all these misadventures, but luck always ran out eventually. That was what his mother didn't want to think about.

That night, Clover struggled to find his way into sleep. He kept imagining all the ways his father and brother might be killed—stabbed through the stomach and slit open at the neck, hanged from a tree and hacked into bits, starved and tortured and drowned and burned and choked and beaten. These fantastical horrors proliferated and ramified, growing ever more byzantine and gruesome.

Only after he'd spent hours tossing and turning under the blanket did it occur to him: all of this was happening for a reason. Here he was, only half a dozen miles from where he'd started out that morning, and wide awake while everyone else was asleep. The signs were too obvious to ignore.

A few minutes later he tiptoed past his mother's tent, past the soft shushing sounds of the Poplin children breathing. The moon overhead was bright and full, milky white, benedictory. He carried the saddle from the wagon over to where the animals were tied up.

But something wasn't right. There were only three horses here; the chestnut called Dart was missing. Clover looked around and spotted the animal standing at the crest of a hill just a little ways up the road. Someone was mounted on her back, and they were moving slowly enough that Clover was able to catch up on foot.

"Gemma?" he whispered.

She turned the horse about. "Clover?"

"What are you doing?"

"Sneaking off, obviously. How'd you catch me?"

Clover held up the saddle. "Because I came out here to do the same thing."

"Huh," Gemma said. "Well, ain't that something."

They stood there in silence for a moment, marveling at the coincidence. Whatever trepidation Clover had felt melted away. Clearly, the Lord was telling him he had a job to do, one that required him to be alone with Gemma, possibly for days.

He went back to the other horses and untethered Almondine.

"Your ma won't be able to move that wagon with only two horses," Gemma said, once Clover had rejoined her at the top of the hill. "We're stranding them here."

"Better to be without horses than without a husband," he said, then gave a little tug of the reins and trotted off into the darkness.

8. Clive

THEY MADE CAMP AN HOUR AFTER SUNSET. OTHER THAN a couple of broken-down shacks and the rotted remains of a silo, they hadn't seen any sign of human habitation since Amestown.

Clive was given the first watch, apparently because it was the easiest. He thought he'd be frightened, staring out into that panorama of darkness, but the gravity of the task made his fear seem insignificant. These three men were trusting him with their very lives, and that made him want to be the kind of man who deserved such trust. He'd never been more awake or alert than he was during those four hours; a squirrel could have leaped off a tree a mile away and he would've heard it.

He woke Eddie when the fire was burning down low and then unrolled his blanket and lay down. The events of the past twenty-four hours scrolled by in his head: blowing out the candles of his birthday cake, the dark vortex of the painted woman's bosom, Arthur Edwards screaming as Burns crushed his skull, the stranger threatening Clover in the streambed, the soft cushion of Gemma's lips. This last thought lingered, the same way her smell did after she'd left a room—saddle leather and horsehair, jasmine from a bottle of scent Eddie had given to her on May Day.

No red-blooded man could have failed to notice the way Gemma had grown into herself over the past few years, and that passionate kiss they'd shared had revealed a side of her Clive hadn't known existed. Yet he still wasn't sure how he felt about *marrying* her. They'd spent their whole childhoods together, like brother and sister almost, and there was an inevitability to their pairing that had defused any sense of tension between them. The boys he knew back at the Anchor were always talking about the girls they liked, and whether those girls liked them back, and whether their parents could be convinced to arrange it officially. Clive could never play along, because there was no fun in saying, *This is the girl I'm meant to be with. I guess she likes me and I guess I like her. We get along just fine.*

But he did love her. Of course he did. She was beautiful and musical and as good with a horse as any Wesah warrior. But his love for her was all muddled up, not only because everyone seemed to take their eventual nuptials for granted, but also because of how Clover felt about her.

At least the kiss had been good. Clive could think of a lot of things worse than kissing Gemma. He allowed himself to relive the moment, to hear her voice low and soft in his ear—*we can do whatever we want*—and the sweet promise of it was just enough to put him to sleep.

><><

By the time the sun succeeded in hoisting its pale pink frame above the jagged horizon, they were already back on the move, following the vague outline of a trail. The silver snake of the Ivan slithered along the valley floor to the west, while to the east, hills dotted with ponderosa pine and cottonwood trees rolled past. Summer made itself known that day with a heat that descended early, landing on the back of the neck and slinking slug-slow down the spine. The warmth from the animal beneath him was almost unbearable, making his legs sweat and then chafe with each step. But *almost* unbearable was still bearable, when it came down to it. Clive was ready to drop by the time they stopped for lunch, but all he said was, "We done already?" The food fortified him, so he barely groaned when the time came to mount up again.

They didn't really know what it was they were looking for, and if it had been winter, with the short days and the road all covered with snow, odds were good they would've missed it. But even a rarely used road makes itself known in the slanting afternoon light of July. There weren't any ruts from wagon wheels or telltale footprints, just a slight sparseness to the yellow grass and a smoothness to the dirt beneath it.

"Could be a homestead," Eddie said, stopping at the intersection.

Burns pulled up next to him. "Could be. But I don't see any farmland."

"Only one way to find out," Honor Hamill said, and kicked his horse's flank.

The trail curved around a gnarled finger of gray stone and over a stream, then passed through a wood made up primarily of aspen trees, their white trunks ringed and layered, as if they'd been wrapped in bandages. After about an hour, the trail bent upward, growing steeper as it went. The trees grew more thickly here, aspens augmented with ash and white oak, and the path itself was blanketed with leaves and branches and acorns. Finally the ground leveled out again, but just as it did, the trail ran straight into a wall of rocky earth about ten feet high.

A small cabin had been built against the escarpment, topped with a healthy thatch of moss-covered straw that angled gently upward. There didn't appear to be any windows, but the column of rocks piled up on the thatched roof was almost certainly a chimney. Honor Hamill tried the lichen-dappled door, but it was locked, and nobody answered when he knocked. Meanwhile, Burns clambered up on the roof to see if there was any sort of trapdoor or skylight.

"Who would wanna live way out here?" Clive asked.

"You kidding?" Eddie said. "This is paradise. No people around to muck everything up."

"What do you think this is?" Burns shouted down to them. He pointed to a slim gray tube that protruded from the corner of the thatching, running along the edge of the cliff face and then arcing off a dozen yards or so to the east, where it connected to some sort of bracket built into the boughs of an oak tree. From there it stretched over to yet another tree, and then on again, until Clive lost track of it among the branches.

"Could be for water," he said.

Eddie snorted. "There's a stream not a hundred yards back down the trail. Nobody's *that* lazy."

"We need to get inside," Burns said, climbing back down from the roof. "So unless one of you has a better idea, I think I'll get to kicking in that door."

"You'd break your foot first," Eddie replied.

"That's what you think."

"It's what I think *and* what would happen."

"The point's moot," Honor Hamill interrupted. "Our suspicions don't give us the right to break into a man's home."

"I didn't know the Filia had a problem with violence against *doors*," Burns sneered. "Could you quote me chapter and verse on that?"

"We've passed beyond the official borders of the Descendancy, Sergeant. I won't have these people's first introduction to us be vandalism."

"So what do you suggest?"

Honor Hamill pointed off into the woods, back the way they'd come. "On the way in, I noticed a rabbit hanging from a snare. It couldn't have been more than a day old. Someone'll be coming to check on it before long. All we have to do is wait."

"Wait, huh?" Burns put his hands behind his head and gave a derisory snort. "I fucking hate waiting."

"That's a fine stone you've got there."

Clive jolted awake. They'd been sitting outside the hut all day, and the heat, coupled with his general exhaustion, had conspired to put him to sleep. Now the sun had set, and the air was beginning to turn chilly.

"What'd you say, Da?"

TOMMY WALLACH

"That stone there. It's nice."

Clive hadn't even realized he was holding Clover's crystal; he must've been worrying at it before he passed out.

"Clover gave it to me. And told me he'd want it back in the very same breath."

Honor Hamill laughed. "Well, I'm glad to hear you two are getting along." Clive thought about correcting his father's misconception, but decided against it. "Truth be told, I've been worried about him. He took your birthday harder than I'd expected. And I'm sure he didn't much like seeing Gemma kiss you good-bye back there."

"Probably not."

"I'm a younger brother myself, you know. It's like being born into second place. You always feel like you have something to prove."

"Clover doesn't have to prove anything to me. He's smarter than I'll ever be."

His father didn't deny it, but Clive wasn't offended; saying Clover was smarter than the rest of them was like saying that grass was green. "Yes, our clever little Clover. He's got more brains than most anyone I know, but he still can't figure out what to do with them."

"Other than be jealous of me."

"*Num custos fratris mei sum ego?*"

"Am I my brother's keeper?" Clive translated. Anyone preparing for a life in the Church was expected to have a working knowledge of Latin and Greek.

"I recognize that one," Eddie said. "Kayin and Hevel."

"Indeed," Honor Hamill said. "Clive, why don't you tell us all the tale."

"Right now?" Clive asked.

"It'd be good practice. An Honor must be ready to speak at a moment's notice."

Though Clive had given short sermons at some of the smaller gatherings, a horde of vicious butterflies would still kick up in his stomach every time he rose to the ambo. He could feel them there even now, though his audience was only three members strong. "So Kayin and Hevel were brothers," he began. "They were the children of Aleph and Eva. Both of them wished to marry their sister, the beautiful Aclima, so Aleph suggested they both present a gift to God, who would then choose which man deserved her. Hevel was a shepherd, and so he gave Aclima his fattest sheep. Kayin, a farmer, could give her only a handful of seeds. The Lord preferred Hevel's gift to Kayin's, and bestowed Aclima upon the shepherd."

"I don't blame him," Burns said.

"Soon after, Kayin and Hevel were out working in the fields, and Kayin picked up a rock and smashed his brother's head in." Clive realized he was still holding the stone his brother had given him. It was white as bone. "Afterward, the Lord appeared to Kayin and asked where Hevel was. 'I don't know,' Kayin said. 'Am I my brother's keeper?' But Hevel's blood screamed out from the ground, and the Lord knew what Kayin had done. And so he set a mark upon him, and all his descendants unto the fifth generation, that they would be known as murderers. And that's the end of the story."

"Very good," Clive's father said, "but I have one correction. The mark wasn't there to warn people that Kayin was dangerous. It was there for his safety. Otherwise, anyone who saw him would kill him. The mark warned others that Kayin still had the Lord's protection."

TOMMY WALLACH

Clive frowned. "But why would the Lord protect him and curse him at the same time?"

"Because death is a release," Honor Hamill said. "The Lord wanted Kayin to suffer. Now tell me this, why was the mark also put on Kayin's children? After all, they were entirely innocent of their father's sin."

"I don't know."

"Think about it."

Clive replayed the story in his head. The Lord was just. He didn't punish the blameless.

"Well, maybe it was his way of telling them that the world was going to mark them anyway," Clive said hesitantly. "That when you do something terrible, it doesn't just stop with you. There are . . . echoes."

Honor Hamill smiled. "Yes. I like that. Echoes."

Everyone was silent for a moment.

"If something interesting doesn't happen in the next five minutes, I'm gonna smash my *own* skull in," Burns said. He slid over and pounded the door with the back of his head. "Hello! Is anybody in there? Save me from all these preachers!"

"Heathen," Eddie muttered.

"Actually, I think the sergeant might have a point," Honor Hamill said. "Whatever this place is, we've marked it on the map, so the Protectorate can check on it the next time they come through the area. Maybe it's time for us to move on. Clive, what do you think?"

"What?" Clive said, before realizing that his father was soliciting his opinion. It was strange to suddenly be included in the decision making, just because he'd turned eighteen. "I don't want to leave the others any longer than we have to," he said, after pausing long enough to make it clear he wasn't taking the question lightly.

"Fine by me," Eddie added. "We've still got a couple hours of light left."

Clive's father nodded. "True enough. Let's pack up our things and get moving."

But just as they were untethering the horses, there was a loud creaking sound from behind them. Clive turned to see the door slowly swinging open, spilling a wedge of yellow light onto the path.

A silhouette, and a glint of a blade.

"Well, look at that," Burns said. "Guess somebody's home after all."

9. Clover

H E FOUND HIMSELF HYPNOTIZED BY THE MUSIC OF Gemma's inhalations and exhalations—the measured cadence, the expansion and contraction of the lungs— and wondered how it was possible that even someone's *breathing* could be beautiful. Neither of them had said a word since they'd left camp. The practical silence they'd started out with, so as not to wake anyone, had shaded into a kind of philosophical silence, a reverence for the peaceful soundlessness of the dead hours after midnight.

He would've preferred that they go around Amestown, but they needed to keep to the trail. At least it was late enough that most everyone in town was asleep. The only signs of life were the few forgotten candles in the windowsills, left to burn down to nubs. Once, Clover caught a flash of movement in the bushes and nearly kicked his horse into a gallop—some part of his brain was waiting for Dominic to reappear, to finish what he'd started down by the river—but it was only an old dog chasing after the horses for something to do.

Just outside of town, the road diverged.

"What do you think?" Clover asked. His voice was husky; it was the first time he'd spoken in hours.

"No way to know, is there?"

"One way maybe." Clover dismounted. He walked down the path on the left a few hundred yards, scanning the ground as he went. He found what he was looking for almost right away, but just to be safe, he checked the path on the right, too.

"It's the left one," he said, remounting Almondine.

"How do you know?"

"They've got four horses. One of them was bound to"—he hesitated, his mother's voice chiding him in his head—"you know."

Gemma laughed. "I see. Couldn't it belong to some other horse?"

"You think I don't know fresh horseshit when I smell it?"

"Didn't mean to offend you. I forgot you're a horseshit expert."

Clover felt a warm bubbling in his blood, as he always did when joking around with Gemma—foolish hope. Then the image of her and Clive kissing came back to him, and the bubbling stopped. She'd had to get up on tippy-toe to do it—because you had to reach and reach to kiss a tall boy like Clive. Clover still hadn't had his first kiss, outside of the meaningless ones everyone got in primary school, when the girls still chased the boys instead of the other way around. A strange transformation, from pursuer to pursued, occurring with a kind of choreographed simultaneity, as if everyone had agreed upon it beforehand. And what was at the root of it? What made the voice drop and the thoughts stray, the hair sprout and the pimples proliferate? What made you so disgusted by the girls begging you for a hug in the school yard,

TOMMY WALLACH

then suddenly so desperate for just a scrap of attention from one of them?

Bernstein said there were hundreds of volumes in the anathema stacks devoted to the subject known as "biology"—the science of life. Clover had the feeling that the answers to all his questions could be found in their pages, but he wouldn't be allowed to read them until he became an attendant himself, which was at least a decade away. Might as well be forever.

They rode hard through the night, stopping every couple of hours to stretch their legs and have a bite to eat. Only after the sun was high and starting to scorch did they look for a place to settle down for a few hours of shut-eye. They found a glittering benison of a stream (*The river is sacred, for it cleaves always to the ground, seeking out the bosom of the Lord*, as the Filia said) and, after watering the horses, arranged their blankets in the spotty shade of a chokecherry. Gemma lay down close enough that Clover could smell the jasmine-tinged sweat on her skin.

"You worried about your brother?" she asked. The question seemed to come out of the blue, but Clover figured there was something about lying down next to someone, the shift from vertical to horizontal, that lent itself to intimacy.

"Of course."

"Me too." She put her hand against his cheek. "I sure gave you a doozy of a black eye."

"It was nothing."

She smiled, then nestled her head down into the blanket. "Let's not sleep too long," she said, already halfway gone.

"All right."

He woke up again in the full heat of the sun, the shade having slunk away across the grass while he slept. Gemma was down by the stream, cupping water in her hands and splashing it across her face. She'd taken off her dress, leaving her in nothing but smock and knickers. The water threw spangles of sunlight across her skin, little diamonds dancing on the sinews of her exposed calves and the graceful curve of her neck. She looked over at him, and because he didn't want to seem as if he'd been caught at something he was ashamed of, he held her gaze. She gave him a little wave before returning to her washing.

He got up and saddled the horses, and before too long they were on the road again. The sun was already dropping, and when it hit the line of the horizon, the whole sky seemed to burst into flame. They had to slow down when the darkness came; the road was almost invisible even in the daylight. If they weren't careful, they'd lose it and never find their way back again.

It was Gemma who first spotted the glimmer in the distance—a spark of orange light moving slowly across the plain.

"Is it them?" she asked.

"Could be, only I think that light's coming toward us."

"They could be on their way back already."

"Maybe."

They kept on riding, and the light only grew brighter as they went. Just when it seemed they were about to run headfirst into whoever was behind it, the light veered away from the road and floated off to the north. A few minutes after that, it winked out completely.

"Should we follow it?" Gemma said. "I mean, if it's not them—"

TOMMY WALLACH

"It has to be them. Who else could it be, all the way out here in the middle of nowhere?"

"I couldn't say. Bandits? Wesah? Ghosts?"

She smiled, a pale crescent glimmering in the starlight. Clover wasn't about to look like a coward in front of her. "We've come this far," he said. "Guess we have to see it through."

"Well, consider me officially inspired. Lead the way, my hero."

They turned the horses in the direction the light had gone, keeping their eyes glued to the ground until they located the vague outline of a trail. Tall, spindly trees blocked out much of the light, so they navigated by sound. There was the gurgle of running water, the crunch and shuffle of the horses walking through dry leaves, the wind soughing through the aspens. Almondine and Dart were breathing more heavily now, as the trail had turned steeply uphill. It plateaued in a small clearing, where ten or so horses were tied up to nearby trees. Even in the dark, Clover recognized the four ministry horses, but the other animals were unfamiliar.

"Look over there," Gemma whispered. She pointed toward the escarpment about a hundred feet beyond the horses. A wan rectangle of light floated in the center of his vision.

"Is that a door?"

Gemma nodded. "They must be inside."

The breeze died down, and Clover could make out the sound of muffled, angry voices—an argument.

Gemma jumped down from her horse. "Da's in there," she said, more loudly than was safe. "I have to help him."

"Gemma, no!"

But she was already running headlong for the door.

10. Clive

"WHOOEE, BUT Y'ALL GAVE ME A FRIGHT! THOUGHT I was about to meet my maker!"

His name was Harry Pardo, and once he'd gotten over the surprise of finding a whole Descendant ministry on his doorstep (and put his puny dagger away), he'd invited them inside. Apparently, this was his hunting cabin; there were a whole lot of nasty-looking traps hanging from hooks on the walls, and a small table near a thin tick mattress bore the remains of a hearty dinner: apple core, rind of cheese, strip of gristle. Against the back wall was an assortment of ramshackle cabinets and a large wardrobe, all shut. The place had a strange smell to it—cloying, with a layer of toxicity beneath the sweetness, like a ripe red berry you knew was poisonous—but otherwise it was pretty cozy.

Harry looked to be about twenty-five or so, dressed in canvas overalls smudged with black dirt. The lantern in the corner of the room inflamed his ginger hair and the million tiny freckles dotting his face.

"Didn't you hear us knocking a few hours back?" Burns asked.

"I'll confess I was having a bit of a snooze. I keep pretty strange hours out here."

"Doing what, exactly?"

"Hunting. Foraging. This and that."

"I'm surprised you can get any sleep at all with that stench," Eddie said.

"Eh, you get used to it. It's a powder I make from mixing up a couple of local berries—keeps the rats from eating me out of house and home. Speaking of which, you boys hungry? I should have something around here. . . ." He poked around in the cabinets and came up with a wooden bowl of cherries. "They may be a day or two past their prime, but nothing's rotten yet." He set the bowl down in front of them and popped one of the cherries into his mouth. Clive tried one himself: sweet and tart at once.

"What sort of things do you forage for?" Burns said. His tone was only a couple of shades shy of outright interrogation, but Harry didn't seem to mind.

"Oh, there's all kinds of valuable stuff, if you know what to look for. I scout for this carpenter out in Amestown, name of Timothy Horsefall. Just a few miles from this cabin, there's a grove of pine you could make a whole town out of. And there are firs farther up north that two grown men couldn't get their arms around. Then there's the fruit trees, of course. The apples aren't good eating, but they make a mean cider. . . ."

Harry kept nattering on as they tore through the bowl of cherries. At some point, Clive noticed his father trying to catch his eye. Honor Hamill made a subtle gesture with his head, toward the place where the rear wall of the cabin met the thatched roof. The gray tube they'd seen outside ran from the ceiling to somewhere behind the wardrobe.

"So tell me about yourselves," Harry eventually said, after having described just about every plant that grew within fifty miles of the cottage. "You're really from the Anchor?"

"Born and raised," Honor Hamill said. "But now I'm in charge of a traveling ministry. We bring the word of the Lord to those who are ready to hear it."

Somewhere close by, a wolf howled; Clive shivered.

"Hey," Harry said, snapping his fingers. "I just remembered I've got a bit of shine up in here somewhere. I was saving it for a rainy day. You boys interested in a drink?"

"Always," Burns said.

Clive watched to see if Harry would go for the wardrobe, but the bottle was in one of the smaller cabinets. "I don't have any glasses, so we'll have to do it the old-fashioned way. To the Daughter." He raised the bottle in a one-man toast before taking a deep draft. "That's how you Descendancy folks put it, isn't it?"

"Sure is," Eddie said, taking a swig and passing the bottle on. Clive's father took only a tiny sip (*An Honor can drink in the spirit of fellowship, but never to the point of impairment*), so Clive did the same. The shine was surprisingly smooth, almost as good as the stuff they made in the Anchor.

"So, Harry," Burns said, "what do you do when you're not out here hunting?"

Harry grinned. "You sure have a lot of questions, Mr. Burns."

Burns grinned right back. "I've got a curious personality. And it's Sergeant Burns."

For some reason, Clive found himself listening intently for

another wolf call—they seldom sounded all alone like that—and maybe that was why he was the first to hear the clicking. It was a bit like the noise certain insects made, only more mechanical, and a little too loud.

"Anybody else hear that?" he said.

"Hear what?" Honor Hamill asked.

"Something's clicking."

"It's just the bugs," Harry said. "I tell ya, this place is nothing but spiders and skeeters—"

"Quiet!" Burns said. They were all listening now. Sure enough, the sound was coming from the back of the room. Only before any of them could get up to investigate, Harry let out a loud sigh.

"I suppose I should just show you," he said. He walked leisurely over to the wardrobe and pulled the doors open, revealing a small device made of metal and wood. A long brass arm rose and fell at irregular intervals, bouncing against a bronze pad mounted in the base: that was where the clicking sound came from.

"Anathema," Clive said.

"Sure is." Burns crinkled up his nose. "And I recognize the stench in here too. It's Blood of the Father."

The Filia said the Lord had set the Blood running through the branches of the Great Tree, warning Aleph and Eva never to drink of it. But the devil had tempted Eva, and she had succumbed, and so humanity was banished from Eden. After the garden was destroyed, the Blood spread into all the veins of the Earth. A second time the Lord warned humanity not to drink of it, and a second time he was ignored. So he sent his Daughter to cleanse the Earth, and humanity was reborn from the seed of

Noach—the only man who'd obeyed God's admonition.

"Blood of the Father," Harry said, and smiled. "I'd forgotten that's what you all call it."

"You extract it here?" Honor Hamill asked.

"Sure do. Pump's in the basement. I'm out here to fix it when it breaks down, then collect the juice and take it where it needs to go."

Clive suddenly remembered what Clover had overheard at the gathering, and the last pieces of the puzzle came together. Blood of the Father was said to burn with a supernatural intensity; in the Gospel of Jiehae, it was referred to as *strange fire.* "Your name's really Riley, isn't it?" he said.

Their host acknowledged the truth with a resounding smack of the knee. "Hot damn, kid! How'd you work that out?"

Clive ignored the question. "You were responsible for some sort of fire near Amestown."

"You heard about that?" Riley chuckled. "See, I was carrying a jug over to Arthur, as a personal favor. I got a late start, and he was asleep when I got there. I didn't want to wake him, so I figured I'd camp out for the night just outside his house. But like a damn fool, I set the jug down too close to the fire. One spark got in it and *fwup.*" Riley threw his hands in the air. "Nearly singed my eyebrows clean off."

"Is that what you're running out of that tube up there?" Burns asked, pointing to the gray cable.

Riley shook his head. "That machine in the wardrobe is called a telegraph. It sends messages along that cable, faster than you can imagine. In fact, I used it to send a message to some friends of mine the moment you first knocked on my door."

It was worrying just how serene Riley seemed to be. Didn't he realize he was admitting to blasphemy? The punishment for extracting Blood of the Father was death.

"So why'd you even open the door?" Clive said. "We were just about to leave when you invited us in."

"I know you were. I could hear everything you were saying. But don't you see? I couldn't let you go. Not after you'd found this place." As he was speaking, Riley had gone to stand by the door. Now he reached into his waistband and withdrew something: an L-shaped piece of wood, inlaid with iron. It had to be a weapon of some sort, though it was like nothing Clive had ever seen.

"Are you threatening us?" Burns said.

"I'm afraid so." Riley pointed the hollow end of the weapon at the sergeant's chest.

Burns laughed. "Well, I don't know much about that doohickey you're holding, but I doubt it'll take us all out faster than we can get to you. You're all alone, Riley. Put that thing away and let's talk civil."

"But I'm not alone, Sergeant Burns. Didn't you hear the wolf howling outside? That's our signal. There's half a dozen men waiting on the other side of this door."

Clive had maintained his composure up until then, but now he felt his blood running cold. He could hit a wild turkey at a hundred feet with a bow and arrow, and Burns was said to be an absolute demon with a sword, but on Honor Hamill's insistence, they'd come to Riley's cabin unarmed. ("The first blow is struck as soon as you unsheathe the sword," he'd said, quoting the Filia.) That meant they had no way to defend themselves.

Was this really it? Was this how he was to die, only two days after he'd finally become a man? Would the Lord really allow something so unjust?

"I'm a Descendant minister," Honor Hamill said. "What you're doing here is wrong. You have to let us go."

"If it were up to me, Honor, I would. Honestly. But this is bigger than us. I don't have a choice."

"Of course you do." Honor Hamill took a step forward, his hands up in a gesture of conciliation. "I can see that you're a good man, Riley. You wouldn't kill us all in cold blood."

"You're right," Riley said. "That's why these men are here."

He pushed the door open with his free hand. Shadows moved out in the darkness, and Clive could hear the jangle of men dismounting.

Under his breath, Honor Hamill began to speak. "Father in the ground, whose fist is the Daughter, whose love is Gravity, thank you for your gift. . . ."

11. Clover

IT WAS A STROKE OF LUCK WHEN GEMMA TRIPPED AND FELL as she dodged between the black masses of the horses, because just afterward, the door opened and two unfamiliar men emerged. Clover ducked out of sight, but not before seeing his father and brother through the doorway. They were still alive at least.

"Hello?" one of the men called out.

"Careful! Someone else is out here!"

It was a girl's voice, coming from somewhere back in the woods; the horsemen must've set up some kind of rear guard. Clover mentally berated himself for not thinking of that sooner. If it hadn't been for the cloud cover blotting out the moonlight, he and Gemma likely would've been picked off on the way in.

The two men at the door of the cottage were talking, but too quietly for Clover to make out the words. Then one of them began moving along the face of the escarpment, while the other came toward the horses. Gemma would be unable to move now without being spotted. Clover pulled out the knife he kept in his boot and crept toward her.

"Whoever's there, just come out peaceable," the man said. "We don't want trouble." When he came up close to the horses, they moved aside to make room. Clover heard a little yelp that could only be Gemma; the horse must've stepped right on her.

"Who was that?" the man said.

Gemma jumped up and began to run out from the scrum of animals, but she only made it a dozen feet or so before the man caught up with her and threw her back to the ground. The light from inside the cottage glinted off a piece of metal in his hand—some kind of weapon.

"You shouldn't have come here."

"I—I got lost," Gemma said.

"Is that right?"

"Yeah. I was on my way out of Amestown and I—"

"Quiet, girl. You're not fooling anyone."

As they were speaking, Clover circled around behind the man, the sound of his movements masked by the loud panting of the horses. He changed his grip on the knife, preparing to strike . . . but hesitated. Though he knew that there was no time to lose, that every passing second could be Gemma's last, his whole upbringing was conspiring to stay his hand. He'd spent a lifetime praying to the Daughter, reciting the proverbs of peace: *Whosoever raises his hand against his brother or sister is a pretender to the Godhead, and so shall be rendered bereft.*

"I want you to know I don't take any pleasure in this," the man said.

"Then why do it?" Gemma asked.

TOMMY WALLACH

This simple question seemed to give the man pause, and Clover knew this was his last chance. All he had to do was swing the knife.

But his body refused to move.

"Stop right there," he said weakly, because it was all he could manage to do.

The man turned. "What the hell—" he started to say.

His eyes widened and bulged outward as Gemma plunged her own knife into his neck. There was a quiet gurgling in the back of his throat, not unlike the sound made by a happy baby, before he went down on his knees and fell face-first into the dirt.

Gemma still had a death grip on the knife, which she'd followed all the way down to the ground. Now she let go and scooted quickly backward.

"What have I done?" she whispered. "Oh Lord, what have I done?"

Clover knelt at her side. "We both did it."

"It's not true."

"Then I did it. It was me. That's what we'll say."

She moaned softly. "No, no, no, no . . ."

He wanted to comfort her, but there wasn't time. "Come on," he said, getting his hands under her armpits and pulling her to her feet. As he tried to lead her toward the cottage, his foot bumped against something hard. He reached down and picked it up—the weapon the man had been holding. It was heavy, built to fit perfectly in the hand. Clover had never seen anything like it before, and yet he understood its nature implicitly, as its purpose was inherent to its design. *And the name of that nectar was science.* This was the darkest manifestation of the anathema, the very thing the

Church had been established to oppose. There was no way to know how precise its aim was, nor at what distance it operated, but one thing was for certain: it had been built to kill.

A plan was beginning to coalesce in Clover's mind. It would all come down to the weapon, and whether or not his instincts about it were correct.

"Gemma, I need you to cut their horses loose and give 'em a good kick. Then make sure ours are ready to ride. If this works, we'll be moving fast."

Gemma nodded her acceptance.

Clover crept onward toward the cottage and peeked around the edge of the open door. The men of the ministry had their backs up against the wall, facing four of the strangers, three of whom held their own versions of the L-shaped weapon.

"I'm telling you the truth," Honor Hamill said. "We're just a ministry looking to bring new folks into the flock."

"Then what's the soldier doing here?" one of the strangers demanded.

"He's here for protection! That's all! I swear it on the Lord and his Daughter. And if you let us go tonight—"

But Honor Hamill's plea was interrupted by a piercing shriek. "He's dead! They killed him!"

Clover recognized the voice: it was the rear guard again. She must have discovered the body of the man they'd killed.

"I knew he was lying," another of the strangers said. He pulled back a small comma of metal on the top of his weapon and took aim.

Of course! There was a priming mechanism, like the drawing

TOMMY WALLACH

back of a bowstring. Clover quickly matched the action and then stepped into the doorway. He pointed his weapon at the lantern hanging near the back of the cabin and squeezed his index finger.

The explosion that resulted was deafening, and the reverberation nearly shook the weapon from Clover's grasp, but it had worked. The lantern was extinguished, and the cottage was cast into sudden darkness. A chorus of grunts and shouts ensued, but because no one could see where anyone else was, the strangers couldn't risk firing their weapons. Bodies came rushing out of the cottage, one after another after another.

Clover could make out Burns's voice close by. "I knocked 'em around a bit. We should have a few seconds before they can shake it off."

"Over here!" Gemma shouted.

They followed her voice back down the trail, to where she held the leads of all their horses. Clover climbed up onto the closest animal.

Quick footsteps from behind them were followed by three more explosions in rapid succession. Two of the bolts whizzed past, but the third found flesh.

"Agh!"

"Eddie, you all right?" Honor Hamill said.

"It's just my leg," Eddie replied. "Keep moving!"

And then they were galloping back along the trail, as fast as they dared in the scattered moonlight. Clover was right at the center of the pack, his brother next to him, Gemma out front, and the other men bringing up the rear. By some miracle, all of them had made it out alive. Someone was giving chase, firing blindly into the dark.

Clover could hear the bolts as they passed—the sound reminded him of the spectral blur made by a hummingbird's wings. Minutes passed, protracted and terrible, accompanied only by the patter of hooves on dirt and Eddie's agonized grunts.

Clover didn't consciously register the moment when their pursuer fell away, but the next time he turned to look back, there was nothing to see but the silvery sheen of moonlight on the aspens. A few seconds later, he heard the most awful scream of his life—shrill and unearthly, impossibly long.

Somehow he knew that scream was directed at him and Gemma, for what they'd done tonight. He wondered if they would ever outrun it.

12. Clive

THEY FOUND THE BIG WAGON BY THE SIDE OF THE ROAD only a few miles west of Amestown; for once, Clive was glad that his mother was such a worrywart. As soon as they saw their father, Michael and Flora came hurtling out at him like a couple of puppies, jumping up on him before he could warn them about his leg. Meanwhile, Clive's mother embraced him with tears in her eyes.

The reunion didn't last long; there was too much to be done. Clive helped with the heavy lifting, unloading anything and everything that wasn't absolutely crucial to the journey ahead. It was a painful business, though not nearly as painful as the thought of all their musical instruments, which were still inside the small wagon they'd abandoned outside Amestown. Eddie was having a lie-down on account of his injury—a ragged hole blown into the flesh just above his knee—so it was almost noon by the time they set out again. Though the Anchor was only about six hundred miles away as the crow flew, the Southern Tail zigged and zagged worse than a drunk stumbling home at the end of the night. They could manage about twenty miles a day if everything went smoothly, but a bad summer storm could slow them down considerably, and trouble with the wagon or the horses could see them stranded indefinitely.

In other words, they were going to be on the run for a good long while.

Even if the specter of death hadn't been circling above them like a vulture, the ride would've been uncomfortable. Nine of them were now stuffed into the big wagon—three people up in the driver's seat, exposed to the sun, and the other six packed in the back with the supplies. Though the Southern Tail was a relatively well-kept road—graded and smoothed every three years by order of the Anchor—it still jostled you hard enough to rattle your brain every minute or two.

The first couple of days passed in a haze of anxiety and fear. They rode through Grandsville at night and skirted around Framington entirely. Clive would've traded every shekel he had for a couple of hours in a real bed, but he understood why they couldn't risk it. Amestown had seemed wholesome enough, and yet Arthur Edwards had lived there, and that man Dominic, and who knew how many other heretics and traitors. There was no telling how deep the corruption went.

As if things weren't bad enough already, four days after the altercation at the pumphouse, Eddie's condition suddenly took a turn for the worse. He'd insisted his injury wasn't all that serious, but ever since the softleaf ran out, he'd been losing strength. They'd set up a nice big pile of blankets for him in the back of the wagon, but the low-grade fever he'd been running for days had begun to

TOMMY WALLACH

intensify, and he wasn't able to keep down more than a few spoon-fuls of chicken broth.

When they stopped that evening, Honor Hamill called every-one but Michael and Flora together for a parley. They made sure they were far enough from the wagon that Eddie wouldn't overhear.

"We're coming up on Wilmington tomorrow," Honor Hamill said. "It's the biggest town until Two Forks, which is another fifty miles on. I don't think we can afford to wait until then. Eddie could lose his leg."

"We're likely to lose a lot more than that if we stop for too long," Burns said.

Clive didn't want to be seen as always agreeing with his father, but he'd never be able to look Gemma in the eye again if he didn't make an effort on behalf of Eddie.

"We've put a good fifty or sixty miles between us and that pum-phouse," he said. "And for all we know, those men gave up following us a long time ago."

"What if they sent word on ahead, with that telegraph contrap-tion of theirs?" Burns asked.

"We can't make decisions as if the whole world has gone crazy," Ellen Hamill replied. "If you're so worried, Sergeant, you go on alone."

"You know I can't do that. You're all my responsibility."

Burns could be confusing that way; Clive figured it was part of being a soldier. Sometimes, your sense of duty made you seem like a hero. Other times, it made you seem like a monster. Burns had sworn an oath to protect them, and Clive believed the man would willingly lay down his life to honor that oath. But if the order ever came down from the Grand Marshal that the whole ministry had to be killed,

Burns would carry out the directive without a second thought.

"All of us except my father, I guess," Gemma sneered.

"Your father, too. I'm here to keep *everyone* safe."

"Like you did at the pumphouse?"

"We're all alive, aren't we?"

"No thanks to you."

"That's enough, Gemma!" Honor Hamill said. "Burns is right. We have to be sensible."

"But—"

"And *you're* right that we have to see to Eddie. We'll stop in Wilmington, but not for a second longer than we have to. That work for everyone?"

Clive could tell Gemma and Burns had plenty more to say on the subject, but both were smart enough to keep quiet.

"Good," Honor Hamill said. "Then it's decided."

The Wilmington church was a typical Descendant house of worship; beneath a low-roofed dome painted a pale, flaking blue— unlike the domes in the Anchor, which were all elaborately tiled—pews were arranged in curved rows that stepped downward as they went, describing the two-thirds of the room that an Honor could comfortably address at once. The ambo was always given pride of place at the room's lowest point. Above it hung an enormous annulus made up of tiny twigs braided together; it looked like a bird's nest with the bottom sliced off.

"Hello?" Clive's father called out. The sound echoed around the room.

After a moment, a woman emerged from a door behind the apse. Her head was shaved down to the skin—an odd tradition among some outerlands ministers—and the thinnest layer of silver fuzz had begun to grow back. As always, Clive found it strange to see a woman in the flame-red robes of an Honor. There were no female ministers in the Anchor proper, though it had been more than half a century since the Distaff Encyclical had granted women the right to seek ordination.

"Can I help you?" she asked. Then recognition flooded her face. "Honor Hamill!"

"Afternoon, Honor Epley."

"I didn't expect you this early in the season."

"That makes two of us." He quickly related the broad strokes of their story, eliding the details of what they'd seen in Riley's cottage.

"Well, thank the Daughter you got here safe. We've got guest quarters in the basement. Nothing extravagant, but they'll keep you warm."

"I'm afraid we won't be staying the night," Burns interjected. "We just need to see the doctor and get moving again."

"That's a shame. I was hoping I could convince the Honor here to give the sermon tomorrow morning."

"Next time around," Honor Hamill said.

"I hope so. Now, Dr. Brinton is just down the road from here, in the blue house with the gables. He's a fine physician, Anchor-educated. Meantime, I'll send Novice Dawson out to the sheriff, and he'll let us know if any unfamiliar faces come sniffing at the gates."

"Thank you kindly, Honor."

Dr. Brinton's house was only a few minutes' walk from the

church. When he answered the door, it was clear he'd just risen from a midday nap; his fluffy white hair had matted into a surprisingly tenacious crest. Thankfully, his apparent drowsiness evaporated when he learned who they were and why they were there, and his examination of Eddie—which he insisted take place behind a large paper screen, for the sake of the patient's privacy—was anything but cursory. Clive held Gemma's hand the whole hour they spent waiting for the doctor's diagnosis. She stood up swiftly when he came back around the screen.

"Can you save the leg?"

"I believe so," Dr. Brinton said. "But there's a small pellet of what I believe to be iron buried deep in the muscle. I'll have to take that out right away."

"Will you use chloroform or ether?" Clover asked.

Dr. Brinton chuckled. "Chloroform, of course. It's much faster."

"But it's more dangerous."

"Speed is of the essence, Doc," Burns said. "We need to get back on the road tonight."

Dr. Brinton took off his spectacles, the better to display his frown. "Oh, I can't recommend that. I'll need to see how Mr. Poplin responds to the surgery. If the infection doesn't improve, the leg will have to go, and that's not exactly a procedure you can carry out on the road."

"How soon then?"

"Twenty-four hours at the very least."

"We don't have twenty-four hours!" Eddie shouted out from the other side of the screen. "Just get this thing out of me and we'll take our chances."

TOMMY WALLACH

"But Daddy—" Gemma began to say.

Only Eddie wasn't in the mood for arguing. "Everybody who isn't pulling metal out of my leg get the hell out of here right now! We're wasting time."

Clive saw the first tear spill down Gemma's cheek, just before she went running out of the room. A moment later the front door slammed shut.

"Clive," his mother said, a note of censure in her voice.

"What?"

"Go after her!"

"Oh. Sure."

If it were him, he would've wanted a bit of time on his own. But girls were strange that way; they never seemed to want to be alone. He took off at a jog—down the hall and out the front door, off the porch and through the little wrought-iron gate. Distracted by thoughts of what he'd say when he caught up with Gemma, he smacked right into someone walking the other way.

"Sorry," he said.

"That's all right."

It was a girl, licking at a sugar-on-a-stick she must have bought at the town general. She wore a white poncho and a dark wide-brimmed hat, and her skin was the color of wet clay. She was the sort of girl who made you realize that all the other girls you'd called "beautiful" hadn't really deserved the label. And somehow Clive could tell that she knew he was thinking along those lines.

"I'm chasing after someone," he explained.

"Lucky girl."

The smile she gave him was both open and sly at once, and his mind went blank as a tightly fitted sheet. "I'm Clive," he finally managed to say.

"Irene. See you around, Clive."

She walked on, toward Wilmington's main street, and Clive paused a moment to watch her go. In a different world . . .

Gemma. He was looking for Gemma. It seemed unlikely she would've headed toward the center of town, which was still pretty busy even though the sun had just begun to set, so he went in the other direction. There were only a few houses out this way, and you could see across the prairie for miles—thousands of cacti, each one standing there with its arms up, as if it were denying some wrong-doing: *Don't look at me, buddy.*

It was a good thing that Gemma was a whimperer; Clive never would've found her otherwise. She'd hidden herself behind the knee-high turret of a well, sitting with her legs akimbo and her face all splotchy from crying.

"What am I?" Clive asked, then put both of his arms up at right angles. "Can you guess?"

"Clive, please."

"I'm a cactus!"

She wiped at her nose, trying to conceal the shadow of a smile. "You're an idiot."

"That too." He sat down next to her, leaning back against the uneven stonework. "Your da's tough, Gemma. He's gonna be fine."

"I don't think so, Clive. I think this is my punishment."

"Punishment? For what?"

"For what I did outside that pumphouse."

"You mean the man that Clover killed? That wasn't your fault."

"It was, though. Otherwise why would I feel so bad? Why would I see his face every time I close my eyes?"

"Because you're good, Gemma. And it's right to feel guilty sometimes. It means your conscience is working. But take it from a future Honor: the Daughter forgives you for what you did."

He couldn't tell if she believed him or not, but after a moment, she let her head fall onto his shoulder. "I'm never leaving the Anchor again after this. I mean it. If you end up having to preach on the circuit, you can damn well do it on your own."

Clive laughed. "Deal."

"And when I get home, I'm gonna sit out in the Maple Garden every day for a month."

"Oh yeah?"

Her voice got softer, dreamier. "Absolutely. I won't do a single thing, either. No thinking, or reading, or *anything*. I'll just sit there, being a person. And you can come too, of course. Unless you think your father will want you to start seminary right away."

"I'll make time."

"It's exciting, isn't it? Finally starting your career in the Church? This is what you've been waiting your whole life for."

"Sure. But it's hard to get too excited about something you've always known was going to happen."

She lifted her head abruptly off his shoulder, but it wasn't until he saw the hurt in her eyes that he realized what he'd said. "That's . . . that's not to say that . . . you can't be excited," he stammered out, "only it depends on the exact, you know, thing . . . that you're talking about."

"Sure," Gemma said quietly.

"I mean . . . there's plenty of stuff that isn't like that. Like you and me."

He reached out to take her hand, but her fingers lay limp in his own.

Idiot, he thought, silently berating himself. He had to do better. It wouldn't be long before he and Gemma were married. They had to figure out how to speak to each other like a husband and wife.

"Gemma, I'm sorry—"

"Shut up," she said, rising quickly to her feet.

"But I'm trying to apol—"

"I said shut up!" She was staring out over the prairie, her eyes wide and fearful. "Look out there."

Clive stood up next to her. They couldn't have been more than a mile or two away—six horses, black as nightmares beneath the wide crimson sky. A cloud of dust loomed up behind them like a sandstorm.

The riders had come.

13. Clover

CLOVER GAZED OUT THE BACK OF THE WAGON AS IT bucked and bumped along with every stone and divot in the road. He had his satchel next to him, the weapon from the pumphouse still hidden away at the very bottom. He'd told his father he'd dropped it during their chaotic escape in the dark.

On the rare occasions when he could manage a bit of privacy, he would take it out for examination. Every time, he was struck by the sheer craftsmanship of the thing: the grip of dark polished wood, the complex floral tracings in the metalwork, swelling smoothly up to the cheek-like bulge of the barrel, which popped out to reveal the twelve small cavities where the pellets were kept. Only one of these holes was empty at the moment—the pellet he'd discharged to extinguish Riley's lantern. The others were each plugged with a small cylinder of copper, a gritty white powder, and the pellet itself. His guess was that the trigger mechanism caused the hammer to slam into the copper, creating a spark that ignited the powder and expelled the pellet. Of course, *how* it worked wasn't important—only *if* it did.

They'd left Wilmington within ten minutes of Clive and Gemma spotting the horsemen—not west along the Southern Tail, as would be expected, but north, making use of a treacherous and boulder-strewn old mining road that ran all the way to the Northern Tail.

The black hours of night passed uneasily; Clover managed only a few hours of sleep. There was an unfamiliar tension in the wagon—a silence heavy as guilt. Eddie was restless with pain (the doctor had managed to get the pellet out, but there'd been no time to treat the wound), and Clover's parents were still bitter over the argument they'd had back in Wilmington.

"We'd be safe hiding out in the basement of the church," his mother had insisted.

"And if they found us?" Honor Hamill had said. "What then? I won't endanger every man, woman, and child in town."

At least Honor Epley had provided them with fresh horses, and promised to do everything she could to persuade the men from the pumphouse that the ministry had stayed on the Southern Tail.

And yet, as the sun rose the next morning, Clover caught sight of something, moving toward them from the direction of Wilmington. It was a single rider, coming on fast.

"There's someone out there," he announced.

Clive leaned out the back of the wagon, squinting into the distance. "If those strangers were coming for us, they wouldn't be coming alone."

That made sense enough, but Clover went on watching anyway.

TOMMY WALLACH

The shapeless speck gave up its secrets one by one over the course of the next half hour: a horse the color of rainclouds, a white poncho flapping in the breeze like a sheet on a line, a wide-brimmed hat. And finally, a sun-reddened face . . .

It was a girl. And now she was raising her hand, hailing them.

"I think she's trying to wave us down," Clover said.

Clive raised an eyebrow. "It's a she?"

"Honor, you want me to stop?" Burns asked from the driver's seat.

"Might as well," Honor Hamill said. "She's overtaking us anyway."

Burns slowed the wagon to a halt, and all of them got out. The girl caught up with them a couple of minutes later.

"You the minister's family?" she said.

Burns rested his right hand on the hilt of his sword. "Who's asking?"

"Irene Pirez of Eaton. Honor Epley sent me." The girl dismounted in an easy swoop and took off her hat, releasing a long, loose braid of jet-black hair. Her lips were bright red, chapped from the wind, and the smooth skin of her forehead was sheened with sweat. She looked to be Clive's age, or maybe a little older.

Everyone introduced themselves. When it was Clover's turn, the girl took hold of his hand with an odd, almost masculine firmness.

"Good to meet you, Clover Hamill."

He felt embarrassed, though he couldn't have said why.

"So you've got a message for us?" Burns asked, once the pleasantries were finished.

"The Honor knew I was heading north this morning, so she

caught me before I left and asked me to bring you something. You all disappeared in such a hurry, she didn't have time to get it out from the church pantry."

"Is it candy?" Michael asked.

"Close," Irene said with a smile. She went back to her horse and unhitched what Clover now saw was an extra set of saddlebags. They were filled with biscuits and jams and dried fruit. "I only hope it tastes half as good as it smells. I nearly stopped to sneak a few things, I'll admit. Though that's probably just because I skipped breakfast."

"That's mighty kind of you," Honor Hamill said, taking the saddlebags.

"Well, it's been a real pleasure meeting you all." She put a foot up in the stirrup. "Safe travels to you."

"We were just about to eat, ourselves," Clive said. "You should join us."

Irene hesitated. "You sure? I wouldn't wanna inconvenience you."

"Least we can do is give you a bite to eat, after you came all this way. Isn't that right, Ma?"

Clover could tell his mother was a little surprised at Clive's sudden hospitality, given their situation. "Of course it is. But we won't be stopping long."

"That's fine by me," Irene said, stepping back down to the ground. "I'm in a bit of a hurry myself."

The girl was reserved at first, but she warmed up before too long. She told them her father was a vegetable farmer, and that he'd sent her out to talk to other farmers along the Tails, to see what was

TOMMY WALLACH

growing well and bring back the seeds for next season's planting.

"Doesn't your mother worry about you?" Ellen asked.

"My momma's dead," Irene said. "And my da knows I can take care of myself."

"I guess with that hat on, a lot of people mistake you for a man," Gemma said.

If Irene was insulted by the comment, she didn't show it. "That's one of the reasons I wear it. Same with the poncho. It hides the curves." She smiled, and suddenly Clover couldn't help but wonder what kind of curves she had. "But that's plenty of talk about me. What about you? You spend most of your time out on the road?"

"We live in the Anchor," Michael said. He always got excited talking to somebody new, particularly when that somebody was a girl. "Have you ever been there?"

"I haven't," Irene said. "But I've heard plenty about it. Is it true there's a whole castle there full of nothing but books?"

"Sure is."

"It's called the Library," Clover interjected. "And it's not really a castle. And there aren't that many books."

"My brother is apprenticing there," Clive said. "He's the scholar of the family."

"Oh, is he? So what does that make you?" Her tone was light, flirtatious even.

"I'm studying to be an Honor."

"A scholar and an Honor. What a distinguished company. Cheers."

"Cheers," Clive said, and the two of them tapped leather flasks.

After they were done eating, Irene excused herself to answer the call of nature. Michael waited until she was just out of sight, then made a theatrical collapse onto the dirt. "She's so pretty," he said, staring up at the sky. "How is she so pretty?"

"Michael!" Eddie chided. "It's rude to talk about people like that."

Michael turned over onto his stomach. "But I'm saying nice things!"

"Even so."

"Don't listen to him," Burns said. "You're just saying what everybody's thinking."

"I wasn't thinking it," Gemma said.

"That's just because you're jealous," Michael countered.

"She is not," Flora said, leaping to her sister's defense.

"Is too!"

"Is not!"

"Both of you shut up!" Gemma shouted. She must have realized how harsh she'd sounded, because when she spoke again, it was in a more placatory tone. "I mean, what will that girl think if she hears you talking about her like she was nothing but a slab of beef?"

"Sorry, Gemma," Flora said, and even Michael looked appropriately chastened.

Clover figured Gemma was just anxious because her da was still running a fever. The last thing she needed right now was some strange girl making eyes at Clive. Luckily, when Irene came back, she immediately announced her intention to leave.

"Thank you all so much for the meal," she said. "It was real pleasant."

Clive stood up just a little too fast. "Hold on, though. I thought you were taking this road here up north."

"I am."

"Well, so are we. We should all go together."

Irene looked to Honor Hamill. "Only if I wouldn't be a bother."

"Not at all," Clover's father said. "But I'll warn you, this wagon doesn't move nearly as fast as your horse."

"What good's moving fast when the time moves so slow? The road gets awful boring with no one to talk to. Just let me know if you get sick of me, and I'll be out of your hair straightaway."

They got on the move again a few minutes later. Irene rode just behind the wagon, chatting with Clive and Michael through the opening in the canvas. Clover's parents were up in the driver's seat, while Burns was jotting down some notes in a little logbook he kept in his jacket pocket. Clover once again reached the end of the only book he'd kept with him after the fracas at the pumphouse—an adventure story about a boy from the Anchor who discovers an ancient treasure map—and immediately started it over again from the beginning. Morning turned to afternoon, passing in a fraught but uneventful quietude.

He woke from a daydream of the Library reading room to find most everyone else in the back of the wagon asleep—Flora had her head on Gemma's shoulder, mouth leaking a shiny ribbon of drool; Eddie snored loudly on his pallet; even Ellen and Honor Hamill had left the driving to Burns and snuck into the back for a bit of shut-eye. Only Michael and Clive were still awake, the former talking up a storm with Irene, the latter just listening. Clover watched his brother out of slitted eyes. There was a brightness in Clive's expression, a palpable excitement, as he gazed unblinkingly at the new girl. And every once in a while, she would look back at him with the same odd intensity. Though they weren't even speaking to each other, Clover felt the urge to intervene, to defuse the tension somehow.

But just when he was about to try, there was a loud snapping sound from somewhere close by. The rear of the wagon dropped a few inches, and the whole thing came to a shuddering halt. Suddenly everyone was wide-awake.

"What the hell was that?" Honor Hamill said.

"We must've hit a pothole or something back there," Burns called out from the driver's seat. "I'll take a look."

Clover jumped from the lip of the wagon—which was closer to the ground than it used to be—and found the sergeant kneeling down next to the right back wheel.

"Shit on a stick," Burns said.

"What is it?"

"Look for yourself."

Clover came closer. The wagon wheel lay there on the ground like a dead animal, a nub of splintered wood sticking out from the center bore. The damn thing had broken right off the axle.

They were stranded.

14. Clive

SHE'D FOLLOWED HIM. SHE'D FOLLOWED HIM ALL THE way from Wilmington because she'd felt the same spark that he had. And now here they were, stuck together in the middle of nowhere. It almost would've been romantic, if not for everything else that was going on.

"No offense, Honor, but I'm the faster rider," Burns said.

"And you're the only one of us who knows how to fight, should it come to that."

A week ago they could have abandoned the wagon and continued on horseback, but Eddie couldn't possibly ride in his current state. Their only hope was to get a new axle, but that meant somebody had to go back to Wilmington to pick it up.

Irene was over by the wheel, examining the break. "You all expecting trouble?" she asked.

"We had an incident," Clive said. "Some dissidents. We think they might be following us."

She stood up and brushed off her hands. "Well, maybe I should be the one to go back, then. Ain't nobody looking for me."

"Thank you, young lady," Honor Hamill said, "but it's our problem to solve. Besides, you said you had business up north."

"All respect, but you're an Honor, and you're in danger. I think that's a good bit more important than vegetables."

Clive's mother and father shared one of their famous long looks, communicating mind to mind. "Well," Ellen said, "if you really don't mind—"

"Are you joking?" Clive said. He couldn't believe what he was hearing. "She can't go back there on her own. What if those men got it out of Honor Epley that we came this way? She'd run right into them."

"I'll take the risk, Clive," Irene said. "It would be a privilege."

"You don't understand. These men . . . they kill people. You can't go."

Irene smiled. "If we're gonna be friends, you should know I don't have much patience for being told what to do." She gave a whistle, and her horse trotted over. "I'll be back before you know it," she said, swinging into the saddle and immediately taking off back down the trail.

"Damn it," Clive said. He unhitched one of the horses from the yoke and jumped up onto her unsaddled back.

"What are you doing?" his mother said.

"She could die, Ma. Least I can do is warn her what she ought to be on the lookout for." He touched his boot heels to the horse's flanks, and she was off like an arrow. Passing by the opening in the back of the wagon, he saw Gemma tending to Eddie, and his eyes met hers for just a moment. . . .

But there was no time to think about that. Irene wasn't far in

TOMMY WALLACH

front of him, but she was moving fast—far faster than was prudent. The mining road was pocked and pitted, barely wide enough to accommodate a wagon, with a sheer drop-off on the right side. Far below, a silver thread of river wound its way between towering sandstone boulders.

"Hey!" Clive called out. "Slow down!"

Irene glanced over her shoulder, then turned to face forward again. There could be no mistaking it: she was racing him. The road angled precipitously downward, so they were picking up speed whether they wanted to or not. It wouldn't take more than a single slip to send either one of them over the edge.

Down and down they went, accompanied by the rhythmic flutter of hooves striking hard dirt and the rumble of loose rubble rolling in their wake. Irene's hair had come loose beneath her hat and was streaming out behind her like a comet's tail. Lord, but she was fast; she might actually get away from him! And the strangest thing was that Clive didn't feel angry, or even scared—there was only the exhilaration of the chase, of the danger, of being away from Gemma and Clover and his parents and all the trouble they were in.

The trail curved sharply to the right ahead of them. Clive watched to see when Irene would slow down, but she never did; it was only her horse's sense of self-preservation that saved them both. Just a few feet shy of the curve, the animal pulled up short, sending Irene flying off its back. She landed once on the horse's neck, then again on the trail. Her momentum sent her tumbling—once, twice, three times—straight toward the drop at the side of the road. Her legs went over the edge, but she managed to get a hand around a little shock of yellow grass just before the rest of her was carried along with them.

Clive rode right up to the edge of the cliff and dismounted. Irene was trying to pull herself back up, but the grass was starting to come loose. He still had a grip on Orion's reins, and now he looped his right foot through the leather strap and went down on his belly. He reached out to Irene.

"Grab on to me," he said.

She glared up at him, a fear in her eyes so profound it looked like rage.

"What are you doing, Irene? Grab the hell on!"

With a grunt, she threw her hand into his. Clive pulled as hard as he could, using the rein around his ankle and the weight of the horse for resistance. It took everything he had—the race down the canyon had tired him out more than he knew—but at last he got her back up onto the roadway. They both lay there for a moment, gasping with effort.

"Why were you chasing me?" she asked.

"Why were you running?"

He rolled over, supporting himself on his forearms just above her. There was a cut under her left eye from when she'd rolled across the road. Blood dripped down the side of her face. He wiped it away with his thumb, smearing it across her cheek. Her lips were salty, dry, but when she turned her head to kiss him more deeply, he tasted chicory and the sweet bite of tobacco. Then her hands were against his chest and she was pushing him away, so hard he fell onto his back. She towered over him, flushed and panting.

124   TOMMY WALLACH

"What the hell are you doing?" she demanded.

"I don't know." And that was the truth: he had no idea why he'd kissed her. It was wrong in about a thousand different ways.

"You think I owe you something?"

"No."

"Because I don't."

"I know."

"Good."

She slapped her dusty hands together a few times and limped back over to her horse. "Don't follow me this time," she said. Then she was riding off again, down the twisting corridor of the trail, no slower or more carefully than before. Clive was left with the taste of her in his mouth, and a bright crimson stain on his thumb.

On the way back to the wagon, he passed the two younger Poplin children playing out among the cacti. Flora was pretending the plants were people—friends of hers who for some reason refused to move—while Michael was whittling a gnarled piece of old wood into another equally unrecognizable shape. Meanwhile, the rest of the party was carrying things out from the broken wagon to a spot just a few hundred yards away, hidden from the road by a boulder the size of a house. There was an uncomfortable silence that hadn't been there when he'd left.

"What's going on?" he asked his father.

"It's Eddie," Honor Hamill said quietly. "His fever's back. Apparently it got bad almost as soon as we left Wilmington, but the fool didn't say anything until now. He figured—"

"We might try to go back if we knew," Clive said, finishing the thought.

"Exactly."

"So what does that mean for us? What happens next?"

Honor Hamill let out a heavy breath. "I don't know. For now, you should be with Gemma. She's . . . struggling."

Clive found her sitting in the back of the wagon, holding a wet cloth to her father's forehead. Eddie looked to be somewhere between sleep and waking. He said something incomprehensible, a mumble like a prayer. Clive was newly struck by the sheer size of the man; it seemed impossible that someone so big and strong could be brought low so easily. And though it didn't make a bit of sense, Clive couldn't help but feel guilty, as if he'd made this happen by kissing Irene. He felt even worse when he sat down next to Gemma and she immediately curled into him, collapsing against his chest, sobbing hard.

"It'll be all right," he said, stroking her soft hair. "It's gonna be just fine."

She didn't answer him, just went on crying; both of them knew he was only saying what she wanted to hear.

They ate dinner in the wagon that night, doing their best to keep the conversation light. Eddie woke up now and again, always making sure to crack a joke or two, trying to keep the twins from worrying. But it was far too late for that. In the middle of the meal, Flora began to cry, and nothing anyone said could comfort her.

Clive stayed with Gemma at Eddie's side all night, but sometime during the wee hours he allowed his eyes to close—just for a second—and he woke up again with the sunrise. Eddie was tossing and turning on his pallet, his forehead hotter than ever against the back of Clive's hand. They couldn't get any food into him, though he would take sips of water now and again. At some point late that afternoon, he woke up with a wild look in his eyes and grabbed Gemma's hand.

"Viola!" he said, almost as a gasp.

"No, Daddy. It's me. It's Gemma."

"It's been so hard, darling. It's been so hard without you. I've missed you."

Gemma wiped away a tear. "I know. I've missed you, too."

Thankfully, that was all Eddie needed to hear, and soon enough he drifted back into fitful sleep.

"I'll be back in a minute," Clive said.

Gemma was so intent on her father, she didn't even notice Clive leaving.

He found his own father reading the Filia in the cool darkness just behind the boulder. Clover was next to him, also reading: some damn book of stories or poems that had exactly nothing to do with anything that mattered.

"He's dying!" Clive shouted. His father looked up at him. "You know that, don't you?"

"Yes."

"And?"

"And what?"

"Well, shouldn't we go back to that doctor or something?"

"We can't," Clover said, without looking away from his book.

"Why not?"

"You know why not," his father said. "Because even if Honor

Epley convinced those men we kept going along the Southern Tail, it won't take them long to figure out we didn't. All they'll have to do is ask anyone they pass about a minister and his family farther up the road. Then they'll likely be back in Wilmington with more questions."

"So you're just gonna sit here reading while Eddie dies?"

"The Scriptures are where I go for solace in the face of tribulation," his father said quietly.

"The Scriptures aren't worth a copper shekel if we all end up dead!"

Finally, Honor Hamill closed the cover of his Filia. Its gold-leaf annulus suddenly looked cheap, meretricious—a symbol for the Lord's inability, or refusal, to help them.

"We're hundreds of miles from the Anchor right now, Clive, and yet we're still within the boundaries of the Descendancy. More than a hundred thousand people, spread out over thousands of square miles. All those souls. All that space. Yet we have peace. Do you understand how incredible that is?"

"Sure," Clive said. "But I don't see what that has to do—"

"It has *everything* to do with it," Honor Hamill said sharply. He held up the Filia. "This book you think so little of at the moment is the alpha and omega of that peace. And perhaps you don't yet appreciate the effort that is required to maintain it."

"Effort like letting a good man die?"

"Yes, Clive. Effort like that. Should Eddie pass, he will find his reward in heaven, as will all of us who cleave to the path laid out for us by the Lord. Think on that." He tossed the Filia at Clive, who caught it on instinct. "And think on that, too, son."

TOMMY WALLACH

That night Clive lay awake in his tent, idly flicking through the Book of Ivan. Outside, he could hear Eddie coughing—a terrible hacking sound, as if the man were trying to cut his way out of a jungle that was only growing denser with every passing moment.

"It won't be long now," Clover said.

"No," Clive replied. Then, because he didn't want to think about Eddie: "You could've spoken up for me earlier. With Da, I mean."

"But you were wrong," Clover said.

And the strange thing was that Clive found himself smiling; it was such a quintessentially Clover-ish answer. "I know I was."

They were silent for a minute, while Eddie had another coughing fit.

"I wish we had some music," Clive said. "I miss playing."

"Me too."

It was a few seconds before Clive realized his brother had begun humming the verse melody of "I Came Me Down to Ground." Ever since he was a toddler, it had been Clover's favorite song. For years their mother had sung it to them both before bed every night.

"*The night is dark, the sky is deep,*" Clover sang, "*the stars are small as crumbs. But if I e'er begin to grieve, the Daughter to me comes.*"

Clive joined in after that, and the two of them sang the next verse together. Then, halfway through the chorus, Clive heard his father's rumbly bass voice, and soon after that, everybody else in their little party, all of them singing as loudly as they could, trying to drown out the sound of Eddie's coughing, the claustrophobic hush of the night, the fear.

"*Grant me sleep, oh holy round, and so I came me down to ground.*

This humble fire by light be drowned, and so I came me down to ground. To ground, to ground, Oh Lord, to ground. How soft I came me down to ground."

The song ended, and the silence that came afterward was better somehow, less menacing. Before too long, Clive found his way into sleep.

In his dreams, a flock of ravens loomed overhead, like a black cloud. They circled, cawing, then dove down at him one by one, talons grasping at his coat and piercing the skin underneath, clenching and dragging him up into the air. Their screams resolved into human voices, and he woke confused, angry, swatting at the air. His hand caught something in the dark.

"Get up, Clive," a voice whispered. "Get up now."

Clover. It was only Clover.

"What are you talking about?" he said groggily.

"They're here, Clive. The men are here. We have to run."

15. Clover

FOR THE REST OF HIS LIFE, CLOVER WOULD REMEMBER every detail of the next few minutes, each one seared into his memory as if with a branding iron. How he pulled on his trousers and threaded the belt through the loops, missing half of them in his hurry. How he stepped out of the tent and into a night that seemed full of dark, scuttling things. How he caught hold of his mother's arm as she ferried saddles over to the horses.

"Where are they?" he whispered.

"Close. Burns saw them coming up the road from the canyon."

"We gonna try—"

"There's no time for questions. Just get yourself ready. Leave everything you don't absolutely need."

"Yes, Ma." She hurried off, just as Clover remembered Eddie, who was still sleeping in the wagon smack-dab in the middle of the road. "What about—" he began to say, but his mother was already too far off to hear him.

And the truth was, he didn't really need to ask. Eddie was too weak to walk on his own anymore, which meant he'd need to be carried out of the wagon. And would he have the strength to stay on a horse's back at a gallop?

No. There was no way around it: Eddie would have to be left behind.

They worked as quickly as they could in the darkness, but only a couple of minutes later, Clover heard the hoofbeats out on the road. The horsemen were probably approaching the wagon gingerly, wary of an ambush. What would they make of Eddie, twisting feverishly in the back, so obviously helpless that he could only be some kind of decoy?

"We still have a chance," Honor Hamill whispered. "Move slow until I give the signal, then ride like hell. If we're lucky—"

"Where's Michael?" Gemma interrupted, her voice low but frantic. "Has anyone seen him?"

"Oh, sweet Daughter," Clover's mother said.

She was peeking around the edge of the boulder; Clover joined her there a moment later, and together they watched the tiny silhouette moving toward the wagon. Gemma didn't hesitate, sprinting out after her brother, Clive right on her heels. But they'd started much too late to ever catch up. Clover could only look on in horror as Michael approached the wagon, brandishing the little stick he'd spent the past couple of days whittling to a point.

"Michael, stop!" Gemma shrieked.

Maybe if the horsemen had known he was only a child, they wouldn't have done what they did. But all they could see in the darkness was a shadow creeping toward them with a weapon in its hand.

A burst of lightning. A crack of thunder. Michael didn't make a sound as he slumped to the ground.

"No!" Gemma screamed. "God, no!"

Clive had caught up with her by then, and he half carried her back toward where the rest of them were hidden. A fresh set of explosions sounded, bolts ricocheting off the rocks around them.

There could be no escape now without some sort of engagement. Clover knew of only one thing that might save them. He plunged his hand down into his saddlebag, delving through the layers of dirty clothes. The hoofbeats were getting louder and louder, fast as fluttering wings. The men barked out orders to one another; they were splitting up into two groups so they could come around the boulder from the north and south at the same time. Clover felt a rush of relief as his hand closed around something hard at the bottom of the bag, but it turned out to be the crystal he'd pulled from the stream outside Amestown, which his brother had duly returned to him a few days ago.

Meanwhile, Burns had positioned himself at the northern end of the boulder and drawn his sword. Oddly, instead of holding it by the hilt, he'd laid it out horizontally on his palms, as if he were about to offer it up to someone. A moment later the first horseman came into view, and Burns launched the sword like a spear, catching the man in the stomach and knocking him from his mount. The horse just behind reared back, nearly throwing its rider, and by the time it steadied again, the sergeant was ready, leaping up and wrestling the second man to the ground.

At last Clover's fingers found the smooth wood of the weapon's handle. He pulled it out just as three more of the horsemen came around the southern end of the boulder. He didn't aim for the riders—afraid that his courage would fail him as it had outside the pumphouse—but their horses instead. His first shot sent the nearest animal tumbling, pinning its rider's leg beneath its thrashing bulk. While his next few shots didn't seem to hit anything, at least they forced the rest of the men back around the boulder.

There was the sound of steel clashing with steel—a sword fight. If Burns kept up his diversion to the north, the rest of them might have a chance of escaping.

Unfortunately, most of their horses had spooked during the tumult; only three were left. Clover's parents mounted up together, as did Clive and Gemma. Clover helped Flora up onto the remaining animal's back, then climbed up in front of her.

"We're going to make it, aren't we?" she asked.

Clover's mother smiled. "Of course we are, sweetie."

Another explosion sounded, and Clover saw his mother shudder with the impact. A small sigh escaped her lips.

"Momma?" he said.

She listed and fell off her horse. Honor Hamill immediately jumped down next to her. "Ellen! You have to get up. You have to get up now. Ellen? Ellen?" His voice grew increasingly desperate. Clover felt paralyzed; his hands were like blocks of ice at the ends of his senseless arms. Then his father looked up at him, eyes full of emotion.

"Go!" he shouted huskily.

It was a voice Clover had learned to obey on instinct, and before he knew it, he was riding as hard as he could, blowing past the north end of the boulder, his brother and the surviving Poplin chil-

TOMMY WALLACH

dren just behind him. The horsemen caught on eventually, but by the time they started shooting, Clover and the others were out of range. Even so, Clover pointed his own weapon behind him and squeezed off a couple of shots. Then he molded himself to the horse's back as the world turned to fluid motion. He tasted salt water on his tongue.

They made it to the top of the ridge and kept going, farther and farther, mile after mile. Clover hoped they would never stop, because stopping would allow this nightmare to resolve into reality. Stopping would turn them into children without parents, stranded many hundreds of miles from home. Better to keep on riding forever.

Clive's horse gave up first, simply stopping in place and lowering itself onto its belly. Clover slid out of the saddle and lay down on the cold ground, and it wasn't long before he sensed Gemma and Flora there beside him, and then Clive, too. They all put their arms around him, around one another, but he couldn't derive any warmth or comfort from the contact. The sorrow was simply too deep to be touched.

He pulled away, stepping back from the cacophony of the girls' sobbing, and that was when he noticed it—just beyond their little huddle, out there in the trees, something was moving.

He drew the weapon from his belt.

"Come out here with your hands on your head," he shouted.

A rustle in the branches, a silhouette resolving into familiarity. Clover lowered the weapon.

"I'm sorry," Irene said. She was standing just in front of her horse, her cheeks glazed with tears that shone bluish and ghostly in the moonlight. "I tried my best."

They walked. They walked because their feet could carry them places the horses couldn't follow. They walked because the only way to make sleep come was to be too exhausted at the end of the day to grieve. They walked because there was still a home out there, across the continent, and it was all they had left to cling to. They walked through a lush landscape of crystalline streams and swaying trees, mountain caps floating in the distance like doves. And with each step, Clover felt himself retreating a little further into himself, away from a world that took what it wanted from you whenever it wanted to take it. He didn't speak. He didn't smile. Maybe for the first time in his life, he didn't even think. He'd discovered a vast cavern inside himself, and all he wanted to do now was sit in the darkness of that cavern and listen—to the plinking of water drops forming stalactites and stalagmites, to the leathery fluttering of the bats, to the roar within the silence.

He wasn't angry, as his brother so obviously was, nor was he in mourning, as Gemma kept insisting he ought to be. He'd found a sort of peace on the other side of caring. Even the thought of dying didn't bother him anymore. In a way, it would be fitting. The land would swallow them up, as it had swallowed up so many before them. As it swallowed up everyone, sooner or later.

On and on, they walked.

16. Clive

THE CHURCH IN VIRGIL WAS WIDELY CONSIDERED TO BE the most beautiful house of God outside of the Anchor's Notre Fille. It had taken more than two years of digging to lay the foundation—a full fifty feet below ground—and the dirt removed in this excavation had been used to construct an enormous annulus of raised earth just in front of the church; locals affectionately referred to it as the Cupcake. The pews were built of solid mahogany, polished to a shine, and the ambo had been carved out of a single piece of alabaster. Overhead, a row of windows, each one as tall as a man standing, ran around the circumference of the church, just below the dome. During the days, they filled the room with a liquid yellow luster, through which dust motes danced as madly as tadpoles.

But when Clive entered the church, it was dark outside and dark within. The only light came from the handful of oil lamps left burning in sconces along the walls. He scanned the room until he spotted the Dubium, squirreled away in a crevice just below a painting of the beatification of Saint Ivan.

Clive had never made use of a Dubium outside the Anchor before, had never felt the need. But the last few weeks had been the most spiritually demanding period of his life. After that terrible night on the mining road, he and the others had continued traveling north, through a miasma of fear and hunger and grief. And by some strange belated mercy on the part of the Lord, they'd made it to the Northern Tail, where they turned west. They traveled only by night after that, always out of sight of the road, until they reached a town large enough to absorb them without comment: Virgil. For the first time in a long time, it seemed possible they might survive to see the Anchor again.

Clive rented a couple of rooms above a tavern, and immediately slid under the covers of the first soft bed he'd touched in months. But in spite of his exhaustion, sleep wouldn't come. After a few hours plagued by terrible memories and even worse premonitions, he realized what he had to do.

The Dubium was a small two-chambered box, each chamber screened off by a velvet curtain so heavy as to cut out any light from outside. Before entering, Clive tugged at a braided golden cord that hung from the ceiling just next to it. The cord would cause a bell to ring in Honor Ferdjoukh's bedroom, elsewhere in the church. Clive regretted having to wake the man at such an hour, but attending to the Dubium was one of an Honor's foremost responsibilities. Someday, it would be Clive dragging himself out of bed to speak to some guilt-ridden petitioner in the middle of the night.

It was at least fifteen minutes before he heard the curtain in

TOMMY WALLACH

the other chamber slide open and shut again. Candlelight glowed through the lattice separating the chambers, projecting little orange rings onto Clive's folded hands.

"Good evening," Honor Ferdjoukh said, his voice still thick with sleep.

"Forgive me, Honor, for I have doubted."

"To doubt is to question God."

"I know, Honor."

"And what have you doubted?"

"I have doubted the wisdom of our Lord's injunction against violence."

"I see. And have you practiced violence?"

Clive had known this question would come—it was standard practice with this particular doubt—but that didn't mean he had an answer. How responsible was he for what had happened with Arthur Edwards? Technically, he hadn't done anything to the old man. Nor had he directly hurt anyone at the pumphouse, or even during the skirmish on the mining road. Yet to be present for so much violence was, in a way, to condone it. And hadn't he spent most every night since then dreaming of murdering the men who'd murdered his parents, of tying them to a tree and slowly scraping off their skin, of making them bleed rivers?

"Yes, Honor."

"Was this violence done for personal gain or private grudge?"

"No, Honor."

"Do you repent of this violence?"

"I do."

"Then I absolve you of your doubt, in the n—"

"Honor, I—" Clive hesitated. He wasn't sure why he'd interrupted, only that he couldn't stand to be given some easy answer, when everything in his mind was chaos and convolution. "I don't think I deserve to be absolved."

"All men who seek absolution deserve it."

"I guess I doubt that, too."

Honor Ferdjoukh chuckled. "You didn't wake me up for nothing, did you?"

"No, Honor."

"You sound young. Have you spoken to your father about this?"

For a moment, Clive thought that Honor Ferdjoukh had somehow recognized his voice. Then he realized it was just a general admonition; when a boy was confused, he spoke to his father. Clive gritted his teeth against the tears. "My father's dead, Honor. And it's important to me to do right by him. I want to live the way he taught me to. But I've got so much anger in me right now, and he never seemed to have any."

"To be angry is to believe the world is not as it should be. But the Lord made this world especially for us, through the love of his Daughter. To wish it different is just another form of doubt."

"I know, Honor."

"The Filia tells us a violent man can no more easily enter the Kingdom of God than a mule can pass through the eye of a needle. You have to let your anger go."

"I'm not sure that I can."

"And yet you must." Clive sensed the note of finality in the Honor's voice, so he wasn't surprised at the familiar words that

TOMMY WALLACH

followed. "Your penance is twenty Trinity Prayers and two copper shekels."

"I'm afraid I don't have much money to spare, Honor."

Honor Ferdjoukh sighed. "Thirty Trinity Prayers, then. Through the ministry of the Descendant Church, I absolve you of your doubt, in the name of the Father, and of the Daughter, and of Holy Gravity. Amen."

"Amen," Clive said, making the sign of the annulus on his chest.

He listened as the curtain was pulled aside again, as Honor Ferdjoukh's footsteps receded. He'd hoped talking with the Honor would calm the tempest in his mind, but their conversation hadn't resolved anything.

He exited the Dubium. In the short time he'd been inside, someone else had come into the church, a robed figure kneeling in the front pew. Clive shuffled out as quietly as he could, so as not to disturb the man's prayers.

It was colder than he'd expected outside—colder than it had any right to be. There was no one in sight, but Clive had barely made it to the bottom of the steps when he heard the church doors creak open behind him. He glanced over his shoulder and saw the hooded figure step through. The inn where he'd taken rooms was all the way at the other edge of town, but Virgil was only about half a mile from end to end. Clive quickened his pace. As soon as he did so, the hooded figure sped up as well. Then Clive was running, and the figure behind him was running too, much faster than Clive had anticipated. The steep margin of the Cupcake loomed before him, and he clambered up it in a few easy leaps. But when he looked back from the top of the ring, to see if he could make out any sort of weapon in the other man's hand, his foot caught in a divot, and he went tumbling down into the center of the annulus. He turned over just in time to see the stranger looming above him.

"It's really you," the man said. "God damn."

He pulled back his hood.

"Sergeant Burns?" Clive said.

Burns stretched his arms out wide, as if he'd just performed a miracle and was now basking in the crowd's adulation. "In the wasted flesh," he replied.

The bottom floor of the inn was empty but for the rough-looking girl serving drinks and a couple of men speaking in low tones at the bar. Clive staked out a corner table and Burns brought over a couple of pints.

"Good thing you showed up when you did," he said. "I was gonna start back home in the next couple of days."

"How'd you know we'd be here?"

"Call it an educated guess. I figured you'd stick close to the road, and Virgil here was your safest option for a warm bed and a good meal."

"But if you worked it out that easily, won't the people chasing us be able to do the same?"

"Maybe. Maybe not. I only left a couple of them standing. Besides, they don't know you like I do. Though even *I* didn't expect you to go to church in the middle of the night."

"So what were you doing there?"

Burns smiled. "I made some friends in the past couple days.

They gave me word the moment you got into town, but I wanted to keep an eye on you from a distance at first, just to make sure nobody else was watching."

"And?"

"Nothing so far."

Clive had a question he needed to ask, though he wasn't sure he wanted to know the answer. "I take it you're alone?"

"How do you mean?"

"I mean . . ." He took a deep breath. "They shot Ma just as we were leaving, but Da was still alive."

"I'm sorry, Clive. Last thing I saw was one of those men give your father one right in the belly. That's when I took off. I'd done everything I could." Burns gave Clive a moment to take this in, but no more. "And the rest of you, your brother and the Poplin sisters, you're all well enough?"

"I suppose so. Alive, anyway."

"They have you to thank for that. Not easy leading a bunch of moody children across the country."

"It was only a few days. And I couldn't have done it without Irene. She knows the land better than any of us. There were a few times—"

"Hold up a minute," Burns interrupted. "You're telling me that girl from Wilmington is still with you?"

"Yeah."

The sergeant laughed, loudly enough to draw the attention of the men at the bar. "Well, she sure knows what she wants, doesn't she?"

Clive frowned. "What are you talking about?"

"Use your head, Clivey. A farmer's daughter is out on the road, and she happens to run into the son of an Honor. Odds are he's got a healthy living coming his way, not to mention a fancy place in the Anchor. Sure beats marrying some hick and dying young in a shack in the woods, doesn't it?"

The thought had never occurred to him, that Irene had only stuck around because she had designs on him. She'd insisted it was her duty as a God-fearing member of the Descendancy.

"That's crazy," Clive said.

"Women are crazy. But that one sure is easy on the eyes, isn't she?"

"I guess."

"Come on, now! You really gonna sit there telling me that girl doesn't get your blood boiling?"

"I haven't really thought about it."

But that was a lie, of course. Even with everything else that had happened since, he'd spent more than a few nights thinking about what had transpired between him and Irene out on the mining road.

"Sure you haven't," Burns said with a smirk. "Say, you want another drink?"

Clive hadn't even noticed he'd finished his beer while they'd been talking. "Thanks, but I should get to bed."

"Suit yourself. Just be sure to have everyone downstairs by first light."

"I will. Night, Burns."

Only sleep didn't come for a long time that night; Clive couldn't keep his brain from spinning out possibilities. His parents had prepared a life for him, one that he'd accepted without question. He'd be an Honor, and Gemma would be his wife, and they'd churn out a gaggle of little ones as quick as they could. Meanwhile, his father would be nominated to the Gloria, and someday, Clive would follow in his footsteps. Cut and dried. Pure and simple.

Only that life was gone now.

For the past couple of weeks, he'd been looking at his newly uncertain future as yet another aspect of the tragedy that had befallen him and his family; but now he wondered if it might also be a kind of gift. He'd been granted what so few people ever got: a chance to start again. The future was no longer predetermined; he could choose the one he wanted.

It was a terrifying thought—and a strangely exciting one too.

Interlude

ANDROMÈDE OPENED HER EYES. THE FUGUE STATE WAS receding, along with the visions. Reality reasserted itself, heavy as a winter fur worn in summer.

She sensed someone in the tent with her, which was unexpected. Euphrosine, the elderly otsapah who'd brewed the dreamtea and carried out the ceremony, would have left hours ago, and there was only one other person who would dare enter Andromède's tent while she was still journeying.

"Athène," she said, "you've returned."

"It seems we both have, Mother. And how were your dreams?"

Andromède thought back on what she'd seen; already the images and sensations were fading. "I'm not certain. The signs were contradictory."

Athène smiled impishly. "Aren't they always?"

"Perhaps. But what of the raid? I take it from your good humor that it went well."

"Two men and six women. Twenty-five horses. A week's worth of food. And this beauty." She held up her right hand to display the jewel sparkling on her middle finger: a ruby.

"You should wear it on your left. It has greater properties of protection there."

"This is a trophy, not a charm. There's no magic in it."

"There's magic in everything. It's said a woman who wears a ruby too often will see her beauty fade."

"As will the woman who wears anything too often."

Athène maintained an exaggeratedly serious expression for as long as she could, but it soon dissolved into laughter. The collection of copper bangles on her right arm laughed along with her.

Andromède repressed her own smile. Her daughter had always been too quick for her own good; the last thing she needed was encouragement. "How long until the others arrive?"

"Any moment. I only rode ahead so I could deliver the news personally. You should begin preparing yourself for the feast."

"Must I?"

"The tribe will be expecting enthusiasm, Mother. Put on a show."

Athène was one of the few people who knew Andromède's secret: that she preferred silence to noise, fasting to feast, solitude to companionship. They were very different people, mother and daughter, yet Athène had always been Andromède's favorite child, doted on as only the youngest can be. Of the chieftain's five daughters, Athène was the only one who still traveled with her mother's naasyoon, the largest in the Wesah nation. She'd have to be pushed out of the nest soon, before her playful impieties could develop into outright insubordination.

Athène picked up the humble brass crown that was the only visible symbol of her mother's chiefdom. "I don't know why you insist on wearing something so plain. They say the Archbishop wears a headdress of gold that reaches two feet into the air."

"Men have always been so concerned with length," Andromède

said. "Yet it's the edge of a blade that cuts, the point that pierces. What good is the shaft?"

Athène laughed. "We both know the answer to that."

"Such is our curse."

Andromède took the crown and placed it on her head. Then she swept out of her private tent and on across the prairie where they'd been encamped for the last month, planning tonight's raid. She was pleased that it had come off so well: eight prisoners and twenty-five horses was a fine haul, and the beasts would come laden with a bounty of food and weapons. The Wesah eschewed traditional valuables, and ornaments such as Athène's new ring could only be taken from a kill—one piece per life. The girl already wore a small graveyard on her long, limber arms, mostly accrued in a bloody run of raids they'd carried out up north.

Andromède hadn't killed in many months. She didn't miss it.

To celebrate the raid, the naasyoon would feast deep into the night. And when all the "liberated" wine had been drunk and all the songs of their ancestors sung, they would pack up and travel in darkness for as long as it took their otsapah to tell the tale of the flame deluge in its entirety—usually eight to ten hours. Only then would they allow themselves to sleep. It was a show of strength, of course, but also a necessary precaution; the enemy would eventually rally and come looking for retribution. They would find nothing. No Descendancy man moved as fast as the Wesah.

Andromède bypassed the large canvas tent in which the feast would be held, as well as the roasting pits where the nisklaav lamoor were putting the finishing touches on the meat. She inhaled the fragrant smoke, and her mouth filled with saliva; tonight would mark the end of her three-day fast. It was one of the many rituals her daughter was so skeptical of, like the visions granted by the dreamtea, or the ostapah's divinations. Yet who could argue with the results? Their raid had succeeded, and Athène had returned alive. Andromède's fasting was a kind of prayer, and her prayers had been answered.

She hiked up to the top of the mesa to look out over the valley beneath their encampment. Her warriors were close now. Andromède could see the captives, too, tied one to the next in a despondent daisy chain. They believed that tonight marked the beginning of their enslavement; before long, they would come to think of it as the dawn of their emancipation.

"Li boon jheu paardoonaan," she whispered under her breath.

She returned to the feasting tent. There were no thrones among their people, so Andromède sat where she would; the ever-shifting hierarchies below her would determine who had the privilege of sharing her blanket tonight. Only Athène had a permanent seat at her mother's right hand, though she was still missing when the nisklaav began to bring in the food. Soon after, the first of the returning warriors entered the encampment. They were loud, high on survival, shrieking their victory. Andromède could smell the blood on their armor, the blood in their veins. Nephra, who'd been charged with executing the raid, came to sit at Andromède's blanket, greeting her chief with a slight nod. She was a large woman, her shoulders wide and ropy with muscle. Andromède raised an eyebrow and Nephra responded by holding up four fingers. More than a hundred warriors had gone out today; a loss of four was a good outcome.

Athène didn't enter the tent for an hour, and when she did, Andromède was surprised to see Noémie on her arm, a suspicious bloom in their cheeks. Andromède knew her daughter had amused herself with the girl on occasion, but that they'd delayed feasting in order to make love meant there might be more to it now than mere amusement.

Nephra noticed the girls as well.

"Youth," she said.

"Indeed."

"Can you remember it?" In Nephra's eyes, Andromède saw a glimmer, harkening back at least a decade, to a time when they would often find occasion to visit one another's tent in the dead of night. "Perhaps we could stand to rediscover our own childish ways."

Andromède allowed herself a thin smile. "Perhaps. But I have other duties tonight."

"Of course."

Duties she'd already put off long enough. She stood up, realizing only then that she hadn't eaten more than a few bites of the venison. Her stomach growled, but the meat would keep. Once Andromède had set herself to a task, nothing could distract her from it.

The prisoners were roped to a simple iron T stuck into the ground at the edge of camp. The women were all between the ages of twelve and twenty; most of them would be converted within the week. Put a few hundred miles between a girl and her home, show her a world in which her sex was slave to no one, in which she could fight and feast and fuck at her own discretion, instead of simply keeping her husband's house and spreading her legs at his whim, and she would be yours for life. As the Wesah saying went, *A Descendancy girl is as easy to break as bread.*

The males were a different story. In a perfect world, they wouldn't be necessary at all, but babies had to be made somehow, and because the Wesah never raised boys within the tribe, every nisklaav had to be captured. As for baby boys born to Wesah tribeswomen, they were occasionally sacrificed, but more often left with some sympathetic dahor the tribe knew to be friendly.

As Andromède approached the captives, she saw one of the men tugging for all he was worth at the bottom of the iron T. His fellow prisoners, exhausted after hours of marching, regarded his struggle with the apathy born of despair.

"You aren't nearly strong enough to pull that out," Andromède said. Not all Wesah chieftains spoke English, but Andromède had made sure all her daughters were fluent in the tricksy, guttural tongue. It made certain tasks significantly easier.

The man looked up at her, the veins in his neck throbbing from his fruitless effort. He'd seen thirty winters at most, and his hair and beard were both wiry yellow mops, the color of a duckling's fur.

"Come closer and I'll show you how strong I am."

Andromède allowed herself to laugh, full-throated. "A fine threat," she said. "Now wake up your fellow male over there. I won't waste my time speaking to you separately."

"Do it yourself."

Andromède walked around the T, careful to stay just beyond the reach of the duckling. She kicked the other male, who sat up immediately. He was even younger than the first man, docile-eyed and anxious: practically a nisklaav already.

"Men, my name is Andromède, and I am the chief of this nation."

"Nation?" It was the duckling's turn to laugh. "What do you have here, a couple hundred souls at most?"

"This is but a single naasyoon, just one finger on one hand of our body. And I am the head. Many would consider it an honor to be captured by me."

The man spat into the dirt. "That's what I think of your honor."

Andromède knew of two ways to make a man submit. He could be warmed up gradually, like metal in a crucible, then poured into the mold you wanted. Or he could he hacked into shape like an arrowhead, his undesirable qualities hewn off one by one. Andromède didn't have a preference one way or the other, but something about her mood today inspired her to mercy. She remembered a fragment of one of her teadreams—a dove flying across an icy blue sky and coming to rest on the snout of a black horse.

"Do you know what we Wesah are?" she asked.

"A bunch of dirty bitches," the duckling said.

"Warriors. We don't need men to do our fighting for us. But we do need men. Why?"

"To do all the thinking for you?" He laughed at his own joke.

Andromède was glad to see the twinkling of anger in the eyes of a couple of the female prisoners. That rage would be the seed of their conversion.

"Only if you think with what's between your legs."

The man's smile faded, hardened into hatred. "I wouldn't let you anywhere near what I got between my legs, you godless whore."

Instinct moved faster than thought. The duckling hardly had time to widen his eyes before the blade was buried in his chest,

TOMMY WALLACH

just deep enough to pierce the heart. Here was the secret third way to win a man, short-lived as the victory might be. And there were benefits, in spite of the loss. The fear in the eyes of the remaining male made it clear that he wouldn't be giving them any trouble; a few hours alone with one of Andromède's warriors, and he'd be ready to die for the tribe. And though one of the captured women had screamed as the duckling crumpled to the ground, Andromède knew that nothing would more efficiently convey to them the possibilities of this brave new world in which they found themselves. But perhaps the greatest benefit of all was for Athène, whom Andromède had noticed watching from just outside the feasting tent. As chief, Andromède no longer went out on raids herself, so her daughter rarely saw her flex her muscle. It was good to remind the girl that her mother was still a warrior.

Andromède bent down and pulled the knife out of the man's chest. Then she used it to cut the brass chain of his necklace, freeing a plain silver annulus.

"What do you think of it?" she called out to Athène.

Her daughter approached the prisoners. She took the ring and held it up toward the crescent moon, appraising. Andromède noticed, with no small satisfaction, that her daughter had transferred the ruby to her left hand.

"Cheap," Athène said. "Cheap and ugly." She let the annulus fall to the dirt, then ground it beneath her heel.

The duckling gurgled something wordless and furious through a cloud of red foam.

"The wise woman knows that all lives must end," Andromède said, kneeling down next to him. "Time is an illusion. Beyond the reach of our sun, there has only ever been a single day, in which all are born and die. The gods watch their world unspool in an instant. To them, one death weighs less than a grain of earth."

The man's gurgle intensified for a moment before it abruptly stopped.

Andromède stood up again, smiling as a strange thought rose to her mind. She'd been wrong; all this time, she *had* missed killing.

"Now are we finished here?" she said to the other captives. "Or does anyone else want to call me a whore?"

Part II
ORPHANS

And seeing ignorance is the curse of God,

Knowledge the wing wherewith we fly to heaven.

—*Shakespeare*, Henry VI, Part 2

1. Paz

MEMORY AS NIGHTMARE. NIGHTMARE AS MEMORY. Paz stood atop the family home in Coriander, watching her older brother launch his kite into the cobalt sky. She knew what was about to happen, but though she wanted to run to him, her body refused to obey. She tried to scream instead, but the sound was drowned out by the wind, rising quickly now, and when the inevitable gust came, the silk of the kite puffed out, strained at its leash, and then Anton was ripped from the roof, falling fast and silent as a hailstone.

Paz woke, but the paralysis lingered. She knew from experience that no amount of willpower or physical strength could bring her out of it—her brain had simply woken up a few seconds before her body—but she couldn't help but fight against it, straining whatever muscles she had control over, hyperventilating, sometimes even screaming so loudly that her father would come running in to see what was the matter.

At last, she managed to pull herself up to a sitting position, breathless with the effort. She got out of bed and padded out into the empty kitchen, where she put the water on for porridge. Frankie, Terry, and Carlos were already up; she could hear them knocking around in the bedroom that the three of them shared (as the oldest child and only girl, she got her own room). Carlos, the youngest, poked his tousled head around the kitchen door.

"Where's Da?"

"In the garden, most like."

Carlos grinned. "Why?"

It was one of his favorite games, asking *why* over and over again. Paz knew he didn't really care about the answers so much as the infinite regression of the inquiry. He was seeking the moment when causality gave way to magic, which always seemed to occur when whoever was being interrogated lost her patience. She could remember one particular series of questions that began with *Why is grass green?* and ended with her grudgingly admitting to the possible existence of angels.

"Well, if you don't get the watering done early, the sun scorches everything."

"Why?"

"Because the water droplets magnify the light somehow, just like you can use a piece of glass to set a leaf to burning." Or an ant to writhing, as Terry had been known to do.

"Why, though?"

"I guess, well . . ." And here was the funny thing: every now and again, Paz reached a new understanding through Carlos's catechism. It was why she still bothered playing along; the rest of the family had given up months ago. "I guess light and heat must be the same thing somehow."

TOMMY WALLACH

"Why?"

Paz flicked a bit of water at him. "Because I said so, goblin. Now go tell your brothers that breakfast is almost ready."

The morning proceeded like any other. Paz's father, José, came inside a few minutes later, already smelling of sweat and fresh earth, and planted a kiss on the top of her head. Just after that, her brothers burst in, and then it was the usual pandemonium through to the end of breakfast, when José assigned the chores that would keep them occupied for the rest of the morning. Paz cleaned up the dishes, then saw to the chickens. She pulled a bucket of water from the well. She carved up the rabbit that Terry had caught in one of his traps last night. And when all her chores were out of the way, she went back into her bedroom and took down one of the precious books she'd borrowed from the schoolhouse in Sophia. The one she was reading now was all about something called calculus, which as far as she could tell was a way of tracking how fast a changing thing was changing. It was difficult to wrap her head around without having access to pen or paper, but she was trying her best. After all, if somebody at the academy had gone to the trouble of writing it down, the least she could do was try to understand it.

Paz couldn't have said how long the siren had been ringing when Carlos finally showed up. She lost track of reality when she was reading—particularly something as complicated as that book on calculus. "What is it?" she asked, annoyed at the distraction.

"The siren's going," he said. "Don't you hear it?" And now she *did* hear it: a distant ringing, like church bells gone mad. "Daddy says you better come quick."

She doubted it was anything important—probably just some

sort of mechanical problem with the siren, or else a drill. But she knew the protocol well enough, and quickly packed up a satchel with what food they had at the ready. Then she buckled her gun belt and slid Silverboy into its holster. A few minutes later she met her father in the stables, and together, they rode for the sheriff's place.

The rest of the town guard was already assembled when Paz and her father arrived: Sheriff Evan Okimoto, the brothers Eli and Leo Ferrell, crusty old Sam Downing (known by everyone as Gramps), Raff Park (who was a year younger than Paz but looked ten years older on account of his pitted skin and thin hair), and Catriona Lipez. They were the eight best gunslingers in town, as determined by an annual competition held out behind the smithy—a competition Paz had won three of the last four years. The year she'd lost, it was only because her revolver had malfunctioned in the middle of the contest. She'd vowed never to be caught flat-footed again after that, which was why she'd designed Silverboy all on her own.

"Took your time," Gramps said.

"That's my fault," Paz said. "I was reading."

"Reading?" Raff scoffed, as if Paz had just admitted to something shameful. "What for?"

"You know what for," Eli said. "She's angling for a spot at the academy."

"Fat chance."

"Shut up, every one of you," Sheriff Okimoto said sharply. "Nobody's late. Telegram only came in from the pumphouse a few minutes ago."

TOMMY WALLACH

Paz's heart skipped a beat; this was no drill.

"The pumphouse?" Paz's father said. "What's going on?"

"Apparently, Riley has visitors."

"Is he all right?"

"He is. For now, anyway."

Paz liked Riley. She'd gone out to visit him a bunch of times, though truthfully that was only so she could learn how the telegraph machine and the pump worked. By now, she probably could've built either one from scratch, if she had the materials on hand.

"Nobody's getting in there without a battering ram," Raff said.

Paz hated how men were always so *sure* about things. In her opinion, certainty was for fools; it left you unprepared for the unexpected. "Wesah could've taken him by surprise," she said.

"It's not Wesah," the sheriff replied. "It's an Honor, from the Anchor. Apparently he and his people set up camp just outside the pumphouse."

Just the mention of the Anchor set Paz's blood boiling. If not for their mad laws, Anton would still be alive today.

"What are they doing there?" she asked.

"Don't know. But something must've set them sniffing."

"Probably that 'gathering' of theirs over by Amestown," Catriona said with a sneer. "They pass around the shine to get people talking. And they call themselves men of God." She spat loudly into the dirt.

About fifteen years back, Catriona had lost her husband and all three of her children to the plague. After that, she'd heard a rumor that the Library had developed a cure that they administered only to senior members of the Church. Paz had no idea whether the rumor was true—though the elderly Archbishop *had* somehow managed to survive the disease while plenty of younger folks had succumbed—but Catriona had certainly believed it. She'd moved out to Sophia soon after.

"Anyway, we should get moving," Sheriff Okimoto said. "I sent a telegram up the hill, and the message from Zeno came back loud and clear."

"No survivors?" José said.

The sheriff nodded grimly. "That's right. No survivors."

It was a journey of almost six hours from Sophia to the pump-house, and Paz knew every twist and turn of the road, every thicket and crevice and hillock, every graceful catenary described by the thin telegraph cable. The corpse of Raff's old horse, Merrily, was still visible at about the halfway point, right where it had turned its ankle. Its thin, rotting skin was stretched over an armature of bone that practically glowed in the light from Sheriff Okimoto's lantern. Though Paz had seen the skeleton plenty of times before, something about it disturbed her today, or maybe it was just the lingering anxiety from last night's dream. Either way, she'd begun to notice a churning in her stomach. At first she mistook it for fear, only that didn't make sense; she'd once run into a mountain lion while alone in the woods and hadn't felt even a flutter of alarm— only wonder at being so close to something so foreign, so savage and beautiful and irreproachable.

No, her anxiety now wasn't fear in the traditional sense, but fear's mirror image: she dreaded what she might have to do. Though she had more hatred for the Church than just about anyone in Sophia, she knew many of its representatives were good men. And it was no small thing, killing a good man.

It was an hour past sunset when the posse reached the unmarked road that led to the pumphouse. The trail was just wide enough for two of them to ride abreast, and Paz ended up next to her father.

"You all right?" he asked.

"Why wouldn't I be?"

"Don't know. But you had this look on your face back there that told me maybe I oughta ask. Your momma used to get the same one when she was bearing down to do something she didn't wanna do."

"Like marry you?"

Her father put his hands up against his heart, as if he'd been shot. "Ooh, that's vicious. You're a vicious child."

"And I got plenty more in the cylinder, so watch yourself."

"Message received."

She would've liked to tell him what she was really feeling, but she couldn't; if one person showed weakness in the face of what they had to do, it might rub off on the others.

Sheriff Okimoto extinguished his lantern as they crested the final hill and the pumphouse came into view. There were four horses tied up out front, but no sign of any people. Evan made the wolf call that was their signal; if Riley was still alive, he would know that they'd arrived. In spite of the urgency of the situation, they took the time to tie up their horses; otherwise the sound of gunshots would likely set the animals running.

"Don't forget," Paz's father said. "They may not have guns,

but that doesn't mean they aren't dangerous. Don't give them the chance to fight. Don't give them the chance to run. You hear me?" Paz nodded. "Good. You'll be covering the retreat."

"Very funny."

"I look like I'm kidding?"

It took all of Paz's self-control to contain herself to a whisper. "Hell, no! I'm going in with the rest of you!"

"Hey now." He took her face in his hands. "Someone's gotta hold back, Paz. And you and I both know you're the best shot we've got."

Paz gritted her teeth. "Fine. Just be careful."

"Always."

She hiked uphill into the woods a ways, to where she could see both the front door of the pumphouse and a good hundred feet back down the trail, then drew Silverboy, who hissed like a snake against the leather of the holster on the way out.

"Evening, darling," she said to the gun. "How you feeling tonight?" She extended her arm and squinted along the sight. The weight of the weapon was perfect in her hand, and she could feel her anxiety melting away. No one would get out on her watch.

She looked on as the rest of the posse stalked quietly past the Honor's horses and up to the threshold of the pumphouse. They paused there for a moment, then Sheriff Okimoto flung the door open.

"Nobody move!"

The lantern inside threw a wedge of buttery light out onto the leaf-strewn dirt, the shimmery bark of the aspens, and . . . something else: two silhouettes, creeping low up the trail. Animals, maybe, only what were the odds of that? She trained Silverboy on

TOMMY WALLACH

one of them, but just then the wind kicked up and set the branches to swaying, muddling up the shadows.

The voices coming from the direction of the cottage grew increasingly heated. And now the two silhouettes reappeared, much farther along the trail than Paz had anticipated. One of them unfurled to human height and began hurtling pell-mell for the pumphouse, like an angry piece of night. It disappeared among the horses. Paz couldn't risk the shot—it would be just as likely to hit one of the animals—but she had to warn the others.

"Careful!" she shouted. "Someone else is out here!"

Her father and Eli Ferrell were still standing in the doorway, and she could see that they'd heard her. Eli set off along the edge of the escarpment, while her father began to walk toward the horses, who were stamping about and snorting with disquiet.

"Whoever's there, just come out peaceable," he said. "We don't want trouble."

"No, no, no," Paz said under her breath. Though she knew she was meant to stay back and cover the retreat path, this was her father, walking straight into danger. She began to climb back down the hill toward the trail. Her father said something and was quickly answered by a female voice, quavery with terror. Paz listened for the crack of a gunshot, but it never came. What was her father doing? And why had everything suddenly gone so terribly silent? A prickle ran up Paz's spine, as if someone had touched a handful of snow to the back of her neck.

She took off running, but the snarls of ivy at her feet were treacherous, and she had to slow down or risk tumbling. When she finally reached the trail, she crouched and crept forward into the heavy, pungent breath of the animals. She could hear the muffled movement of the strangers somewhere close by, but she didn't care anymore, because here was her father, lying face-down in the dirt.

"Da," she said. A knife had been sunk deep in his neck. Around the edges of the blade, blood pulsed blackly out into the earth. "Da," she said again, more loudly this time, though she knew he could no longer hear her.

The grief loomed up inside her, a grizzly bear rising onto its hind legs, opening its mouth wide: to roar, to rend, to ruin. She shouted something, though she had no idea what it was, or if it had even been made up of words, and began sprinting for the pumphouse. Then a gun discharged and everything went dark. Paz raised Silverboy and aimed it at the pumphouse doorway, but there was no way to tell friend from foe. Someone crashed into her, knocking her onto her back. A fusillade of footsteps falling around her head. The jangle of horses being mounted. Barked commands. She sat up and fired a few times into the darkness.

"Shit," she heard Sheriff Okimoto say. "They cut the horses loose."

But Paz had tied up her own horse separately, up where she'd been on lookout. She sprinted uphill, sawing at the tether with her knife just to save the few precious seconds it would take to unpick the knot in the dark.

"Move, you damned stupid animal!" she said, climbing up onto its back. The Honor and his people had a head start on her, but she could still hear them not far up the trail. She drew her gun again and fired—once, twice, three times—but it was no use. She was losing ground. Already her horse had begun gasping for breath;

TOMMY WALLACH

the creature had been pushed to its limit just getting her out to the pumphouse so fast.

"Don't you dare," she whispered in its ear.

But there was nothing for it. The animal was already slowing, and a few minutes later, it gave up entirely.

"Move!" she shouted. "Move!"

When it refused to listen, she jumped down and took off running, not caring if she lost the horse or the rest of the posse, not even caring if she ended up dead. On and on into the night she ran, as fast as she could, until her legs turned numb and finally buckled beneath her. Sprawled out there in the hard, cold dirt, knees childishly akimbo, tears streaming down her face, she let out a scream, as loud as she had inside her. She screamed until her throat was raw and there was no breath left in her lungs, and then she kept on screaming. She hoped the Honor and his people were still close enough to hear that scream, and to fear the source of it.

Eventually, she went back to the others, but only to tell them she'd be riding ahead on her own. Sheriff Okimoto started hollering something about obeying orders and chain of command, but she ignored him. Likewise did she ignore the voice inside her, the one that said she had a responsibility to return to Sophia and take care of her brothers. She had a higher calling now: to make the Descendancy pay for everything they'd taken from her.

Over the course of the next week, she scarcely ate or slept, which was how she was able to outpace the rest of the posse and catch up with the Honor and his family even before they reached

Wilmington. She was there when they got into town, and she followed them to the church where they met up with Honor Epley. She was there when they brought their injured man to see the town doctor, and when the pale, yellow-haired girl came running out with tears in her eyes. She was there a few seconds later, standing just outside the gate, when the boy blindsided her.

And from the way he looked at her in that very first moment—fear and desire and shame all swirling around in his big brown eyes—she knew what she had to do. She could already see herself flagging down the ministry wagon. She'd play up her country accent and flirt as well as she was able. When the opportunity arose, she'd file down the spindle on one of the wagon wheels, so it would snap at the slightest bump in the road. She'd make up some excuse to return to Wilmington, where she'd have left a message for the rest of the town guard to wait for her. Then she'd lead them back to the broken wagon and watch with a smile in her heart as the Honor and his fellow zealots bled out in the dirt.

She would achieve her vengeance, and at the same time, her dream: Director Zeno would be so grateful, she'd have no choice but to admit Paz to the academy.

"I'm chasing after someone," the boy said, his tongue practically hanging out of his mouth.

"Lucky girl."

She gave him a smile that promised the world.

"I'm Clive," he said.

It just came to her, the perfect name for the perfect monster she was about to create. Its meaning was the same as her real name, the name her mother and father had given her on the day of her birth, their hearts full of blind hope, as if they had no idea what the world was really like.

Peace.

"Irene," she said. "See you around, Clive."

2. Clive

CLIVE LET OUT HIS BREATH AS THEY PASSED BENEATH THE Anchor's Eastern Gate, waiting for the inevitable wave of relief to wash over him—only it never came. He was numb with exhaustion, too anxious about the future to celebrate the present, and he could tell most of the others were feeling the same way. Only Irene seemed to be genuinely delighted at their arrival.

"Daughter be praised," she whispered, gazing up at the massive stone arch overhead.

Clive had forgotten that this would be her first time entering the capital. It was strange—though they'd been on the road together for nearly two months, he didn't know her much better now than he had after that very first day. They'd never discussed the kiss they'd shared, and any further flirtation had been precluded by their circumstances. But she was still here—that was the important thing. Clive had told her again and again that she was free to go back to Eaton, and every time, she'd insisted she wanted to stay;

what else could that mean except that she wanted to stay with *him*? When they'd reached Corning, at the foot of the Teeth, she'd sent a message back east, explaining to her family that she would be gone on official Descendancy business for the foreseeable future. Clive couldn't even imagine how upset his own father would have been to receive a letter like that, but Irene was surprisingly unconcerned.

"I've got four brothers," she'd said. "The farm'll get along fine without me."

Gemma had agreed to take Irene in once they got back to the Anchor. Clive would've offered himself, but because he and Clover would be living alone in their parents' house, such an arrangement wouldn't be proper.

"It's all so big," Irene said, gazing around in wonder.

"You know anything about how the city's laid out?" Clive asked. She shook her head. "So it's one big circle, walled all the way round, with gates at the four points of the compass. There's one big road that runs all the way around the, uh . . . the . . ."

"Circumference?" Irene suggested.

"Circum-what?"

"It's geometry," Clover said, as if this were obvious. "You wouldn't understand."

Clive bit his tongue. His brother had only grown more sullen and difficult since their parents had passed; it was his way of grieving, Clive knew, but that didn't make it any easier to put up with.

"It means the edge of a circle," Irene explained.

"Oh." Clive could feel his face reddening. "Didn't realize they taught math out there in Eaton."

Irene put on a little show of being offended. "Not everyone

outside the Anchor is an ignorant lump, Clive. Farmers gotta know things too."

That was another thing about the girl; Clive felt slow around her, the same way he'd always felt slow around his little brother. It didn't bother him with Clover—he could always smack the kid around a bit, to remind him who was top dog—but it was different with Irene. He didn't want her to think he was stupid; he wanted her to be impressed by him, dazzled even. Maybe that was what he liked best about her: she made him want to be better than he was.

"Anyway," he said, "the road that runs around this *circumference* of yours is called the Ring Road. It's what we're walking on now. Then there's the roads between the gates, north-south and east-west, and two more that run diagonally."

"Those are called diameters," Flora said.

"You gonna start too?" Clive asked. Flora grinned in response. "So the four roads make for eight slices, which we call quarters, even though that doesn't make a lick of sense. The roads all meet at Notre Fille, the cathedral right in the middle of the city."

"You left out Portland Park," Flora said. "It's the best thing in the Anchor."

"Where's that?" Irene asked.

Flora pointed. "Sorta in the corner back that way, where the river comes under the wall."

"Circles don't have corners," Clover and Irene said at the exact same time.

Clive groaned. "I don't know which of you two is more annoying."

It was midday, and the streets were raucous with the lunchtime crowds: vendors hawking their wares and haggling over prices, ever vigilant for the cutpurses who plied their trade in the busy squares and alleys of the city; protectorate peacekeepers in their immaculate red-and-gold uniforms, always on hand to settle a dispute or toss a drunkard in a cell to dry out; a clutch of seamstresses, their fingers insensate with calluses, dividing up a huge, steaming flatbread with mushrooms. Clive had expected to feel comforted by the familiar sights and smells of the Anchor, yet for some strange reason, it all left him cold. He'd spent enough time on the road to know that no physical place could ever really be your home; your *family* was your home, and his family was fractured now, irrecoverable. So what was the Anchor, really? Just an empty vessel with a familiar handle and a fading warmth.

He quickened his pace so he could walk parallel with Burns. "There are some things I'd like to discuss with you, when you've got the time," he said quietly.

"Go ahead."

"Not now. Not around the others."

Burns looked back at Clover, who was talking to Irene. "You're keeping secrets from your brother now?"

"We don't tell each other everything."

"Well, you know where to find me, when you're ready to spill your guts."

They kept on walking, until the red sandstone blocks of the Bastion became visible over the tops of the houses that ran between the Ring Road and the Anchor wall. Clive realized he was following Burns automatically, still attached to the idea that any nearby adult could be trusted to lead him in the right direction.

He stopped in place, and the others bunched up behind him. "Where are we going, Burns?"

"I've got no idea where *you're* going," the sergeant said, "but I've gotta make my report. I imagine you've got your own duties to attend to."

He walked away without so much as a pat on the back for any of them.

There was a time when Clive would've been surprised or even offended by the sergeant's brusqueness, but he'd come to understand Burns better over the past couple of months. He knew now that there was a profound empathy in the man, hidden away beneath the layers of scar tissue and crudity.

"We should probably get going too," Gemma said. "Granddad should hear about Da from us, not the gossip around town."

"You really don't think he'll mind putting me up?" Irene asked.

"Of course not. He's gonna love you."

Mitchell Poplin was a kindly old furniture maker who'd only become more doting in his dotage, and who would welcome the opportunity to regale a pair of fresh ears with his lifetime's worth of meandering stories. He still lived in the big shambly house at the edge of the city where he'd raised his eight children—plenty of space for an extra body.

"We can walk you there if you want," Clive said.

Gemma smiled. "We know the way just fine."

They all hesitated for a moment, knowing that no gesture or speech could encompass everything they'd been through together. Eventually they started hugging one another, making sure not to miss anyone, like when you were seeking out everybody's glass

TOMMY WALLACH

during a toast. When Clive had finished hugging Gemma, she gave him a quick peck on the corner of his lips. "Come see us tomorrow?"

"Of course."

Clive watched the three girls walk on along the Ring Road. Just as they were about to disappear around the curve, Irene glanced back over her shoulder. Her eyes found Clive's, and she smiled.

A half-familiar novice was seated in front of the visitor's log, making notes in the margins of a Broken Book. He had beady black eyes and a downturned mouth that allowed him to maintain a sort of perpetual scowl—the kind of face that started arguing with you before you'd spoken a word.

"We need to see the Archbishop," Clive said.

The novice kept scribbling for a few seconds, then shut the tome and looked up at them. "The Archbishop doesn't meet with strangers off the street."

"He'll meet with us. Tell him that Honor Hamill is dead, and his sons seek an audience."

The novice's expression made it clear that the name Hamill still carried weight here. He wondered if anyone would even recognize it a year from now.

"Take a seat," the novice said. "I'll see what I can do."

The two of them sat down in the high-backed, torturous chairs reserved for supplicants. Even for urgent news such as this, the novice would have to go through the proper channels. Every bishop in the Gloria was assigned an *innocent*—a simpleton who acted as a kind of assistant. The Archbishop's innocent was named Preston. He had strange, overly broad features, and his vocabulary was limited to a few hundred words.

The novice returned after a few minutes, but only to deliver the message that someone would be with them shortly. An hour passed before the door swung open to reveal Francis—Bishop Allen's innocent. He was completely bald, with blue-black skin and sad, sunken eyes. His stutter sometimes made him difficult to understand.

"Buh-Buh-Bishop Allen will speak to you," he said.

Clive tried to hide his disappointment. Allen was the last person he wanted to see right now. "What about the Archbishop?"

"He is unuh . . . unuh . . ."

"Unavailable?" Clover said.

The innocent nodded gratefully, then gestured for them to follow him. But before they could pass beyond the door, the novice reached out a hand to bar their way.

"Sorry," he said, imbuing the word with a sadist's joy. "But the bishop doesn't grant audiences to children. The little one will have to wait out here."

"'Little one'?" Clover said, eyes flashing. "You pompous, ignorant—"

"Can you make an exception this once?" Clive interrupted. "My brother might remember things I don't. I could really use his help."

The novice shrugged. "Do you want to see the bishop or not?"

Clive turned to his brother. "I'm sorry, Clover. Just stay here for now. I'll see if I can convince the bishop to let you—"

"Don't worry about it."

Clover strode out of the waiting room before Clive could say another word.

The novice chuckled. "That boy needs to watch his temper."

"One more word," Clive said, "and I'll make you swallow every tooth in your head." The novice was too shocked to respond, which Clive figured was probably for the best. "Come on, Francis," he said, and pushed open the door.

The innocent led him quickly past the wide arcade of the scriptorium, where novices sat copying out Filiae by hand, then down a wide set of stairs. The lower floor was all narrow hallways and small offices; here, the various members of the Holy Order toiled away at the Lord's busywork. In the evening, they would scatter across the Anchor to perform vespers at one of the city's twenty-four chapels, or to a nearby township without a full-time Honor.

Clive's father's chambers were just down that passage there. Sometime in the next few days, Clive would have to come here and empty them out. The thought filled him with dread.

Down another set of stairs, they came to the floor where the bishops had their chambers. Francis knocked twice on Bishop Allen's door, which was artfully inscribed with a collection of bland Filial verses.

"Come in," said a voice from inside.

Immediately upon entering the bishop's office, Clive remembered why it was he'd never liked Allen. The room was terribly ostentatious, dominated by a large desk with brass fittings, lighted by a large annulus of wrought gold in which three or four dozen candles had been mounted. The bishop sat in a velvet chair with gold tassels hanging from the upper corners. He was short and plump, with round, shiny cheeks; in his flowing purple robes, he looked a bit like a freshly washed grape. Back when he'd been an Honor, Allen had often come to the Hamill home for dinner—but they'd seen little of him since he'd received the bishopric of the West three years ago.

"Thank you, Francis," he said, after Clive was seated. "You may go."

The innocent left, shutting the door behind him. "Novice Dawson tells me your father is dead," the bishop said without even a trace of pathos or empathy.

"Yes, sir. And my mother. And our—"

"*Requiescat in pace*," Bishop Allen intoned, making the sign of the annulus on his ample chest. "Tell me everything."

There was something unsettling about telling the story from start to finish; Clive felt as if he were performing somehow, as if all the people he'd loved and lost were just made-up characters in a novel, rather than flesh and blood. He kept the account as brief as possible.

"I'd like to recommend Burns for an official commendation from the Church," he said, once he'd reached the end of the tale. "He's the only reason I'm standing here today."

"That's never going to happen. We aren't exactly handing out medals to Protectorate soldiers these days. Honestly, it might have been better if he hadn't come back at all."

Clive felt offended on Burns's behalf. "What does *that* mean?"

"Grand Marshal Chang has arranged another plebiscite on the subject of Protectorate autonomy. It's scheduled for six weeks from now."

Clive could remember his father complaining about the Protectorate's constant political agitations: for a larger standing army, for clearance to organize random sorties against the Wesah, for a loosening of Library restrictions on anathema that might aid in the defense of the Anchor.

"So what?" Clive said. "The Protectorate always loses those votes."

"In the past, yes. But this news, that one of our most senior Honors was murdered? It could shift the balance of things."

"But it's the truth. People have to know."

"There are many truths the people emphatically do *not* have to know, Clive. What happened to your family was terrible, but spreading the word of God in godless lands is, by nature, a dangerous task. By your own admission, you were operating outside the borders of the Descendancy."

"That's what traveling ministries do. It's our job to spread the gospel."

"And you did that job admirably. But we will not allow a single tragedy to compromise the very foundations of Church doctrine. We do not actively seek out conflict."

"The conflict came to us!"

Bishop Allen leaned across his desk, his expression darkening. "I understand that you're upset, but you will never raise your voice to me again."

Clive could feel his insides churning. He wanted to scream. He wanted to cry. He wanted to jump across the table and grab hold of this fat old man by the neck. But he wouldn't risk his future, not to mention his brother's, for a single moment of satisfaction.

"I'm sorry, sir," he finally said. "It's been a difficult few months. I'm not myself."

The bishop leaned back in his chair and tented his fingers. "A memorial service will be held this coming Sunday, with all the pomp and circumstance a man of your father's stature deserves. Until then, tell no one else what you've just told me. I'll expect a full written report by the end of next week."

"Yes, sir."

"Good boy. You may go."

Clive stood up and gave the bishop a small nod in parting; he was afraid if he spoke at all, everything he was feeling might come pouring out. He was already halfway out the door when he caught the bishop's final words, spoken like the afterthought they were.

"And I'm truly sorry for your loss, Clive."

Sure you are, Clive thought, and pulled the door shut.

3. Clover

T HE DAY AFTER HIS RETURN TO THE ANCHOR, CLOVER appeared at the Library gatehouse at the crack of dawn. Given the momentous nature of his visit, he hadn't considered the possibility that no one would be there to let him in when he arrived, yet the post stood empty. He sat down on the cobblestones to wait.

The streets were quiet, the air so still and fresh it felt as if you could collect dew on your fingernails. Yet as the minutes passed, a sense of apprehension began creeping up on him. It wasn't just because of what he'd brought with him either; this feeling had been with him ever since that night at the pumphouse—a constant anxiety that he was being pursued by someone who wished him ill. In some ways, it had been easier out in the country, where you could see for miles in every direction. Here in the city, everything was shadow and periphery. Danger could come from anywhere and everywhere, and when it did, there would be nowhere to run.

"Hamill!"

He jumped at the sound. A man was glaring out of the gate-house window—Denver Suchland. Like many who worked at the Library, he'd always been slightly resentful of Clover's precocity. "You have business, or you just loitering?"

"I'm here to see Attendant Bernstein."

"You mean *Grand* Attendant Bernstein?"

So the old man had gotten a promotion during Clover's time away. Good for him.

"Yes."

"Is he expecting you?"

"Yes." Only that wasn't quite true. "And also no. He isn't expecting me at this exact moment, or even anytime soon. But he's expecting me in a more general sort of—"

"Daughter's love, Hamill," Denver interrupted. "Talking to you is like watching grass grow."

Clover frowned. "I've never understood that saying. Grass is actually very interesting. Did you know that blades of grass grow from the base, rather than from the tip, so the underlying plant isn't damaged by grazing animals?"

"Ugh. I'd rather do my actual job than listen to more of this."

Denver disappeared out the back of the gatehouse, and Clover sat down once again to wait. Beyond the gate, a path wound its way across the Library gardens to a guardhouse built into the walls of the Library itself. Denver would describe Clover's business to the soldiers stationed there, then *he'd* have to wait while the message was passed on into the Library itself.

If only they had a machine like the one at the pumphouse; then Denver wouldn't have had to leave his station at all. To pass the time, Clover brainstormed other uses for such a device. Novices working in far-flung corners of the Descendancy could recite sermons provided to them by Honors working in the Anchor, rather than their own second-rate compositions. The weather at Borst could be communicated to all the towns west of the mountains, so no one would waste their time trying to cross the Teeth when the pass was snowed in. Restaurants and public houses could make specific orders for produce, so that local farmers would only have to transport exactly what they knew they could sell. On and on, the ideas unspooled, until finally Clover glanced up to find that Denver had returned.

"Miracle of miracles," Denver said. "The old man wants to see you."

The path meandered between tulip trees, their buds just about ready to burst. Above their branches, Clover caught sight of the Library, and in the rush of relief that followed, he realized that he'd doubted he would ever see the place again.

The Library was a messy building, all in all, profuse and unpredictable as moneywort, abloom with balconies and balustrades, bridges and spires and parapets—as if its architects had been allergic to the very notion of symmetry. In a way, the edifice functioned as a metaphor for knowledge itself: contradictory, idiosyncratic, inexhaustible. And for Clover, it was also a kind of second home—only figuratively for now, but senior members of the institution were required to live here full-time, abandoning the outside world completely. Once upon a time, that thought had terrified Clover;

these days, it was almost comforting. Last night, following his brother into their house for the first time in more than six months, entering the swirl of must and dust, he'd been assaulted by the phantoms of past happiness. His mother and father haunted every room, every piece of furniture, every floorboard. Though Clive had done his best to return some warmth to the place—setting a fire in the hearth, sweeping the grit out of the halls with their mother's old birch broom, mixing the dough and setting a loaf of bread baking in the oven—Clover doubted it would ever feel safe or homely again. The house was a husk now, empty as a grave. Could living in the Library really be worse than that?

The soldiers outside the guardhouse waved him through, and once inside the building, he was escorted by an apprentice through the subject sections for botany and horticulture. The hallway forked, and the apprentice took the left path, which led up a set of stairs.

"C and F is down that way," Clover said, pointing to the right.

"Grand Attendant Bernstein works in divinity now," the apprentice replied.

Clover stifled a laugh; working in divinity was considered a great honor, but it was an honor Bernstein was almost certainly miserable to have received. He'd always claimed to find the Scriptures "as dull and painful as a headache." Now he spent his days surrounded by annotated Gospels and Filial exegeses. Poor man.

Up the stairs and down another long hallway, Clover was finally led into Bernstein's office. The grand attendant sat at a massive maple U of a desk, which surrounded him on three sides. Books were piled up everywhere, along with loose-leaf paper, material for binding, a little bowl of gold leaf, and the various other paints and pens the monks used to illuminate manuscripts.

"Your guest," the apprentice said.

Bernstein didn't look up. "Leave us alone."

The apprentice retreated without another word. Clover took a random book down from a shelf and began to read; Bernstein would continue working until he reached what he considered a reasonable stopping point—which could easily be an hour from now.

Clover owed his relationship with Bernstein to his fourth-form teacher, Mrs. Rogel, who'd recognized not only her pupil's intellectual gifts, but also his isolation; she'd brought him to the Library as much for his emotional well-being as his edification. At the time, Bernstein had been working in C and F—construction and fabrication. After a brief but wide-ranging conversation with his prospective pupil, he'd agreed to become the boy's mentor. That was five years ago now.

Twenty minutes passed before Bernstein finally set his pen aside and leaned back in his chair. "Can you believe this nonsense?" he said, gesturing around the room.

"At least they moved you to a *higher* floor. That's not how promotions work in the Church."

"I demanded it. It's ridiculous to have monks working by oil lamps in the middle of the day. The Descendant faith overturns millennia of precedent in this regard."

"So you've told me," Clover said.

Bernstein sighed loudly. "Look at this." He gestured toward the page he had in front of him, on which a few verses from the Book of Armelle had been artfully elaborated with various colored inks.

"Lord only knows why it has to come gilded and gussied up like a street-corner whore."

Clover smiled. He'd missed Bernstein.

"I'm wasted here, Clover. Just as I was leaving C and F, we discovered a critical improvement to our process for making lime—ten percent increased efficiency in an instant!"

"That was more than two years ago," Clover said.

"Was it? No . . ."

Clover watched as Bernstein's gaze turned inward, riffling the musty pages of his own history. The attendant was at least sixty-five, and though his analytical mind was as sharp as ever, he'd begun to forget things. After a moment, he waved the error away. "It doesn't matter. I'm in divinity until the bitter end now. For my sins."

"I'm sure you'll find something useful to do."

"Perhaps." Silence. Bernstein took a deep breath. "I suppose I'm meant to say something now, about your . . . misfortune."

"You already heard?"

"Bad news travels fast. People love a good tragedy."

It stung to know the death of his parents had already become fodder for gossip. "Well, I didn't come to you for sympathy."

"Good. I've never been much for handing it out."

"I came to show you this."

Clover unclasped the flap of his satchel and pulled out the weapon. He slid it across the desk toward Bernstein.

The attendant pushed back his chair so suddenly he nearly fell over. His eyes were as big as dinner plates.

"It can't hurt you just by being close to you," Clover said. "That's not how it works."

TOMMY WALLACH

"You know how it works?"

"More or less, except for the chemistry."

"Where did you get it?"

"I . . ." Clover once again saw the paltry resistance of skin and sinew as Gemma's knife plunged into the stranger's neck. The gurgle and sigh as he fell. The blood spouting, pooling, crying out from the earth.

"Take your time." Bernstein's voice was gentle now. "Daughter knows I've got plenty of it."

Clover took a moment to calm himself, and then he began to tell the story, or a version of the story, at any rate, one in which he glossed over all the parts he wanted to forget—not just the stabbing, but also breaking his promise to Clive, and the brief burst of black vapor around Michael's head when he was shot, and the light leaving his mother's eyes as she fell from her horse. When he was finished, Bernstein was quiet for a long time.

"The sergeant didn't want the weapon for himself?" he finally asked. Clover was grateful for the simple pragmatism of the question; the attendant really had no interest in discussing emotions.

"I told him I lost it. He was furious."

"Of course he was. He knew Grand Marshal Chang would've used it to gin up support for narrowing the parameters defining anathema. Imagine a public demonstration of this thing. The people would insist we start developing our own."

"But what is it? Have you seen one before?"

"I've never *seen* one, no."

"But you know what it is."

The attendant pursed his lips. "We're in dangerous waters here,

Clover. You aren't even an official apprentice yet. You shouldn't know about things like this."

"But I do, don't I? I think I've earned the right to at least know what it's called."

"I suppose that's true." Bernstein leaned down, examining the weapon more closely. "Technically, it's called a gun, but its true name is far more sinister."

Clover furrowed his brow. "It has a second name?"

"In a sense." Bernstein gingerly picked the weapon up between his thumb and index finger, as if it were a snake that might just be playing dead. "It's called history repeating itself."

4. Paz

"**H**AVE I TOLD YOU ABOUT THE TIME I WAS CHASED UP A tree by a sheep?"

Mitchell Poplin was standing between Paz and the bread bin, threatening to subject her to yet another of his interminable stories. At this point, she was starting to believe he was just making them up; in the two days she'd been staying in the Poplins' guest room, she must've heard a hundred of the damned things. Better to go hungry.

She smiled contritely. "You know, I should probably get moving."

His face fell. "You sure? Roosters aren't even crowing yet—"

"Sorry. I have somewhere I need to be."

Which wasn't technically true. She only wanted to get out of the house before Gemma and Flora woke up, so she could have a bit of time to herself; the girls had scarcely let her out of their sight since she'd arrived. But even though she'd crept downstairs a good hour before sunrise, she'd still ended up waylaid by the stupid old man, who apparently didn't sleep at all.

"At least take this," he said, reaching into the deep front pocket of his overalls and excavating a few copper shekels. "Growing girl needs to eat."

"Thanks," she said, and slipped out the front door before he could parlay her gratitude into a grudging audience for another soporific soliloquy.

Though her family had left for Sophia when she was only six, Paz had been born less than a full day's ride from the Anchor. It was strange to be visiting it for the first time only now, more than a decade later. She'd only managed to see the bits right around the Poplin house so far; today, she hoped to really explore.

She'd expected the streets to be empty, but it turned out the Anchor rose early. Paz visited a fruit vendor who'd already set up shop in an otherwise sleepy square. She lifted plums to her nose, sniffing deeply—funny how the best ones were those just on the brink of rotting—then took her plunder to a wooden bench nearby. Skin split beneath her teeth; juice gushed. The taste—tart, sweet, earthy—was transporting. She felt a sudden ache of nostalgia for Sophia, for her father, for Terry and Frankie and Carlos and long-lost Anton, from whom she'd received her first lesson in grief.

The guilt rose up inside her, heavy as stone. She'd abandoned her brothers, her responsibilities. Her father would've been so disappointed in her.

"But I'm doing this for them!" she said, needing to hear the words aloud, though a couple of people passing by looked at her as if she might be mad.

How had she ended up here, alone in the throbbing black heart of everything she hated most in the world, living a lie? It never should have come to this. It should have ended that night on the mining road.

What remained of the Sophian town guard had been waiting for her in Wilmington, just as she'd planned, and she led them straight to the crippled wagon. But she'd underestimated Burns, who'd taken the Ferrell twins out of commission single-handedly, and then it turned out that Clover had gotten hold of her father's gun. In a matter of moments, what should have been an unlosable battle was lost. Paz had chased after the survivors, of course, but when she'd caught up, and they were all looking up at her from their tearful little huddle, she'd frozen. Was it the practical realization that even a crack shot like her wouldn't be able to take out all four of them on her own? Or was it something far more dangerous: the unexpected trust in their eyes triggering a sudden swell of compassion?

No—anything but that. Besides, Sergeant Burns had survived the battle as well, so even if Paz *had* managed to kill the others, the location of the pumphouse still would've gotten back to the Anchor. So she'd done the next best thing to slaughter. She'd maintained her mask. She'd retained their confidence. Clive was preparing for a life in the Church, after all. Who knew what opportunities that might afford him, and Paz by extension, if she stayed close to him? Perhaps she'd missed her chance to pay her father's murderer back in kind, but that had always been a petty sort of vengeance. Better to keep her eye on the true prize: the war to come, and her place in it. She would return to Director Zeno with enough information to ensure herself a spot at the academy, or else die trying.

She sucked the last bit of flesh from the second plum, then

rolled the pits across the dirt like a pair of dice: snake eyes.

A few minutes later she reached the Purple Road, a wide boulevard lined with grand stone buildings. They weren't all that tall—Church doctrine limited any new construction to three stories—but most were bedizened with stone sculptures, glistering windows, and fanciful iron scrollwork. Beneath these elaborate facades, the citizens of the Anchor strode about in a rainbow display of rich fabrics and furs. In a wide-open plaza with a fountain in the center, Paz's attention was drawn to a pair of men sitting at a table, absorbed by a set of tiny figurines that they moved around a board of checkered squares as if the fate of the world depended on it. She watched them for a while, then followed a group of screaming children until they were swallowed up inside a veritable castle of brick and mortar. Through the window, she saw them come to sit before a great black slate on which a severe-looking woman began to write out a few simple arithmetic equations.

Paz felt sorry for them; they lived and died in a darkness that masqueraded as light. The young people of Sophia were educated by a rotating group of scholars from the academy, where nothing was considered anathema. The very best students were eventually invited to continue their studies at the academy itself, while those who weren't selected remained in town, helping to provide the labor and raw materials the scholars needed to continue their research. The results of this collaboration—electric lights, medicine, farming equipment—benefited everyone.

She followed the Purple Road southeast all the way to the cathedral, Notre Fille—great granite jewel at the center of the Descendant diadem. However she may have felt about the teachings of the

Church, there was no denying the magnificence of their houses of worship. Paz tiptoed through the narthex and past the donation box, past the guardsman tasked with protecting the place from vandals and thieves, past the elaborate frescoes that told the story of the Daughter's coming—a flame-haired girl rising up from the bowels of the Earth and disappearing into the stars, then crashing back down and setting the world ablaze—past the mostly empty pews, and all the way up to the kneeler. A massive silver annulus, as big around as the trunk of an old oak, was mounted on the apse. It glittered in the light from a dozen chandeliers, their candles smoking with the sweet scent of bayberry.

She felt a strange urge to jump up on the altar and tear the thing down.

"Irene?"

A momentary sense of dislocation—*who's Irene?* She turned. At the end of the kneeler, Clover was watching her with his steady, searching gaze. She tried to look relaxed.

"Hello, stranger," she said.

"What are you doing here?"

She sidled down the row, so they could speak quietly. "What do you think? Praying, of course."

"I've never seen you pray before."

Oh, but he was an observant one, wasn't he? "I don't make a performance out of it," she said, a note of chastisement in her voice. Sometimes, the only way to defend yourself was to attack.

Clover seemed to accept her answer. He looked up at the annulus. "I don't believe in it, you know."

Paz was momentarily stunned. Was the son of an Honor

admitting to heresy while kneeling in the very front row of Notre Fille?

"I mean praying," he explained. "Bernstein says the Daughter isn't likely to have time to answer every single person who asks something of her. But I suppose you never know if you'll be the one she listens to that day."

"Bernstein?"

"He's the man I work for at the Library."

Paz hadn't given much thought to Clive's brother before, but as soon as she heard the word "Library," something began simmering in the back of her mind.

"What do you do there again?" she asked.

"This and that. Tinker around in the chemistry lab. Build things in the workshop. Read whatever books I can."

"They allow a boy your age to do all that? You must be very advanced."

She thought it would be easy to play on the boy's vanity, but his eyes immediately narrowed. "It's not that interesting," he said. "Anyway, how have you been doing? You didn't come downstairs when Clive and I visited Gemma yesterday."

"I was sleeping," Paz lied. In truth, she'd watched Clive out of the guest-room window as he approached, and felt an odd fizz of excitement in her belly. It was the same fizz she'd felt that day along the canyon road, when she'd been thrown from her horse and nearly gone over the edge. When Clive had loomed over her with a perfect combination of concern and desire in his eyes, and she'd allowed herself to be kissed. Part of it was the game, of course— she enjoyed how thoroughly she'd fooled him, how he'd just saved

TOMMY WALLACH

the life of someone who was trying to take his. But there was no getting around the fact that he was a handsome boy, and for a moment there, maybe she'd forgotten what was fake and what was real. Anyway, it didn't matter now. A new plan was coalescing— one that would eliminate the temptation of messing about with Clive entirely.

All the secrets of the Descendancy were hidden inside the Library—everything they knew and everything they didn't know. And this damaged, self-conscious little boy just happened to be a favorite there.

"You know, I still haven't seen the Library," she said. "When you're done here, maybe you could show it to me?"

She rearranged her skirt beneath her, and in so doing, brought the outside edge of her leg to lie against Clover's.

"Okay," he said. "Just give me a few minutes to finish praying."

Paz smiled. "Take all the time you need."

5. Clive

LIVE SAT ALONE IN NOTRE FILLE'S SPACIOUS SACRISTY—
"backstage," as his brother used to call it—just a few minutes before the memorial service was to begin. He looked at himself in the glass and spoke the first line of his eulogy.

"I loved my father more than I loved God."

Wrong. Arrogant and melodramatic and *wrong*.

"I loved my father more than anything," he said, trying the alternate opening line.

But that was even worse, as trite as it was saccharine. Maybe he should cut the line altogether. Or why not just cut the whole damn thing and simply stare at the audience for twenty minutes? He'd spent the last few days agonizing over this speech; or more accurately, agonizing over *two* speeches, and which of them he ought to give. Almost funny how often he'd thought, *I should really run this part by Da*. But that was the whole point, wasn't it? There was no longer a Da to run things by. He was on his own.

"I loved my father more than . . . than . . ."

Someone knocked on the door of the sacristy: a welcome interruption.

"Come in," Clive said.

Gemma was dressed all in black, her hair artfully braided and tied back with ribbon. The tiny crystal earrings Clive's mother had given her last Landfall Day dangled from her earlobes, sparkling in the candlelight. She shut the door behind her.

"Evening, Clive."

He'd been expecting someone from the Church hierarchy, not the soon-to-be fiancée he'd been neglecting ever since he got back to the Anchor. It was the last thing he needed right now, but he did his best to appear pleased to see her.

"Evening, Gemma. How are you?"

"Okay, I guess, aside from, you know, everything." She stayed by the door, as if unsure whether she should come closer. "I thought maybe we'd see you yesterday."

"Yeah, there's just been—"

"Or the day before."

Clive glanced down at his notes. "I've been busy."

"I know."

"Between getting this service ready and making the house a place we can actually live—"

"I know, Clive. And it's fine. I just miss you is all. You doing all right?"

"Sure." He straightened the bottom edge of his papers on the table. "What about your sister? How's she?"

"It's been hard. She cries herself to sleep most every night. But the days aren't so bad. And we're lucky my granddad's so generous.

At least we got a comfy place to stay." She laughed a little, and Clive laughed in sympathy, but neither of them were quite sure what was funny, so their laughter trickled off into uncomfortable silence. "Your brother brought a few of your ma's dresses over this morning, but I couldn't even bring myself to touch them."

"They'll look pretty on you, though."

"Thanks." Another awkward silence. "And how's Clover holding up?"

"Your guess is as good as mine."

"He's never known how to talk about what he's feeling. Neither of you are much good at it, to be honest. I was thinking just yesterday, I don't believe I've ever seen you cry. Not since we were little, anyway. Why do you think that is?"

Strange, how all it took was her asking that to bring a lump to his throat, a sting to the back of his eye. He swallowed it down, blinked it away. "Somebody has to be strong."

Gemma smiled at him, almost pityingly. "You think it's weak to cry?"

"Of course it is." And had she noticed the catch in his voice just then? Best to change the subject. "Anyway, I know Ma woulda wanted you to have those clothes. You know how much she loved you."

Gemma started to speak, then stopped. That one word— "love"—had left little ripples in the air between them.

"I don't think I could stand to see myself in them," she finally said. "It just wouldn't feel right. Would you mind if I gave them to Irene?"

"Of course not. They're yours to give."

"Thanks."

"How is she, by the way? Irene, that is." Just saying her name, Clive felt his heartbeat quicken, as if he were doing something wicked.

Gemma looked surprised. "You haven't spoken to her?"

"No. Why would I?"

"Well, because she and Clover always seem to be together these days. I figured you'd be seeing her all the time."

A pinprick of jealousy, quick and keen. "Like I said, I've been busy."

"She went off with him when he came by to drop off the dresses earlier today." Gemma put a hand over her mouth, as if she'd just had a revelation; her voice took on the playful cadence of the schoolyard gossip. "Do you think he likes her? I mean, in a *romantical* sort of way?"

"I sure hope not."

"Why?"

"I don't want him to get hurt. Lord knows he's been through enough."

Damn it all—that lump in his throat was back. And this time, Gemma could tell. She took a couple of steps toward him.

"You all right?"

He tried to smile. "You already asked me that."

"I know, but people are always saying that sort of thing, just because. I'm really asking. I really wanna know." She reached out and placed her small, cool hand against his cheek. A hand he'd known practically all his life. He could feel his eyes starting to burn again. If she didn't leave soon, she'd see . . .

"I really should focus on this," he said huskily, holding up the sheaf of papers.

"Of course."

She stepped away, embarrassed. He could tell he'd stung her, and he wished he knew the words to make it right again, to make *everything* right again. But he suspected there were no such words, and anyway the bells of Notre Fille had begun to chime, signaling that the service was about to start, and there was no time left for apology or atonement.

Gemma hurried out the door a moment later, with a wave and a mumbled "Good luck."

Bishop Allen delivered the opening prayer, then launched into a brief, rote sermon on the subject of the sacrifices required of true men of God.

"He coulda put a little effort into it," Clover whispered.

"Quiet," Clive said.

After the speech was over, Allen led the congregation in a few of Honor Hamill's favorite hymns. Throughout, Clive kept glancing between his two speeches, so deep in thought that he didn't even notice when the singing stopped. Only after everyone around him had already stood up did he do the same: the Archbishop had arrived, stepping lightly down the aisle between the pews, his golden robes sparkling celestially in the light from the chandeliers. His wrinkles were deep as trenches, his hair cloud white, but the way he carried himself belied his years. It wasn't exactly that he looked healthy, but more that he looked to be beyond the very notion of health—ageless as a bronze statue.

"You may be seated," he said. "We are gathered here today to commend Honor Hamill and his wife, Ellen, to the care of our Lord and his Daughter, who rule eternal in the great below. Amen."

"He didn't mention Eddie or Michael," Clover muttered.

"Daniel Adams Hamill was born sixteen hundred and fifty-four years after the founding of the Descendancy," the Archbishop said. "He married Ellen Ali Andrews twenty-one years later, right here in Notre Fille, and soon after, was ordained as an Honor. Since then he has been responsible for overseeing a critically important traveling ministry. Daniel and Ellen had two children, Clive and Clover, aged eighteen and sixteen respectively, who are both here with us today. It is to Clive Hamill, who plans to one day follow in his father's most noble footsteps, that I now cede the floor. Please join me in welcoming him."

Clive stood up and was struck by a wave of dizziness bordering on nausea. He didn't want to be here. He didn't want to commend his father's spirit to the Lord. He wanted his father to be alive again. He wanted his family back. But his shaky legs were carrying him forward, as if on the current of time itself, and suddenly he was standing face-to-face with the Archbishop, waiting in front of the ambo with his arms open. Clive allowed himself to be enfolded in the old man's embrace, redolent of scent and tobacco.

"Do your duty," the Archbishop whispered, just before releasing him.

Clive hadn't the slightest idea what that meant, so he could only nod in response. A moment later he found himself standing at the ambo, where a small scrap of paper was waiting for him:

Clive Hamill,

You will tell this congregation that what happened to your family was a tragic anomaly, and that it would be wrong to vote in favor of empowering the Protectorate to engage in any form of reprisal. It's what your father would've wanted.

Clive ran his finger over the red wax seal at the bottom of the note. Something began smoldering in his chest—the fathomless fury he'd been suppressing for the last month. How dare the Archbishop try to manipulate him like this, and at his father's memorial service no less. Besides, it didn't matter what Honor Hamill would've wanted, because he was gone. And in his absence, Clive would have to navigate by his own compass.

He clenched his fist, crumpling up the note. There was no question now what speech he would read.

The room was a black mass of pity and boredom, dusty with whispers. Clive waited, staring dead-eyed at the congregation until they quieted out of sheer nervousness. He let the silence build, like the pressure you felt diving deeper and deeper into a lake.

"I loved my father more than I loved God," he finally said, and enjoyed the small thrill of consternation that ran through the audience. "I think most children do. They can't help it. If someone had told me that only one of them could continue to exist, God or my father, I would've chosen my father in an instant. I know that was

TOMMY WALLACH

wrong. I know it *is* wrong. But it's the truth." This was the point of no return. Clive looked to his brother; if he went through with this, things would get even harder for Clover—but could that be helped? *Num custos fratris mei sum ego?*

He slammed both his palms down on the angled surface of the ambo. "My father was killed in cold blood!" The word "blood" echoed around the room, like a bird seeking escape. "So was my mother, Ellen Hamill. And Eddie Poplin, who was like a second father to me, and his little boy Michael, who was like my brother. They were cut down by a cult of violent infidels who spit on the laws of God, who use the anathema to kill."

Clive scanned the faces in the frontmost pew: bishops and Honors only just beginning to understand what was happening; Gemma and Flora wiping tears from their eyes; Clover watching him with a wary, censorious expression; and Irene, so ravishing in her hand-me-down mourning clothes it was almost profane.

He put all of them out of his mind. It was time to bring it home. "And ever since that day, the day I lost the two people I loved most in this world, there's something I've been trying to understand. We're all taught that the Lord desires peace above all things. Our Protectorate is tasked only with defending us in the case of attack. Yet when the Daughter came, she did not come peaceful."

"Amen!" someone in the congregation shouted.

Clive raised his voice, allowed himself to fall into the fiery rhythms of the preacher he'd never be. "She came in smoke and fire and blood. She burned the wicked and the innocent alike, because that was the only way this world could be cleansed. And so I honor her when I say that there is no other way forward now but the way of smoke and fire and blood." The congregation was a pot coming to a boil—bubbling over now with cries and curses, hisses and hurrahs. Clive saw the Archbishop rise from his pew and begin walking briskly toward the ambo. Time was running out. "My father was the best man I ever knew, but I realize now I can never be what he was. I plan to honor him in the only way I can, by fighting for what he believed in!"

"That's enough," the Archbishop whispered angrily.

But Clive wasn't quite finished. "Those who would seek to destroy the Descendancy must be stopped by any means necessary. For the Father, and the Daughter, and the Holy Force of Gravity. Amen!"

"Amen!" The response sounded as if it had come from every mouth in the room. Clive swept past the Archbishop, through the raucous commotion of the crowd, and out onto the street. He felt terrified and exhilarated at once. He'd done it. He'd finally chosen his own path.

First thing tomorrow morning, he would enlist as a soldier in the Descendancy Protectorate.

6. Clover

THEY LAY BACK ON THE GRASS, STARING UP AT THE SKY.

"What makes it blue?" he asked.

"I don't know," Irene said. "But I know that the ocean only looks that color because it's reflecting the blue of the sky."

Clover tried to remember the ocean, but he'd only seen it once, and that had been almost a decade ago. Hadn't it been black? Or silver? Certainly he'd been able to see right through it up close. How could something be blue and black and silver and colorless all at the same time?

A flock of starlings wheeled about overhead in an ever-shifting constellation of brown and cream. "I wish I could fly," Irene said, then smiled mischievously. "Don't tell the Archbishop."

"It wouldn't be so great."

"Oh no?"

"People think it would be easy, just gliding around with the wind in your hair. But have you ever tried to lift your body off the ground just by flapping your arms?"

"I'd need wings, obviously."

"Even so. It'd be work. A lot of work. Like you were running really hard all the time. And if you ever got tired out, Gravity would be right there to pull you back down again. And then you'd die."

The birds disappeared behind the trees. "You know, there's a difference between being smart and ruining a perfectly nice daydream," Irene said.

Clover grimaced. If he had a copper shekel for every stupid thing he'd said to Irene, he'd be the richest boy in the Anchor by now. Yet she insisted she enjoyed spending time with him.

Why? he wanted to ask, but he wasn't about to draw her attention to the utter implausibility of their affiliation.

It had all begun that day she'd caught him praying at Notre Fille. They'd started talking, and not ten minutes later, he was showing her around the city, starting with the church itself, then leading her through the familiar side streets of the Eighth Quarter, pointing out all his favorite landmarks along the way: the house with the conical roof on which a single pigeon always seemed to be sitting, as if the house beneath it were an egg that refused to hatch; the pub with the broken sign that was called the Broken Sign; and best of all, the topmost spire of the Library, where the Epistem was said to reside.

Since then, they'd explored almost every corner of the city, though they never failed to return to the Library at some point during the day, just to look at it and talk about what went on behind the walls. His one complaint was the way she kept asking to be snuck inside. He felt bad saying no to her, especially because he still didn't have the slightest idea why she wanted to be his friend

TOMMY WALLACH

in the first place. After all, he was the kind of boy who talked about how terrible it would be to fly.

"It could still be nice, though," he said, "soaring around like that. Even if it *was* a lot of work."

Irene smiled. "There you go. Was that so hard?" She sat up, brushing a few stray dandelion seeds off her skirt. "Let's keep walking. I want to see the sights."

"Okay."

It was Irene's first time in Portland Park, and the weather was nearly perfect—bright and clear, chilly only when the breeze picked up. They walked close together down the wide gravel pathway.

"You see your brother this morning?"

Clover shook his head. "Training starts before sunrise every day."

"Are you still angry with him?"

"I don't know," Clover said, though that wasn't quite true. Of course he was mad. Clive had turned his back on the Church, on everything they'd been raised to believe in. Worse than that, he'd turned their parents' death into a cause. "I guess he did what he had to do."

"Just means you'll have to spend more time with me, I guess," Irene said, threading her arm through his. "Say, what's this?"

Just next to the small lake at the center of Portland Park, an elderly couple with a little clapboard stand were selling prepackaged picnic baskets—two egg sandwiches, two pears, two sugar cookies, two bottles of apple beer.

"Shall we?" Irene asked. "I'm starving."

Clover hesitated. This was the kind of thing boyfriends and

girlfriends did together. Irene wouldn't want people thinking the two of them were a couple. "Maybe we should just eat at home."

"Don't be silly. We're right here."

"Okay. If you really want to."

"I do."

He handed over eight bronze shekels to the woman behind the counter. "There's a blanket in there, just at the bottom," she said. Then, so quickly that he almost missed it, she gave him a knowing wink.

"Thank you," he said.

They crossed a bridge that arched steeply over the Tiber, which flowed out of the city beneath the portion of the Anchor wall that bordered Portland Park. A sign pointed the way toward the Maple Garden. In that direction, the gravel pathway became a tunnel, delving through a perfect bower of golden maple trees.

"Let's go in there," Irene said.

Clover held his ground, pulling her back by way of their linked elbows. "We really shouldn't."

"Why not?"

He could feel himself beginning to blush, so he looked up and away, toward the oddly feminine curves of the cumulus clouds overhead. "The Maple Garden is where people go . . . I mean, where boys and girls go . . . when they want to . . . be alone."

Irene gaped. "You mean they . . . ?" She left a pause that became more and more translatable as it went on.

"No!" Clover finally said. "No, of course not!" Then, because he wasn't completely sure of that: "I mean, I don't actually know. I don't think so. It's just, well, the place has a reputation."

"Why doesn't the Church do something about it?"

"They've tried, but it never works. You see, there's this rule—everybody in the Anchor knows about it. If you're in the garden and you spot someone on the hunt for, uh, misbehavior, you give a holler. Anyone who hears it gives a holler too, and pretty soon everybody knows to clear out."

"How exciting!" Irene pulled her arm out from his and set off skipping down the path. Her shiny black hair was pulled back into pigtails, tied at the ends with purple ribbon, and they bounced against her back as she went. "Come on, Clover!"

He knew he should call her back, but something even stronger than the rigid moral code he'd inherited from his father had glued his top lip to his bottom. If he let her get just a bit farther along, he'd have no choice but to go in after her. Was it the scientist in him, always eager to research a new subject, or just the sinner?

By the time he caught up with her, the path had narrowed, hemmed in by the last flowers of summer. The smell of them was thick and urgent; the air felt almost humid. When his fingers accidentally brushed up against Irene's, he jumped, scratching the back of his left hand on a rosebush. Overhead, the boughs of the trees made a patchwork quilt of crimson and saffron leaves, studded with sapphires of sky and pearls of cloud. Small trails snaked away from the main path here and there. If you looked closely, you could see couples through the branches, though never quite clearly enough to know what they were up to.

"Let's try this one," Irene said, choosing one of the paths at random. Clover had lost all sense of restraint or self-command. He could only follow.

A moment later they found themselves in a glade surrounded by alders and bigleaf maples. Long grasses fluttered in the breeze, thin as eyelashes. Clover laid out the blanket and pinned it down with the picnic basket. Irene sat down and took off her shoes. She wiggled her stockinged toes.

"Do you bring all the girls here?"

"It's my first time," Clover said, blushing again. He sat down as far away from her as he could, at the other edge of the blanket, opening up the picnic basket just to have something to do.

"Really? You never brought Gemma?"

"Why would I bring Gemma?"

"Because you like her." She put up a hand even as Clover was opening his mouth to deny it. "Don't bother. A girl can tell."

He was embarrassed and curious in equal measure. "And who does Gemma like?"

Irene laughed. "I don't know *everything*, Clover."

"It's Clive. I know it is. They're promised to each other. And you saw how jealous she got as soon as you showed up."

"Jealousy's complicated, in my experience. You can be jealous about something you don't really want." Irene pulled out the two bottles of apple beer. She handed one to him. "Cheers," she said, looking into his eyes as they clinked.

The beer was sweet, if not very cold. Clover felt a drop of sweat run down from his armpit to the waist of his pants. Irene moved the basket out from between them and slid closer.

"Let's play Questions," she said.

"Okay."

It was a game she'd taught him a few days ago, in which the par-

TOMMY WALLACH

ticipants traded questions they believed to be unanswerable back and forth, until one person actually knew the answer, which was worth a point.

"Why does the world seem to keep on spinning when you turn yourself in a circle a bunch of times and then stop?" Clover asked.

"Why does your heart beat so fast sometimes it feels like it's trying to jump out of your chest?" Irene replied. Clover actually knew the answer to that one, but he wasn't interested in scoring points.

"Why is grass green?"

"Why is blood red?"

"Why do you hear a roar when you put a cup over your ear?"

"Why do your pupils shrink when you get excited?"

As she asked this, Irene leaned across the blanket, bringing her eyes up close to his. Suddenly he couldn't think of another question.

"Oh, look what you've done," she said, noticing the scratch on the back of his hand.

"A rose did it."

"Roses are soft."

"The thorn, I mean."

"Poor boy." The wind picked up. Irene had untied the ribbons around her pigtails, and now her hair was whipping wildly around her face. Slow as honey, she lifted his hand to her lips. "Poor, poor boy."

Clover hadn't had romantic thoughts about any girl but Gemma in as long as he could remember. But what was the point of a love that would never be reciprocated, that broke your heart into pieces every time you so much as thought about it?

Irene kissed the scratch on his hand, still fresh enough that it left a bead of blood clinging to her bottom lip. This didn't make any sense. She was two whole years older than him, and impossibly beautiful. Besides, Clive wanted her. And didn't Clive always get what he wanted? Didn't he always do what he wanted and say what he wanted and get what he wanted?

"Why are you doing this?" Clover asked.

He'd meant it as a real question, but Irene interpreted it as part of the game, and countered with one last question of her own.

"Why does blood taste like metal?" she whispered, and then he tasted it himself: his own blood on her lips, his first kiss.

7. Paz

P AZ HAD MET DIRECTOR ZENO ONLY ONCE, FOUR years after her father had moved the family out to Sophia. The woman had shown up unannounced at the schoolhouse to administer a brief examination. She'd been dressed plainly—a gray homespun shift, leather sandals, no jewelry or adornments whatsoever—but her hair was a deep, vivid shade of red that Paz had never seen before.

"How did you do that?" Paz had asked, awestruck.

"With henna," the director said, her voice crisp and slightly condescending. "It's a natural compound derived from *Lawsonia inermis*, which we grow in a greenhouse. The colorant is formed by drying and milling the leaves, then mixing the resulting powder into some liquid medium. In this case, I used lemon juice, which seems to work slightly better than water, perhaps because of the acidity."

Paz followed this explanation only well enough to understand that the director was terribly clever, and that she'd used that cleverness to do magic.

The students were then asked to write down answers to a series of seemingly unanswerable questions: the origin of the game Paz would one day teach to Clover. When this was finished, the director had collected their papers and made them wait in silence while she read through them.

"Nothing definitive, I'm afraid," she said, once she was finished. "But which of you is Paz Dedios?"

Paz raised her hand.

"How old are you, Paz?"

"Ten, Miss Zeno."

"Well, I thought you'd like to know that you were correct about number seven. Snakes shed because their skins don't grow along with their bodies. Very good. Keep studying."

"I will."

She'd already been the brightest child in the classroom, but that day, her brilliance and drive finally found a worthy objective: admittance to the academy. She began reading every book she could get her hands on (the scholars of Sophia would occasionally lend a treatise or two to the schoolhouse) and making herself an honorary apprentice to whatever tradesman or hobbyist would have her. Within a year, she could tan a bearskin, hammer a horseshoe, throw a pot on a kick wheel, and construct a sturdy dining table. This obsessive drive to self-improvement may not have won her many friends, but she didn't care. She had a dream now, born the morning Director Zeno came to visit—and in no small part because ten-year-old Paz Dedios thought she'd look particularly lovely with red hair.

Unfortunately, when her mother died a few years later, Paz had

TOMMY WALLACH

to give up most of her educational pursuits; there was simply too much to be done on the farm. She still read at least a couple of hours every day, but by that time, she'd already devoured most of what the schoolhouse library had to offer.

Which was why she had to catch her breath when she first stepped through the doorway of Pettigrew's Bookshop, tucked away in a quiet corner of the Anchor's Seventh Quarter. In a space no bigger than that old schoolhouse in which her love of learning had first been kindled, more books than Paz had ever imagined existed in the whole world were arranged willy-nilly—against the walls, on tables, under tables, bursting from the crammed bookshelves, and even piled up *above* the bookshelves, reaching all the way to the cracked and browning ceiling.

"Do you like it?" Clover said.

Paz could only nod. She stepped deeper into the rich funk of it all—paper and leather and cloth and ink and mildew—running her fingers along the smooth spines. There were practical books about farming and cabinetry, compendia of herbal remedies and recipes, biographies of the Descendancy's so-called "great men"— every Archbishop, Epistem, and Grand Marshal who'd ever lived (with the conspicuous exception of Duncan Leibowitz). There was a tome listing all the games one could play with a deck of cards, a whole bookcase full of Filial commentaries that Paz made sure to pretend to be interested in, and best of all, hidden away in the very back of the shop, as if illicit: shelves upon shelves of stories. She scanned the titles, arranged alphabetically, in search of one volume in particular.

When she found it, she actually squealed.

"What is it?" Clover asked. She held it out for him to see. "Fairy tales?"

"My momma used to read this to me and my brothers every night. But we lost it after we moved."

"Moved where?"

"Moved to—"

Paz caught herself just in time. As far as Clover knew, Irene Pirez had lived in Eaton her whole life; she'd never moved from Coriander to Sophia. This was the danger of combining real history with invention—sometimes Paz forgot what she'd been honest about and what she'd made up. She'd been in the Anchor more than five weeks now, and in that time, she'd spun a web of truths and half-truths and bald-faced lies so abstruse she couldn't have re-created it if she'd wanted to. She could only hope that nobody was paying enough attention to spot the inconsistencies.

"To a new house," she improvised. "Our old one burned down."

"Was it bigger? You said all four of your brothers shared one room before."

All four *of your brothers*—how easy it turned out to be, to bring the dead back to life. Paz had resurrected Anton on a whim, a passing fancy while padding out the shadowy corners of her fabricated history. Since then, she'd managed to create a whole detailed backstory for him: the life he'd been robbed of. In the process, she'd created a fictional version of herself, too—a Paz who'd never been traumatized by her brother's death, who had never watched her father grieve, who had never moved to Sophia. A simpler, happier Paz.

"Yeah. Lots more space."

"Burns was in a fire too," Clover said, continuing down the aisle. "His chest is scarred something terrible."

"I saw it. You have any idea how it happened?"

"No. He doesn't like to talk about that stuff."

Clover knelt down to examine a certain title more closely, and Paz kept exploring. She did a full circuit of the shop before returning to the shelves concerned with scientific subjects. Perhaps there was something here that the academy could use.

"Clover, I need your advice."

"What is it?"

She waited until he was close, then spoke under her breath. "Do you think any of these books might have anathema in them?"

His eyes went wide. "You can't say things like that in public," he whispered. "Besides, it's illegal to sell that sort of thing."

"But there's at least a thousand books in here! Something could've slipped through. Think about it. Use that big brain of yours." She raked her fingers through his hair until his outrage melted away, replaced with the usual puppyish desire to please.

"Well . . . I guess I could look."

"Thank you."

He took his time, pointing at each title and reading it aloud. *Cattle Husbandry. The Four-Season Harvest. Root Cellars in Wet Climes. On Wood and Woodworking. On the Laying of Foundations.* Paz wished she could've sat down and read every single one of them, but she comforted herself with the thought that she would have plenty of time for scholarship when she was accepted into the academy.

"This might fit the bill," Clover finally said, a few dozen titles later.

He pulled out a short volume, bound in red leather: *100 Uses of Fire*, by Grand Attendant Garen Zilafra.

"Really?" Paz said. "Everybody knows about fire."

"Sure, but it's still a dangerous subject. Maybe there's something in it about Blood of the Father."

Paz was disappointed. The scholars of Sophia would already know everything there was to know about Blood of the Father.

"You sure there isn't something else?"

"It's the best they've got. You want it or not?"

"That's okay." She gave him a playful smile. "I'll be a good girl."

Outside the shop, a group of four soldiers were walking down the road shoulder to shoulder. Paz found herself unconsciously seeking out Clive's face and experiencing an irrational disappointment when she didn't find it.

The Protectorate seemed to be everywhere these days, engaged in a comprehensive variety of civic tasks; Clover said it was because Grand Marshal Chang wanted to show the people how useful an expanded military could be. Earlier today, Paz had seen at least a dozen soldiers sweeping up Annunciation Square, where the plebiscite was to be held. The vote was only a few days off now, and if it went Chang's way, a Protectorate contingent would be sent east soon after. In that case, Paz would have to go back too; someone had to warn Sophia what was coming.

"Daughter's love! Is that who I think it is?"

Just on the other side of the road, a boy around Paz's age was beaming at her like an idiot.

"It's me! Charles. Chuck. From Coriander."

Paz's mind began racing. Though she hadn't seen him in more

TOMMY WALLACH

than a decade, this was undoubtedly Chuck Barker, eldest son of Coriander's town drunk. He'd been a nasty little boy—the kind who was always pulling your hair or stepping on your heel—and something in his expression betrayed the fact that he hadn't changed much since. He looked to be down on his luck; his clothes were dirty and threadbare, and he was in desperate need of a haircut and shave.

"I think you've mistaken me for someone else," she said.

Chuck laughed, then realized Paz was being serious. "Are you joking? I'd know you anywhere. You're as pretty now as you were back then."

"Sir, my name is Irene Pirez. And I'm from Eaton, not Coriander."

Chuck's smile was giving way to a grimace now, angry and confused. "You say you're from Eaton?"

"I do."

"Then I say you're lying."

Clover stepped up to within a few inches of Chuck. "Her name's Irene, and she said she doesn't know you."

Chuck's eyes narrowed, and for a second, Paz worried he was going to take a swing at Clover. But then he let out a sharp bark of a laugh. "All right," he said. "Then I guess I'll go. *Irene.*" He said her name as if it were the punch line to a terrible joke, then turned and continued walking along the Ring Road.

"That was strange," Clover said.

Paz watched Chuck go, heart hammering in her chest. Then she looked back at Clover and gave him what she hoped was a carefree sort of smile.

"I sure hope he finds whoever he's looking for," she said.

8. Clive

CLIVE WAS ONE OF MORE THAN FIFTY SOLDIERS stationed around the edge of Annunciation Square, there to ensure a safe and orderly polling process. At the center of the plaza, registrars sat at wide wooden tables, preparing the logbooks inside of which were written the names of every citizen of the Anchor and the twenty-five largest surrounding towns. The names would be crossed off as each citizen voted, and if all went well, the results would be known before midnight.

It was Clive's first time wearing his uniform outside the Bastion, and he was enjoying the sensation. People were looking at him with that familiar combination of respect and fear he himself had shown toward soldiers all his life. Last night he'd spent an hour sharpening the blade of the slim sword that now hung at his waist. Though he had six weeks of swordsmanship drills under his belt, he still wasn't particularly good with it, but he figured he knew enough to do what had to be done: chop like this, skewer like that.

The bells of Notre Fille began to toll—nine chimes echoing

loudly across the hard red tiles of the plaza. Soon after, the voters began to arrive in numbers, arranging themselves into twenty-six uneven lines, one for each letter of the alphabet. Eventually these lines extended from one end of the square to the other. There was an excitement in the air, a restless tension Clive hadn't expected. Though the Protectorate had sponsored a number of similar plebiscites in the past, this was the first time it had a real shot at winning. Clive was proud to think his speech might have helped the cause; all over the city, people were talking about what had happened to Honor Hamill and his family. If one of the Church's most senior members could be murdered without repercussions, what would stop their enemies from striking again?

Around noon, the Archbishop appeared with his usual retinue of novices and retainers. His innocent took a tomato to the face from some Protectorate sympathizer in the crowd, but otherwise the first few hours of voting remained peaceable enough. Clive had nothing to do but stand at attention and look serious.

"Dull as a prude, isn't it?"

The boy who'd spoken was dressed in the same red-and-gold uniform as Clive, but for one important difference: a laurel pin on his lapel, marking him out as a third-year soldier. He had frizzy black hair and ears so incongruously big they looked like they'd been taken off someone else's head and stuck on his. Clive had seen him around the mess hall a few times, but they'd never interacted.

"Garrick Schwid," he said, offering a hand.

"Clive Hamill."

"I know. You're the Honor's kid. Talk of the town."

"I guess."

"So how are you finding the soldierly life?"

Clive wasn't sure how to respond—in part because he couldn't tell yet if Garrick was making fun of him, but also because the answer was complicated. It wasn't that he regretted joining the Protectorate, exactly, but the experience hadn't been at all like he'd expected. It seemed stupid now, but he'd really believed the other soldiers would be grateful for what he'd done at his father's memorial service. He'd imagined being welcomed into the fold like a hero. But as far as he could tell, the other soldiers weren't appreciative at all. In fact, they seemed downright resentful of him. And the truth was, he really didn't have much to recommend him as a soldier. Though he could shoot a bow and arrow well enough, only second-year recruits were allowed to train as archers. He was by far the slowest around the obstacle course and the weakest with the weights, and the first time he'd crossed swords with another recruit, he'd lost his grip on the hilt, earning himself the unfortunate nickname Dropsy.

"It's fine," he said.

"Yeah? I hear everybody hates your guts."

Clive laughed. He would've been insulted if it hadn't been the truth. "You didn't ever meet my father, did you?"

Garrick shook his head.

"He had a way with people. Everybody liked him, or respected him at least. Guess the talent didn't rub off on me."

"Eh, don't be so hard on yourself. It's not your fault they're all jealous."

"Jealous? Of what?"

"Word around the barracks is you've got friends in high places.

With your background, that means you're a shoe-in to make officer before long."

Garrick was talking about Burns, of course. Since their return to the Anchor, the sergeant had been promoted to marshal; rumor was he'd be in charge of the mission back east, if the plebiscite went the Protectorate's way.

"They hate me because I know a marshal?"

"And because your da was an Honor. And because of the way you talk to them. And because you grew up in the Anchor. And because apparently you can't keep hold of your sword."

"I dropped it one time!"

"Once is enough, Hamill. No second chances at first impressions." Clive smiled grimly. "You really tell it like it is, don't you?"

"I like to think so. Dare you to ask me how long my willy is."

"I'll pass, thanks."

Clive's attention was suddenly arrested by a mane of black hair moving through the crowded square: Irene. He'd scarcely seen her over the past month; his training took up all his time. Besides, there was no easy way to visit her without running into Gemma.

"Oh my," Garrick said, following the direction of Clive's gaze. "She's something special, isn't she?"

"I know her."

"Well, aren't you lucky? Though not half as lucky as that kid."

Through an opening in the milling throng, Clive saw Irene's companion: Clover. They were standing close together, shoulder to shoulder, hand in hand, and now she was turning her laughing face toward him, and he was smiling back at her, and they were both leaning in . . .

The very nature of the world shifted. Clive's stomach felt hollow, and he had to swallow down the sip of bile that had risen to the top of his throat.

"You all right?" Garrick asked.

"Yeah. It's just . . . that's my brother."

In a way, he was saying it to himself, as a reminder. It wasn't right to be covetous. That was Clover—his own flesh and blood. And didn't Clover have every right to love? Hadn't he spent the last couple of years making himself miserable over Gemma? Shouldn't Clive just be happy for him?

Only that was impossible. Irene and Clive had a history. Could she really have forgotten what had transpired between them, that day on the mining road? And now she was cozying up to his brother? It didn't make a lick of sense. Clover was the clever one, the peculiar one—not the one the girls wanted. Irene had to be after something; she had to be playing some kind of angle.

Or maybe that was unfair. Maybe Clover had changed over the past few months—matured in a way Irene could see but Clive couldn't. Watching the two of them kissing out in the middle of the square, looking for all the world like any other infatuated young couple, Clive wondered if he knew his brother at all anymore.

"I hate to distract you," Garrick said, "but I think we may need to do our jobs."

"What?"

"Over there."

Clive wrenched his gaze away from the horror of Clover and Irene together. Near the front of one of the voting lines, a thickset

TOMMY WALLACH

man in dirty overalls had begun shouting at the registrar. Clive and Garrick drew closer.

"But I live here," the man was saying.

"I'm sorry, sir," the registrar said. "You're not on my list."

"So add me. I only moved two weeks ago."

"It's too late to register for this plebiscite. But if you come to the Office of the People tomorrow, we can get you on the rolls for next—"

The man pounded on the table. "Do you know why I moved my family to the Anchor, missy?"

"No, sir."

"Because I was tired of the fear. You know what I'm talking about?"

"No, sir."

"Have you ever spent more than a day or two outside this city?" He didn't even give her time to answer. "Of course you haven't. Well, let me tell you what it's like. When it's not bandits, it's the Wesah. When it's not the Wesah, it's dying of the flu because there's no doctor worth a damn within fifty miles. And now we've got this new nonsense out east? I say enough is enough."

"I'm actually in agreement with you, sir. And if you'll just wait for the next—"

The man swept the registrar's logbook off the table. "I'll be damned if you're gonna silence me—"

"Sir," Clive said, stepping forward, "let's not make a scene."

The troublemaker turned to face him and smiled patronizingly at what he saw. "Shut your mouth, boy. A man is speaking."

It was the first time Clive had ever punched someone, so he

was surprised at how naturally it came to him. Time seemed to slow. He could feel the man's stubbly cheek under his knuckles, the give of flesh and the intransigence of bone. In his mind's eye, he saw Clover and Irene kissing again—long and lingering. The man was on the ground now, and Clive delivered a sharp kick to his stomach—and another, and another. He would've kept going too, only someone had grabbed hold of him around the armpits and was dragging him away.

"What the hell were you thinking, Hamill?" Garrick said.

"That man disrespected me."

"So what? Welcome to the fucking Protectorate."

Garrick didn't let Clive go until they were back out at the edge of the square.

The anger had receded, and guilt was flooding in to fill the empty space. What if that man had really gotten hurt? And what if Irene and Clover had been watching?

"Daughter's love," Clive said quietly. "I don't know what came over me."

"Don't beat yourself up, Hamill. In fact, maybe don't beat anyone up."

Clive grimaced. "Should I go back, to make sure he's okay?"

"He'll be fine. Let's you and me take a little walk, yeah? You can tell me all about your brother's girl."

"There's nothing to tell," Clive said.

Garrick threw a chummy arm over his shoulder. "Somehow, I doubt that."

9. Clover

"A VOTE FOR THE PROTECTORATE IS A VOTE AGAINST God! It is a vote against the Daughter herself! So it is written: he who unsheathes the sword has already struck the first blow. Repent before it is too late!"

The lay preacher stood on an overturned crate, screaming his lungs out. He'd been at it all day.

"I can't believe he's got any voice left," Irene said.

"He'd tell you it's the power of the Lord working through him," Gemma replied. "And who's to say it isn't?"

Clover wasn't yet old enough to vote in the plebiscite, but Bernstein had given him the day off anyway, so he'd brought Irene to Annunciation Square to watch the proceedings. He figured she'd enjoy seeing how the vote was carried out, given how curious she always seemed to be about every little aspect of life in the Anchor. He'd forgotten just how cramped Annunciation Square could get—teeming with humanity, the air a pungent fog of perfume, tobacco, body odor, and spiced meat smoking over hot coals.

Though there was always something to watch, be it a heated argument between citizens or a puppeteer's dumb show, he would've rather been curled up at home with a good book. Thankfully, the day was finally drawing to a close. They'd made plans to meet up with the Poplin sisters for dinner, and now they all sat together at a small stone table in a corner of the square, watching the last straggling citizens perform that most fundamental civic duty.

"Hey, Clover," Flora said, "how would you have voted, if you were allowed to?"

"For the Church, of course."

"Really? Gemma says she would've voted for the Protectorate."

"Flora!" Gemma said, blushing with embarrassment. "That was a secret."

"It's fine," Clover said. "Your sister is smart, Flora. She just wants to be on the winning side."

Flora frowned. "The Church is going to lose?"

"It looks that way."

Irene raised her hand, as if they were all in school. "You'll have to excuse a poor backward country girl, but I don't even understand who's up against who. Isn't the Protectorate just another part of the Church?"

"Sort of," Clover said. "The Church established the Protectorate as a peacekeeping force. They're only supposed to act defensively, but it's getting less and less clear what qualifies as defense. If Grand Marshal Chang had his way, we'd incorporate towns by force and slaughter every Wesah warrior on the continent."

"And that would be bad?"

"Well, the Filia says violence only begets more violence."

"Then why'd you kill that man out at the pumphouse?"

Clover was taken aback by the sharpness in Irene's voice, the challenge in her eyes. He looked to Gemma, who met his gaze only for a moment. Everyone still believed *he* was the one who'd stabbed the stranger that night, and he was glad for that. He'd wanted to, after all; he just hadn't had the courage.

"I didn't have a choice," he said quietly.

"You did."

"It was them or us!"

"And you chose yourself!"

Before Clover could argue any further, he was interrupted by a faint, uneasy voice. "C-C-Clover Hamill?"

Clover turned around in his chair. Bishop Allen's innocent, Francis, was standing just behind him. "What is it?"

"You've b-been summoned."

"Awwww!" Flora said. "Now he's gonna miss hearing the results!"

But in truth, Clover was grateful for the excuse to leave. Irene had been getting oddly worked up, and he didn't have the slightest idea why. Funny, in spite of all the time they'd spent together, sometimes he felt as if he hardly knew her at all. Maybe every romantic relationship was like that—two people trying to clasp hands across an unbridgeable divide. Or maybe romance had nothing to do with it. Maybe *all* human relationships were like that.

When he leaned down to kiss her good-bye, she turned her face to receive it on the cheek.

"I'll be back as soon as I can," he said.

Clover followed Innocent Francis through the streets around Annunciation Square, still raucous with anxious debate and premature celebration. Near Notre Fille, he saw a man lying in the gutter, his face bruised and bloodied; he'd likely been beaten for having the wrong opinion at the wrong time. Francis passed the cathedral and kept walking.

"Aren't we going inside?" Clover asked.

"N-no. The L-library."

"That's where Bishop Allen is?"

Francis didn't answer, but Clover supposed it was logical enough; tonight the Church and the Library were as one, a singular bulwark against the Protectorate's power grab. It took them another twenty minutes to walk the length of the Black Road to the Library, where they were ushered through the gate and past the guardhouse without question. Then they were inside, threading their way across the ground floor, to a door Clover had never seen before. Francis unlocked it with a large key he wore on a chain around his neck. On the other side, a set of stairs led steeply upward.

Clover began to climb.

"I'll w-w-wait for you here," Francis said, then quickly shut the door and engaged the dead bolt.

There was nowhere to go but up—floor after floor without a single door or window. Clover was at first surprised, then flummoxed, then simply exhausted. His calves were on fire by the time the stairway leveled off, dead-ending at a set of regal red doors. They looked too prestigious to be left unlocked, yet they opened at Clover's touch.

He found himself in a very large room, at least thirty feet long by thirty wide. Two walls were made up of little else but windows, providing a stunning view out over the fertile farmland to the north of the Anchor. The other two were devoted to bookshelves that stretched all the way up to the room's second floor, which was accessed by a sharply spiraling staircase.

It was simultaneously the chamber of a scholar and a king—and only one citizen in the Anchor fit that description.

"Ah, good. You're finally here."

He was sitting at a large desk just in front of the windows, pen poised over a notebook. His mane of silver hair reached down past his shoulders, and he had a few days' growth of salt and pepper stubble. The eyes behind the thin-rimmed spectacles were maniacally bright; when he blinked, it seemed a conscious action, as if he were watching the world so intently that he hated to lose even that millisecond of vision.

The Epistem, Hal Turin, in the flesh.

"Good evening, Clover," he said, offering his hand. Clover noticed the man's knuckles were crosshatched with tiny scratches.

"Good evening."

They shook hands.

"I'm—"

"I know who you are," Clover said, then winced. "Sorry, sir. I didn't mean to interrupt you."

The Epistem smiled. "It's quite all right." He motioned for his guest to take the seat across from him, a big leather chair that made Clover feel even smaller than usual. "I have something of yours," he said, and, reaching into one of the drawers of his desk, produced the gun. Clover hadn't seen it since he'd given it to Bernstein. It had been polished in the meantime, and sparkled now like a shard of obsidian.

"It's a stunning design," the Epistem said. "I thought when this day finally came, our enemies might have developed muskets. And here we find they've progressed to the six-shooter. Or the twelve-shooter, as it turns out." He set it down on the desk. "You understand how it works?"

Clover hesitated. Men had been put to death for misuse of the anathema. But he'd already told Bernstein he knew how to use the gun, so there was no point in lying. "Yes, sir."

"Explain it to me."

"Oh. Okay." He picked up the weapon. "It's pretty simple, actually. You just have to squeeze this bit at the bottom—"

"The trigger," the Epistem said.

Trigger: logical enough. "Right. So you squeeze the trigger, and that causes the hammer up here to collide with, well, some sort of reacting agent. The resulting force expels the metal pellet out the end of the tube."

"The pellet is called a bullet. And the tube is called a barrel."

"After that, you just pull the hammer back, which causes this cylinder here to rotate, and that brings the next bullet into line, so it can be discharged again. And . . . that's it."

Clover replaced the gun on the desk, to the sound of Turin's surprisingly energetic applause. "Oh, that's very good, Clover. Bernstein wasn't wrong about you."

"Thank you, sir."

"But our examination isn't quite done yet. Do you have any idea who that is?" He pointed to an oil painting mounted in the

TOMMY WALLACH

middle of the bookshelves on the east-facing wall. The subject was a middle-aged man, captured in the standard pose of a Library monk: seated at a desk, holding a book with PRINCIPIA written in gold letters on the spine. The light from a candle glimmered on the skin of an apple resting on a corner of the desk; the fruit was puckered with rot.

"No, sir."

"His name was Duncan Leibowitz. He became Epistem about ninety years ago, long before you or I were even born. But his administration of the Library was one of the shortest ever recorded."

"He died?"

"Eventually. But no, that wasn't why he left. He fled, you see, along with a few hundred volumes from the anathema stacks."

"Why?"

"Because Leibowitz, not unlike our current Grand Marshal, believed that the laws of our Church were too onerous. But where Chang wants more freedom in deploying our soldiers, Leibowitz wanted more freedom in his research."

"Where did he go?"

"For the longest time, no one knew. Then, about twenty-five years ago, we began to hear rumors of an academy dedicated to scientific inquiry, one that cared nothing for God's laws. He'd named it Sophia."

"Why didn't someone stop him?"

"How? By slaughtering his people like sheep? By bringing them back to the Anchor in chains? We had no choice but to wait, to hope they would fall apart on their own. Unfortunately, they don't appear to have done so. Nor will they. Not without help."

The Epistem went silent. When he finally spoke again, he seemed almost nervous, rasping his fingers back and forth across his stubble. "Clover, I'd like you to go somewhere for me. It's a place only the most senior members of the Church have ever seen."

"Why?"

"I apologize for what may seem a needless obscurity, but I can only tell you that after you've returned."

On this last word, the Epistem glanced pointedly toward the back corner of the room, where a small wooden door was half-hidden in the wainscoting. An elaborate rendering of Aleph and Eva beneath the Great Tree had been carved into its surface.

"What's in there?"

"The truth. Would you like to know it?"

The question wasn't rhetorical, the Epistem was sincerely offering Clover a choice—innocence or experience, ignorance or knowledge. The Filia said learning was a lightening, and the past few months had borne that out. Clover would've given anything to return to the days before he'd heard about that pumphouse, when his parents were still alive and his biggest fear was of Clive and Gemma getting married. But time only flowed in one direction, and his innocence was long since lost.

"Yes," he breathed.

The Epistem smiled. "Good. Then please strip."

"Strip?" Clover hoped he'd heard wrong. "You mean my clothes?"

"No, I mean your skin." The Epistem clapped once, derisively. "Of course your clothes."

"Why?"

"Because the path must be walked as the garden was walked."

TOMMY WALLACH

The Epistem turned around and covered his eyes.

Clover did as he was told, quickly shedding his shirt, pants, shoes, and socks. He hesitated only a moment before unbuttoning his undersuit, ashamed by the childishness of his body: all protruding ribs and stick legs.

The Epistem kept his gaze averted as he produced a large iron key from a pocket of his robe and set it on the desk behind him. Clover picked it up—heavy, old, inscribed with a short phrase in Greek: ἔσεσθε ὡς θεοί.

"What's it mean?" he asked.

"'And you shall be as Gods.' Now go."

"Yes, sir."

Clover approached the door. Up close, he could make out the details of the carving. In the branches of the tree perched a falcon— one of the traditional symbols for the Daughter. The snake was portrayed as a vine twisting its way around the trunk, with large diamond-shaped spines just like what you saw on the skin of a rattler. A stream of nectar appeared to flow out of a knothole that also served as the keyhole. Clover inserted the key, but before he opened the door, he looked back over his shoulder.

"Thank you for your faith in me, sir."

The Epistem was still facing the windows. "Don't thank me yet," he said, a forbidding solemnity in his voice.

Clover turned the key.

10. Paz

THEY WATCHED AS CLOVER WALKED AWAY WITH THE strange stuttering man.

"What in the Daughter's name was *that* about?" Gemma said.

Paz shrugged. "Don't ask me. I never understand what he gets up to."

She wished she could have gone with him, but of course that was impossible. No matter how close she got to Clover, she would never be allowed into the Library; there were some risks even a lust-addled teenage boy wouldn't take. Still, the sudden summons, tonight of all nights, seemed to signal something important. And Paz would be there to ask him about it when he returned. Maybe she'd finally learn something worth knowing.

Flora screwed up her face in disgust. "I can't believe you kiss him!"

"Clover is a fine kisser," Paz said, which was true enough, though it had required a fair amount of hand-holding to get him there.

"Is he really?" Gemma asked.

"Sure. Isn't Clive?"

"I suppose. But he's always poking his tongue around. And his face is all scratchy."

Paz had quite liked the experience of kissing Clive, but she wasn't about to tell Gemma that.

"Ew, ew, ew!" Flora screamed.

"It doesn't matter anyway," Gemma said. "I can't remember the last time we really kissed. He's always so busy these days."

"Who's so busy?"

Paz's heart jumped when she saw the Protectorate uniform—was her deception about to be revealed?—then again when she realized who was inside it. Hidden behind that short beard and high-collared jacket was a familiar face: Clive. It had only been a matter of weeks since they'd last seen each other, but he looked different from before. Harder. Older. Paz hated the way some animal part of her thrilled to the unexpected meeting.

"Hi, Clive," Flora said. "We were just talking about kissing!"

"That's not important," Gemma quickly interrupted. "How did everything go today?"

"Nothing we couldn't handle," Clive said, "though it'll probably get uglier when the results come in." The soldier behind him gave a little cough for show. "Oh, sorry. Everyone, this is Garrick. Garrick, this is Gemma, Flora, and Irene."

"A pleasure to meet you," he said, taking Gemma's hand and giving it a kiss. "And you," he said, doing the same for Paz. "And you." Flora pulled her hand away before he could get at it, but she was grinning ear to ear. "And now that we're all introduced, let's get drunk, shall we?"

"Are you allowed to drink in uniform?" Gemma asked.

Garrick cocked an eyebrow. "If I said yes, would you believe me?"

They all left the square as a group, yet as they turned down one road, then a smaller street, then an even smaller alleyway, the line broke up, and Paz suddenly found herself alone next to Clive.

"It's been a while," he said.

"You've been learning to be a soldier."

"And you've been spending all your time with Clover."

An accusation of sorts, but she refused to recognize it. "He's a wonderful boy."

"I know he is. But don't you think—"

"Why are you being all slowpoke-y?" Flora asked, using that magical power little kids always seemed to have, sensing the exact moment they would be least welcome.

"I'll show you who's a slowpoke," Clive said, chasing her back toward the others.

The pub was only a few minutes farther on, at the place where one crooked alley met another: the Stag's Head. It was terrifically crowded, so much so that a dozen people had been relegated to the cobblestones outside. Paz followed the others through the throng to the back of the establishment, where they secured a small table just in front of the fireplace. There weren't enough chairs, so Paz and the Poplin sisters sat on the edge of the hearth, their backs slowly scorching as Clive and Garrick went to order drinks. After a couple of minutes, the boys returned with an iced

TOMMY WALLACH

maple for Flora and frothy mugs of ale for everyone else.

All her life, Paz had heard the Anchor had the best beer in the world, and her first sip of the ale didn't disappoint: wintergreen and ginger on top of the usual bite of the hops. Flora had just asked Garrick where he was from, and now the boy was in the middle of an entertaining, if unnecessarily comprehensive, life history. He'd grown up a good ways south of the Anchor, moving to the capital a few years back in order to join the Protectorate. A good old country boy like so many Paz had known, sending his extra shekels home to his family every month.

His autobiography was interrupted by a bawdy chorus that began in some corner of the pub and quickly overtook the whole room: *"Soldiers come and soldiers go, be there war or no."*

"So what's going to happen when the results come in?" Gemma shouted over the singing.

"We're gonna win," Garrick said.

"And then?"

"And then we'll go back east and figure out what's what."

"Damn right," Clive said, raising his glass to toast his fellow soldier.

Paz could almost laugh at the thought of these callow, arrogant boys marching on Sophia. They'd come in all puffed up like roosters, and leave with their tails between their legs.

Or more likely, they wouldn't leave at all.

"I'll get the next round," she said. Her drink wasn't quite empty, but she needed to get away from them all for a moment. Only no such luck . . .

"I'll come too," Gemma said.

The crowd parted for them easily enough—two young, pretty women bent on inebriation were not to be detained. Once Paz had gently and then not-so-gently declined the offer of a drink from the hirsute man sitting at the bar, she and Gemma ordered another four ales.

"Does Clive seem strange to you?" Gemma asked while they were waiting.

"What do you mean?"

"I don't know. Cold or something?"

"I'm gonna answer your question with one of my own," Paz said. She knew she was about to say more than she ought to, but she didn't care. That was the terrible thing about alcohol: it erased your inhibitions while simultaneously convincing you that inhibitions were a terrible burden in the first place. "Why do you worry about him so much?"

Gemma looked hurt by the accusation. "What do you mean?"

"You're always thinking about him. About how he's feeling and what he's doing—it's all you talk about. I mean, what would you have done if he hadn't made it back to the Anchor at all?"

"Irene!"

"What? It's just a hypothetical question."

It was almost funny, how genuinely confused Gemma looked.

"I don't know," she said.

"Well, what would you do if you never ended up getting married? If you just had to be on your own forever?"

"I guess . . . well . . . I really love horses. I like taking care of them, I mean. When I was Flora's age, I thought about trying to breed them."

The bartender finally brought the ales, but Paz immediately asked him to pour them a couple of glasses of shine.

"I really shouldn't," Gemma said. "Sometimes liquor brings on my fits."

Paz raised her glass. "Gemma, we're drinking to your dreams here. To horses!"

Gemma rolled her eyes, relenting. "To horses!" They clinked glasses.

The shine wasn't as smooth as the stuff they made up at the academy, but it sure was strong.

"Whooee," Paz said, blinking away tears. She slammed her glass back down on the bar.

A moment later, Gemma drew her into an embrace so tight it crushed the breath from her lungs. "Thank you," she said.

"For what?"

Gemma pulled back, frowning. "I don't even know."

That set both of them to laughing, so hard that Paz didn't notice the man calling out her name until he'd said it three or four times.

"Irene! Irene!" His tone was odd: mocking almost, playful. She recognized it even before she found his face in the crowd. "There you are," Chuck said, pushing his way up to the bar. "My old friend, *Irene*. What are the odds of that?"

Paz quickly weighed her options. Did she pretend to know him, but only as the stranger who'd harassed her last week? Did she play along, now that he was at least calling her Irene? Or did she plead total ignorance again?

Chuck leaned in close, putting a proprietary hand on her hip, and whispered into her ear: "You'll come outside with me right now, or else I'm going to start talking to everyone you came here with."

Gemma was watching them with a quizzical expression, still unsure if Chuck was a real friend, or just some drunk. Paz laughed flirtatiously, giving Gemma a look that said everything was just peachy. "I'll be back in a minute," she shouted. Chuck had hold of her wrist and was pulling her toward the door. "I'm coming," she hissed. "You don't have to drag me like a mule."

She wrested her arm free but followed him outside—down the alley, farther and farther from the pub, until he found an unoccupied stretch of road and drew her into a doorway. She'd had to abandon Silverboy during the trip to the Anchor (the discovery of the weapon would've exposed her as a spy), but at least she wasn't completely defenseless. Only a fool didn't keep a knife in her boot for special occasions.

"Time to lay your cards on the table, Paz," Chuck said. "Just what in hell are you playing at here?"

She couldn't tell him the truth, of course, but he'd already seen through her original lie. Some imagination would be required. She pushed him away, just hard enough to seem angry instead of afraid.

"I'm running a con, obviously. And you're about to muck the whole thing up."

Chuck grinned conspiratorially, revealing three wide gaps where teeth should've been. "What's the angle?"

"It's none of your business, actually, and that's all I'm saying."

She'd only taken one step into the road before he grabbed her

TOMMY WALLACH

by the shoulders and pulled her back, slamming her head against the door.

"You'll say as much as I want you to say."

She hadn't expected to get away that easily, but it had been worth a try. "Fine!" she said. "You don't have to get rough. That boy you saw me with is the son of a very wealthy Honor. And I've got him wrapped around my finger."

"So you've come into some money."

"Not yet. That's why you're barking up the wrong tree. You gotta leave me be for now, and I'll cut you in if it all pans out. Deal?"

She put out her hand to shake. Chuck snorted, then gave her a backhanded slap that sent her spinning. It was just the opportunity she'd been waiting for; she bent over, as if in pain, and slid the knife out of her boot and up her sleeve.

"You think you can fool me," Chuck said, "but I know where your heathen family went after you left Coriander. And you won't be marrying no Honor's son if they find out about *that*. They'd kill you first."

"What do you want from me?" she said, straightening up again.

"I haven't decided yet, in the long term." He put a hand on her belly, exhaling rank tobacco breath into her face, then ran it down along her hip. "But I've got some ideas about the here and now."

As he leaned in to kiss her, she slid her hand up his chest and plunged the knife into his heart. The smile died on his lips. His breath caught.

"You brought this on yourself," she said, twisting the hilt. A bubble of blood expanded in the corner of his mouth and popped redly. She stepped backward as he fell onto his knees and tilted forward, coming to rest with his head propped up against the wall, almost as if he were praying.

And just behind him, in what had previously been an empty alleyway, stood Clive.

11. Clive

IS FIRST THOUGHT WAS THAT SHE WAS FOOLING around with someone behind Clover's back—and was some part of him pleased at the notion? Only now the boy was slumping forward, and Irene stepped aside to let the body land heavily on the stoop. She looked up, and her eyes met Clive's. For a moment, he found himself staring into cold black holes in a perfectly composed face, a vague disgust the only visible emotion. Then her countenance crumpled, the knife clattered onto the cobblestones, and she threw herself sobbing into his arms.

"He attacked me," she gasped. "He knocked my head into the wall. Feel." She took one of his hands and placed it gently on the back of her head; sure enough, a lump had already begun to form. "He was drunk, and he was trying to force himself on me, and I pulled the knife—"

"Shh," Clive said. "You don't have to explain."

"I just wanted to make him stop."

He put his hands on her wet cheeks and pushed her gently away. "Why'd you leave with him?"

"Because I know him. We grew up together. He said he'd come here with a whole bunch of people from Eaton, and he was going to take me to see them. But then, once he got me alone . . ."

She choked up, dropping her head onto his shoulder again.

"It's fine, Irene. It's all going to be fine."

He stroked her hair, careful to avoid the lump on her head. Sometime in the past few minutes, a light rain had begun to fall, pattering gently on the cobblestones. Away from the mass of bodies in the pub, Clive could smell it—the acrid zing that signaled a storm on the way.

"Did anyone see you two come out here together?"

"I don't know. Just Gemma, I think. But other people might've noticed."

"I doubt they'll remember much of anything come morning," Clive said. "We just need to get clear of this quick."

He went over to the body and flipped it onto its back, then knelt down, threaded his arms through the armpits—still so warm—and heaved it up into a sitting position. It was a believable enough pose for a passed-out drunk, except for the blood that had soaked his creamy white shirt to a dark, vivid red. There was nothing for it but to wrestle off the boy's thin woolen coat, shaking the heavy sausage arms out through the sleeves, then drape it back over him like a blanket. The head lolled heavily forward, and Clive almost retched when he pushed it back up into a more natural attitude.

"You should empty his pockets," Irene said quietly.

"I don't want his money."

"I know. But when the body's found, won't it look better if he was robbed?"

She was right, as usual. He hastily rifled the boy's pockets and took the dozen bronze shekels he found there.

"Take them," he said to Irene.

She shook her head. "I couldn't."

"They won't do him any good anymore. You know that."

As she reluctantly took the coins, something compelled him to grab hold of her hand, crushing the metal between their palms. Both of their fingers were stained red with blood: but had she transferred it to him, or had he transferred it to her? He looked up into her eyes. They had a secret now. A bond. Her pulse fluttered hotly in her wrist. Their faces were so close he could smell the ale on her breath.

"Clive," she whispered, "we—"

But he'd never know what she'd been planning to say, because at just that moment, the entire city seemed to erupt with sound— screaming and shouting, crying and clapping, somehow coming from above and below and around them all at once. Irene pulled her hands sharply away from his, as if waking from a nightmare.

"What's happening?"

"The results of the plebiscite must have come in," Clive said.

"And?"

"Isn't it obvious?" A soulful howl went up from a nearby roof-top: the shattering of the old order in one livid thunderclap. "The Protectorate won."

Clive saw himself propping the body up against the wall, repositioning the head, going through the pockets. He saw that dead look in Irene's eyes. . . .

"Clive!" Garrick said.

He shook the memory away. "What?"

"You think we should do something?"

They'd made it about halfway across the city—obeying their directive to return to the Bastion after the plebiscite results came in—but it was slow going. The Anchor had been entirely transformed in the space of the last hour. Clive had never known the citizens of the Capitol were capable of such wanton destructiveness. Fights were breaking out left and right. Looters could be seen skulking away from shops with whatever they could carry. The sparkle of shattering glass was a constant accompaniment to the bellows of the vindicated and the wails of the disappointed.

But now they'd come upon something much worse than a little fistfight. People had been building bonfires in the streets, and just off the Silver Road, the fire had gotten out of control, spreading to a nearby house whose roof was just beginning to catch.

"You think there are people inside?" Clive said.

"Maybe."

"Shouldn't we help?"

"How?"

The whole bottom floor was already a raging inferno; there was no hope for those left inside. Still, the two of them stood there for a while longer, watching it burn.

Eventually they moved on, into the darkness beyond the fire's reach. The Silver Road was usually lit with lanterns, but rioters had taken most of them out already, smashing the protective panes of glass and allowing the pelting rain to extinguish the flames inside.

"Hey, Clive," Garrick said. "I wanted to ask you something, before we get to the Bastion."

"What is it?"

"I was wondering if you'd put in a word for me, with Marshal Burns."

"What kind of word?"

"Well, you and him are close, right? And everybody knows he's gonna get the nod to lead the mission east. So just tell him I should go too."

Clive was nonplussed. "But . . . why?"

"Because I want to."

"I get that. But why?"

"Because my other options are falling asleep doing guard duty in the city for the rest of my life, or else chasing Wesah around until one of them catches me with an arrow in the gut. This here is the first opportunity a Protectorate soldier has ever had to do something really valuable."

"Who's to say it's valuable?"

"Well, aren't *you* going?"

"I've got my own reasons."

"So do I! And I'm not asking for much. Just tell Marshal Burns I'm the finest soldier you've ever seen and you can't survive without me. Which is obviously true, by the way. Already today I saved you from a court martial *and* got you a moment alone with that honey-pot you're trying to steal off your brother."

"It's not like that," Clive said.

Garrick smirked. "Sure it's not, Dropsy. Just think about what I said, okay?"

"I'll think about thinking about it."

A few minutes later they reached the plaza outside the Bastion. Unfortunately, there were about a thousand people standing between them and the compound—a pullulating mass of protesters, screaming Filial verses and throwing whatever they could find at the soldiers posted on either side of the gate.

Clive suddenly felt terribly exposed in his uniform. Doing his very best not to draw attention to himself, he slipped into the crowd and began moving as quickly as possible toward the Bastion. He lost sight of Garrick almost immediately. After about a hundred feet, the first gob of spit hit him in the cheek, followed by a stream of obscene invective. He sped up a bit, which only made him more conspicuous. Someone grabbed him by the shoulder, and he lashed out with his fist on instinct, realizing too late that it was an old woman. She held a hand to her nose as red streams of blood streaked the front of her white dress.

He broke into a run, cries of "heathen" and "devil" going up all around him, an outstretched foot that almost sent him sprawling, hands grabbing at his clothes and his hair, and then something whistling through the air, a bright burst of pain, and everything went dark.

A nightmare. He was being chased through the alleyways of the Anchor by some sort of monster—when he looked over his shoulder, all he could see was the moonlight reflecting off the glossy black fur. Shapeless. Nameless. It lunged for him. . . .

He woke into quiet, calm—a shadowy sanctuary of white beds and black windows, lit by a single oil lamp hanging over the door like a charm. There was a dull pounding in his head. The racket of a city in crisis could still be heard, but it was blessedly muted.

Someone sat in a chair just next to the bed, smoking a cigarillo.

"Where am I?" Clive asked.

"The Bastion infirmary. You took a bad hit. I thought you might be out for the night."

That distinctive voice, like the sound you got scraping the black off a piece of charred toast: Burns. Clive had seen him only a handful of times since he'd joined the Protectorate, and always from afar. Strange to think, but he'd actually missed the man.

"How's the celebration going?"

Burns grunted. "Chang's insufferable even on the days he isn't gloating."

"I thought you'd be happy. We won."

"We didn't win shit. Winning is when you're still standing up and somebody else is on the ground. Or in it." He took another long drag off the cigarillo, expelling the smoke in a narrow beam of white that swirled up toward the ceiling. "I was born in a town called Emmetsville. Tiny as a freckle. Way up north. Our family worked a little seam of coal my granddaddy found, way back when. It was hard work, but good business. Too good, in fact. Some of my da's customers didn't like the terms he gave. So one day, while we were down in the mine, someone started a fire up around the mouth. Sucks the air right out of your lungs. My father died, along with a lot of my kin. I only got out 'cause

I was on my way up at the time, and I had to run two hundred feet of pure fire to make it. Wouldn't have survived, only we had this Anchor-trained doctor who'd just moved to town. He said I looked like a piece of chewed up gristle when I showed up. Still do, really."

Burns laughed, though Clive couldn't see what was funny about it.

"See, the problem up in Emmetsville was there wasn't no order to things. Every man was out for himself and his kin and to hell with everyone else. And that's no way to live. We all knew about the Descendancy, of course. My daddy said it was a bunch of crazies who sat around praying about God's kid. But I'd also heard it was civilized, or at least trying to be, and that was more important to me than the nutty religious stuff." He stopped for a moment, as if to underline whatever he said next. "I believe in order, Clive. I believe in civilization. And if you're gonna fight, that has to be what you're fighting for—not something as petty as revenge. And that's why I can't let you come east."

It was, by a significant margin, the most Clive had ever heard Burns say in a single go. And yet all he could focus on were those last six words: *I can't let you come east.*

"That's bullshit," Clive said.

Burns stubbed the cigarillo out on the arm of his chair. "It's not. You just started your training. And I feel"—the words clearly didn't come easy for him—"a responsibility toward you. Toward your parents."

"My parents are dead. That's the whole point." Clive threw off the blanket and climbed out of bed—wavering a bit when the ache in his head intensified to a pounding. "I'm going whether you want me to or not."

Burns stood up too. "It ain't your decision, kid."

Clive felt his fists ball up of their own volition. How dare Burns treat him like a child? Why did he think Clive had even joined the Protectorate, if not to be part of the mission to avenge his parents? If he ended up stuck here in the Anchor, he'd done it all for nothing—thrown away his future with Gemma, renounced his life in the Church, abdicated his responsibility toward his brother.

He would die before he'd be left behind.

Burns saw the sucker punch coming a moment too late; it caught him full-on in the kidney.

"Fuck," he gasped, bent double and wheezing.

The pounding in Clive's head receded; the lingering haze of the alcohol cleared. When Burns snapped upright, Clive was ready, dodging an uppercut and landing his own glancing shot to Burns's temple in the process. He weaved successfully around a flurry of jabs before a quick kick to his left knee buckled the leg, and Burns followed up with a whirling haymaker that sent him sprawling.

He allowed himself one deep breath before rising to his feet again. Burns was smiling now, bouncing on his toes. Clive charged, narrowly avoiding a straight fist to the nose when a broken floor tile threw him slightly off balance, and found himself staring at an open cheek. His momentum was off, so he couldn't put much strength into it, but it was still a clean blow, and it knocked Burns back a step.

He shook the pain out of his knuckles, which was all the time Burns needed to recover. The marshal feinted once, then again—a playful sort of taunt, but with a wariness to it now, a respect. Clive did the same, and Burns actually flinched. It was his enjoyment of that moment that ruined him; in the half second of satisfaction he allowed himself, Burns's left hand came hurtling like a stone from a slingshot, faster than the eye could even make out, and with the full weight of genuine outrage behind it. Clive didn't even remember falling—only a hideous flash of white. Then he was on his back, staring up at the ceiling.

He could hear Burns's breathing, slowing now, measured.

"It matters that much to you?"

"It's all that matters," Clive said.

A long pause. "I'll see what I can do."

Clive turned his head to spit, leaving a pink froth on the white tile floor. The world spun, slowed, centered. Burns was gone— had been gone for a long time now. Through one of the infirmary windows, Clive could see the sky: a gory spatter of stars. They all winked out at once, as if the end of the universe had come, when he closed his eyes.

12. Clover

CLOVER FOUND HIMSELF ON A COVERED PARAPET, buffeted by a chill breeze that made his skin break out in goose pimples. He walked quickly to keep the blood flowing to his extremities. Through the narrow embrasures to his left, he could see the Tiber sparkling blackly beneath a lowering sky. A couple of torches shone far off in the darkness—travelers coming to or going from the city's northern gate. The parapet continued to trace the outline of the Library where it extended slightly beyond the plane of the Anchor wall; then the walkway began to angle downward.

A sweet smell seeped up from somewhere close by, pleasant at first, but growing into an overwhelming miasma as he continued to descend. The moonlight that came through the battlements far above him was scarcely enough to see by, so it wasn't until he felt the first sharp pain in his foot that he stopped and allowed his eyes time to adjust.

As the scene ahead of him clarified, his awe gave way to a grim comprehension: now he understood Turin's order to strip, and the tiny scratches he'd noticed all over the man's hands. Stretching out before him was a single unbroken thicket of blackberries, its flowers dead and drooping, its berries overripe, rotting on the ground like corpse flesh. The plants had been cultivated to grow somewhere beneath the walkway, then trained through holes in the floor and walls to form an impenetrable snarl of vines.

Clover took a step forward. He was so cold that the first cuts only reached him as a sort of dull pinching. But then the body went to work: pain triggered the heart to pump harder, and the blood brought warmth along with it, so that every step he took brought more pain, which only accelerated the cycle. Another step, then another. His only choice was to use one hand to cup the sensitive region between his legs while he waved the other in front of his face to protect his eyes. Unfortunately, this left the rest of his body exposed, and the sheer density of the branches meant every inch of forward motion brought three or four inch-long scratches somewhere or other.

He tried to distract himself from the pain. What did he know about blackberries? If he remembered correctly, they weren't berries at all, but an aggregation of tiny stone fruits—like miniature peaches all bunched together. Also, they were the victim of a common misconception made in the classification of spinescent plants: namely, that all sharp protrusions were thorns. In fact, blackberry bushes, like rosebushes, had *prickles*, which were like the plant equivalent of hairs. Hairs that sank deep into the flesh of your foot when you stepped on them, that drew blood the same color as the juice of the fruit itself.

Clover realized he had begun to moan. The pain was amplifying, ramifying, not unlike the tumescent beads of the blackberry fruit, joining together to form something so much greater than the sum of its parts. He picked up the pace, though it only made the agony worse. A prickle at his forehead seared a line of fire back across his scalp. Blood and berry juice dripped off his chin and spattered on the ground. Everything burned. His moan grew into a prolonged shout, one that he rejuvenated every few seconds with another deep gasping breath.

It couldn't go on forever, could it?

Of course not. But it could go on longer than he could stand. He'd never been so aware of his fragility. Not just physically—though it was humbling to see the damage one seemingly innocuous plant was capable of inflicting, how easily it punctured the thin membrane that was all that kept his insides inside—but mentally, too. In his childhood games with Clive, he'd often played at being captured and "tortured" for information. In those scenarios, he'd always managed to hold his tongue, and he'd honestly believed he could do the same in real life. Now he knew better. Pain rendered all promises null and void.

The end came without warning or fanfare. Clover simply brushed past one last vine and suddenly his vision cleared. The world was so much brighter here, but before he could investigate exactly why, his eyes alighted on a pool of clear water just to his left; it seemed only natural to jump in. He'd expected it to be ice cold (and he still would've been grateful for it), but the water was unaccountably warm, soothing as a cup of tea in winter. He opened his eyes underwater and watched the stains leach out of his skin in little crimson clouds. A great sense of peace came over him, and he allowed himself to simply hang there, suspended, not kicking or flapping, until finally the pressure in his lungs forced him to surface.

At least twenty feet overhead, a band of sky—blanketed by dark clouds that looked to be on the brink of storming—could be seen through a peaked glass window. And bordering that skylight was something entirely impossible: a series of large glass bulbs, each one shining with a keen, unwavering light, like a bottled stare.

Only how could a room this large be hidden outside the Library proper if it wasn't underground?

The answer was far-fetched but inescapable: he was inside the Anchor wall. Whatever secrets this chamber held hadn't been squirreled away deep beneath the earth, but girdled the city like some kind of protective charm.

He tore his gaze away from the lamps to look at the rest of the room. It was only about fifteen feet wide, but so long that he couldn't see the end of it from this vantage point. A single tall bookcase ran down the center like a long wooden spine. The sight of it confirmed Clover's suspicions, and his heart began to hammer in his chest.

Whenever an attendant wanted to consult a volume containing information pertaining to the anathema, he had to file a formal request. If that request was approved, the volume would be delivered in a couple of days. Clover had always wondered where those deliveries originated, and now he knew. Here was the real library within the Library: the infamous anathema stacks.

TOMMY WALLACH

Clover glanced back at the thicket, the infinite vines twisting around one another like a nest of snakes. Before the night was over, he'd have to travel that path again. But for now, there was respite. Just next to the pool, a dozen white robes hung from a simple wooden rack. He got out of the water and used one to dry himself, then donned another. Passing his arms through the sleeves, he saw that the inside of the garment was stained a permanent pink: blackberries and blood.

A few shallow steps took him down to the level of the bookcase. It was a few inches taller than he was, and divided up at irregular, esoteric intervals. Clover took down a book at random: *The Special Theory of Relativity*, by Albert Einstein. It began with a couple of recognizable principles—parabolas and planes—but quickly devolved into gibberish—electrodynamical phenomena and the Lorentz transformation, heuristic values and four-dimensional space.

He kept walking, scanning the titles of the books in order to get a general sense of how the room was organized. The natural sciences—biology, chemistry, and physics—gave way to pure mathematics, then philosophy. And just beyond that . . .

"Blasphemy," Clover whispered.

A large brass annulus had been built directly into the shelf; the books contained within appeared to pertain to pre-Descendant history.

Clover reached for a volume bound in cracked black leather, half expecting to be struck by lightning as soon as he touched it. Hopefully the Lord couldn't see what went on way down here, amidst the anathema. Or maybe he couldn't bear to watch.

Cataclysm, by Sydney Glickman, the title page read.

In the following text, I seek to consider the most likely outcome of our impending disaster, based on historical corollaries (insofar as they exist) and the most up-to-date understanding of the damage the Earth is likely to sustain. As should be obvious, I side with the more hopeful wing of the scientific establishment, taking as a first principle that the impact winter will be mild enough to allow for the survival of limited pockets of humanity large enough to eventually reestablish some semblance of civilized society. My conclusions must therefore be considered speculative, penned in the spirit of Isaac Asimov's Hari Seldon, who sought to treat history as if it were an equation that could be, to some extent, solved.

To those who would ask why I should bother writing anything in light of what's to come, I offer the following quote by Schopenhauer: "We can regard our life as a uselessly disturbing episode in the blissful repose of nothingness."

Though Bernstein had never been the most poetic of men, there was one metaphor he was particularly fond of: that learning was a kind of illumination. In his conception, every human being lived in an immense mansion of shadowy rooms, each one representing a field of knowledge or understanding. As one learned about a given subject, that room slowly filled with light. It would never be entirely elucidated, of course, and no matter how many rooms one managed to brighten, there would always be thousands upon thousands left in darkness.

TOMMY WALLACH

Bernstein also said that revelation was rare; knowledge usually came like the dawn, in gradations so small you didn't even notice them passing.

But as Clover read on, he felt a sun rising within him, laying bare the solution to a puzzle he hadn't even known existed, whose pieces were so myriad and motley that he never would've guessed they would fit together so cleanly.

Before the Descendancy, there had been a grand civilization on Earth—and its corruption had run far deeper than was ever described in the Filia. The first generation of men hadn't just extracted Blood of the Father and abrogated Holy Gravity; their civilization had mastered technologies Clover couldn't even begin to fathom. Through these technologies, they had foreseen the coming of the Daughter, and in books like this one, had investigated not only the mechanism of their own destruction, but the world to follow.

Many of the predictions made in Glickman's book turned out to be uncanny. Her research pointed to a post-disaster civilization arising somewhere on the western edge of the continent, where various ecological factors would be especially conducive to supporting a larger population. She also guessed this society would be highly religious, and would likely fold the cataclysm itself into some preexisting religious paradigm.

"If we use Rome as a model," she'd written, "it could be a millennium or more before the survivors rediscover manufacture, trade, or a system of law more complex than *lex talionis*. And even this might be wishful thinking, as the post-impact environment will likely present practical difficulties that even the Romans didn't have to contend with. It is likely that many of the luxuries we currently take for granted will never be rediscovered—not on *this* planet, at any rate."

Clover put the book back on the shelf. He was vibrating with excitement, with fear, with horror. Everything going on outside that room—the results of the plebiscite, the rioting that would follow, the inevitable mission to Sophia—receded into irrelevance. He wanted to shout his discovery to the rooftops, to let everyone know the truth. And at the same time, he wished he could scour that truth from his mind, to retreat to the reality he'd occupied only an hour ago. In that reality, the Daughter was a divine being sent by the Lord, and the Church was the earthly manifestation of his will.

In *this* reality, the Daughter was just a rock, hurtling randomly through space, and the Church was built on lies. The Archbishop was a liar. Even Clover's father had been a liar—well, a liar or a fool.

But that was the thing about reality: it wouldn't be denied.

Clover took down the next book.

13. Paz

PAZ HELD HER HANDS PALM UP IN THE RAIN, WATCHING as the droplets slowly rinsed the blood away into the street. She felt oddly numb. Was this like that moment just after you stubbed your toe, before the pain forced its way into your consciousness like a drunken latecomer to a party? Or was this just what she was like now, the kind of person who could kill someone in cold blood and then go on about her day, remorseless as an animal?

Either way, it wouldn't do her any good to hang around the body waiting to get caught. Clive had been summoned to the Protectorate at least ten minutes ago, when the plebiscite results came in, and she'd been standing here ever since. Once she was sure her hands were clean, she went back to the Stag's Head. Gemma and Flora were alone at the table now, looking demure and delicate among all the drunkards.

"I thought you left with your friend," Gemma said.

"No. He . . . had other plans."

"I don't like it here anymore," Flora interjected. "Everybody's shouting."

"Shall we go back home?" Gemma asked.

"Fine by me," Paz said. It would be best to put as much distance between her and Chuck as possible, just in case he was discovered before morning.

The three of them forced their way back through the crowd. Outside, a woman was vomiting into a ceramic flowerpot, while nearby, a couple of men were engaged in a spirited fistfight, cheered on by a small knot of onlookers. And only a few hundred feet away, the body of a boy Paz had played tag with as a child was growing colder every second.

Good riddance.

The Poplin house was a fifteen-minute walk from the Stag's Head, nestled up against the Anchor wall. Inside, it was silent and cold.

"Where's Grampy?" Flora asked.

"Probably off protesting somewhere," Gemma said. "He was pretty upset at the notion the Church might lose the vote."

"Shouldn't we go find him?" asked Flora.

"Not a chance, little one. In fact, it's long past your bedtime."

Flora put on a sulky expression. "I won't be able to sleep."

"We'll see about that." Gemma turned to Paz. "Give me a second to put her to bed, yeah? There's something I want to talk to you about."

"Take your time," Paz said.

The two girls went upstairs together. Paz threw a few pieces of wood into the stove and stuffed the empty spaces with kindling.

Back home, she'd have had to set it alight with flint and steel, but here, there were always plenty of matches on hand. They were kept in a little tin box on a shelf above the stove, and each one was as long as Paz's middle finger. She struck one and watched it burn. The flame wavered, dancing in the drafts that blew through the chinks in the creaking old house, and ignited crescent embers beneath her fingernails—blood.

She lit the tinder, shook the match out into smoke, then went to the kitchen and dipped her fingers in a clay pot of wash water, scraping out the telltale corrosion beneath her nails. The half-full bottle of honey wine on the counter was calling to her, promising oblivion. Her hand shook as she filled a glass. She took the drink over to the window and gazed out onto the street, breathing deeply to calm her ragged nerves.

Footsteps on the stairs behind her. "More liquor? You sure that's wise?"

Paz turned. Gemma had changed into a white nightgown; she looked like a ghost, or an angel. "Not at all. Care to join me?"

Gemma smiled. "Why not?"

She poured herself a glass and joined Paz by the window. A group of young men went running past, their torches guttering in the rain. A stray cat, its orange fur matted to its gaunt frame, skulked from one shadow to another.

"Did something happen between you and Clive?" Gemma asked.

An inevitable question, really. Only how to answer? There were so many stories Paz could tell. There was the truth that soothed and the truth that cut. The lie that illuminated and the lie that obscured. The most important thing was to say something quickly. The longer she hesitated, the more dishonest she would sound. Wait long enough, and there was no point in answering at all.

"Because it would be all right if it did," Gemma added. "I mean, it wouldn't be ideal, of course, but it would be all right, if that makes any sense. He doesn't belong to me. And you're so pretty. Really. So I would understand—"

"Nothing happened," Paz interrupted.

"Oh. Okay then."

Did she detect a note of disappointment in Gemma's voice, or was it just that her answer hadn't been convincing?

"He won't be here long anyway," Gemma said after a while. "He wants to go east."

"I know. How do you feel about that?"

Silence. Then, a solitary sniffle—Gemma had started to cry. The drops slid steadily down her cheeks and pattered onto the wood floor. Paz watched them fall, and as she did so, something primal seized hold of her—that base animal longing to comfort and be comforted. She forgot what she was doing in the Anchor, forgot that this girl was the same one she'd been trying to kill three months ago, and opened her arms. Gemma fell against her, a consolatory warmth in the shape of a girl. She was saying something between sobs, gibbering about all the things she'd lost, but Paz couldn't make out the details. They probably didn't matter much anyway.

It didn't last longer than a minute or two. Then Gemma wiped her eyes against Paz's shoulder and stepped away, taking the warmth with her. "Daughter's love, it's been a bad few months."

Gemma shook her head as if to clear it of sadness. "But you're right. I need to grow up. I need to figure out what it is I want out of life."

"We all do."

"Yes. Yes, I suppose so." She leaned forward and kissed Paz on the cheek. "Good night, Irene."

"Good night."

Paz watched the girl go, and couldn't for the life of her summon up even a shadow of her former hatred. Things couldn't go on like this. The walls were beginning to crack. Between her and Gemma. Between her and Clover. Between her and Clive. Between Irene and Paz.

She had to get back to Sophia, before she lost track of herself entirely.

14. Clive

HE WOKE INTO THE ANTICIPATORY DARKNESS OF THE wee hours, head pounding. Someone must have carried him back to one of the infirmary beds, many of which were now occupied—casualties of the evening's riots. Most of the patients were asleep, but a pair of soldiers near the windows were talking quietly, their words drowned out by the patter of the rain against the panes.

Someone had left a glass of water next to the bed, and he drank it down greedily. There was a low hum of anxiety in the back of his mind, as if he'd forgotten to do something important. But what? So much had happened over the last few hours: the altercation in Annunciation Square, his discovery of Irene and the boy she'd killed, his hapless but ultimately effective fistfight with Burns.

A strange feeling of melancholy came over him; he realized he'd gone the whole day without thinking about his mother or father once. That was how forgetting began, wasn't it? It stole up on you, slow as molasses, promising an end to sorrow. But it turned out that forgetting hurt as much as it healed, because memories were a comfort, even when they caused pain. Gemma said she hadn't been able to picture her mother's face for years. How far off was the day when he would try to recall his own mother's smile and come up with only some hazy approximation—somebody's smile, but not hers?

He wondered how Clover was coping with the grief. The two of them had scarcely spent more than a few minutes at a time together since Clive joined the Protectorate—he hadn't even known about his brother's romance with Irene until this afternoon.

It was yet one more thing to feel guilty about. One more way in which he'd let their parents down.

Where had things gone wrong? How had he gone from the happy son of an Honor—his whole life laid out before him like a birthday feast—to this bruised and baffled Protectorate soldier, shirking his familial obligations and infatuated with his brother's sweetheart?

The answer came to him—a flash of insight, stark as a bolt of lightning—and immediately he was up and walking, out of the infirmary and the Bastion, striding briskly along the Silver Road. The cobblestones were slick with rain, gleaming in the starlight. Clive passed a party of drunkards, arms thrown over each other's shoulders, singing bawdy parodies of hymns in celebration of the results of the plebiscite.

Gemma's grandfather's house was in the Seventh Quarter, all the way across the city, but that was probably for the best; the long walk in the rain would give him time to think.

What did he want to say to her?

That he was sorry.

For what?

He wasn't sure.

And what would he say after that?

He would ask her to marry him.

Just the thought made him laugh out loud. It made no sense, and at the same time, it made all the sense in the world. Somewhere over the course of the past few months, he'd lost track of himself. But he and Gemma had known each other for almost their whole lives. If anyone could help him find himself again, it was her.

The sun was a tangible threat on the horizon by the time Clive reached his destination. Though the rain had nearly stopped, his uniform was already soaked, pulling heavy on his shoulders. His once shiny black boots were caked with mud. He picked out the attic window and began to hurl pebbles at it. But when no one seemed to notice, he found a slightly larger rock under a hedgerow and threw that instead. As soon as it left his hand, he knew he'd miscalculated; the stone went straight through the pane.

A moment later the window was pushed open.

"Gemma," he shout-whispered.

But his eyes were playing tricks on him: the same dandelion hair and pale complexion, but the wrong size.

"Clive," Flora said, neither surprised nor pleased.

"Go get your sister for me. I've got a question for her."

"Come back in the morning."

"It *is* the morning," he said.

She glared at him for a few seconds more, then rolled her eyes. "You better pay my grandfather back for what you broke."

She pulled the window closed again. Clive ran his fingers through his wet hair, slicking it back. It wasn't the way he would've wanted to propose—clothes clinging to his skin, his breath still sour with ale, no ring to put on her finger—but there could be a kind of perfection to imperfection, couldn't there?

Time passed, enough that Clive began to wonder if Flora had actually told her sister anything. But at last the front door of the house swung open. Gemma, dressed in a thin white nightgown, stood in the doorway.

"Gemma Poplin," he said.

"What do you want, Clive?"

"I want to talk."

He took a few steps toward her.

"Stop there," she said.

Clive was hurt. "You're afraid of me now?"

"You look like the devil himself. Did somebody beat you up?"

"It doesn't matter. I came here to ask you something important."

"So ask it."

"Come closer."

She shook her head.

"Gemma, how long have we known each other? Give me a little credit."

"It's all muddy, though." Her tone was more conciliatory now, and when Clive gave her a little smile, she capitulated, crossing about half the distance between them. "That's as far as I go."

"Fine. I'll just have to do it from here then." He dropped to one knee in the mud, almost falling over in the process. "Gemma Poplin, would you do me the great honor of becoming my wife?"

She stared at him hard for a few seconds, and then a smile began to creep onto her face. The smile soon became a giggle. Clive's heart leaped up in his chest—she was grateful, she was happy, she was going to say *yes!* He could feel his mother and father beaming at him from the great beyond.

But laughter can mean a lot of things, and it didn't take long for Clive to catch the edge of the razor blade hidden away inside Gemma's; it sliced his hopes wide open.

"What's wrong?" he said, standing up. "You're saying no?"

"Yes, I'm saying no," she answered, still giggling.

"Well, you don't have to laugh at me."

"Oh, don't I?"

"No. It's cruel."

It was that last word that finally put a stop to her laughing. Only what replaced it was so much worse: an icy calm, beneath which ran a roiling current of fury. "And it isn't cruel how you've been treating me? How long have we been back in the Anchor, Clive? How many chances have you had to spend time with me? And how many times have you come to visit?"

"I've been busy—"

"And I've got eyes in my head. The whole way back from Wilmington, you were mooning around Irene like you'd never seen a girl before. How do you think that made me feel?"

"I'm sorry, Gemma. I know I've been a damn fool. That's why I'm here—"

"I'm not done talking!" she shouted, the anger breaking to the surface. "Don't you understand? Everything's different now. I saw my little brother shot right in front of my eyes. I—I killed a man."

TOMMY WALLACH

"You mean at the pumphouse? But it was Clover—"

"No, it was me. I let Clover lie about it because . . . I don't even know why. I guess so I could pretend I wasn't the kind of person who could do something like that. But I did do it, and I'm not sorry. I'm done playing pretend. See, you're not the only one who gets to change, Clive. I may've disappeared from your mind until now, but that doesn't mean I disappeared. I have my own thoughts when you're not around."

"Of course you do." He traversed the rest of the distance between them, coming to stand as close to her as he dared. "But this—you and me here—this is meant to be. It's what our parents wanted."

"Is it what *you* want?"

"Yes!"

"Why?"

"Because . . ." He was thrown off by the question, unable to hide his exasperation. "Because I just do! I mean, what kind of thing is that to ask, anyway?"

"The most important question there is."

"But how can you ever know the real why of something? It's all so complicated."

She shrugged. "You just do, Clive." There was such a deep sadness in her voice when she said it, a sympathy bordering on pity, and at last he understood his mistake. He'd assumed that whenever he came around to Gemma, she'd be there waiting for him.

"You don't want me," he said wonderingly.

Gemma shook her head. "I'm sorry."

"Did you ever?"

She turned her eyes upward, that way girls sometimes did when they were trying not to cry. "I don't know anymore. But I do know this—us getting married, I mean—it won't bring any of them back. We're on our own now. So we gotta find our own way."

Clive didn't bother trying to hide his own tears; he'd relinquished his dignity the second he got down on one knee. "So where does that leave us?"

"I guess we've got two choices. Either this is the end right here, or else we try and make it some sort of new beginning."

"Beginning of what?"

"I don't know. We'll have to figure that out."

She reached out to him—a simple handshake, an offer of friendship—and some petty part of him wanted to push it away, to refuse to accept any sort of compromise. His heart ached to think of all the things they would never be to each other, the chance at happiness they may have missed. But he'd lost so much in the past few months—his intended, his mother and father, his calling, even his brother, in a way—he didn't imagine he could survive losing anything else.

He took her hand in his. It wasn't the same as it had been before, but at least it was something. A comfort. A reminder. A new beginning.

TOMMY WALLACH

15. Clover

A T SOME POINT IN THE NIGHT, THE CLOUDS OVERHEAD burst open and the rain began to drum a dense tattoo upon the roof. If Clover had looked up, he could've watched the rivers of rain running down the peaked glass, smearing the starlight. But he didn't look up. There were simply too many books to read. Books about religion and books about war and books about technology. Books about ways to think, to learn, to live. Books about books and books about books about books, hinting at a past so dense with knowledge that it was a wonder anyone had done anything *but* read.

He understood the inscription he'd seen on the door now—*and you shall be as Gods*. It wasn't a promise, but a curse. God knew all the dark secrets of the world, and now Clover knew them too. He felt drunk on that knowledge, almost sick with it. If learning was a lightening, as the Filia had it, then by now, Clover was floating up around the clouds.

Sometime just after sunrise, he realized he was no longer reading the words in front of him, but tracking the line of pink light creeping across the page. His mind was glutted, saturated—like a tea towel soaked in water. He simply couldn't absorb another word.

He stood up, bones cracking, and replaced the book on the shelf. Over the course of the night, he'd traversed the full length of the chamber—about a quarter mile from end to end—but only now did he notice the door at the far end of the room. It was no more than a black rectangle cut into the stone beneath a small sculpture of a hawk, with a keyhole bored around hand height. Clover knelt down and stared into the aperture, but he could see only darkness.

He was turning away when he heard it—just a rustle, really, yet impossible to miss in the sepulchral silence of the anathema stacks. He returned to the door and put his ear up against the stone. The ghostly susurrus that came whenever something was held up to the ear, the thunderous beating of his heart . . . and voices. Unquestionably, what he was hearing were people speaking. He stepped away from the door, as if whoever was on the other side might burst through at any moment.

But who could it be? Were there prisoners kept down here? And if so, why? How terrible must their crimes have been to merit such isolation?

No. That didn't make any sense. He must've misunderstood the geometry of the room as it related to the city. This door undoubtedly opened onto some empty back alley behind the Library, hidden here so the Epistem would have a secret means of escape, should he require it. The voices were just ordinary citizens going about their day.

The mystery solved, Clover finally returned to the entrance,

TOMMY WALLACH

pausing next to the rack where the robes were kept. When he'd first seen them, he'd been relieved—now he'd have something to wear on the way back through the brambles. But that was wrong, wasn't it? As the Epistem had said, the path was to be walked as the garden was walked.

He hung up his robe, took a deep breath, and stepped back into the passage.

There was a towel waiting on a hook inside the door, and his clothes had been folded up just beneath it. Epistem Turin was at his desk, looking for all the world as if he hadn't moved since Clover had left.

"I had some tea brought up," he said, "but it may've gone cold. I expected you to return sooner."

"Thank you."

Clover sat down across from the Epistem and picked up the red clay mug. He sipped: peppermint and pine. It was such an oddly commonplace thing to be doing, after everything he'd just been through.

"Well?" the Epistem said. "Ask what you need to ask. I'd like to get to sleep at some point."

Clover had a million questions, but one was more pressing than the others. "The Filia, is anything in it real?"

"Everything in it is real."

"But . . . but it isn't. I learned the truth last night. You showed it to me."

"Ah yes. The truth." With a groan, the Epistem rose from his chair and went to stand by the windows. The sky was pink at the horizon, shading to peach up above. He took off his spectacles and rubbed at his eyes. "I have terrible vision, you know. It's been that way since I was very young. Right now, all I see out there is a field of color. It's beautiful, but not very practical." He put the spectacles back on. "When I was your age, I became fascinated by the field of optics. I decided to apprentice as a glazier, but my master kicked me out when he discovered I was spending all my time grinding lenses instead of making glassware. I realized the only place I could pursue my research in peace was here, at the Library, so I began my apprenticeship as soon as I turned sixteen. I was insatiable, just like you. I read everything I could. But like so many precocious learners before and after me, my mind had begun to outpace my soul."

"I don't know what that means."

"True learning requires one to question, Clover, and I learned far too much too quickly. I began to doubt everything, so much so that my apprenticeship was in danger of being suspended. As a last resort, I took my questions to the Library Dubium, and by sheer chance, our Honor at the time was a man named Carmassi."

"The Archbishop," Clover said.

"Eventually. He saved my faith, Clover, and that faith has saved my life more times than I can say. It will do the same for you. Knowledge alone will not sustain you, whatever you may think now. Trust in God. Trust in his Daughter."

"But the Daughter was just a stone."

The Epistem sighed. "And your mother was just a complex arrangement of proteins resulting from a simple evolutionary process that took place over an untold number of millennia. And the love you felt for her was just the honeyed mead brewed up by

TOMMY WALLACH

the chemicals and electrical impulses in your brain. That is what knowledge tells us is true. But does that feel like the whole truth to you?"

After a moment, Clover shook his head.

"Exactly," the Epistem said. "With everything that's to come, you'll have to hold fast to your faith. Otherwise, you'll be lost."

"Everything to come?" Clover's mind had reached the breaking point; he couldn't solve any more mysteries tonight. "I don't understand."

"While you were in the wall, we lost the plebiscite. The Protectorate will send a contingent to Sophia, and that act will read as a declaration of war."

"But what does that have to do with me?"

"You will accompany the contingent under the pretense of doing research for the Library. And when you reach your destination, you will surrender yourself to the enemy."

Clover would've laughed, but there wasn't a glimmer of humor in the Epistem's voice. "What?"

"We've learned that Sophia is always on the hunt for promising new students. These recruits must be young and exceptionally intelligent, like you."

"What good would I do as a prisoner of Sophia?"

"Not a prisoner. A student. And you'll do what any student does: learn. How far has Sophia's technology developed? How many soldiers can they muster? What is their chain of command? At the moment, we're completely in the dark."

"They'd suspect me right away."

"Of course. But the Archbishop and I believe you can convince them of your sincerity by sharing some of what you've learned tonight. That's why you were allowed to explore the anathema stacks."

"You want me to give up the Descendancy's secrets?"

"Nothing in our books is a secret to them, I'm afraid. Leibowitz saw to that."

"And if it doesn't work? If they don't believe me?"

The Epistem sighed. "I think you know the answer to that."

Paths through the future zigged and zagged, a lightning tree of possibilities. Clover saw himself bleeding out from a bullet wound to the head. He saw an arrow protruding from his chest, loosed by the Protectorate soldier who'd caught him in the act of offering himself up to the enemy. He saw himself in some dank basement, facing whatever hideous tortures the scholars of Sophia had devised. And yet . . . to sneak right under the noses of the people who'd killed his parents, to destroy them from the inside, wasn't that worth the risk?

And there was something else, too, a thought he would never dare speak aloud. In Sophia, he could do more than read about the anathema; he could *touch* it. He could learn how the telegraph machine worked. Maybe he could even build his own. For the first time in his life, he would be entirely free.

"I need to think."

"Of course you do. Just remember, no one is to know of this, especially not your friend Marshal Burns."

"You're keeping secrets from the Protectorate?"

"We're keeping our options open. That's all you need to know. I'll expect your answer within the next couple of days."

TOMMY WALLACH

"Yes, sir." Clover rose to his feet, feeling weightless and disembodied and dazed.

"Before you go," the Epistem said, "would you mind praying with me?"

"Of course."

The Epistem closed his eyes, cleared his throat, and recited the first few words of the Trinity Prayer. And all at once, Clover was transported back to his childhood, sitting around the campfire on some tour around the Tails, surrounded by the loving faces of his mother and his father, of Clive and Gemma and Flora and Eddie and Michael, all speaking the prayer in one voice. What he wouldn't have given to be with them all again.

But there could be no going back; there was only the future. Clover already knew he would accept the Epistem's mission. He would go east with the contingent, carrying this fraught new knowledge inside him, like one of the terrible bombs he'd read about in the anathema stacks. And at the gates of Sophia, he would pretend to betray the Descendancy. No one could know the truth—not Gemma, not Irene, not even Clive, who was too deeply involved with the Protectorate now to be trustworthy.

Oh, but there were dark days ahead.

Clover bowed his head and joined in with the prayer.

Interlude

A T THE VELVETY, BLUE-BLACK HOUR JUST BEFORE dawn, the boy climbed out of bed and quietly pushed his bedroom window open. The roof was steeply pitched, and the previous night's storm had left the shingles slippery as eels, but he was adroit at such maneuvers; he sometimes made a few shekels sweeping out his neighbors' chimneys with a long-handled broom he'd secretly named Sir Sweepy.

The boy sidestepped to the very edge of the roof, then sat down. From this position, he could tap his boot heel against the window of his younger sister's room. After a moment, she tapped back, and a minute later she emerged onto the roof. Her wild shock of black hair and long white nightdress were both whipping around in the wind as if they were fixing to fly away.

"You must be freezing," he said.

His sister ignored him. "Is it ready?"

"Yeah."

"Then do it already."

The boy stepped up to stand on the crest of the steepled roof, holding the kite in one hand and the spool in the other. This was the moment of truth. He closed his eyes and listened for the ripple of leaves along the pathway below that signaled an upswell of breeze; when he heard it, he cocked his arm and threw the frame out into space. The wind took hold of it immediately, and the boy was so surprised that he nearly lost his grip. The kite fought hard against him, a prisoner being dragged to the gallows, but he held fast to the spool, playing out the line in order to give his captive a bit more room to breathe. The black fabric was more conspicuous than he'd expected, reflecting the moonlight in white waves up and down its skin. It bucked and banked, once dipping down below the line of the roof, then whipping back up toward the sky with a breathtaking swiftness.

"It's so beautiful," his sister said, her voice gone soft with reverence.

"Isn't it?"

The boy understood now why such an activity was banned; this pleasure was far too keen to be holy. He felt himself becoming one with the kite, carried aloft by some impossible force. Unable to help himself, he let out a single loud *whoop*.

This joyful noise did not go unheard. Just next door, Emilia Cardacci happened to be awake as well. She was penning a letter to her paramour, a young man with whom she'd become a little too well-acquainted three weeks earlier, and whom she was now attempting to cajole into proposing to her, when some animal part of her brain registered movement beyond the thick glass of her window. She looked up. Something was moving out there, causing the stars to blink. A bat? Impossible. No bat had ever danced like that. Nor would a bat allow itself to be leashed by the foot, as this one had. Emilia had no word for what she was seeing, and yet she eventually worked out the gist of it: someone on the roof of the house next door had built a flying device. And who else could it be but that strange little boy?

He's lucky it's only me seeing this, Emilia thought, glancing over at her sister, Lily, still sound asleep, dreaming of doing chores and obeying rules, most likely. If that little prude had spotted the boy's misdeed, she would've gone screaming for their parents in an instant.

But no—this moment was reserved for Emilia alone, suddenly connected to something greater than herself by this sparkling black diamond capering through the early-morning darkness. She felt something lighten inside of her. When the boy let out his whoop, it took everything in her power not to whoop along with him. If flight was possible, then everything was possible. She didn't have to marry some boy she scarcely knew just because of a single unfortunate tryst. She didn't have to do anything she didn't want to do. She could be like that . . . that *thing* up in the sky: free.

For many weeks afterward, Emilia would wonder if everything that came next really happened as she remembered it. For in her memory, the horror gripped her as a kind of prophecy, even before the wind gusted and the black diamond suddenly puffed up like an angry rooster. She was already on her feet, hands against the window, as the kite pulled the boy down the steepled roof, holding the leash in his hands.

Let go, she wanted to scream, and at the same time, she understood why he couldn't. The kite had opened a doorway, a glimpse into another, better world.

The boy disappeared over the edge, down past the gable and out of Emilia's sight. And then his little sister appeared at the very spot

TOMMY WALLACH

where he had fallen. She must have been up on the roof too, and had seen it all happen from just a few feet away.

Emilia had never liked the girl much: pretty as anything, too pretty really, but just as strange. Stared at you like she was seeing into your soul. Never bothered saying good morning or good evening. Even now, she wasn't screaming or crying, just standing there, gazing downward.

It took Emilia a moment to remember herself, then she ran downstairs and out into the chill of the morning. The boy lay in the alley between their houses. His eyes were open, as if still hungry for another few seconds of vision through that doorway, and his neck was bent at an obscene angle. The spindle had been crushed beneath his body, and by some miracle, the kite continued to gambol in the air above them, like an oblivious animal.

Ever so slowly, Emilia reeled it in. When she had the kite safely in hand, she dropped it to the ground and trampled it underfoot, shattering the thin wooden braces. She reached down and tore out the silk, rubbing it between her fingers: impossibly soft.

"Give that to me."

It was the boy's sister, who'd slipped into the alley as silent as a shadow. Her tone was flat, her expression impassive. Was she in shock, or simply heartless? For an instant, Emilia entertained the thought of refusing the girl's demand. She would've liked to keep the silk, as a sign or symbol of something. But of course that would be crazy.

"I'm sorry," she said, offering up the piece of fabric. The girl tore it out of her fingers and ran back into the house without a word.

Emilia registered the tears leaking slowly but unceasingly down her face, and she realized she wasn't crying for that brief moment of absolute freedom she'd felt while watching the kite, or even for the boy lying breathless and broken at her feet. She was crying for that strange little girl, who couldn't cry for herself.

Part III
TRAITORS

And Nadab and Abihu, the sons of Aaron,

took either of them his censer,

and put fire therein, and put incense thereon,

and offered strange fire

before the Lord, which he commanded them not.

And there went out fire from the Lord,

and devoured them,

and they died before the Lord.

—*Leviticus 10:1–2*

1. Gemma

EMMA STOOD IN FRONT OF THE GLASS, TURNING FIRST one way and then the other, watching her double do the same. Lord, could they have made this getup any less flattering?

"Momma would be spinning in her grave," she said under her breath.

Viola Poplin had had such high hopes for her daughter—that she would leave behind the nomadic ministry life and become a normal Anchor society girl, married to the estimable Honor Clive Hamill, peacefully growing fat in a well-appointed Anchor home with a gaggle of children around her. And here she was in a Protectorate uniform a size too big for her, her engagement broken off, preparing to head out once again into the wilderness.

"You look terrible," Flora said.

"That's not very nice."

"I'm not trying to be nice."

The contingent would be departing for Sophia (a place Gemma

had never heard of, but that the Protectorate now claimed was behind the ambush at the pumphouse) in less than an hour, and Flora still hadn't forgiven her older sister for agreeing to go. Gemma had tried to explain that the trip wouldn't be all that dangerous— she'd be surrounded by soldiers the whole time, and her only jobs would be cooking and cleaning—and that Burns had practically ordered her to come along. But she got the feeling her little sister had guessed the truth: that far from being forced into the mission, Gemma had actually gone to the Bastion of her own volition and begged Burns to allow her to come.

"Why?" the marshal had asked.

"Because those boys are my family," she'd answered. "Somebody has to look out for them."

"And that somebody has to be you?"

There'd been a playful sort of challenge in his eyes, as if her professed selflessness was nothing more than a bad Hallows' Eve costume. And maybe it was true that she'd grown used to life on the road, that some small part of her found the daily dullness of life in the Anchor as claustrophobic as a coffin. But one truth didn't cancel out another; it was possible to have both a duty *and* a desire.

Of course she felt guilty about leaving her sister behind. But Flora had their grandfather, and her school friends. She would survive.

Gemma laced up her boots and shouldered her rucksack. "I guess this is it, then."

"I guess so," Flora said. From behind her back, she presented a tiny parcel wrapped up in a paper flyer and tied with brown string. "Here."

TOMMY WALLACH

"What is it?"

Flora only gestured impatiently at the package. Gemma pulled the string and let the paper fall open. Resting in the center was a small annulus, only it was different from any annulus Gemma had seen before: weightless and thready, yellow as wheat baking in the sun. She had to touch it to understand; it was made of braided hair.

"I've been plucking 'em out for the past couple of weeks," Flora explained. "And I took a lock of Ma's hair and wrapped it up in there too."

"Where'd you find *that*?"

"It was in with Da's stuff, from some old love letter. Guess she sent it to him when they were courting."

Gemma wiped a tear out of the corner of her eye. "I love it," she said. "And I love you, too. You know that, right?"

"Yeah."

They hugged. Then Flora put the string she'd used to wrap the parcel through the center of the annulus and tied it around Gemma's neck. She stood back to admire her handiwork.

"Well, at least now you've got one nice thing to wear."

Gemma worried at the annulus, rubbing its softness between her thumb and index finger, and instinctively turned to look back over her shoulder, as if her eyes might pierce the hundred miles that now separated her from the Anchor, slip through the Eastern Gate and the walls of her grandfather's house, and find Flora curled up like a kitten in the bay window of the attic, dreaming of flower fairies.

But all she saw was the company's rear guard, cracking wise and spitting into the reeds at the side of the road, surrounded by the riotous colors of the season. The cold turn had come five weeks ago and, in that backward way it had, set the world ablaze. Leaves turned the yellow of afternoon sun, then the red of sunset, falling to the ground to rot and dissolve back into the black. Sickle Lake, which they'd had on their left for the last day or so, sparkled with flecks of white gold. In the air, a crispness that didn't yet cut, a fresh bouquet of pine and lavender, occasionally overwhelmed by the homely pong of skunk.

Burns said they'd have to keep off the main roads once they made it over the mountains, so as not to telegraph their approach to Sophia, but for now, their progress was swift. On their tenth day out from the Anchor, they reached Borst, at the foot of the Teeth. The snows wouldn't begin for another month, so the pass was clear.

There were eighty-eight of them in the contingent: seventy-five members of the Protectorate, one Honor (the Church required that an ordained minister be present with any large company traveling the outerlands), one poet (a long-haired, sallow man named Carlsbad, who had already subjected Gemma to half a dozen of his terrible compositions, including one that he claimed to have written just for her), five merchants, three officers of the people, Clover, Irene (who was finally returning to her home in Eaton), and one poorly qualified cook by the name of Gemma Poplin.

All the soldiers traveled on foot, though most of the other members of the contingent were on horseback. Gemma didn't have anything to ride herself, but she *was* in charge of leading one of the pack horses, an easygoing piebald named Valerie. Already she'd

TOMMY WALLACH

begun to daydream about climbing up onto the animal's back and falling asleep to the gentle rhythm of her trot.

"You thinking about Flora again?" Irene said, cantering up beside her and sliding down from the saddle so they could walk together.

"Is it that obvious?"

"Whenever you start playing with that necklace, I know she's on your mind." Irene reached over to touch the annulus, her fingers grazing Gemma's collarbone.

"You think about your brothers a lot?"

Irene nodded.

"Tell me about them."

"What do you want to know?"

"Anything."

"Well, let's see … Anton's the oldest. He's just about the smartest person I ever knew, before Clover, that is. Frankie's the worrywart of the family—weight of the world on his shoulders. Then there's Terry. He's a bit of an odd duck, really. Got a mean streak in him a mile wide, but then sometimes he can just be the sweetest thing. And Carlos is the youngest. All he ever does is ask questions."

Gemma smiled. "I remember when Michael went through that phase."

"Michael?" A second later, Irene covered her mouth in embarrassment. "I'm so sorry, Gemma. It just slipped my mind."

"That's all right. You didn't know him for long."

"I still shouldn't have forgotten." She put a hand on Gemma's shoulder and squeezed her through the uniform jacket. "You'll forgive me, won't you?"

Her eyes were big and brown, so full of contrition it almost looked like an act. Sometimes when Gemma was talking to Irene, she found it difficult to focus on anything other than the girl's physical presence. There was something magnetic about her, a beauty that was equal parts glamour, charm, and mystery. People had been telling Gemma how pretty she was all her life, but pretty was to beautiful as perfume was to fresh flowers, and she would've traded her looks for Irene's in an instant.

Maybe that was why she always felt a vague sort of envy when she saw Clover and Irene together—which was almost all the time now. It seemed the two of them could hardly stand to be away from each other for more than five minutes at a stretch.

"Of course," Gemma said. "It was an honest mistake."

"Anyway, all I meant to say was that I miss my brothers like crazy."

"Well, it seems you've found a decent enough replacement."

"How's that?"

Gemma gestured over her shoulder, toward Clover.

"Oh, him! But Clover's a *much* better kisser than my brothers."

Gemma wrinkled up her nose. "Ew."

Irene laughed. "Isn't that what you Anchorites think about us country folk? That we're all marrying our cousins and such?"

"I've never heard anything like that," Gemma said, but of course she had, and pretty soon she was laughing too.

"Don't you girls know this is a serious military engagement?" Clive said, coming up behind them. "No laughing allowed. And no secrets. What's so damned funny?"

"Nothing," Gemma said, but one look at Irene set her to laughing all over again.

It took them almost two weeks to make it through the mountains. In that time, their company shrank by three—a soldier who broke his leg trying to run down a wild goat and had to be left in a nearby village to recover, and two Church officials with business in Corning. From there, the contingent headed southeast toward Trinity, where the Northern and Southern Tails separated. The weather turned colder as the invincible verdure of the evergreen forests around the mountains gave way to the mortal trees of the lowlands, bruised golden by the changing of the season. Clover, who was engaged in some sort of research project for the Library, kept them all informed about the minutiae of this ecological shift.

Gemma had assumed that traveling with the Protectorate would be like traveling with Honor Hamill's ministry, but it turned out to be an entirely different experience. Any time the contingent stopped, there was a never-ending list of chores to attend to— watering the horses, seeing to the soldiers' swords, finding wood for the fires, rinsing out smelly undershirts and scouring the mud from boots and preparing meal after meal after meal and wearing a smile on her face the whole damn time. ("Keeping up morale is the most important part of your job," Burns had explained.)

In spite of all that, she enjoyed the rhythms of military life. There was an honesty to her exhaustion at the end of the day, a purity of purpose she'd missed during her time in the Anchor.

The contingent skirted around Trinity and began marching across the wild territory between the Tails, hoping to remain undetected by Sophia for as long as possible. There was no sign of civilization out here but the occasional abandoned homestead—barn open to the elements, silo scoured clean by mice, gravestones garlanded with dried-out reed annuli.

One evening a few days later, the contingent stopped to camp in the middle of a vast sagebrush plain, stained here and there with patches of purple wildflowers. Gemma was watching Clover and Irene, who'd wandered a little ways off to marvel at a desert willow. Clover plucked a bloom off the branch and gently slipped it behind Irene's ear.

"Daughter's love," Clive said under his breath, coming to stand beside Gemma. As always, Garrick was right behind him. "It's enough to make a man sick."

"I swear he spent two hours last night just rubbing her goddamn *feet*," Garrick said. "But maybe he's getting two hours of something in return."

"Something like what?" Gemma teased.

Garrick smiled angelically. "I would never sully your delicate ears with filth, Gemma."

She still hadn't decided how she felt about Clive's friend. He was an incorrigible flirt, but that could be fun sometimes; she only wished he wouldn't stare at her quite so much. "Well, Irene'll be back in Eaton soon enough. I suppose we should let 'em have their fun."

Clive grunted, a bad habit he'd picked up from Burns. "I still don't like the way she's got him wrapped around her finger."

"My daddy always said you should never judge a man for anything he does in the name of love," Garrick said. "Of course, he spent a week in the stocks for putting it to a married woman, so he may not be a trustworthy source of wisdom on the subject."

Gemma had a couple of follow-up questions to Garrick's confession, but just then, all of them were distracted by the sound of someone shouting. It took a few moments before anyone was able to locate the source: a lone man on horseback, riding toward the campsite from the east. He was repeating something—a single, unintelligible word—over and over again. As he came closer, Gemma recognized him as the forward scout who'd gone out that morning.

An arrow protruded from his shoulder like a flag of conquest, its fletching shivering in the breeze.

"Wesah," he said one final time, then slumped sideways and slid to the ground.

2. Clive

"THE IDIOT DREW HIS SWORD," CLIVE SAID. "WHOLE thing's on him, far as I see it."

"He was scared," Gemma argued.

"That's no excuse—"

Just then Burns finally swept out of his tent. For the past hour, he'd been inside with the contingent's medic and Nathan Federle, the scout who'd gotten himself skewered by the Wesah.

"He dead?" one of the soldiers asked.

"No," Burns replied. "But he will be if he ever wakes up. Everyone gather round!" The marshal kept talking as the contingent drew close enough to hear. "So that shit-for-brains in there just made us an enemy, and that enemy is currently sitting smack-dab between us and where we're trying to go. We've got no choice but to head out there tomorrow morning and try and make nice."

"Can't we go around them?" Garrick said.

"Then they'll just be behind us. And only a fool marches into trouble with trouble already breathing down his neck."

Honor Gordon, who'd been summoned from his tent in case Nathan needed last rites, gave a loud harrumph. Clive didn't much like the man, who seemed to think his primary role in their company was criticizing those who weren't comporting themselves in a godly fashion.

"You have something to say, Honor?" Burns said.

"Well, perhaps it's not my place to weigh in on this, but I'm a little confused. Are you honestly afraid of a few heathen women in loincloths? I thought you were soldiers."

"We've got nothing to gain from making trouble with the Wesah, Gordon." The marshal's voice thrummed with barely contained hostility.

"So what are you planning to do? Beg them to spare our lives?"

"Oh, it won't just be me," Burns said, allowing a smile of satisfaction to creep across his face. "You'll be coming too."

"Me?"

"That's right. Along with our lovely ladies and whatever food we can spare. Speaking of which, will someone get dinner started already? I'm starving."

With that, the marshal ducked back into his tent.

"Did he say 'ladies'?" Clive said to Garrick.

"Sounded that way."

Clive stood up and strode in after Burns. The marshal's tent was dark, lit only by a single lantern. It smelled of rosewater and softleaf. Nathan was laid out on a pile of blankets in the corner. Burns had already taken a seat nearby, watching as Waverly, the contingent's medic, strapped some sort of poultice to the wounded soldier's shoulder.

"What lovely ladies?" Clive demanded.

"Are you unclear about which members of our company are women?" Burns asked. "Or is it more that you're questioning their loveliness?"

Someone else entered the tent. Clive turned to find his brother, and just behind him, the two ladies in question.

"You aren't trading them away," Clover said. "I won't let you."

Clive couldn't help but smile. Clover was capable of many things, but intimidating Burns wasn't one of them. "If I ever offer the Wesah a human being," the marshal said, "it'll be for something a lot more valuable than safe passage."

"Then what do you want us for?" Gemma asked.

"If I show up there with a bunch of soldiers, it'll look like an attack. You and Irene make it clear we're coming peaceful. Besides, the Wesah get along better with women."

"Well, they're not going anywhere without me," Clive said.

"Or me," Clover added.

"Or me," Garrick said. At some point, he'd slipped inside the tent too.

Burns sighed. "Only because you three and Honor Gordon are the least threatening men in this whole contingent. Just wear your civvies, all right? And no swords, for fuck's sake. I doubt you'd know what to do with them anyway."

Clive was glad to have a horse beneath him again; the day was shaping up to be the coldest of the year so far, and the animal's warmth was a welcome convenience. According to Nathan, the Wesah

TOMMY WALLACH

encampment was about four miles east of their campsite: no more than an hour at an easy trot. They rode in silence at first—Burns's preferred mode of travel—but it wasn't long before Gemma started talking.

"So what exactly *are* the Wesah?" she asked. "I've seen a few of them over the years, but I've never actually met one."

"Godless heretics," Honor Gordon answered. "That's all you need to know."

"I don't wanna tell you your business," Burns said, "but you're wrong about that. They got plenty of gods."

"There is only one God, Marshal Burns, and his aspect is threefold. First—"

"We're here for a sortie, not a sermon, Gordon. Besides, I think we've all heard that one."

Honor Gordon gave a little grumble before going silent.

"The Wesah aren't to be underestimated," Burns said. "That's the most important thing to know about them. They travel in these small bands they call *naasyoon*, which can be anything from a handful of warriors to a few hundred, and each one can wander pretty wide. Captured warriors claim their people cover the whole continent."

"Sounds like a bunch of bullcrap to me," Clive said.

"How many of these *naasyoon* are there?" Gemma asked.

"I bet if you asked them, they'd say it's as many as stars in the sky, or grains of sand on a beach," Garrick scoffed.

"And maybe it'd be the truth," Burns said. "Never assume you know something about something you know you don't know nothing about."

Garrick frowned. "What?"

"Anyway," Burns continued, "all the *naasyoon* meet up once every two years, down south by the ocean. They call it the *tooroon*. It's the only time most of them see their chief."

"There's just one?" Clive said.

"Well, each *naasyoon* has its own leader, but then there's one chief above all the rest. No matter who she is, they call her Andromède."

"Is it true the Wesah keep male slaves?" Irene asked.

Of course that was what she wanted to know about, Clive thought. She already had a male slave right here: Clover, waiting on her hand and foot, bowing to her every whim. Or maybe she had two slaves, come to think of it. After all, it was Clive who'd helped her cover up a murder, taking her at her word that it had been committed in self-defense. And since that night, had she ever bothered to thank him? Of course not. That would have required spending ten seconds away from Clover.

Thank God the girl was finally going back to Eaton, where she couldn't manipulate either of them anymore.

"*Lii nisklaav lamoor*," Burns said. "Love slaves. But in the Descendancy, we call 'em missives. They do all the cooking and cleaning, and whatever grunt work the tribe requires. And of course . . ." He trailed off.

"Of course what?" Gemma asked.

"Use your imagination, girl."

After a moment, Gemma gasped. "Really?"

"Sounds like a damn fine life for a man," Garrick said.

Burns chuckled. "Depends on the man."

"And how does this Andromède stay in power?" Clover asked. "I

TOMMY WALLACH

mean, if nobody ever sees her, she doesn't have much opportunity to prove her value to the tribe."

"I can answer that one," Gemma said. "Because women don't waste all their time fighting amongst themselves to prove who's got the biggest willy."

"Well, if the Wesah are so smart, how come they don't have their own city?" Clive asked.

"Maybe they don't want one."

"Who wouldn't want his own city?"

"*Her* own city."

"Quiet," Burns said. "I think I heard something."

They'd entered a small, sparse copse of gold-leaf aspens and stumpy ponderosa pines. Clive watched a sparrow slip like a dead leaf from the end of a branch, then swoop upward just before touching the ground. There was a moment of expectant tranquility, then a phalanx of slim shadows separated themselves out from the larger shadows cast by the trees. Faces emerged, each one bifurcated by the thin line of a bowstring. Though Clive knew they were all women, many weren't recognizable as such at first glance; most had cut their hair short or shaved it off entirely, and the furs and cured leather they wore would've fit as naturally on a male body as they did on a female's.

Burns jumped down from his horse, bowed his head, and began to speak. At first Clive thought he couldn't understand the words because the Marshal was mumbling. Then he realized that Burns was speaking in the tongue of the Wesah. When the marshal had finished, the tribeswomen conversed among themselves for a surprisingly long time.

"They're as chatty as all the other women I've met," Garrick said.

"Shut your mouth," Burns said sharply.

A moment later one of the Wesah warriors lowered her bow and stepped forward. She was young—no older than Irene, probably, and with far fewer tattoos than most of the other tribeswomen—but it was immediately clear she spoke for the *naasyoon*. In spite of the thick mantle of white fur over her shoulders and the dozen copper bracelets around her left arm, Clive could see the girl was all muscle.

"I lead this tribe," she said, in a heavily accented but intelligible English. "I am called Athène. Now who are you, *chee*."

"Marshal Burns, from the Anchor. *Taanishi, kaniikaniit*."

"*Taanishi*, Marshal Burns of the Anchor. It is your man comes to us with steel yesterday, *chee*."

Clive realized she was talking about Nathan.

"Yes," Burns said. "And for that, we apologize." He laid a canvas sack of deer meat and dried fruit on the ground between himself and Athène. "*Lii prayzaan*, in the hopes of peace between us."

Athène ignored the gift. "Your people always travel by the roads. Now you move through the rocks, *chee*."

"We don't wish to be seen. Our business is our own."

The chieftain laughed, and her tribeswomen laughed along with her. Somehow, their arrowheads hardly wavered.

"Your business is our business today, Marshal Burns."

Clive heard his brother whispering to Irene just a few feet behind him. "That *chee* sound seems to signal a question. They don't inflect their terminals."

"We have reason to believe there is a city to the east that threatens the Descendancy," Burns said.

TOMMY WALLACH

"Your Descendancy does not extend from water to water," Athène answered.

"The Descendancy knows no physical boundary!" Honor Gordon announced. "It is the Lord's Kingdom on Earth." In retrospect, Clive was surprised the man managed to keep quiet as long as he did.

"What the hell are you doing?" Burns murmured.

"Teaching them to respect the one true Lord and his Daughter."

"Your Daughter is a story!" Athène said. Again she laughed loudly, and again her fellow tribeswomen followed suit.

"The Daughter is your savior and redeemer, savage!"

Athène's laughter died as suddenly as it had started. She raised her left hand and made a small twisting motion. A twang and a whistle sounded from the woods. The arrow caught Honor Gordon in the center of his Adam's apple, stopping halfway through his neck. Wide-eyed, he looked desperately from side to side, as if a solution to his present difficulty might be found somewhere near at hand.

Clive took a step forward but was pulled up short by Burns's whispered command. "Don't move. Nothing to be done."

That reality seemed to be occurring to the Honor now too. A strange light had come into his eyes, like a revelation. Was he feeling the pull of Holy Gravity? Seeing God? Touching the Daughter's face? It looked as if he wanted to tell them something—to deliver a message from the other side—but his last words were reduced to sputters and clicks, and finally he slumped sideways and fell from his horse.

"Much better," Athène said.

3. Clover

SILENCE. STILLNESS. THE HONOR LAY HEAPED ON THE ground, blood oozing down his neck to disappear beneath the collar of his purple cassock. Clover thought about the man that Gemma had killed so many months ago, outside the pumphouse. Was the Wesah chieftain feeling any sort of remorse for what she'd just done, or had she and her tribe transcended such simplistic morality? And which was more barbaric: to kill as a rational being, or to kill like an animal?

The girl called Athène went on talking as if nothing had happened. "I am told you don't believe in war," she said. "Now you go in search of it, *chee.*"

"We're only investigating a rumor," Burns said. "Please allow us to pass through your lands without further violence."

"We have no lands."

Burns conceded the point with an open-handed gesture that also happened to serve as a subtle reminder of the gift they'd brought.

Athène stepped forward and, slipping off a moccasin, nudged

the flap of the canvas sack open with her foot. When she'd finished examining the contents, she stepped back again and raised her right fist. Clover braced himself for an arrow through the chest, but apparently the gesture had the opposite meaning. The Wesah warriors behind Athène dropped their bows. Two of them came forward and picked up the canvas sack.

"They hold fire in their hands to the east," Athène said. "Their arrows fly faster than sight. You go to your death, *chee*."

"Because we must."

Athène nodded, as if this response made perfect sense. "Then you may go."

"Thank you," Burns said. "May all your dreams be nightmares."

Athène nodded. "*Kahkiiyow pawatamihk kiishkwayhkwashi*," she said—and the cadence made it clear this was a repetition of the same phrase in the Wesah tongue. She turned away and began walking toward the trees.

"Look at her! Look at her shine!"

Athène spun back around, seeking the source of the shout.

"You sparkle," Gemma said directly to the chieftain. "You sparkle so lovely."

The Wesah looked bewildered, but Clover understood what was happening. Over the years, he'd learned to recognize the bizarre eruptions that sometimes preceded Gemma's fits. Sure enough, her eyes rolled back in her head a few seconds later, and then she was on the ground, shivering and kicking as if something evil inside her was doing its damndest to get out.

Within a few seconds, the general mumble of consternation among the Wesah had grown into a dreadful cacophony, one in which the word *dimoon* seemed to feature heavily. The warrior women sounded fearful and angry at once, chittering away in their high-pitched, consonant-heavy tongue. Clover glanced over at Clive, but his older brother looked as bewildered as everyone else in the glade. Only Irene had had the presence of mind to actually do something useful; she'd been closest to Gemma when the fit started, and she'd immediately rolled the girl onto her side and slipped a hand under her head.

A few of the Wesah warriors were reaching for their quivers now, frightened by what they couldn't comprehend. Burns advanced on them with his hands up.

"She's not a demon!" he said. "She has a sickness! Shit, what's the word for sickness? *Malaajhii. Malaajhii!*"

For her part, Athène also seemed to be trying to convince her fellow tribeswomen not to shoot, waving at them wildly, but not all of them were paying attention. Clover noticed one warrior in particular—a woman at least twice as old as Athène, with a wild thatch of curly hair and a slight but palpable madness in her eyes— who'd already nocked an arrow. Clive saw her too, and he immediately dove forward to shield Gemma's body with his own. Only just then, Gemma bucked particularly hard—a shudder that seemed to start at her belly and ripple outward like a double whip crack—and Irene, who'd been holding the girl's hand, was wrenched to the side, knocking Clive over and putting herself directly in the line of fire.

Clover reached into his saddlebag and pulled out the gun—a parting gift from the Epistem—then pointed it at the curly-haired warrior.

Squeeze the trigger.

"What are you doing?" Irene screamed. "Shoot her!"

Squeeze the trigger.

The Wesah warrior squinted her right eye and drew the bowstring back.

Squeeze the trigger.

Oh God: it was the pumphouse all over again. And though he knew there would be blood on his hands either way, he couldn't bring himself to take that final leap. A plangent twang sounded as the arrow was loosed.

"No!" Clover shouted.

But the arrow flew well wide of its target, disappearing into the trees.

A moment later, the Wesah warrior dropped to her knees and coughed up a thick gout of blood. And now Clover could see the black leather hilt sticking out of her chest. Thirty feet away, Clive had yet to move, his arm frozen in the position from which he'd thrown the knife. The injured warrior coughed wetly a few more times, then lay still. The glade went silent.

Clover found the presence of mind to point the gun at Athène. Hopefully she hadn't noticed he didn't have the guts to actually use it.

"One man for another," Burns said softly. "*Balaansii.*"

Athène's lower lip quivered with rage. Her eyes were wide as moons. "*Balaansii, chee.*" She took a step toward Clover. Then another. He didn't move; even if he'd been capable of shooting, it would have meant all of their deaths. Athène was close enough to touch now. He saw the delicate tracery of a tattoo on her neck: a swirling pattern, like water eddying behind a boat.

"*Paa balaansii,*" she whispered, then leaned forward and pressed her forehead into the barrel of the gun. Her lips curled up into a terrible smile. "*Paa miina,*" she said. Then, pushing even harder against the gun, she let out a long, piercing scream. Then she turned her back on the gun and followed the rest of the *naasyoon* back into the woods. It seemed an eternity before the foliage finally swallowed her up.

As soon as she was out of sight, Irene came rushing into Clover's arms, squeezing him tightly. "We're okay," she said. "We're all okay."

"What did she say there at the end?" Clive asked Burns. "It sounded like a threat."

"It was," the marshal answered. "She said 'Not even. Not yet.'"

Everyone was silent for a moment. Then Garrick snorted loudly. "Look at that." He pointed to a nearby tree, where the canvas bag had been left hanging from a leafless branch, its contents completely intact. "The bitch didn't even take her present."

Clover gently stroked the spines of the prickly pear plant—they were sharp and unyielding, eminently practical. This was a healthy specimen, with big purple flowers and dark green paddles. The fruits, brownish-red cylinders that were a favorite of plains animals, had all been eaten, but more were already growing.

It was the cover story he'd been provided by the Epistem: the Library had sent him along with the Protectorate contingent in order to scout the flora of the eastern reaches of the Descendancy for potential medicinal components. For the sake of verisimilitude, he'd spent his last couple of weeks in the Anchor reading up on

TOMMY WALLACH

botany. He now knew over a thousand different Latin names for plants. He could prescribe herbal treatments for more than twenty-five common ailments, from headache to pinkeye. He'd learned to classify various monocots by the size of the florets and the shape of the leaves. All so he could lie just a little bit more effectively.

"A shekel for your thoughts?" Irene said, appearing out of the darkness.

The rest of the contingent was camped out about a quarter mile away. They'd spent the day traveling east as fast as they could manage, expecting a Wesah counterattack at any moment. But either Athène had decided they weren't worth the trouble, or she was simply biding her time. Whatever the explanation, the situation had left all of them tense and exhausted.

"My thoughts aren't worth that much."

"Don't be so modest." Irene knelt down next to him in the tall grass. "You ever eaten prickly pear?"

"No. Have you?"

"Sure. Tastes a little like watermelon. My momma used to make jam out of it."

"She use it for anything else, like when you were sick?"

Irene shrugged. "You know how we outerlands folk are. Everything's a miracle cure."

It was meant as a joke, but Clover couldn't rally a smile. Irene put her hand over his. "What's wrong, darling?"

What was wrong? Everything, obviously. His parents being dead was wrong. Clive being a soldier was wrong. It was wrong what he'd learned that night in the anathema stacks, and it was wrong what the Epistem had asked of him, and it was wrong that he'd have to leave everyone he loved behind when they reached Sophia.

Irene began to gently stroke his arm. "It's lonely, isn't it?"

"What is?" His voice sounded husky in his throat, and he realized he'd been about to cry.

"Keeping secrets."

"I don't know what you—"

"Shh." She put a finger against his lips, then slid it down to his chin so she could give him a lingering kiss. "You think I haven't been able to tell? Ever since the night of the plebiscite, you've changed. You've been hiding something."

He didn't know what to say. He'd promised he wouldn't say anything about what he'd learned inside the Anchor wall, or what he was meant to do in Sophia. But what a relief it would be, not to be alone with the weight of it anymore.

"Marry me," he said.

Irene frowned. "What did you just say?"

"I said marry me. I love you, Irene. And a husband can tell his wife whatever he wants. So if you and I get married—"

She cut him off, kissing him again, pushing him back onto the ground and straddling his hips. After a while, she sat up straight, looming over him, backlit by the gibbous moon.

"Yes," she said. "My answer is yes."

"Really?"

"Of course." She leaned down, embowering his face with her hair. "Now what's this big, bad secret of yours?"

But even then, after they'd promised themselves to each other for life, Clover felt hesitant. In telling Irene his secret, he would be breaking his word to the Epistem—and to God, in a way. Per-

　　　　　　　　　　　　TOMMY WALLACH

haps it would be better if he said nothing after all. At least now he knew she'd wait for him. If he survived his mission, they could settle down together. He'd work in the Library, and she would stay home with the children, and they'd need never discuss the risk he'd taken for the Descendancy.

"Clover," Irene said, a note of chiding in her voice, "I'm starting to think you don't trust me." She ran her hand down his cheek and neck, his chest and belly, the waist of his trousers. He could feel his resolve melting away.

"Silly boy," she whispered. "Don't you know you can tell me any- thing?"

And so he told her everything.

4. Paz

MARRY ME. I LOVE YOU.

He'd said it just before he relinquished his last secrets and became hers entirely. And now she lay next to him in his tent, restless and tense, the hours passing slow as clouds. In that small space, Clover's even breathing was like a bellows, and she began to imagine it was only getting louder with each exhalation, as if something were chasing her and slowly catching up. She escaped into the fresh night air, into the tranquil chaos of the sylvan biome: arrhythmic clicking of crickets, plangent hoots of owls, gentle flutter of bats winging overhead. The campfire was still smoldering, but the makeshift benches of dead wood the soldiers had placed around it were all empty.

Paz sat down and warmed her hands at the embers, trying to get her head around everything she'd learned in the past twenty-four hours. She'd long known that the Filia was just a collection of fables, and that the first generation of men had been destroyed by *some* sort of natural disaster—Clover's revelation just filled in the details. Apparently the "Conflagration" had been caused by something called an *asteroid*, which was nothing more than a big rock. Interestingly, Clover still believed that both explanations for this disaster—Daughter and asteroid—could be true at the same time. Funny how the mind could rationalize almost anything.

The other piece of information Clover had gleaned in the anathema stacks—that the first generation of men had been far more technologically advanced than the Descendancy would have people believe—was more interesting. It made Paz wonder how many of Sophia's discoveries were new, and how many were simply reconstructions of past breakthroughs.

Either way, she had to assume that everything Clover had learned would be old news to Director Zeno. More important was his disclosure that the Epistem had sent him to spy on Sophia. A dangerous stratagem, surely, but it wasn't entirely without merit; Clover was intelligent enough to pass the academy's entrance examination, and once inside, who knew what he might learn? Luckily, it wouldn't matter, because Paz would be there to unmask him.

Marry me. I love you.

Some part of her had known it already, of course. Making him love her had been a necessary part of the plan. But to actually watch it happen proved to be more disconcerting than she'd expected: the difference between finding a dead rabbit in a snare and being there when it was caught.

Perhaps that was the most disturbing of the day's revelations. When she'd thrown herself into Clover's arms just after the Wesah had retreated, it had only been half performance. Some shameful inner aspect of her had craved the comfort of his embrace, and by extension, his feelings for her. And earlier tonight, when she'd been in the tent with him, she'd glanced over at his sleeping face and realized she could no longer see the monster who'd murdered her father—just the poor boy she'd fooled into loving her.

That was the strange thing about pretending to be someone else: you could only do it for so long before the character you were playing began to infect the person you really were. You became something new, a sort of hybrid of the real and the invented, which only made the invented part that much closer to real.

Paz's meditation was interrupted by a crunching sound from the woods. She turned around, half expecting to see a Wesah arrow screaming toward her head. But it was only Clive. He'd grown a light beard over the last few weeks that suited him.

"Call of nature," he explained gruffly.

She turned around again, hoping he would go back to his tent and leave her in peace.

"Beautiful night, isn't it?" he said, sitting down next to her.

"Sure is."

"Clover asleep?"

"Like a baby."

"I'll tell you, Irene, I know we got off to a bit of a, well, *interesting* start, but I'm glad you and my brother found each other. After he spent all those years pining after Gemma, he deserves a bit of happiness."

Paz was wary, but decided to take Clive at face value for the moment. "I'm glad you think I make him happy."

"Of course you do. And it's good of you not to be jealous—of Gemma, I mean."

TOMMY WALLACH

"Everybody's got a childhood crush."

Clive scratched at his beard. "You mean Clover isn't the only boy *you've* ever cared about?"

Paz had answered a few personal questions over the past few months, but she'd avoided talking about herself whenever such reticence wouldn't look suspicious. She'd also tried to cultivate a general air of absentmindedness on which any factual inconsistencies could be blamed. Lying in her sleeping bag at night, she'd ask herself random questions and then invent answers, knowing full well that at some point, her very life might depend on her ability to improvise convincingly.

Clover had never worked up the courage (or the curiosity) to ask about her previous romantic experiences, but she'd had answers ready since day one.

"There was one other boy, a few years ago."

"Oh yeah? What was he like?"

"What are all boys like? Handsy."

Clive whistled. "And you found him right in your hometown? Lucky girl."

"I guess."

"How many people live in Eaton anyway?"

"Round about three hundred, counting the farmers nearby."

"Farmers like your father?"

"That's right."

"Remind me, what crops did he tend?"

She tried to sound playful. "You sure got a lot of questions this evening, Clive."

"Just making small talk."

She considered putting an end to the conversation—complaining of a headache or answering her own call of nature. But the truth was, some part of her thrilled to the challenge. She would've rather avoided the game entirely, but if Clive was going to force her to play, then she was going to *win*.

"Well, it's damned dull, Clive."

He laughed. "All right then. I got one more question for you. And it's a lot less dull."

"We'll see about that."

"You planning on marrying my brother?"

She could feel the surprise spreading across her face, making a fool out of her. "What makes you think that?"

"Yesterday I asked him if he was broken up that you'd be leaving soon. And he said it might only be temporary."

Paz shrugged. "Anything could happen. Life is long."

"Not always." He smiled when he said it, but not sincerely enough to dull the edge of the threat. There was no doubt now that he was probing her, but Paz wasn't sure if he was doing it because he'd begun to doubt her story, or simply because he didn't like the idea of a country bumpkin like her marrying his fancy little brother.

She tried for a tone somewhere between impish and imperious. "And if I did marry Clover, would that be a problem?"

"I suppose that would depend on why you were doing it. I'm just looking out for him."

"You sure? 'Cause this all sounds like a bad case of the green-eyed monster to me."

"Don't flatter yourself."

"I'm not. You say you're looking out for him, but everybody's noticed where you're really looking. Why else do you think Gemma threw you over?"

As soon as the words were out of her mouth, she regretted them. Where she might've used this conversation to mollify Clive, now she'd gone and provoked him.

He stood up. The dying embers in the fire pit reflected in his eyes—rings of bright orange around the black. "You've given me a lot to think about, Irene. Have a good night."

He left the circle of the firelight, disappearing back into the darkness.

"Shit," Paz said.

5. Gemma

EMMA STOOD UP, ARRANGED HER HANDS ON THE HARD leather of the saddle, and slowly raised her legs over her head. It was a trick she'd seen performed by a rodeo clown years ago, and one that had taken her more than a month to master. She held the headstand for ten seconds or so, then lowered herself back down again.

"Bravo," Burns said. "We oughta take this show on the road."

"I thought that's what we were doing. Is this not the circus?"

She wasn't entirely sure how it had happened, but sometime in the past few weeks, she and Burns had become friends. It was a relationship born out of necessity: the last civilian members of their cohort had peeled off to the south after the confrontation with the Wesah (though not before Burns had requisitioned their horses and finally given Gemma a mount of her own), and as for the Hamill brothers, Clover was always off in his little world with Irene, and Clive spent most of his free time with Garrick and the other soldiers. This left Gemma with a serious dearth of recreational options.

The last time she'd traveled the outerlands, it had been in the clement days of summer. But winter had come upon the contingent like a shroud, darkening the soldiers' spirits as it shortened the days. Now that the sunshine was gone, conversation was the only thing that made the hours bearable. And say what you would about Burns, but the man sure had stories to tell. Up until he'd joined the Protectorate about ten years back, his life had been one harrowing adventure after another. (Or else he was just a really good liar. For her part, Gemma didn't care much either way.)

Mostly they just chewed the fat, talking about whatever came up in the course of the day's march, but they'd managed to get a little personal now and again, like the time she'd said something offhand about Clive's "new girlfriend" Garrick, and Burns casually dropped the question he'd clearly been hankering to ask ever since they'd left the Anchor.

"So what went on between you and him, anyway?"

"Between me and Clive? What do you mean?"

"Your daddy was dead sure that the two of you would end up married before too long. Now it's like the thought never crossed your mind."

"It's complicated."

Burns grunted. "Nothing's all *that* complicated. Either you went off him or he went off you. No shame either way."

"I guess I realized I was never really on him in the first place," she said. Then, seeing the beginning of a smirk on Burns's face: "Don't say it. You know what I mean."

"Sure I do."

They'd let the conversation drop after that.

But even though she'd begun to enjoy Burns's company, she

wouldn't have said she really *liked* him until a few days later, when a blustery evening in early December found the contingent on a narrow road that ran along the edge of a canyon. There was something familiar about it.

"I've been on this road before," Gemma said.

"That's right," Burns replied. "It was a little out of our way, but we've got some unfinished business to take care of here."

"What unfinished business?"

He didn't answer, just looked at her, something like sympathy in his eyes, and at last she realized where they were, and what they were about to do.

"Daughter's love," she whispered.

It was just the four of them now, walking in a row—the last surviving members of Honor Hamill's ministry (except for Flora, of course, blessedly safe back at the Anchor). Garrick and Irene had stayed with the rest of the contingent, just out of sight down the road. Gemma clung to Clive's arm as they rounded the curve.

It looked the same as when they'd left—a moment frozen in time. On their right loomed the large boulder where they'd made their last stand. To the left, the carcass of the wagon lay wasting, its canvas skin sagging and water-stained, braces protruding like ribs. And in the scrubby field between one and the other . . .

"I hate to think they've just been laying out here," Gemma said. The tears had already begun to flow, pouring down her cheeks like they had somewhere important to be.

"There's no shame in it," Clive replied, taking hold of her hand.

TOMMY WALLACH

Clover was on her other side, so she grabbed hold of his hand too. The younger boy's eyes were glazed and impassive, and Gemma wondered what was going through his mind. He'd kept everyone at a distance since the day he lost his parents, or everyone except Irene, anyway. Gemma hoped he'd at least managed to open up to her, to express the grief he hid from the rest of them. No one should have to handle so much pain alone.

Burns had brought a spade with him; likely he'd carried it all the way from the Anchor with just this purpose in mind. He handed it to Gemma. "We'll get the bodies. You start digging. One hole, unless you've got something against a common grave."

Gemma shook her head: in death as it was in life. Burns and the boys headed toward the back of the wagon, where her father's corpse would be waiting. She was grateful not to have to touch him, to lift him, to feel the lightness he'd achieved in death.

She cast about for an adequate location for the grave. At the edge of the road, a yucca tree reached its myriad of viridescent arms up toward the sky, as if in supplication; it would make a fine headstone. She stuck the spade into the hard earth at its roots and tossed the first half scoop aside.

The boys returned and laid her father's body down nearby, and though she didn't want to look, she felt a strange responsibility to acknowledge it. The corpse had been preserved by the enclosed space of the wagon. A ghastly mantle of skin still clung to the bone, tufts of yellow hair waving delicately as cornsilk.

That is not my father. My father is with the Lord and his Daughter in heaven. That is just an empty vessel.

She turned away, dug in harder with the spade, placing her right foot on the back of the blade and using her weight to break through the frigid crust of the earth. She wept openly but quietly, imagining the tears softening the soil for her, consecrating it somehow. They brought Ellen Hamill's body next. The framework of the woman's beauty, the slim figure Gemma had always coveted, now lay starkly revealed—narrow hips and long legs, high cheekbones and those tiny, birdlike feet. Her husband came a few minutes later. His thick purple cassock had kept better than she would've expected; it looked as if it had only been outside for a week or two.

"Was he really this small?" Clover asked.

"I guess so," Clive answered.

Neither of them cried. Why was it men always seemed so concerned with coming off strong? Wasn't there a sort of weakness in that—the fear of being seen as you really were?

The hole was only a couple of feet deep, but Gemma's hands had already been rubbed raw by the splintery handle of the spade, and she was soaked in sweat. Clive took over the digging, while Clover and Burns went to recover the last of the bodies. This was always going to be the hardest one to bear—her baby brother, lionhearted to the very end. Her breath caught in her throat when she saw what was left of him—scarcely anything—and she lost all semblance of self-control after that. Sobs racked her body so violently she worried they might trigger a fit. At some point Clover sat down next to her and put an arm around her shoulders. She just went on crying.

When the digging was done, Clive and Burns used a canvas sling to lower the bodies as gently as possible into the cavity, then took turns replacing the dirt. By the time they were finished, the sun had traveled from high in the sky all the way down to the horizon line.

TOMMY WALLACH

Gemma was all out of tears by then, her eyes red and aching, her soul scoured clean by the sheer force of her grief.

Burns went back down the road and summoned the rest of the company. Clive was the closest thing they had to an Honor now, so he spoke a few words from the Filia. Gemma sang the "Remembrance Hymn"—always her father's favorite—then Clive and Clover duetted on "So I Came Me Down to Ground."

As painful as it had been, Gemma was glad that they'd come here. Something felt finished—some part of the past finally mounted on the shelf where it could be gazed upon from a distance, like an urn full of ashes. After dinner, she climbed up to the top of the big boulder and gazed down on the yucca tree and the gravesite, the soldiers' campfire flicking fingers of red toward the half-moon.

"You ain't wearing shoes," Irene said. She'd appeared out of the shadows, like a black cat.

"I wanted to feel the ground beneath my feet."

"Oh yeah?" Irene took off her shoes and socks, squidged her toes around in the earth. "That's not bad." She began climbing up the side of the boulder.

"Careful."

"I will be."

When Irene reached the top, she lay down next to Gemma. They stared up at the stars, so many it looked like somebody had sifted flour out onto the sky.

"You think there are other folks like us out there somewhere?" Irene asked.

"Probably. Hardly matters, though."

"I suppose not."

Something tickled at her hand. She was about to shake it away when she realized it was Irene's pinky grabbing hold of her own. A curious bubble popped in her stomach, rising to a lightness in her head.

"I'll have to go home soon," Irene said. "At least for a while."

"I know. Clover'll be sad."

"He'll survive. Anyone who can kill a man can handle a little heartache."

Gemma had almost forgotten about Clover's lie; it seemed beside the point now. "He didn't kill that man at the pumphouse. I did."

"Oh," Irene said quietly.

"I guess Clover figured if we said it was him, I wouldn't end up feeling guilty about it." She laughed at how naive that sounded. "But it didn't work. I think about that man all the time. I mean, what would I say to him, if I saw him in heaven?"

"You think he's in heaven? A heretic?"

"I guess not. Or maybe. Who am I to say? I don't pretend to understand much of anything anymore."

Gemma felt Irene gently unhook her pinky. "You know, I'm feeling pretty tired. I should get to sleep."

"You don't wanna talk some more?"

"No. Tomorrow, maybe."

Irene stood up and began clambering back down the boulder. Gemma felt terribly sad all of a sudden—as if she'd lost something precious—and couldn't quite understand why.

6. Clive

IN THE DAYS THAT FOLLOWED THEIR MAKESHIFT MEMORIAL service on the old mining road, the weather took a turn for the worse, and the spirits of the contingent followed suit. Clive went to bed with a gnawing in his belly most nights, which made waking up all the more difficult; it felt as if sleep had lost its restorative powers. Their pace slowed to a crawl, which only made everyone more spiky and ill-mannered.

But slow progress was still progress, and after close to two months on the march, the contingent finally reached the pumphouse.

The door was open when they arrived, swinging ominously on its hinges. The whole place had been cleaned out since Clive had been here last—no pump, no telegraph machine, no Riley. Already nature had begun to reclaim the interior. Thick-legged spiders perched in the corners, and the pellet droppings of mice were everywhere. All that remained of the room's original purpose was the ineradicable stench of Blood of the Father.

"So this is where it all started, eh?" Garrick said.

Clive nodded. For most of the contingent, the pumphouse was just the setting of a story they'd heard. But for him, it represented a turning point: the birthplace of his new self. His memories of that day had faded over the past few months, but, being there again, it all came rushing back: sitting outside, talking with his father about Kayin and Hevel; Riley appearing in the doorway, inviting them inside in his folksy outerlands accent; the bowl of ripe red cherries; the howl, and the horsemen, and the certainty that death was only a moment away . . .

He started at Gemma's hand on his elbow.

"You okay?" she asked.

"I'm fine," he said, more brusquely than he'd meant to. Without furniture, the room was smaller than he remembered, claustrophobic. He had to get out. He excused himself and hurried back across the threshold. Irene was crouched a dozen yards off, tenderly touching the dirt with the tented fingers of her right hand. There was a strange hardness in her eyes, almost like anger, and it disappeared with a disconcerting suddenness when she glanced up and noticed him watching her.

A moment later, Burns came out of the pumphouse and addressed the contingent. "This is the farthest east I've ever been," he said. "It's all unknowns from here on out."

"Not entirely," Clover said. "We know that Sophia can't be more than sixty miles from here."

Burns raised an eyebrow. "How do you reckon?"

"Da told me you got here round noon last time, and the horsemen showed up just after dark. That time of year, at this latitude, sunset would come about eight thirty. If Sophia got word right when you showed up at the pumphouse, and the horsemen rode hard, we'd be talking about fifty miles, give or take."

"That would also explain why they couldn't keep up when we ran," Gemma added. "Their horses wouldn't have had the chase in them."

"Makes sense," Burns said. He raised his voice so everyone could hear him. "We're stopping early tonight, boys!" A cheer went up, but Burns spoke over it. "Don't think that means you're getting off easy. Before we eat, I want every stone turned over for a mile in every direction. We might learn something about where we're headed next. So get to work!"

There was some grumbling after that, but wandering around looking for clues was still a whole lot easier than marching. Clive went to set up his tent, but he'd barely had time to lay out the canvas and stakes before Burns cantered by.

"Saddle up, Clivey," he said. "I got something I want to show you."

"Yes, sir."

He finished putting up his tent, then hiked back up the road to where they'd tied up the animals, untethered a dun-gray mustang called Bear, and rode out to meet Burns. The marshal was waiting a little ways west along the escarpment, and they immediately set off in that same direction.

"How far we going?" Clive asked.

"Top of this ridge, if we can find a path. Should be a pretty good view."

"We hunting something in particular?"

Burns looked at him askance. "No, I was just desperate for some time alone with you."

They rode for a while in silence. Through the gaps in the trees to their left, Clive could see out over the fields down below old farmland long since gone to seed and subsequently overgrown with blackberries and wild grasses. The day's brief but drenching rains had left the wide lea so cratered with puddles it resembled a swamp. They reflected the harsh silver light of the clouds overhead, reminding Clive of what he'd seen in Irene's eyes a few moments ago—a secret animus, momentarily revealed.

"Burns, can I ask you something?"

"Why not? I already got more quiet out of you than I was expecting."

"It's about Irene."

"What about her?"

"I don't trust her."

"Good. Any man who trusts a woman deserves whatever he gets, and you can bet a bucket of shekels he'll get *something*, sooner or later."

"This is more than that."

"Sure it is. This is you bein' sore your brother got a girl just when you lost yours."

Clive's anger overwhelmed his good sense. "Open your fucking ears, man! I'm trying to tell you something important!"

Burns leaned over in the saddle and grabbed hold of Clive by the collar of his uniform jacket, nearly pulling him off his horse. "I know we got history, Clive, but I'm still your superior officer. You're lucky there ain't nobody else around to hear you."

Clive was in too deep to apologize now. "Well, there's not. It's just you and me. And this isn't jealousy, or some family squabble.

I'm telling you, something is off about that girl. She's got a darkness inside her." For a moment, he considered telling Burns about what he'd done for Irene the night of the plebiscite, but he knew it wouldn't reflect well on him, either. "She's after something. I feel it in my bones."

"Maybe she is. Maybe she isn't. Ain't really your business either way, far as I can see. Now come on."

Burns rode on ahead, and Clive grudgingly followed. They'd found something like a trail, which cut through the escarpment and then on up the hill. After another fifteen minutes or so, they reached a plateau. From this vantage, they could see for miles back to the southwest, out across the silver-studded fields.

"There it is," Burns said, jumping down from his horse. "Looks like they've stopped for the night."

"Who have?"

Burns pointed out west, directly at the red disc of the setting sun. There was a slight haziness around a copse of pine trees, smoke rising up in almost invisible puffs. "The Wesah. They've been following us ever since the day you killed one of 'em."

"And you didn't say anything?"

Burns bent down to pluck a piece of golden grass from the dirt, then stuck it between his teeth. "Didn't see much point. If they'd been planning a clean slaughter, they would've made a move long before now."

"So what do they want?"

"I honestly don't know."

Clive remembered the child-chieftain Athène, and the way she'd pressed her forehead up against the barrel of Clover's gun. If every

Wesah warrior were that fearless, the contingent wouldn't stand a chance.

"Why'd you show me this?"

Burns didn't answer for a moment, and when he did, his voice was subdued, almost bashful. "It's been weighing on me. I guess I needed to tell someone."

Clive waited for more, but as was so often the case with Burns, there wasn't more to be had. In the silence that followed, he saw his opening.

"I've got a weight on me too, sir."

"Oh yeah?"

"Her name's Irene." Burns started to protest, but Clive plowed on. "You're right I was taken with her. And you're right I was mad that she picked Clover over me. But I'm telling you right now this isn't about any of that. You have to believe me."

Burns mulled this over for a while, then gave one of his signature grunts. "You got suspicions, Clive, but you need proof."

"So how do I get it? Should I talk to Clover?"

"Nah. Girl's got him by the balls. On that much we agree."

"So what do I do?"

"I couldn't say. But I will tell you this: that girl's sharp as a sickle. If she *is* up to something, catching her at it's gonna mean being a whole hell of a lot smarter than I've ever known you to be."

"Thanks for the vote of confidence."

"You're welcome. And you can return the favor by keeping all of this"—he gestured out toward the Wesah encampment—"to yourself. Wouldn't do any good getting everyone worked up when there's nothing we can do about it anyway."

TOMMY WALLACH

"Fair enough."

It was dark by the time they made it back to camp. They tied the horses up and made for the beckoning beacon of the fire. In their last few moments alone, Clive remembered a question he'd been wanting to ask the marshal for days now.

"Sir, when we met with the Wesah, you said something. It was about dreams, I think."

"'May all your dreams be nightmares.'"

"That's right. What's it mean?"

"It's a saying they got. I guess the idea is that if you're living right, any dream is a nightmare, because it makes you live a life that isn't yours."

Clive supposed that made a strange sort of sense. "How'd you learn to speak their language, anyway?"

"My mining days, before I came to the Anchor. In my old hometown, we had an arrangement with a local *naasyoon*. One of their missives worked in the quarry for a while, and he taught me the language."

Clive shook his head wonderingly. "You've sure had some strange friends in your time."

"And some stranger enemies." Burns nodded toward the campfire, where Irene sat with her head resting on Clover's shoulder, whispering her silver words into his ear. "You best be careful with yours."

"I will, sir. Good night."

"Good night, soldier."

7. Clover

THE NEXT MORNING CLOVER WOKE TO THREE INCHES OF snow on the ground and more coming down every minute: fat, furry flakes that homed in with a perverse sort of accuracy on the back of your neck, then ran down your spine and soaked your undershirt. The physical discomfort alone would've been bad enough, but the snow couldn't have come at a less opportune time for their mission: late the previous day, Burns had noticed the hole in the earthen roof of the pumphouse from which the telegraph cable used to run. The cable was gone, of course, but the Sophians hadn't bothered to remove the brackets from the trees where it used to be attached. Those brackets would lead the contingent straight to Sophia.

Unfortunately, the slim bands of iron would have been hard to spot even without the double layer of obscuration: the snow that already blanketed the branches and the snow still coming down. There were times when the soldiers had to clear off twenty or thirty trees before they located the next bracket; this task could easily take an hour.

They made it about two miles the first day, and a little less on the second. Small as he was, Clover couldn't help with the trees, and the snow made it impossible for him to pursue his fake assignment as botanical researcher. He spent most of his free time with Irene, but she'd grown increasingly preoccupied since the night he'd proposed to her. Yesterday, for the first time since they'd left the Anchor, she went to sleep right after dinner, without even saying good night.

So when they found the first foreboding message, four days after leaving the pumphouse, he was secretly pleased: at least it made for a change of pace. The words were written on the side of an empty woodshed in bright red paint: *Turn back, Protectorate soldiers.* Burns ran his finger over the letters, but anyone could see the paint was long since dry.

"Guess that means they know we're coming," he said.

The good news was that they could stop looking for brackets; just past the woodshed, the vegetation parted unnaturally, signaling the existence of a man-made path somewhere beneath the snow. A mile on, they saw the next message, painted around the entire circumference of an old grain silo: *You are trespassing on Sophian territory.*

The following day the snow stopped falling, and sometime in the early afternoon, they found what would be their final warning. It came in the form of a corrugated tin hut, about twenty feet by twenty feet. The metal reflected the harsh winter light so brightly that from some angles it appeared just as white as the surrounding snow. The soldiers stood back a ways as Burns pulled the door open, and then they began to move inside. The hut was windowless but for a wide skylight overhead, and the only furniture was a square table situated directly below that skylight, drawing a theatrical sort of focus to the strange device mounted on its surface.

Clover pushed his way past the soldiers to see it more closely: a circular base, perhaps six inches in diameter, from which sprouted a trumpet-shaped corona, like the outgrowth at the center of a daffodil, growing from a narrow tube at the bottom to a gaping maw at the top. The trumpet was made of brass, a material that tarnished quickly if left on its own. Either the device had been placed here within the last week, or else someone was coming out regularly to polish it.

"It's a weapon," someone said, causing a bit of a pileup at the door as some of the soldiers tried to leave while others were still coming in.

"It's not a weapon!" Burns shouted. As everyone quieted back down, he glanced at Clover and whispered, "It's not a weapon, is it?"

Clover could only shrug; he had no idea what it was.

"Maybe it says there," Irene said, pointing to a small scrap of paper that had been placed beneath a corner of the device.

Burns picked it up and read aloud. "'Please remove the cylinder from the box and position it in the phonograph. Place the needle in the groove. Turn the crank slowly and regularly.'" He looked back at Clover. "What the hell's a phonograph?"

Phono: sound. *Graph:* write. Sound writer? "Something to do with music, maybe? It looks a little like an instrument."

"Why the fuck would they put a musical instrument in an empty building in the middle of nowhere?"

"I don't know."

"Marshal, I think I found something." A soldier was standing over a small trapdoor built into the floor and marked off by a square of red paint.

Burns reached inside and pulled out a small mahogany box, inside of which was a pale yellow cylinder. He offered it to Clover. "Ring any bells?"

The cylinder was rough to the touch, as if it were a spool of very fine thread. It was made out of wax, which perhaps explained why it had been placed underground: such a material would be particularly sensitive to changes in temperature.

Clover carried the cylinder over to the phonograph and looked for a place where it might be mounted. There was a spindle near the base of the trumpet, and with a little fiddling, he was able to swing it outward. The cylinder slid on neatly and clicked back into place. He located the needle next, positioning a narrow spit of iron into the groove on the cylinder (starting from the left, as if it were a book waiting to be read). The crank on the side of the device had a wooden handle that fit nicely in the palm. As soon as Clover began to turn it, an odd mist of sound emerged from the trumpet, eerie enough that the hut immediately filled with the disconcerted cries of the soldiers.

"Get away from it!"

"It's got the devil inside!"

Clover stopped turning the crank and looked to Burns.

"You know what's making that sound?" the marshal asked.

Clover nodded. "It's the needle scraping the bottom of the groove. The trumpet just amplifies it."

"So no demons?"

"No demons."

"Go on then."

Clover returned to the crank, conjuring up that spectral sound again. It almost would've been soothing, but for the occasional crackle that ran through it like a bolt of lightning in a distant storm cloud. And then, from the ether, a voice emerged.

"Greetings, soldiers of the Descendancy. My name is Zeno. As you've probably guessed, I am from Sophia." It was a woman speaking. Her voice was confident, almost arrogant, but rendered ethereal by the medium. "Sophia—from the Greek word for knowledge, is the name of both my academy and the town that surrounds and sustains that academy. And it is true that we were responsible for the killing of some of your people this past summer." The soldiers started clamoring again, and Clover missed the next bit of the recording as Burns struggled to get them calmed down. ". . . in the hope of re-creating the great technological achievements of the past. As evidence of this, I present to you this phonograph machine. The phonograph was invented by the first generation of men, more specifically by a famous native of this country named Thomas Edison. As you can see, it allows for the recording, storage, and retrieval of sonic information." Clover realized he'd started turning the crank faster, which had the effect of both accelerating the woman's voice and raising its pitch. "Unfortunately, these cylinders have a rather limited recording time, so I must get to my point. I know why you've come here, and I've left this message as a final exhortation for you to reconsider. Your position is hopeless, in both the short term and the long. Sophia offers the world light, while your Church offers only darkness. A

TOMMY WALLACH

war between us would be a tragic waste of our limited resources, and the ending would be the same. The Descendancy will fall."

The Protectorate soldiers were shouting now, angry and fearful, lashing out against what they didn't understand. Clover put his ear closer to the trumpet, so he wouldn't miss anything. "In light of your entrenched fanaticism," Zeno went on to say, "I doubt you will take my counsel to heart, but know that any further movement toward Sophia will be interpreted as a hostile action. We cannot promise that a single one of you—"

The crank was ripped from Clover's hand as Burns lifted the phonograph up off the table.

"Wait!" Clover shouted, but too late. The device must've weighed more than the marshal had expected; he only got it up to chest height before it tumbled out of his hands and onto the floor, where it shattered into a dozen pieces.

"That'll shut the bitch up," he said.

A cheer went up from the soldiers, as if destroying the phonograph were analogous to destroying the voice behind it. But all Clover felt was a burning in the pit of his stomach: the fury of the thwarted scientist. Burns couldn't possibly understand how much work must have gone into the construction of that machine. To break it before making even the slightest effort to understand how it functioned was nothing short of sacrilege.

"That should have gone back to the Library," he said quietly.

Burns smiled grimly. "My condolences to the Epistem." He shouldered his way back through the crowd of soldiers. "We camp early tonight, boys. Obviously these Sophians are scared shitless of us, and that's worth celebrating."

Another cheer erupted as the contingent followed the marshal out of the hut. Clover stood for a moment longer over the broken remnants of the phonograph. He felt as if he ought to say some sort of eulogy.

"I'll help you with the pieces, if you want," Irene said. Lord, but she knew him so well.

"Thanks."

He bent down and picked up the cylinder. It had cracked in half when it landed, but he could still trace the delicate etching from which the needle had drawn the voice. Funny how the very existence of the phonograph sent a clearer message than anything in Zeno's incendiary speech. The scholars of Sophia had built this from scratch, as well as the telegraph machine, and the gun. Maybe Zeno was right. Maybe the Descendancy *was* doomed.

The only way to know for certain was to get inside Sophia, and the day was fast approaching when Clover would do just that. Was it wrong that the thought exhilarated him every bit as much as it terrified him?

"All right, master tracker," Clive said. "Where to first?"

Clover licked his finger and held it up. All things being equal, it was best to move against the wind, so anything they spotted wouldn't have already smelled them coming. He pointed toward the densest part of the woods, due north, and they began to walk.

Clover had been more than a little surprised when his brother peeked into his tent half an hour ago and said Burns had ordered them to go hunting together. While it was true that they'd made a good team back in the ministry days, Clive hadn't seemed particularly interested in reprising the activity since the contingent had left the Anchor. In fact, they'd seldom spoken for more than a few minutes at a time over the course of the whole journey.

"Wouldn't you rather go with Garrick?" Clover had said.

"You kidding? His ugly mug would scare off every deer for miles."

So here Clover was, tramping through the snowy woods with his brother, as if they'd suddenly been transported back in time. As the ground leveled off, their route took them straight up to the banks of a fast-running stream about eight feet wide.

"You remember how all this started?" Clive said.

"All what?"

"Everything. The whole reason we're out here. It was in a stream just like this one."

It had been a long time since Clover had thought about Dominic, the man who'd threatened him out by Amestown. "You really think that's when everything started?"

"Isn't it?"

Clover shook his head. "I'm not sure I know how anything starts."

"What's that supposed to mean?"

"Well, take this stream. If we followed it uphill long enough, we'd find the mouth, right? And we could say, 'Here's where the stream starts.' But that wouldn't really be true, because the water still had to come from somewhere else. Somewhere higher up, probably, or maybe from a spring. And you could call *that* the beginning, but that wouldn't be true either, because the water had to get into that spring, or up onto that mountain peak."

"From the rain," Clive said. "Only the rain started in the sea."

"And how did the sea get there?"

"Run far enough in any direction, and you end up meeting God," Clive said, quoting the Filia.

"Something like that," Clover said.

"Or maybe you just run off a cliff."

"Maybe you do."

Clive smiled, and Clover found himself smiling too. For the first time since they'd left the capital, he felt something like warmth toward his brother. But the moment was cut short when Clive dropped into a crouch and put a finger to his lips. He pointed upstream. A few hundred yards off, the river plashed down a series of short waterfalls. In the middle of the flow, waiting with the patience of a saint, was an enormous grizzly bear. There was something weirdly childish in the way it sat on its haunches in the freezing water, yet Clover knew there was no creature more brutal or voracious. The bear was in the final stages of fattening itself up for the winter, its attention entirely focused on the potential feast waiting in the vortex: salmon, fighting their way upstream, leaping and splashing, their scales flashing prismatically in the sunlight. Clover and his brother stood there, stock-still, as the grizzly reached out and scooped a quicksilver curl of fish directly into its mouth. It tipped its head up and swallowed the creature in one gulp. Then it was back to its original position, watching for its next bite.

TOMMY WALLACH

Clive motioned for Clover to follow him back into the woods, away from the water. The wind had died down to nothing, and they wandered east through the woods in silence.

"So I imagine Irene's gonna leave soon," Clive eventually said.

A seemingly idle observation, but Clover sensed something looming behind it. "She said she'd stay with us until Burns ordered her to go."

"Sure. But it must be hard for you. You two have gotten pretty close."

Another long silence. Clive seemed a little like that bear in the stream: waiting patiently for his next opening. And even though Clover was expecting it, when the strike finally came, it still knocked him off balance.

"Did I tell you I finally proposed to Gemma?" Clive said.

Clover's belly lurched. "What? When?"

"The night of the plebiscite. I got in a big ol' fight with Burns, and then I showed up at her house at some ungodly hour." He paused. "She said no."

"Oh." Clover tried to hide his relief. "I'm sorry, Clive."

"All for the best, really. Wasn't meant to be. Besides, it turns out there's a whole wide world of girls out there. Neither of us should settle down with the first one who takes a shine to us."

And there it was, the conclusion his brother had been building to—probably the whole reason they were out here "hunting" in the first place. "I love her, Clive."

"I know. But you shouldn't."

"Why not?"

Clive took a deep breath. "She and I kissed. The very first day we met. She ever tell you that?" Clover didn't have the presence of mind to hide his shock. "She didn't, did she? I can see it in your face."

"Hell with you, Clive."

Clover turned on his heel and stalked back toward camp, but his brother stayed right on his tail, refusing to let him alone. "Just think about it, okay? When she first joined up with us, she said she was meeting with folks in Wilmington about her father's farm. But did you ever see any proof of that?"

"I wasn't looking to doubt."

"And what about when she ran off to get us an axle and came back *right* when that posse did? What if she led 'em right to us?"

"Anyone in Wilmington could've seen us leaving town by that mining road."

Clive stepped in front of him, blocking his way. "And why did she stay with us all this time, huh? Why didn't she go home?"

"Because she loves me!" Clover shouted. "That's what all this is really about. You hate her because she loves me instead of you!"

"That's not true—"

"It is! You wanted her, even though you already had Gemma!" Clover could hear how he sounded—the petulance and the pettiness, but he couldn't stop himself. "Why wasn't that enough for you? Finally somebody likes me and you have to try to ruin it?"

"You really think that little of me?" There was something soft in Clive's eyes, a compassion Clover hadn't seen there for a long time. "I know we've had our differences, but I care about you. I . . . I love you. You're my brother."

Clover's mind was reeling; he didn't know what to believe. All he knew was that Irene had been there for him. She'd seen him through the loss of his parents. She'd taught him he was worthy of love. And now Clive wanted to make her out to be some sort of monster? How dare he!

"I don't know who you are," Clover said.

Clive took this in, and after a few seconds, gave a small nod, as if some terrible truth about the universe had just been confirmed. "All right," he said. "That's good to know."

Clover waited until his brother was out of sight. Then he sank down onto his knees and allowed himself to cry. When he was finished, he wiped his eyes, stood up, and walked back to camp alone.

That night Irene came to him in his tent. He told her about the fight he'd had with his brother, and she comforted him. They drew close beneath the blankets and fell asleep in each other's arms.

He dreamed of the phonograph. In his mind's eye, he divided it up into pieces, each of which floated out in front of him, twinkling like a star. When he woke, it was with a revelation—not just about how the device itself had been constructed, but about the nature of sound itself. He turned over, to share the epiphany with Irene, but she was gone.

He got dressed and went looking for her, but he couldn't find her anywhere in camp, and nobody else had seen her either. Only after he'd returned to his tent did he notice the note pinned to the canvas:

Dearest Clover,

I'm sorry to steal away like this, but I would've had to leave soon anyway, and I don't like thinking I might be causing trouble between you and Clive. Say good-bye to everyone for me. Come find me in Eaton when you've done what you have to do, if you still want me.

All my love. —I

8. Paz

SHE WOKE TO THE SOUND OF THE SOPHIA SIREN—JUST the scream of an owl out in the woods. Clover was fast asleep, turned away from her, curled in on himself like a dog. How many nights had she spent at his side by now? More than she could count. There had been consolation in the closeness, in feet touching under the covers and the familiar smell of him, in having access to a mind as searching as her own. And now that she knew he wasn't the one who'd killed her father, she found it impossible to hate him . . . which meant it was time to go.

Besides, Clive's suspicions were growing more pronounced by the day; it would only be a matter of time before he caught her up in some lie or another. Paz hated the part of her that enjoyed watching him unravel the mystery, that wanted him to know her well enough to see through her deception. It was the same part of her that had kissed him that day on the mining road, and it would get her killed if she wasn't careful.

So she tore a page from Clover's notebook and wrote a quick note explaining her departure—subtly laying the blame for it on Clive. Then she leaned down and kissed her poor deluded "betrothed" on the cheek. From that position, it was easy to slip her hand under his pillow and retrieve her father's revolver.

She checked the cylinder: just one bullet left.

It came on her all of a sudden, as if planted in her mind by some force outside of herself—an intense impulse to put the barrel to her temple and pull the trigger. She indulged the urge, as if it were only a game. The metal burned cold against her skin, the cocking of the hammer sounded as loud as a gunshot inside her head. All she had to do now was move her little finger, splatter her brains across the inside of the tent, and she could save everyone from . . .

From what? From her? From what she might do?

She almost laughed as she lowered the gun again. What had come over her? It was far too late for remorse now. She'd chosen her path; all that remained was to walk it.

She pinned the note, then peeked her head back inside one last time. Clover was just a shadow, breathing evenly, oblivious. Odds were she'd never see him again—not alive at any rate. The thought saddened her, though she knew it shouldn't.

"Good-bye," she whispered.

She didn't travel for long that first night—just far enough so she wouldn't have to worry about some scout from the contingent happening upon her. She aimed south, but the land forced her to bear west as well. It would cost her a bit of time, but she figured it would still be easy enough to outpace the contingent. With a bit of luck, she could make it to Sophia in a few days.

The only problem would be food. She hadn't wanted to risk raiding the contingent's meager stores, which were kept guarded at night, and she wasn't about to use her only bullet to try to bring down a squirrel.

Early the next morning, after a few hours of restless sleep, she found a chestnut tree still heavy with nuts and set to peeling. It was slow going; after half an hour's steady work, she'd only produced a few meager bites. She was about to give up when she caught a flash of white against white in her peripheral vision: a baby rabbit, peeping its head above a rock at the top of an incline.

Full-grown does were usually too quick to catch, but the younger ones hadn't yet mastered the art of the dodge. Paz was on her feet in an instant. By the time she made it to the top of the slope, the rabbit was already a dozen yards off, but there was nowhere for it to hide, so she kept up the chase. She nearly had the creature in hand when she saw a couple of its fellows sitting back on their haunches and sniffing the air just outside a black hole in the snow: their warren. The bunny dove for safety, and Paz dove after it, just barely catching hold of the animal by its ears. She let out a whoop, which immediately became a shriek as the rabbit flipped up and sank its sharp little teeth into the heel of her hand.

She lost her grip—silk slipping through her fingers—and the terrible creature disappeared into the earth.

She slumped down, landing on her knees in the soft snow. There was a chaos of tracks around the hole; each set of paw prints represented a delicious meal she wouldn't be eating. Heavyhearted, she stood up and searched around for her boot prints, so she could follow them back to where she'd been camped. Only something wasn't right—a second set of shoe prints led both toward and away from the warren. Paz was certain they couldn't be hers: her boot made two marks, one for the heel and one for the toe, whereas these prints made only a single impression.

The safest thing would be to ignore the prints, of course, but Paz's curiosity was piqued. What were the odds someone would be this close to the Protectorate contingent by chance? Besides, the stranger couldn't be too far off—otherwise the activity of the rabbits at the mouth of the warren would've scratched the tracks out.

Paz followed the prints across the little glade and downhill. Left. Right. Left. Right. A little trough where the right foot had slid on an icy patch. Funny—it was no different from tracking any other animal, except a human was less likely to sense it was being pursued.

She smelled the meat cooking long before she saw anyone. Her mouth filled with saliva, and for a just a moment, she entertained the fantasy of sitting in front of a roaring fire with a group of friendly strangers, biting into a warm and dripping haunch.

The dream was dashed soon after, when the first few words reached her ears. Even at a distance, she could sense the difference in the cadence: Wesah. She abandoned the trail of footprints after that, following the voices, and caught her first glimpse of the warriors' campsite while peeking out from behind the sappy trunk of a pine, its needles gone the color of dried blood. Pintos and Appaloosas grazed in a field of yellow grass tall enough to pierce the snow. Two men—the famous "missives" Paz had heard so much

TOMMY WALLACH

about—rolled skinned rabbits over a bed of charcoal. Nearby was a massive conical tent made of animal skins, blackened with soot up around the top. Tribeswomen came and went through a flap in the front, through which Paz caught sight of about thirty Wesah arrayed before a large fire.

She wasn't particularly surprised when Athène emerged from the tent a few minutes later, though she had no idea what the girl's *naasyoon* was doing there. They had to be pursuing the contingent, but if that was the case, they should've caught up a long time ago; the Wesah knew this land far better than any Protectorate soldier. Athène's decision to hold back had to be part of some more complicated plan.

You have to warn them.

The thought was an unwelcome guest, rudely invading her self-proclaimed indifference. She didn't care what happened to the contingent, did she? Of course not. The Protectorate was her enemy.

Then again, if Athène's *naasyoon* slaughtered the soldiers before they reached their destination, the war between the Anchor and Sophia might be delayed for years, as the Protectorate turned its bellicose attentions toward the Wesah. And hadn't Paz risked everything in order to hasten the day when Sophia brought the corrupt Descendancy to its knees? So maybe it *would* be best to warn the contingent.

Or maybe you're trying to protect them.

Another uninvited guest, easy to ignore. She wasn't going to picture Clover's face as the Wesah arrow caught him in the back. She wasn't going to imagine Clive reaching out to her in pain. She wasn't going to think about the blood running down Gemma's pale face.

What did she care about Gemma? Gemma had taken her father from her.

No, there was nothing to be done. Even if she'd wanted to warn them—*which she didn't*—she couldn't go back without facing Clive's suspicions again. And those suspicions would be even more inflamed after her sudden departure.

Having reached her decision, Paz knew she should leave right away. Yet she couldn't tear herself away from the sight of the Wesah going about their daily tasks. Sharpening blades. Sparring. Laughing. And all the while the missives dutifully prepared the food. She imagined what it would be like to be born into the Wesah nation—to be one among a legion of warrior women, each in control of her own destiny and beholden to no one—and felt a bittersweet sort of yearning. In another life, perhaps.

She stood up.

And a hand forced her right back down again, firm as iron, until her cheek found the snow and she felt the rough weave of the rope as it was wrapped tightly around her wrists.

9. Gemma

A PALL HUNG OVER GEMMA THAT MORNING, MADE worse by the quilt of dull gray clouds hovering low in the sky, like a premonition of disaster. She'd been upset to learn that Irene had left in the night without so much as a good-bye. The last thing they'd talked about was that poor man at the pumphouse, and Irene had seemed genuinely disturbed to learn that it was Gemma who wielded the knife. Could that revelation have contributed to the girl's decision to leave so abruptly? If so, then Gemma was doubly guilty.

Late yesterday the trail had brought the contingent to the bank of the Ivan, which ran northeast out of Amestown and on across the continent, where it was said to open up onto a lake almost two hundred miles from end to end. Burns figured any city in the area would depend on the river in some way, so they decided to follow its course. They were close to their destination now, and everyone felt it; a new heat had entered the collective bloodstream, almost enough to counter the continued drop in temperature. Gemma had taken to wearing all her clothes at once—a strategy that kept her extremities warm at the cost of turning her torso into a sweaty, sweltering swamp. Nor was she alone in making this sartorial deal with the devil. At the end of each day's march, it was her job to walk around the camp collecting the soldiers' underclothes so they could be washed out in the river. This pile seemed to get a little more pungent with each passing day. Gemma had to carry it as far as possible from her face, or else the smell made her want to retch.

As she passed by the campfire, Garrick noticed her and jumped to attention. "You look like you could use some help," he said. Though Gemma was well aware of the boy's amorous aspirations, he still treated her more respectfully than most of the other soldiers. Besides, a second set of hands meant half the work.

"Much obliged, Garrick."

The Ivan was only a short walk from their campsite. The water was frozen at the edges, cracked in crazy patterns, speckled with tiny air bubbles like the eyes of little fish trying to break through to the surface. Garrick knelt down on the bank, picked up a smooth river rock, and smashed a hole in the ice. Vapor rose up from the black as the cold air met the slightly warmer water. "Hand me those," he said.

She passed him the pile. "You don't want to do this alone, trust me. I'll help."

"And risk those beautiful fingers of yours? Don't be crazy. What if one of them fell off? How would you ever play the fiddle again?"

Gemma was taken aback. She couldn't remember ever telling Garrick she played the fiddle.

TOMMY WALLACH

"I saw you at a gathering in the Anchor once," he explained, "singing like an angel and sawing away like the devil. Gave me sweet dreams for a week." He grinned, then immediately grimaced as his fingers met the water. "Daughter's love, that's cold!"

"What did I tell you?"

"It's all right. I've suffered for love before." He pulled the first shirt out and set it down on the rocks. "Of course, I wouldn't say no to a little thank-you present."

"Cheeky boy! What do you think I am?"

Garrick made a show of being offended. "Not like that! Just sing me something. It'll pass the time."

Gemma hadn't done much singing since that last gathering in Amestown. Part of it was because she'd lost her fiddle, but the real explanation went a lot deeper than that. Music hadn't been just some pastime; it had been her whole life. When her father and Daniel and Ellen Hamill died, it was like the music died with them. "I don't know what to sing."

"Well, hurry up and figure it out. My fingers are already numb."

She racked her brain, and finally an old ballad came to mind: "Dirt on the Grave." It seemed a fitting accompaniment for the cleaning of dirty shirts.

"I saw you first
through the heat in my veins
through the light in my eyes
through the blood in my heart
and I knew love

I saw you next
through the dust of the fields
through the light of the stars
through the dark of the night
and I knew love

I saw you last
through the ice in the air
through the chill in my veins
through the dirt on the grave
and I knew love."

She'd closed her eyes as she sang—and when she felt Garrick's lips pressing softly against her own, she let it happen, ignoring the stubbly roughness of his chin and the icy fingers against her cheek. It was something, anyway—a scrap of solace on a lonely evening.

The lips withdrew quickly, and she opened her eyes to reality. Garrick was on his feet, squinting upriver.

"What is it?" Gemma said.

"I heard something, out in the woods. Could be a deer, maybe." He'd brought his bow along with him, but when he took it off his back and tried to nock an arrow, his hands were shaking. "Shit."

And now she heard it too—movement in the reeds just a couple dozen yards upstream. A flash of black hair between the stalks.

"Don't shoot!" someone said.

A moment later she emerged from the reeds, like a phantom.

"Irene," Gemma said with quiet wonder.

Garrick laughed as he put the bow on his back again. "Lord,

TOMMY WALLACH

girl, I almost skewered you. What the hell are you doing back here? Clover was a wreck over your going, the poor little—"

"Take me to Burns," Irene interrupted, her voice so serious that Gemma felt a prickle at the back of her neck. "We don't have much time."

Gemma had petitioned to stay with the contingent, but Burns was adamant that "untrained girls got no place on a battlefield." And that's what this was now: a soon-to-be battlefield. Apparently, Irene had been on her way back to Eaton when she happened upon a Wesah encampment—the same *naasyoon* the contingent had clashed with before. She said that the warrior women looked to be preparing for some sort of attack, and that they'd mentioned Marshal Burns by name.

"Gemma and I can hide out upriver until it's over," Irene suggested.

"Good idea," Burns said. "If we haven't come for you by morning, head for home."

"You're all gonna be all right, aren't you?" Gemma asked the marshal.

Burns gave a noncommittal sort of sigh. "Well, at least we've got warning. That's something anyway." He placed a fatherly hand on Gemma's shoulder and gave it a little squeeze. "Stay safe, yeah?"

"I'll do my best."

"Good." He stared off into the distance for a moment, lips pursed in a manner that could have signaled either distraction or genuine emotion. "Good," he said again, as if closing a door on something. Then he was heading back toward camp, and Gemma was left alone with Irene.

They walked upriver, crunching over the hard-packed snow. Gemma fingered the annulus at her neck; though the hair had grown brittle since her sister first gave it to her, touching it still granted a measure of consolation. Where was Flora right now? Just sitting down to dinner at their grandfather's house, most likely, scheming how she could get an extra slice of pie for dessert.

And how would she get on if Gemma never came back?

"We should stop here," Irene said. They were passing beneath a picturesque willow, whose branches brushed the icy surface of the river. Only the thinnest layer of snow lay on the ground within the dome of its thousand drooping limbs, like a mantelpiece feathered with dust.

"Do you think it's far enough?"

"Sure. And at least we've got some protection in here. It's starting to snow again."

Gemma reached a hand out beyond the branches, catching one of the flakes in her palm, and brought it back just in time to observe it for a moment. "It sorta looks like candy, doesn't it?"

"Looks can be deceiving."

Gemma wiped the melt off on her uniform trousers, then sat down and leaned back against the trunk of the willow. Irene paced around the rim of the bower, occasionally stopping to glance out through the branches.

"You worried about Clover?" Gemma asked.

"What do you mean?" Irene looked genuinely confused, as if she'd just woken from a dream.

"Well, because of the Wesah, obviously."

"Of course," Irene said, though her voice was strangely devoid of emotion. "Of course I'm worried about him. And the rest of them."

Time passed. The only sounds were the soughing of the willow branches, the fluid hum of the river, the tread of Irene's boots on the increasingly packed snow. Gemma watched the snowflakes dissolving on the surface of the water. Was that what a life was like? Just a tiny particle tossed around by the wind, lifted for a time, but doomed to drop into the darkness, to disappear, to drown?

"Do you think there's such a thing as a bad person?" Irene asked. She was also staring out across the river, her anxious pacing momentarily halted.

"No," Gemma said, though she hadn't realized she'd believed that until she said it.

"Not even whoever it was that killed your little brother?"

Once again, Gemma saw Michael's tiny silhouette sprinting toward the wagon. The flash and the explosion, the burst of blood. His tiny skeleton slipping into the grave. That first shovelful of dirt falling on what was left of his face.

"Not even him."

Irene laughed, a laugh so inappropriate to their conversation that Gemma actually shivered. "And what if it was me who did it?"

"That's not funny."

"Who's joking?"

Gemma felt an emptiness in the pit of her stomach. Why was Irene acting like this? Did she know what she was saying?

A ray of light from the setting sun pierced their little bower, illuminating the glittering diamond of a tear frozen halfway down

Irene's cheek. Behind her, the branches of the willow tree parted, as if by some divine magic.

"Irene—" Gemma began to say, but the words stuck in her throat as she saw the first Wesah warrior step through the gap. Another warrior followed the first, then another after that, until at last Gemma found the presence of mind to stand up and run.

But there were other warriors behind her now.

She drew a deep breath, preparing to scream, but was interrupted by a firm open hand across her cheek, knocking her to the ground. She shook the stars from her eyes and saw Athène standing above her. The chieftain's copper bracelets sparkled gaily, tinkled like music. She spoke a few sharp words to the other warriors, and Gemma felt herself being lifted up by the arms and legs and flipped over like a pancake. When she landed again, it was to find the familiar warmth of a horse under her belly.

A moment later, the animal began to move, swift and silent across the snowy ground. Gemma looked back, and her eyes met Irene's. The girl from Eaton stood just outside the bower of the willow tree, entirely unharmed. She raised her hand in farewell, then turned away.

Gemma began to weep.

10. Clive

THEY'D ARRANGED THE CAMP IN A BULL'S-EYE PATTERN, with a ring of personal tents surrounding Burns's large command tent, where all of them were packed in tight as rats in a nest. The marshal was counting on the Wesah to initiate their attack on the outer ring; just as they realized the shapes beneath the blankets were just piles of dirty clothes and riding gear, the contingent would burst out of the central tent and fall on them.

Crouched breathlessly in the dark, Clive felt a strange sort of giddiness, like back when he and Clover would stay up all night together, talking about nothing, playing a game of chicken with sunrise. He had to keep checking the impulse to giggle. Even stranger, as the minutes passed, and as the minutes stretched into hours, he realized he was *hoping* for something to happen. He'd made a sort of peace with the most likely future—charging out of the tent and immediately taking an arrow in the gut; it was only the interminable present that terrified.

When he first heard the shouting, he assumed it was coming from a wild animal; the Wesah would never advertise their attack so brazenly. It was a while longer before he recognized the voice—the girl who'd run away and come right back again.

His brother pushed past him and out of the tent.

"What are you doing?" Burns said.

"It's Irene!" Clover said.

The marshal cursed. "The rest of you stay here." He followed Clover out of the tent, and Clive was right behind him. They made it only a few hundred feet toward the river before she appeared—sobbing, haggard, heavily favoring her right leg. She fell straight into Clover's arms. "They took her," she said between gasps. "They took Gemma."

"Who did?" Burns asked.

"The Wesah. They said it was a trade for the warrior that Clive killed."

"How long ago?" Clive asked.

Irene put her hands up against her temples, closing her eyes as if she'd been overtaken by a sudden bout of wooziness; Clive didn't buy it for a second.

"How long ago?" he said again, half shouting this time.

"I don't know! At least an hour. They used something to knock me out."

"An hour? A fucking *hour*?" He turned on Burns. "You've got to order everyone to move out now."

Burns put a hand on his shoulder. "You know I can't do that."

Clive shook the hand off. "Why the hell not?"

"The way the Wesah ride, an hour might as well be a week."

"So what? You're just gonna let them have her? You're too chicken to even *try*?"

"Do you have any idea how lucky we are that she's all they wanted?" Burns said, raising his voice to match Clive's. "The whole contingent could be dead right now, including your brother. You oughta be down on your knees thanking the Lord, not shoutin' at me!"

"What's there to be thankful for? Gemma is gone." He pointed at Irene as if he were naming the devil. "And that bitch is still here."

Irene's eyes flashed, but she said nothing.

"Irene came back to warn us about the Wesah," Clover said.

"And what good did it do us?" Nobody had an answer for that. "Well, you're crazy if you think I'm letting those savages have their way with her. I'll go on my own."

But Burns was there now, blocking the way to the horses. When Clive tried to sidestep, the marshal grabbed him by the jacket and threw him to the ground.

"I let you join this contingent because you told me you could be a man. And a man doesn't leave a mission half-finished to chase some private grudge. Sometimes"—and Burns's voice got quieter then, almost soft—"sometimes a man's gotta sit back on his hands. And I think that can be the hardest thing for folks like us. But we still gotta do it."

Clive thought about the moment when Gemma had kissed him, just before he rode east to the pumphouse. He thought about the night he'd asked her to marry him. He thought about everything they could've had together. If he'd only done what his parents had wanted him to do, she'd still be here now.

"You hearing me, Clive?"

"Yeah. I'm hearing you."

"Good man," Burns said. "So stand the fuck up."

Three hours later the contingent still hadn't let up celebrating. Clive sat alone outside his tent, blowing the steam off a cup of nettle tea, trying to calm the churning in his belly.

"Not enjoying the party?" Garrick asked, coming to stand beside him.

"Look at them," Clive said, gesturing out toward the soldiers singing their bawdy songs around the fire, laughing loud enough to wake the dead. Didn't they care at all that Gemma was gone? She'd been cooking for them for months now, enduring their jokes and gibes and come-ons; couldn't they summon up a bit of grief on her behalf?

"They're alive. They didn't expect to be. So they're happy."

"They shouldn't be. We still got Sophia in front of us."

At that moment, Irene and Clover emerged from Clover's tent. Though they at least looked appropriately somber, they still went to stand in front of the fire with the other soldiers, effectively joining in with the festivities.

Garrick shrugged. "You know, I had this terrible flu once—lasted for a whole week. My fever was so bad, I thought my head was gonna melt right off my neck. Then one morning I wake up and *poof*: it's gone, just like that. And I said to myself, 'Garrick, don't you ever forget what a blessing it is not to be exploding out both ends all day.' But you know what happened?"

"What?"

"I *did* forget."

"What's your point?"

"These men just remembered what a blessing it is to be alive. But they'll forget by morning. Let 'em have the moment."

Clive sipped at his tea; it scalded his tongue, but he kept drinking anyway. Garrick was right; the soldiers were doomed to forget their joy, just as Clive was doomed to forget his grief. Everything important would be forgotten eventually, and it followed naturally that the vast majority of the world's injustices would never be made right. That was time's greatest joke: to erase the memory of injury from the mind of the injured.

Remember, Clive urged himself.

He closed his eyes, dipped his nose into the cup, and inhaled the steam. They'd had a lot of nettle tea over the years, the Hamill family ministry. It tasted like spinach water on its own, but improved with a bit of honey or a squeeze of lemon; Flora had always preferred the latter, because it turned the tea pink. Clive remembered Gemma bringing him a mug of the stuff just before that last gathering in Amestown. Oh, the way her eyes used to light up when she saw him, as if they shared some wonderful secret—but that wasn't the memory he was looking for. In his mind's eye, he passed over the week that had followed that gathering, landmarks flashing past—the pumphouse, the reunion with his mother, Eddie's feverish writing—until he found Irene again, standing outside the doctor's house in Wilmington, almost as if she'd been waiting for him.

The next day she'd appeared out of nowhere and agreed to

ride with them, and only a few hours later, the wagon had broken down. She'd offered to go get help, but when she got back, she brought death and devastation along with her. And hadn't the exact same thing happened today? She'd disappeared, taking Clover's gun along with her, and almost as soon as she'd returned, tragedy struck.

It couldn't all be a coincidence. It just couldn't. And that meant every second she remained here was another invitation to further catastrophe. What was it Burns had said, when they went to parley with the Wesah? *Only a fool marches into trouble with trouble already breathing down his neck.*

"Garrick, I need you to do something for me."

"What's that?"

"Distract Clover somehow. I want a few minutes alone with Irene."

"Daughter's love, Hamill, why do you still have it in for her?"

"Because she's a liar."

Garrick made a big show of sighing. "Fine. Just keep my name out of it when you're apologizing to Burns an hour from now."

Garrick set his tea down and crossed over to the fire. Clive couldn't hear what was said, but Clover got up a moment later and went with Garrick out beyond the circle of firelight. Irene stood up soon afterward, just as Clive had expected; she never spent time with the soldiers without Clover close at hand. Clive followed her, away from the campsite, toward her tent. She'd taken to setting it up as far as possible from the rest of the contingent—she said the soldiers' snoring kept her up at night, but Clive suspected it was because she knew he was keeping an eye on her.

When she reached her tent, she didn't go inside, but stood in front of the flap, staring up at the sky. Slim as a reed, or a sapling: a stark brown shoot rising from the snow. She spoke even before he emerged from the shadows of the trees.

"I expect you think that was spectacularly subtle."

He stepped out into the moonlight. "I don't know what you mean."

"Obviously you wanted to get me alone. Once upon a time, I would've thought your motives were romantic. Now I know they're only the same tired suspicions."

"You're saying it would be romantic if I wanted to steal you away from my own brother?"

Irene shrugged. "We love who we love. But you don't love me. You hate me, in fact. All because I chose him over you. It's sad, really."

The conviction in her voice. The arrogance. At first it made him want to grab hold of her by the throat, to break her. But as he let the rage wash over him, he saw something in her eyes—a kind of strain, as if she were trying to keep track of a hundred possible futures at once. This was a game, he realized. It had been a game all along. And Irene's latest play was this seemingly invincible confidence. Take it away, and there'd be nothing left.

"You can stop this now," he said, trying to channel his father's calm, implacable authority. "It's over."

"And what is *that* supposed to mean?"

Clive smiled slightly but said nothing, letting the silence seep into the cracks of Irene's certainty.

"You're acting even stranger than usual," she said, a little more quietly. "You feeling all right?"

"My only question is this," he said. "Why'd you come back? You'd made it out. I never would've known for sure if you hadn't come back."

Irene laughed. "Clive, I'm really not sure what nonsense you've invented in that twisted little head of yours—"

"Enough!" he said, his tone that of an exhausted parent dealing with a stubborn child. "Didn't you hear me? It's over. You're smart enough to see that."

For a few more seconds, Irene kept up the pretense of astonishment. Then, as if by some trick of the light, her face suddenly transformed. There was no sign of diabolical delight or grim solemnity in her expression—only a dismal sort of relief. Her eyes turned watery, and she took a first halting step toward him.

He backed away, placing a hand on the hilt of his sword. "What are you doing?"

She kept coming, until she was close enough to throw her arms over his shoulders. At first he thought she was trying to choke him, but then she began to sob—huge gasping breaths that shook her whole body. He was caught by surprise, and fumbled for an adequate response. "Irene. Irene. It's okay. It's done. You can stop pretending now." His arms felt silly dangling at his sides, so he put them loosely around her, giving her a few consolatory pats on the back.

But now something strange was happening. Her sobs were growing more and more intense, until they reached the point where she was thrashing around in his arms like Gemma during one of her fits.

"No, Clive!" she shouted. "I said no! Let go of me!"

TOMMY WALLACH

"What the hell are you talking about?"

A flash of white—Clive's first thought was that he'd been struck by lightning—followed by an awesome pain that bloomed outward from a point at the back of his head to encompass his whole body. And how had he ended up on the ground? He reached around to touch the place where the pain had originated, and his hand came away wet with blood.

"You touch her again and I swear to God I'll kill you."

Clive's vision was finally beginning to clear, and now he saw Clover standing over him, holding a flawless white stone in his right hand. Clive remembered exactly where his brother had found it, in the streambed near Amestown, the last time they'd been something like happy. If things hadn't gone so wrong, that crystal would've ended up on the mantel in the kitchen, where Clover used to keep his rock collection: the quartz and agate, the chunk of pyrite that he'd tried to pass off as real gold, the topaz and sea glass and azurite, the uncut opal Bernstein had given him as a birthday gift. But Clover had given all of them away a few days after they got back to the Anchor. He said it made him too sad to look at them.

And yet he'd kept this one.

"Clover . . . you hurt me."

Clive felt his stomach turn over, and before he could say anything else, he threw up into the snow.

"Why did you make me do that?" Clover shouted. "Why couldn't you just leave her alone?"

But Clive wasn't listening. He had to get up. Had to stop Irene. And Clover was standing in his way.

Though he still felt shaky, he'd managed to get his feet under him again, and now he sprang at his brother like a cat pouncing on a mouse. They landed hard in a frozen snowdrift, bones bruising against the craggy ice. Clive's head was spinning, but his first punch connected solidly with his brother's jaw, as did the second. He kept swinging even as Clover got a wicked grip on his hair, pulling at it until a great hunk came loose. The pain was so intense that Clive nearly retched again, which gave his brother time to slither out from under him.

"You're a bully," Clover said, panting heavily. He was bleeding from a gash in his left cheek. "That's all you've ever been. That's why Gemma threw you over, and that's why Irene didn't want you. You're nothing but a bully and a killer, and Da would've been ashamed of you."

Words. Clover had always been good with those. He'd always had them at the ready, an inexhaustible quiver of poison-tipped arrows. But words weren't the only thing that cut. Clive launched himself at his brother again, closing the distance between them in the blink of an eye. Clover turned to run, but his foot slipped on the ice, sending him face-first into the snow. He scarcely had time to flip over before Clive was on top of him again. Their hands, raw and red from the cold, scrabbled fruitlessly for a few moments, until Clive's superior strength finally prevailed.

"Stop," Clover said. "Stop, please."

But Clive was beyond reasoning now. He closed his fist and brought it down, jerking his brother's head first one way and then the other, amazed at how his anger only seemed to increase with every blow he landed. Jealousy, grief, shame, regret, despair—all of it was transmuted into a blinding rage, like a tornado pulling

TOMMY WALLACH

everything into its howling vortex, until finally Clover's protestations were silenced and his body went still.

Then Clive stood up, wiping the tears from his eyes and smearing his face with blood. He looked around.

Irene was gone.

11. Clover

H<small>E WAS BARELY CONSCIOUS WHEN THE BEATING</small> finally stopped, and through the narrow horizon line of his half-closed eyelids, he watched his brother duck into Irene's tent and emerge with the gun—one bullet left— then sprint off into the woods.

Clover fell asleep after that, and when he woke again, it was to a chill that was worryingly close to warmth. The moon was high in the sky, beams of light transfixing each individual snowflake as it tumbled lifelessly down to join its fellows. He could feel death hovering somewhere close by, just out of sight, whining in his ear like a mosquito: *Would you like to come with me?*

It took him a few tries to stand up. The snow all around where he'd lain was stained with blood. Droplets led off to the east, like a trail of bread crumbs. Clover knew he had to follow them. If Clive caught up with Irene, Daughter only knew what he'd do to her; after all, he'd nearly beaten his own brother to death just a few minutes ago. Things would've been so much simpler if she'd just run the *other* way, toward the contingent: simpler, and safer . . . and smarter.

And Irene was nothing if not smart. She must have known that Clive couldn't hurt her if the other soldiers were around—so why would she take her chances alone in the woods?

Because she was guilty of something. Because she had something to hide.

The doubts had always been there—so many seedlings, waiting only for a bit of sunlight and water to sprout. What were the odds that their wagon axle would break like that? What were the odds that a farm girl from the outerlands would risk her life for a bunch of strangers? What were the odds that a girl that beautiful and brilliant could really be in love with a freak like him?

The questions proliferated, a forest fire leaping from tree to tree, until finally his whole world was ablaze, and the full ramifications of what he'd done crashed into him like the Daughter herself making landfall.

He'd told her everything. Everything he'd learned in his time working at the Library. Everything he'd read in the anathema stacks. Everything the Epistem had asked him to do for the Descendancy. She knew all his secrets, and she would bring every single one of them to Sophia. The mission would be over before it began.

Unless Clive caught up with her first.

"Irene," he whispered, as if in mourning. And then he had a thought that made him laugh, only the laugh quickly devolved into a thick, bloody cough: "Irene" probably wasn't even her real name.

There was no point in trying to catch up with them; both would be moving far faster than he ever could. Instead he limped back to the campsite. The fire had been abandoned; all the soldiers but the night watch had gone to sleep.

Clover went to Burns's tent and found the marshal kneeling at the edge of his cot, head bowed in prayer, lips moving silently.

"I didn't know you believed in praying," Clover said.

Burns opened his eyes. "Figure it can't hurt," he said, standing up and brushing off the knees of his trousers. Then he noticed Clover's face. "Daughter's love, what the hell happened to you?"

"It was Irene," Clover said, which was technically true, though not the whole truth. The least he could do now was protect his brother, who'd been right about her all along. "She attacked me, then ran off. Clive went after her." Clover hung his head. "I . . . I told her things, Burns. Things I learned at the Library. I'm sorry."

The marshal gave him a gentle pat on the back. "I've done stupider things for a woman. And you beating yourself up doesn't do us any good now. You wanna make it up to me, get everybody out of their tents as fast as you can."

"Why?"

"I don't think that girl would've taken off unless we were close to Sophia. We're gonna beat her there."

The snow stopped falling just as they decamped, and though the sky was still patchy with clouds, the attenuated moonlight was more than enough to see by, illuminating a sparkling snowscape so perfectly serene it was as if time itself had frozen. Though the soldiers were as exhausted as they'd ever been—the combination of near-death experience, sudden salvation, and interrupted sleep—

Clover thought there was a remarkable grandeur to them tonight, as they marched uncomplainingly toward whatever fate God had in store for them. It was the most admirable aspect of humanity, the willingness to be subsumed into something greater than one-self; Clover had never felt more connected to his family than when they played music together.

Oh, but he missed them all so terribly. His parents. Eddie. Gemma. Clive. Even Irene. All of them were gone now: dead or disappeared or alienated beyond recovery.

So maybe it was for the best that he was about to give himself over to Sophia. There was nothing tying him to his old life any longer. Nothing holding him back. No one to be ashamed of his betrayal. And if he did die in the line of duty, there would be no one left to mourn him.

He'd expected a long journey, but scarcely an hour after they'd started marching, still cleaving to the course of the Ivan, there was a cry from the front of the line. A moment later Clover saw it for himself: the infamous Sophia. They crossed a sturdy bridge and passed through a gate, which for some inexplicable reason had been left open.

At first glance, it seemed like any another town built on a hill, its main street like any other main street, its houses like any other houses (though a good ways better constructed than those of the average outerland burg). The top of the hill was obscured by build-ings and trees, but Clover felt certain the academy was up there somewhere, perched like an eagle waiting for him.

There was no one out on the streets at the moment, not a single candle visible through the windows of the houses. Burns ordered the soldiers to knock on a few doors, but no one answered.

"They've emptied out," the marshal said. "Probably holed up in that academy of theirs."

"So what are we waiting for?" Garrick said. "Let's go."

But they hadn't made it more than a few steps up the hill when something truly extraordinary occurred. Though Clover had noticed the lampposts that lined the main street, he'd assumed they ran on gas, like the lamps in the Anchor. But at that moment, every single one erupted with bright white light. Farther up the hill, the face of a small clock tower was also illuminated, revealing the time to be just past ten o'clock. The contingent cried out in surprise, which quickly transitioned to wonder. Clover had seen electric light before, in the anathema stacks, but he hadn't realized until now the full ramifications of the technology. This wasn't a slight improvement on the gas lamp, but a world-changing revelation. With light this powerful, night could be counteracted, cured like an illness.

The soldiers were laughing now, as if they were party to a miracle. But all Clover could think about was *why*. Why turn on the lights now? Did the Sophians really care about impressing a bunch of Protectorate soldiers?

Of course not. This must have been done for a practical reason, and there was only one that made sense.

"Run!" Clover shouted. "Everyone run!"

Garrick gave him a condescending pat on the back. "It's just light, little man."

And that was true: light to aim by.

The first bullet buzzed like a bee as it passed, a high singing

TOMMY WALLACH

whine that ended in a wet thump. There was a look of utter befuddlement on Garrick's face, as if he'd just been told a joke with no punch line. A puddle of darkness spread out from the center of his uniform jacket. He fell onto his knees, hands breaking loudly through the crust of snow as he went down on all fours.

All hell broke loose after that. Clover couldn't tell where the shots were coming from; the Sophians had been prepared, and were perfectly positioned. Soldiers screamed as they or someone near to them was hit. The contingent broke apart, every man running toward whatever piece of cover was closest. Clover tried to do the same, only Garrick had grabbed hold of his ankle.

"Help me," he whispered, then coughed a spritz of red across the white.

Haemoptysis: the coughing up of blood. The bullet must have pierced one of Garrick's lungs. Even with the best doctor in the Anchor to hand, his chance of survival would've been slight. Out here, there was no hope for him at all.

"I'm sorry," Clover said. He tried to pull himself free, but Garrick was holding on too tight. It wasn't until Clover planted a firm foot in the boy's face that he finally managed to get loose.

The gunfire slowed down as the surviving soldiers found something to hide behind, and now they began the slow process of climbing the hill, scampering quickly from one piece of cover to another. More than once Clover heard a bullet carom off the low stone wall he'd just slid behind; more than once he heard the strangled cry of someone less lucky than himself.

By the time they'd made it up the first thousand feet or so of the hillside, a good half of the company had been lost. After that, the structures of the town grew slightly denser—the equivalent of a few Anchor blocks of two-story brick and stone buildings. Those who'd survived the initial assault grouped up in an alleyway behind a smithy. Burns was still with them, though he'd taken a grazing shot to the left leg.

"There's six of them," he said. "Or six with guns anyway. And unless they moved in the last couple of minutes, they're hiding out in three places. In here." He pounded the side of the smithy. "In the big house across the street, and in that clock tower up the hill."

Burns divided the soldiers into three groups, one for each of the gunmen's shelters. Clover waited in the alleyway with Burns as one group of soldiers set themselves to knocking down the door of the smithy, while another headed across the street.

"If I'd known it would go down like this," said Burns, "I would've left you back in camp."

"I wouldn't have stayed there anyway," Clover replied.

Burns smiled grimly. "I suppose not."

The sound of wood splintering, a chorus of shouts, followed by the first couple of gunshots. Burns signaled the remaining soldiers to prepare to run for it. A countdown: five, four, three, two, one . . .

Clover watched them go. The first soldier went down almost immediately—taking one bullet in the chest and a second in the gut. In the end, this was probably a lucky outcome, as it allowed the rest of the company to make it up the hill unharmed.

Burns would notice that Clover was missing before long; it was time to go his own way, to do what he'd come here to do. He waited until the marshal and his cohort succeeded in breaking down the door at the bottom of the tower, then simply took off running up the wide-open street. He wondered what a bullet felt like as it entered the body. Like a blunt force? Like a stab wound? Was it possible to die before you even heard the shot ring out? But the only shots he heard were distant, aimed at someone other than himself, and the loudest sound was the scuttering of his shoes on the snow, fast as his heartbeat.

A half mile or so up the hill, the houses had thinned out completely; it was as if he were back in the woods. And then, coming around a bend in the road, the strangest building Clover had ever seen hove into view. From the front, it looked like a large gray cube, perhaps twenty yards high and two hundred wide; from this angle, there was no way to know how far back it went. It appeared to be made of some kind of concrete, though smoother and more polished than anything they used in the Anchor. The surface was unblemished but for the single set of doors carved into the front and the line of windows up near the top of the structure, glowing with a warm yellow light.

Clover had no doubt he was being watched. Likely there was at least one gun pointed his way at this very moment. He raised his arms, palms facing outward, and approached the building at a measured pace.

"I surrender," he shouted, over and over again, as he came to stand within a few paces of the doors. He sensed movement somewhere on the other side, scrapes and whispers, strangers determining whether he should live or die. The outcome was in God's hands now. Clover bowed his head.

"What the hell are you doing?"

Clover turned to find his brother emerging from the woods at the edge of the road. Clive's face was covered in blood, his hair matted, his eyes wild. He led Irene in front of him, the gun pressed up against the back of her head. Her arms were bound behind her, and a piece of cloth had been tied across her mouth.

"I knew you hated *me*," Clive said. "I had no idea you hated the whole Descendancy."

"How'd you get up here?"

"Paz led me."

"Paz?"

"This bitch here. And it's a damn good thing she did, or I wouldn't have been able to stop whatever it is you're doing. Now walk straight over to me, no hesitating, or I swear to God I'll shoot her."

Clover allowed himself one last long look at the girl he'd thought he would marry. Had anything they'd shared been real? Was it possible to manufacture affection so convincingly? He would've given the world to know the truth. But he had a mission, and it was more important than whatever he'd had with her, more important even than his love for his brother, which remained in spite of everything.

"I'm sorry," he said, to both of them at once, "but I can't go with you." He turned back toward the doors just as they opened—two eight-foot slabs of solid granite swinging soundlessly on invisible hinges.

But before he could take a step, there was a loud crack, and a fiery red flower of pain exploded in his shoulder. He fell forward, stumbling through the opening, and immediately the doors shut behind him. He could feel the blood running torrentially down his back, and the pain crested like a wave and crashed down on him.

Paz, he thought, as his consciousness slipped away. *Her name is Paz.*

Epilogue
Five Months Earlier

THE DOOR SHUT BEHIND HER—*WHOOSH*—AND FOR A moment, Zeno knew perfect peace. Light. Warmth. The sense of homecoming she always felt in the greenhouse, as if its inhabitants had gone silent in honor of her arrival, gifting her this respite from the din of the outside world. Zeno loved the quietude of plants—both in how it contrasted with the constant clamor produced by people, and in how it was really just an elaborate subterfuge; all it would require was a means of amplification to transform that seeming tranquility into cacophony. Roots could drill through solid granite. Sap flowed oceanic behind the bark. Vines spun blind, inexorable circles in search of prey, which was then enwrapped boa-constrictor tight. Plants were like a brilliant mind, in a way: calm on the surface, tempestuous underneath.

Some of Sophia's scholars were censorious of the many hours Zeno spent in the greenhouse. They believed her to be shirking her duties, or at the very least, squandering her talents. To them, the hard work of cultivation, the seeding and pruning, the weeding and the fertilizing, was mindless drudgery. They didn't understand that Zeno's mind was sharpest here. Her thoughts expanded in the humid, molten air, as if her neurons had become free-floating particles of oxygen and carbon, and she could watch the silky dendrites transmitting ideas from place to place, forming connections between distant and disparate nodes.

Throughout history, there had been people believed capable of seeing the future. They were known by many names. Soothsayers. Fortune-tellers. Shamans. Witches. All hokum, of course, and yet at the heart of the matter was the little-understood phenomenon known as intuition. And what was intuition but the ability to read the subtle signs of the universe—not any sort of spiritual symbology, of course, but the material, objective manifestations? You could not *see* the future, but you could *infer* it, in much the same way as the first generation of men had been able to make predictions about the weather, even down to the very hour.

The key was to array the facts before you and contemplate them. You couldn't chase epiphany the way a hunter chased a buck. You had to let the revelation come to *you*, like an old man scattering bread crumbs for the birds.

Zeno gazed upon the bonsai tree. *Juniperus procumbens*—the dwarf Japanese garden juniper. She had inherited it from Duncan Leibowitz himself; between the two of them, the plant had now been trained for over thirty-five years. Its trunk was the off-white color of driftwood, gnarled and streaked, indistinguishable from the source tree in every aspect but size. The upper branches were of a more traditional dark brown, and it was from these that the leaves grew. This particular variety of juniper had needles when it was young, but as it aged, those needles gave way to overlapping scales.

Just like me, Zeno thought. *Prickly when young and scaly when old.*

It wasn't a bitter notion; she'd enjoyed the process of aging. The diminution of one's physical beauty was more than offset by the excuse it gave one to be bad-tempered.

Though Zeno's favorite activity in the greenhouse was pruning the bonsai, it didn't need attention of that sort today, so she allowed herself merely to gaze on it. Slowly but surely, the tumult in her mind calmed, and she found herself looking down upon the chessboard of the future.

Things would have been so much simpler if Sophia's town guard had succeeded in wiping out the ministry. Zeno's informants had long since apprised her of the bellicose aims of Grand Marshal Chang, and of his increasing popularity within the Anchor. She'd hoped to avoid direct confrontation for at least another decade, but now that Chang had his excuse, soldiers would be at her doorstep in a matter of months. At the moment, if the Descendancy chose to mobilize all of its available resources, it would easily overrun Sophia. But Zeno felt confident that the Protectorate force would be relatively meager; the deaths of a minister and his family were tragic, certainly, but not quite tragic enough to turn a whole country of pacifists into warmongers overnight. The Grand Marshal would need more blood on the ground before the people of the Anchor would let go of their noble but doomed ideal. In other words, the incoming force would triumph even in defeat.

Of course, that was only the Protectorate's plan. The Archbishop and his toady the Epistem (or was it the other way around?) would certainly have their own pieces on the board, and those were the pieces Zeno feared. The true capability of the Library remained the most dangerous unknown clouding her vision. Leibowitz had managed to steal only a few hundred volumes when he defected, leaving behind many thousands more. If the Archbishop's hand was forced, and the ban on anathema was lifted, who could say what powers the Descendancy might bring to bear?

And then there was the girl, Paz, who'd apparently managed to ingratiate herself with the Honor's children. If things had gone well for her, she would be at the Anchor now, gleaning what information she could. While it was possible she might return with something useful, Zeno wasn't counting on it. Far more likely that the girl would be discovered, tortured for information, and killed. It was a good thing she knew next to nothing of importance about the goings-on inside the academy, though it would make her death all the slower.

Zeno had been accused of having no conscience, but that accusation was only half-true. She cared little for any particular human, but she cared deeply about humanity. And the best thing she could do for humanity was to protect Sophia until the day it could take its rightful place as the heart of a new civilization—a day that was fast approaching.

She stood up, leaving the bonsai tree and wandering into her vegetable garden. A single light brown mushroom was growing at the base of the tomato plants. It was known as a haymaker—*Panaeolina foenisecii*. She dug out its slender stalk and turned it over in her palm. Beautiful organisms, mushrooms. Their bad reputation sprang from the fact that they were parasites, but what wasn't? Every creature on the planet was a freeloader, sustained by the ever-generous sun, and most weren't even half as lovely as this

　　　　　　　　　　　　　　TOMMY WALLACH

mushroom, with its baby-soft skin and delicate tan gills.

Maybe that was the best thing about a garden—the way it grew metaphors. The mushroom reminded Zeno how many things grew in the dark crevices of the world, weeds that could choke the life out of the healthiest tree, if left unimpeded.

The Church would cultivate its own haymaker in the shadows. But how would this parasite manifest? Cunningly, no doubt. As much as Zeno despised the Descendancy, she knew it was run by intelligent men. But only men, of course. Such a common mistake, failing to see the value in the feminine.

The bell rang, signaling a shift to the second class of the day. Zeno had students to teach, but they would forgive her for being a few minutes late. There was one last thing she needed to do—not a practical matter, but an emotional one.

Down one set of stairs, along the northern side of the building, through two unlocked doors and then a locked one, secured with an ingenious coded device built specially by Sister Balewa. Zeno entered the password—*aliger*—and felt the satisfying click as the tumblers lined up and the bolt slid loose.

The room on the other side was known as St. Nick's, from the old myth about the toymaker who brought gifts to children once a year. Though there were at least twenty-five projects in some state of development scattered across the enormous work floor, only one was of interest to Zeno at the moment.

It was by far the largest object in the room, twenty feet from end to end and twice that across. Covered by a thick canvas blanket, it looked a bit like a giant who'd fallen asleep with his arms outstretched. Zeno grabbed a corner of the canvas and walked backward, pulling it away with a long, steady hiss, until the great secret was revealed.

The future was a dark forest, full of evils crouching in the shadows. But Zeno had faith in her mission, in what they were trying to build here in Sophia. Someday soon, the Descendancy's reign of ignorance and superstition would end, and the people would at last be free. That many of them believed themselves to be free already was simply an error of perspective. True freedom was the right to study what you wanted, when you wanted, in whatever manner you wanted. It was the right to a future that was better than the present. It was the right to fly a kite.

There weren't many things that made Zeno cry, but as she looked upon that magnificent machine, the precocious offspring of her imagination, she felt the tears rise to her eyes. She stepped forward and touched the cool skin of the wing. The contact thrilled her, filled her with confidence and hope. They would not lose. They could not lose.

"Hello, my child," she said, her voice low, as if she were in the presence of something holy. "I can't wait to watch you soar."

TOMMY WALLACH

OCT   2017